What It's About

A mesmerizing work, literarily impressive and historically exacting. -Kirkus

In 1847, the Donner party resorted to eating human flesh to survive entrapment at the base of the Sierra Nevada mountains. They became infamous almost instantly, inspiring hundreds of books, stories, and interviews exploring their misery. But none of them tell the extraordinary story from the first-person point of view of the female survivors.

Until now.

Three women yearned to make better lives in California:

Nineteen-year-old Mary Ann Graves set out west with her family in search of a home that would be free of disease like the ague that had afflicted her mother and sisters for years. If she met a handsome guy along the way, well, she wouldn't complain. As the belle of the Donner party, she certainly had plenty of interest.

Peggy Breen had just given birth to her seventh child, but she wasn't afraid of the two-thousand-mile journey toward prosperity. She'd take care of her children and honor her husband along the trail, because that's what women of faith did. But when supplies became limited, her giving heart and her mother's instinct were at odds.

Virginia Blackstone Reed, the thirteen-year-old daughter of the group's leader, set out in search of adventure, riding her sassy palomino pony alongside the largest double-decker wagon anyone had ever seen. As the adopted daughter of the most influential and prosperous man in the wagon train, she had no idea at the start that her polarizing father with his ostentatious wealth would pave the way for their future devastation.

By the time these women and the rest of the party reached the Sierra Nevada mountains after taking an unproven "shortcut," they were already two months late. They had lost people, oxen, mules, and livestock they couldn't survive without. Then the snow began to fall.

And it didn't stop.

Hungry follows the tenacious protagonists and their miraculous rescue as they fight the elements and one another, highlighting the strength that kept them going when most of us would have been defeated.

Kirkus Reviews said of *Hungry*, "The story's historical verisimilitude is magisterial—the author's research is simply impeccable. This is much more than a recitation of historical facts, though—Baker brings to terrifying life the cruel proximity of hope and barbarism, and the unspeakable things people will do to survive and to save their own. This is a stunning glimpse into a vanished time in American history when every obstacle seemed surmountable and progress assured, despite the awesome danger that lurked everywhere."

Hungry

THE INSPIRING TALE OF THREE DONNER PARTY SURVIVORS

B. E. BAKER

For my darling Jack:
*I would never, ever, **ever** eat you.*

(You're FAR too small.)

Author's Note

During the summer of 1846, eighty-seven people joined forces as they traveled from various places in or near Missouri toward California, a land governed at the time by Mexico. The United States settlers knew that their country was technically at war with Mexico, but that was not near the top of their list of concerns.

For various reasons, all the members of the Donner party, as it came to be known, were late to the trail, and all of them were eager to make up for lost time. That's the main reason why they decided to take the untested Hastings shortcut—to make up for lost time so that they could reach the Sierra Nevada mountains and cross them before winter struck.

The fact that it was a shortcut, along with pretty much all the promises made by an infamous man named Lansford Hastings, turned out to be a lie. The route they took added a full month to their trip instead of shortening it. And worse, they lost the lives of people, oxen, mules, and other livestock on that leg of the journey that they could not afford to lose.

By the time they reached the base of the Sierra Nevada mountains, they were nearly two months late, and when they finally attempted to cross on Halloween, after traveling without rest for nearly seven full months, an early blizzard hit. They retreated after that first attempt, scrambling to make shelters in which to huddle while they waited for a break in the weather.

A break that never came.

In the end, half of the men, women, and children who were a part of that wagon train died. Of those who survived, only eight did not consume human flesh in order to do it.

Many people have told versions of this story over the years, but this one is different. In an attempt to bring the struggles, the perspectives, and the joys of these often misunderstood travelers to life, I'm telling this story in first person point of view, from three of the most interesting members of the party. Thirteen-year-old Virginia Reed, nineteen-year-old Mary Ann Graves, and forty-one-year-old Peggy Breen, mother of seven.

As you might expect with such a large party, the accounts of those involved diverge critically on nearly every key point. Many interests were involved, and many individuals wrote their accounts for different reasons and with changing motivations. It's essentially impossible to know the precise truth of just how or why things occurred. Insofar as it was possible, I maintained truth and accuracy with circumstances, dates, and facts. However, with regard to the thoughts, feelings, and motivations of all the travelers involved, I used my imagination.

But all the things I will write *could* have happened just as they do in my tale. I think that this story is replete with the highs and lows of human nature, and I believe that you, like me, will be able see yourself inside of it somewhere.

As you learn about their harrowing and inspiring story, I hope that you might find a fresh and unique perspective on your own.

A woman who weighs a hundred and thirty pounds, as I did in the spring of 1846, needs roughly two thousand calories a day in order to maintain a healthy weight. If you account for the calories we burned from walking an average of fifteen miles a day alongside our oxen-pulled wagons, you can add another fifteen hundred calories to the mix.

Getting up at dawn and tending to children, packing wagons, hauling water in buckets from the nearest stream for humans and animals, helping our husbands gather firewood or bison chips, preparing coffee and bread for the day, and the myriad other tasks that female travelers completed each morning—not to mention nursing a newborn as I was—meant that we needed even more calories to remain healthy and strong. Disease, accidents, and hostile forces stalked the trails we traveled, so remaining strong wasn't optional.

The weak died.

By the time our company reached the base of the Sierra Nevada mountains on Halloween of 1846, our bodies had already weakened. Most of us had been operating at a significant caloric deficit for quite some time. Even with the extra supplies that Charles Stanton had brought from Sutter's Fort, our stores had been depleted to a dangerously low level.

Long before anyone in the Donner party ever contemplated eating another human, our bodies had already been pulling on our natural fat stores for the nutrients they needed to keep operating for many weeks.

But I didn't know any of that then.

No, on that fateful final day when we failed miserably in our first attempt to cross the massive mountains standing between us and California, all I knew was that I was already very, very *hungry*. I had no idea how much worse that hunger would become, or what such a powerful force could do to God-fearing humans.

But I was about to find out.

CHAPTER 1

Mary Ann Graves

I was always the pretty sister.

My older sister by one year, Sarah, was the funny one. She was the smart one, too, and the one everyone loved best.

That's just how it was.

Everyone thought that I'd be the first Graves girl to get married because of my face and shiny, curly hair. Our family was a little odd, but for a famous local beauty, marriage wouldn't be a problem. That's what women always told me. I couldn't really take issue with their statements.

Our family was a little odd.

Pa insisted on wandering into town barefoot to trade his furs and game, no matter the weather. Our mother wasn't much more conventional. She'd take a boat into town to sell her honey and eggs, even in a snowstorm. We all lived in a one-room farmhouse on the banks of the Illinois river, and there were a *lot* of us. But the same people who called us odd also knew that our family was helpful and supportive. People called on my mother for help with childbirth, new babies, and all sorts of other problems. Pa was handy with, well, nearly everything.

In spite of our family quirks, plenty of men did propose to me. It's just that none of the men ever felt quite right, so I always said no. Sarah and I had each other—we were inseparable—so I didn't have to say yes to the first man who asked. When your best friend is your sister, you're always together.

But one day during Sunday School, I noticed Sarah watching a young man—one we all knew relatively well. Jay Fosdick's family had been living here as long as we had, or perhaps even a few years longer. The Fosdicks were nothing special. Jay himself wasn't particularly tall, or particularly smart, or particularly strong. He wasn't especially handsome either, though he wasn't *un*attractive, I suppose.

But I couldn't imagine why Sarah would stare at him.

It unnerved me.

When Jay stood up that day and began to play *Amazing Grace*, his hands flying across the fiddle, I finally understood. He may not have been an obvious catch, but he was extraordinary in unique, understated ways, just like Sarah herself.

I wasn't even surprised when he proposed the next week.

Or worse, when she said yes.

But I knew we'd still see each other. Every Sunday at church, at least. They'd probably move to a small home on his father's farm. It wasn't far from ours. I started calculating how much I might be able to earn from selling eggs in the next few weeks. I could probably afford a bolt of muslin for a wedding gift, or perhaps a new hat. If I managed to find a beehive or two, I might be able to buy Sarah a new pair of shoes. I was looking over the various things at the General Store when something distracted me.

Or rather, someone.

The man was wearing a strange, cone-shaped hat, and he was piling supplies up on the main counter like he owned half of Illinois. "I'd like two bags of hard candies as well." He was beaming.

So was the store proprietor. "That's quite a lot of candy," Harris said from behind the counter. "Are you sure?"

"My wife has a sweet tooth," the funny-hat man said. "And we're celebrating."

"What are you celebrating?" I was glad Harris asked. I also wanted to know. There weren't many new people around here, and I'd never seen him.

"We've decided to settle somewhere around here—we're in the market for a farm. If you know of someone willing to sell, send them my way.

We're staying at the boarding house across the street with our three children."

"A farm?"

The man leaned closer. "I sold my farm back east for quite a lot, and I'm willing to pay top dollar, especially if there's already a home and barn built. Spread the word."

Before I could even nudge my father, I noticed he was watching.

Pa had read a book about California during the long, miserable winter, and with Ma sick again with the shakes, I knew he wanted to sell up. "Franklin Graves," Pa said, extending his hand. "I have a lovely farm with a home and barn, right on the river. I'd be happy to show you more of it."

The funny-hat man turned out to be deadly serious, and within days, Pa had struck a deal. The man would pay us fifteen hundred silver dollars for our farm. It was a fortune greater than any I'd ever heard of, and Pa was delighted. We'd take most of our animals and all our wagons—we had three farm wagons we could modify to use for a longer journey—and we'd leave in three weeks.

Of course, the real problem came when Sarah told her fiancé. Jay Fosdick's father was adamantly opposed to the notion of traveling west. He loved Illinois and refused to ever leave. As Jay was the only son old enough to help on the farm, he forbade him to leave too, which meant that Sarah would also stay. She swore that one day she'd visit, but we all knew that was impossible. We'd be traveling two thousand miles away— we'd never see one another again.

Every time I thought about Sunday School meetings without her, baby births, or Fourth of July Celebrations, I wanted to bawl. I might be the pretty one, but who cares about that? I wanted the smart one close to help my children with their sums. I wanted the funny one to dole out stories and humor when things got bad. I hated Jay Fiddling Fosdick for taking her away from me.

Ma and Pa were as upset as I was—she was everyone's favorite.

Preparing to leave on this epic voyage into the unknown should've been exciting. We piled up supplies around the house, and we added boards to the wagons. We sewed the shell for the sun and wind shade on each of the wagons while my pa built the frames. I helped when my dad split the wood for the oxen yokes. We traded some of our dairy cows for more oxen. We slaughtered and salted hogs, and we constructed cages to hold our chickens while we travelled. We'd let them out each night to scratch around and find food, but they had to be secured for the traveling.

Pa tried to keep things happy by talking about California. He'd now done his research, and we knew that the ground there was fecund—supposedly, anything would grow. We knew you could secure a portion of land there for a song. With our fifteen hundred coins, we'd be able to buy the nicest of spots, even after the costs of traveling two thousand miles. Bees were everywhere, and grass grew bountifully without irrigation for the cattle, even during the winter. It was paradise, or as near to it as anyone had found.

But instead of becoming more excited as the day to depart drew nearer, my heart grew heavier.

"You should take Nedra." Ma rubbed our dun mare's face, but her eyes were on Sarah. "She loves you more than anyone else, and the terribly long journey would probably be too hard on her."

Sarah sighed and leaned against Nedra's round side. "She's not even old, Ma."

"Fifteen for a horse is different than fifteen for a human," Ma said. But we all knew she was trying to leave Sarah something valuable. Something by which to remember us. "She can have a few more foals, and then you'll be set for years to come, with Graves animals." Ma's eyes welled with tears yet again.

"I can't do that." Sarah straightened.

Mom handed her the lead. "I insist. Your pa and I can spare her, and maybe someday you can ride her out for a visit."

It was a lie we were telling more and more often as our departure hastened.

"Bess and her calf are already too generous a bridal gift," Sarah said. "Plus my hope chest." She shook her head. "We can't take more, not when you and Pa have eight other children to look after."

"Just take her," I said. "It's not like we don't know what we need at this point." I hated how angry I got, but I couldn't help it. I wasn't mad at Sarah—I loved her too much for that. But my anger at the situation had to go somewhere, so every time Jay came over to visit, I nearly bit his head off.

He knew why. He never complained.

The day before we were set to leave, we spent hours stacking all our supplies into the wagons. Bedrolls, iron cookware, dutch ovens, Dad's tools, iron shoes, nails, seeds for the spring, candles, tarps, blankets, and the three salted hogs.

I was tired and irritable when we finished, and I was ready to head inside for something to eat when I saw Jay jogging toward us. Technically it was too far for me to see his face, coming up from the edge of the river as he was, but his big, goofy straw hat was a dead giveaway. I turned to go inside, refusing to greet him with a smile. I should be kind to Sarah's future husband, but I just couldn't.

Sarah grabbed my arm. "Stay, please. He said he wants to go for a walk today, like we used to." Before he declared he'd be staying behind, and keeping my best friend with him.

I gritted my teeth, but I couldn't tell Sarah no. It might be the last request she made of me. "The path will be muddy." The spring had been wet, wet, wet, and I was already sick of it, two weeks into April. "My shoes will get covered in mud."

Sarah rolled her eyes, but she nodded as she said, "Fine. If you go, I'll clean them for you." She hated cleaning muddy shoes, so that offer meant something.

When Jay finally reached us, I could tell he had more 'exciting' news. Yesterday, he came over with the *very exciting* news that their lost rooster was found. The day before, he shared that their cow had given birth to twins. He was practically bouncing, and his entire face was taken up with a lopsided grin. It looked as goofy as his hat.

"What?" I asked. "What happened this time?"

"When we went hunting this morning, Pa and I managed to shoot not one, not even two, but four deer. *And* an elk." His eyes widened, his stupid grin growing even larger.

"Amazing," I said, my voice flat. "What amazing news." I don't roll my eyes, but it's hard.

"It is good news." He folded his arms. "Because with all the good news that kept coming in, my father decided that he shouldn't be standing in our way." Jay dropped his gaze to Sarah's. "He's given his blessing."

"He's—what?" Sarah's mouth dangled open. Her eyes widened. She inhaled sharply. "Tell me exactly what that means."

"I'm late today—I was going to come help load the wagons—but the reason is that Father went through and separated out the things he's sending with us for our journey. . .to California."

I whooped so loudly that people started shooting out of the door of our farmhouse.

"What's going on?" Ma asked.

"Why are you shouting?" Pa asked.

"Sarah's coming!" I'd grabbed her hands and we were spinning round and round.

Within moments, all the kids had joined in, and we were running and shouting and dancing in circles. "I promised Mother and Father we'd be married before we left," Jay said. "They wanted to see it."

"Then we have a wedding cake to make," Ma said. But she didn't look upset at all.

"And I think we should shift some things over," Pa said. "We're giving you one of our wagons as a wedding gift."

It was a very happy day all around.

We had no idea how rare that would be in the months to come.

CHAPTER 2

Virginia Reed

I was only eight years old when Papa bought Billy for me.

Papa and Mama had given me a lot of amazing things, but my little cream pony was *by far* the best gift I'd ever received. Now, as we prepared for an unimaginably long trip from Springfield, Illinois to California, the thing I looked forward to the most was daily rides on Billy. His glossy coat gleamed, and when he tossed his head, the braids I'd plaited along his mane shook. There had never been a golden pony as lovely as mine.

We had spent the last hour and more saying goodbye to all our gathered friends. Papa's hand had been clasped over and over, and all his friends were standing still, watching us leave. My schoolmates had come, some of them crying, and some of them standing with somber faces. A few had already left, unable to stand and watch as we left.

"It's almost time, Virginia." Papa grinned when he gestured for me to climb up into the saddle, and I knew that of everyone in the family, no one was as excited as the two of us. Mama was sobbing, actually. I could hear her from her seat inside the family wagon.

But I smiled broadly back at Papa, ready for the adventure.

Mama's brothers, Gersham and James, were trying to act excited, but we all knew they were upset. Mama's mother, Grandma Keyes, a 'tough

7

old bird,' as Papa called her, insisted that she would come with us. No matter how her sons begged, she never changed her mind.

"Ginny," she called from where her sons had carried her and placed her on a big feather bed inside the family wagon. *"Ginny."*

"I'm here." I waved.

She could only see me from the back of the wagon now because being on Billy made me taller. Our friends had taken to calling the two-story wagon Papa had custom designed a 'Pioneer Palace Car,' which was a ridiculous name, but even I had to admit that it was fitting. Patty's small face was floating next to Grandma's, holding the curtains back. Grandma Keyes smiled her gap-toothed smile and waved.

She'd never been in the best of health that I could remember, and even for a healthy person, this was supposed to be a difficult journey. Last night I had even asked her, "Papa says your cough's getting worse. Are you sure you should come?"

"My dear." She cradled the side of my face with her hand. "You don't have children yet, so I won't fault you for asking." She coughed then, loud and long. Once she could speak, her smile was gentle as she said, "One of my sons already went west, and if God's willing, we'll cross paths with your uncle. But above all things, I won't be parted from your mother. She's my only daughter, and it's that simple." She had patted my hand then, like there was nothing more to say.

My uncles followed us for almost two full days in the hope that she'd change her mind, riding alongside our wagon processional and camping nearby at night.

She didn't.

"At least Reed spared no expense," Uncle James said as they prepared to turn around. "That's the most ridiculous wagon I have ever seen—I hope those oxen can pull it the whole way."

Our wagon was much taller, and it was wider, too. It had storage above each wheel and under the bouncing seats. It had a second floor with beds, and the main cabin had a stove with a pipe that carefully ran the length of it, keeping us warm even on the coldest of mornings.

Because of its size, it took four yoke of oxen to pull it, eight beasts in all, and Papa had hired the finest drover just to manage it. He was a man we'd known for years and years—he had worked for Papa's wood mill, and we all loved Milt Elliott. When we told him we were leaving, he begged to come with us.

We had two more wagons full of supplies, of course, and Papa hired two more men to tend them. After all, he couldn't very well ride with me every day if he was chained to a wagon, directing oxen. The other two wagons were loaded down with our supplies, including everything we could even imagine we might want. In addition to the usual tents, food, blankets, tools, clothing, and so forth, Papa had ordered a brand new cooking stove for when we reached California. Mama's friends had also given her a full-length looking glass, which Papa hung on the far side of the family car so that she could maintain her looks on this long trek.

Our long-time housekeeper and cook, Eliza Williams, came with us, as did Baylis Williams, her albino brother. Poor Baylis had to stay hidden in one of the supply wagons all day, or he'd risk burning his skin to a crisp. He said he'd never been able to go out in the sun, which I thought was the most terrible curse. He was always happy to help with tasks once the sun went down, and he liked to smile as much as his sister. It was nice to have them along to help with the cows and the cooking and the hauling water.

So far, that was the only thing I really didn't like about traveling.

Everything that was already annoying back home was doubly hard when you were traveling. Most days, I rode out on Billy and Papa rode on his mare, Glaucus, moving easily ahead of the ponderously slow wagons. That was especially nice, because all those oxen feet churned up loads of dust when it was dry, and created lots of terrible ruts and bogs when it was wet. We had a job, though. Since we were ahead, we'd look and look for good places to stop. We had to stop twice—once in the middle of the day to give the animals a break and eat something. And again for the night.

At lunch, we mostly just wanted to find shade and water, but after a long day of walking, we needed water and a safe place to stop for humans and animals both. I got really good at finding accessible water and long, rich grass. When things looked safe and protected, like in places where there weren't many Indians, or when we found a nice sheltered area, we didn't have to circle the wagons to keep the cattle in between them. That made things a lot easier, and the ground stayed a lot less messy.

Horses and cows that are eating and drinking also poop a lot.

At thirteen, I'm old enough to keep my eyes open and avoid it, but some of the little kids just don't pay attention. My youngest brother,

Thomas, always came back with poop splattered on his pants, and Mama would exhale slowly and sigh before helping him change clothes. Thanks to a very wet spring, for most of the first few weeks, everything that wasn't covered in poop was covered in mud.

It squelched. It splattered. It just plain stunk.

It kept me and Papa on horseback every second we could be, but we did have to clean Glaucus and Billy's feet off really well each day, or they could go lame. Even with the mud, and later, the bugs, we just kept right on going, even when our poor teamsters, Walt Herron, James Smith, and Milt Elliot, had to shout and whip the oxen to get them moving. Even when the wagon wheels got stuck and we had to double team the wagons, we kept moving ahead. Even when the sun beat down or the rain fell or the wind screamed, we bowed our heads, and we kept going.

Until finally, we reached the Big Blue River.

I think that was around the end of May, and after Grandma Keyes had gotten better for a bit, she wilted again. For nearly a week of wet, miserable, muddy travel, she spent all day every day lying down. She cried about the big lumps, and she moaned through the long, frustrating slogs, and my little eight-year-old sister Patty never left her side. Patty would also describe everything to her, from Indians to wildflowers, and then she'd twitch the window open when Grandma wanted to see things for herself.

But Grandma's cough got worse, and her spirits got awfully low.

When we asked her to tell us stories about her aunt who was captured by the Indians, which she normally loved to tell, she'd just wave us off and then start to cough again. I was praying for her to get better every morning and every night, but God wasn't listening.

Not one bit, apparently, because it only got worse.

When we got to that Big Blue River, it was bigger than ever before, and it didn't even look very blue. "That water looks almost brown," I said, eyeing it sideways so I could also watch Papa's reaction. I liked to know what he thought, so I could know what I thought.

"It's all the rain." He was frowning. "There's no way we can ford it, not like that."

"What will we do, then?"

Papa shrugged. "Not much we can do. We'll have to wait for it to go down."

We waited, and then we waited some more. The river didn't go down, but Grandma Keyes, well, she did something that made us care a little less about the enormous, brownish Big Blue River.

She coughed and coughed and coughed.

And then she died.

Mama was never the strongest or the fiercest, but when she lost Grandma, her grief was definitely the biggest. It hurt my heart to see her sobbing. Patty went from being Grandma Keyes' shadow to being Mama's. She was stuck to Mama like a flea to a dog, so I wasn't sure what to do.

"Come along, Ginny," Papa said. "You and I will make sure Grandma Keyes has a beautiful casket, even out here in the wilds."

Not only did Papa pay someone to build her a mighty fine casket out of a fresh-hewn cottonwood tree, but he also found a man to carve her name and birthplace on a nice, flat, round rock. The man was named John Denton. Papa knew him back in Springfield, and he was working for the Donners. As we were all friends, Mr. Denton really wanted to do it right. He spent all day carving Grandma Keyes' name, birthdate, and death date. It looked real nice when he was done.

By way of a service, a Reverend Cornwall tried to say some nice words, but between Mama's crying and Patty's quiet sobs, I didn't hear much of it. I knew why everyone was sad—she was gone, of course, but they also didn't like leaving her on the trail. I was sad not to be able to visit her grave too, but Grandma knew she was sick, and she got to spend her last weeks with the people she loved the most. I thought that if we could have asked her again, even knowing she'd die out here, she'd do the exact same thing and come with us. That made it less sad to me.

After the funeral was finally past, something else became pretty clear. The Big Blue River wasn't going to settle down any time soon, and we'd waited too long already. Papa set to work after that on making rafts, because we were stuck floating the wagons across.

Milt Elliott was the best driver in the whole company, and he was responsible for our family wagon with almost all of our special things in it. Even though he was good at his job, and even though Papa said not to worry, I was scared that our wagon wouldn't make it across. It was way bigger and way heavier and way *more everything* than everyone else's, and what if the raft just gave out and it sank to the bottom of the stupid, muddy river?

I told Milt, "Make sure those oxen don't miss the raft, alright?"

He laughed so hard, he slapped his thigh. "No, little Virginia, you can be sure of that. I won't let them miss it."

I shouldn't have worried so much. With just three words, "whoa," "haw," and "gee," Milt Elliott could make those oxen do most anything. The men made one twenty-five foot wide raft, cut from the biggest trees they could find, and that was the one we used. Milt had a little trouble, but in the end, he forced all eight of them onto that newly-made raft.

After far, far too long, we were finally on our way again.

If Mama looked back a little more during the next day or two, well, I couldn't fault her for that. I'm sure if I'd lost Mama, I'd be crying for months.

One good thing happened the day after we finally cleared the Big Blue River—I made a friend. Dad and I were scouting a good spot to stop, and we hadn't had much luck, so Papa told me to head back and let everyone know that we'd have to go just a little farther than usual.

"I know it'll be a long day," he said, "but with the delay we had, I imagine most people will be pleased to make a little extra progress."

I was wheeling Billy around to head back around the corner when I nearly ran headlong into someone coming around the bend. It was a boy I'd seen before but not had much chance to visit with. His name was Eddie—Edward Breen—but that was all I knew.

"Whoa." He hauled back on the reins of his horse, who had not taken our near collision in stride. His sorrel's eyes rolled, and her nostrils flared, and she tossed her head and stomped, but Eddie handled her well.

Once both our horses had calmed down, I pointed behind him. "My father sent me back to let everyone know we'll have to make a late camp today."

"Your Pa is James Reed?"

I nodded.

"He's from Ireland."

He wasn't asking. He already knew. I nodded again.

"My father's from Ireland, too. Only. . ." He swallowed. "We're Catholic."

I shrugged.

"You don't care?"

I shook my head slowly.

He watched me for a moment, and then he asked me in a small voice, "Why do we have to make camp later?"

"There's not enough grass here." I tossed my head toward the area beyond. "It's just too rocky."

"And back there, the drop to get to the stream was too steep."

I nodded. "Exactly." I couldn't help my smile. "Did everyone back with the wagons seem exhausted?"

"Don't they always?" He wasn't quite smiling, but almost.

"I can't really blame them," I said. "I feel sorry for the ones who don't have horses to ride."

"My pa and my brother John are stuck driving the wagons, and my Pa says Patty Junior's too small to ride out alone." His smile was smug. "So I'm the only one who can, really."

"My sister Patty's way too small, too."

"Both Pattys are too small." Eddie was really smirking.

"Patrick and Patricia," I said. "It's kind of funny that we both have younger siblings we call Patty."

"We have to call him that, because Patrick Junior is way too long to say, but I bet mine's more annoying."

"I wouldn't count on it." I encouraged Billy to start trotting back, and Eddie kept up admirably. "Mine has this doll she never stops playing with."

Eddie frowned, as if he was mulling over a problem. "Dolls? What's annoying about that? Mine picks his nose."

"Patty steals my sweets." Billy never wanted another horse to pass him, so as Eddy's horse sped up, so did Billy. I kept him from cantering, but we were moving pretty well along.

"Did I just say he picked his nose?" He arched one eyebrow. "He also eats the boogers."

"Eww."

"See?" He chuckled. "I win."

The rest of the ride was just as ridiculous, and I loved every minute of it. By the time we reached the first wagon in our group, Eddie and I were fast friends.

And the next morning, when Papa and I rode out, he was ready.

"Can Eddie Breen come along with us?" I asked Papa.

Papa eyed him up and down. "You're Patrick Breen's boy?"

Eddie nodded slowly.

"You can handle that horse?"

My new friend smiled. "Trixie's not quite as fast or as sure-footed as your mare, sir, but yes. She listens to me most of the time, and I make her listen the rest."

Eddie might not have known it, but complimenting Papa's grey mare was literally the best thing he could have done. Sometimes I thought the only thing Papa liked more than me or Mama or the other children was his horse. I knew he loved us more, but it was fairly close. He'd broken Glaucus himself, and she loved him like he was her mother or something.

"You're alright, boy. As long as your father can spare you, you can ride out with us."

And that's how I became best friends with an Irish Catholic boy. I had no idea at the time how much that friendship would change my life in the months to come.

CHAPTER 3
Mary Ann Graves

It took us nearly a month to reach St. Joe's.

We reached the outskirts of town just before dusk, and we set up camp the same way we always did. When dawn came, we were all buzzing with excitement about going into town. We'd been traveling for weeks and weeks, but they called St. Joe's the launch point for a reason. We hoped to find a wagon train to join here.

Pa woke my seventeen-year-old brother, Billy, and they headed out to round up the oxen and our four dairy cows. One of them was struggling to keep up right now, because she was due to have a calf any day. Another just had her calf a week ago. We had to keep it in the wagon for a few days, but new calves learn to walk fast.

I grabbed two buckets, pouring what was left from the night into the bucket for the cattle, and then heading to the stream with the other. My little sister, Eleanor, was already awake, tossing handfuls of grain to the six chickens to gather them back in. They knew what was coming, and it took them a few moments to decide whether it was worth a handful of grain. They didn't especially like being locked back in their wooden boxes for another day of bumpy riding.

I had to yank the blanket off Lovina—she's eleven, and as different from level, calm, thirteen-year-old Eleanor as can be. "Mary *Ann*," Lovina whimpered. "Just a few more minutes. I'm so *tired*."

"But last night, I slept with Nancy, so you can't say she kicked you all night." I arched one eyebrow. Nancy *did* kick, but being kicked was less annoying than hearing Lovina whine about it.

"This time, it was Johnny kicking. And didn't you hear Frankie? He woke up and kept coughing, *all* night long."

I hadn't, but I'd learned to sleep through most everything years and years ago. Living in a one-bedroom farmhouse had basically prepared us to share a tent, or at least, I thought it had. In spite of every single day of her life leading up to the trip, Lovina had apparently never become used to all the noises and rigamarole of a large family. "Even so," I said, trying to stay calm, "it's time to start working on the flour."

"Why can't we just buy the expensive flour? I hate the middlings."

"Superfine costs too much," I said. "And with a little sifting, the middlings taste just fine." We toss the excess to the chickens the next morning anyway, so there's no waste. Trying to explain the basics of economizing to Lovina had always been a waste of time.

"No," Johnny said. "Don't let Lovina do it. I nearly chipped my teeth on a rock last time she sifted it."

"A rock? Really?" I couldn't help snorting a little.

Johnny exaggerated as much as Lovina complained.

Sarah was carrying another bucket back from the stream. "Did you say you found a *rock* in the bread?" She met my eyes. "Sounds pretty dangerous. Why don't you help her sift, then? You can be quality control. Keep all our teeth safe."

Lovina and Johnny were both muttering, but they were also moving toward the wagon when I started sawing a hunk off the dangling salted pork. By the time I had it cut into smaller strips and was tossing it into the frying pan, Eleanor had returned with three large eggs and a tiny one. My father would be pleased. We only found one yesterday, and somehow it had been cracked. We had to feed it to Ollie, our dog. He was delighted, but wasted food never makes Pa happy.

Mother had the fire going already, and Eleanor set right to mixing the biscuits while I got the pork strips frying. By the time we finished making breakfast, Lovina had the flour ready for us to mix up the bread we'd use for the rest of the day. We'd had a lot of practice, so it was no shock to me to discover that Ma had broken down the tent and stowed it away and the bread was nearly done baking, at about the same time that the boys got all the animals fed, watered, and hooked up to the wagons.

We set the dutch ovens in the back of the wagons and headed out just after we all ate breakfast. Walking fifteen miles every day with wagons pulled by oxen wasn't easy, but we had it down to an art by now. Our one teamster, John Snyder, took control of one wagon, Billy and Pa shared the load of driving the other, and Jay Fosdick drove the third. For years, most people headed to California made for Independence, Missouri, but an increasingly large number of emigrants were now leaving from St. Joseph's. From our part of Illinois, it just made sense to launch from somewhere a bit closer.

It had been a cold, dirty, damp month getting here.

But St. Joe's was thankfully dry, and blessedly full of people, and those people were eagerly selling all the supplies we needed. I was already heartily sick of eating biscuits, a bite of egg, and salted pork every morning. Because Pa had sold his farm for quite a lot, we had enough to buy what we needed, but that didn't mean Pa *wanted* to spend a dime more than necessary. That was just who he was.

Sarah and Jay made their own decisions on supplies, but Ma left Eleanor and John Snyder, our family friend turned paid helper, to watch the kids while Ma and Pa and I went to buy supplies for the rest of us. It was a lot to buy, but we needed all of it. Sugar, twenty pounds a person, flour, at least two hundred pounds more than what we had per person, ten pounds of salt, brandy for Ma, whiskey for Pa, vinegar, crackers, hard tack, a wheel of cheese, in case our mother cow doesn't make much milk for a while on travel rations, saleratus, raisins, and some hard candies for the youngest kids when they had bad days.

It was almost alarming to see how fast the cost added up, and I wasn't even the one paying. Even still, once we hauled the supplies out, we had to find a place for all of them in the two wagons we shared. Pa wound up storing a bit of it with Jay and Sarah, and I realized the bit he 'stored' was really what he thought they would be short.

My Pa wasn't perfect, but he loved his kids. We were lucky to have him.

After buying food, we bought three new pairs of shoes, a few new coats, socks, a few blankets, and then Pa had an axe mended. He also bought a few new tools, and a whole stack of iron shoes for the oxen. With eighteen oxen between the three wagons, we had a lot of animals to care for. The last thing you want to be without in the middle of a long-distance trip is the shoes your oxen or horses need to walk comfortably.

That night, none of us were bone-tired, because we hadn't walked fifteen miles like usual. Instead of dropping right to sleep after dinner, Jay got his fiddle out. As much as it annoyed me that he stole my sister away, I could always understand *how* when he played. It was like everything else disappeared.

There was a youngish man in a wagon a few down from us who walked down to join us with a smile on his face. He had longish, brown hair, and bright hazel eyes. "That's amazing," he said, glancing at Jay.

"He's my brother-in-law," I said. "He knows his way around a fiddle —that's for sure."

"He's married to your sister?" He glanced at Sarah.

I nodded.

"But then, you're. . ." The man raised his eyebrows.

I could feel the heat rise in my cheeks. "I'm not wed."

John Snyder stood up then, and without saying another word, yanked the wide, flat piece of wood that formed the back of the wagon out of its place and set it on the mostly-flat but grass-covered ground. "Play a fun one, Jay."

John Snyder had been the handsomest man in our small town before we left, and since we set out on the trail, I'd yet to see someone better looking. He had sandy-blond hair, sky-blue eyes, and a dusting of freckles across his nose. His eyes were a bit close-set, but they lent him a kind of boyish charm. And when Jay began to play *The Rose of Allendale*, faster than I'd usually heard it played, John started to dance. I had no idea he was an accomplished dancer.

The dancing attracted even more travelers. Before I knew it, more wagon tails had been dropped down next to ours. And when Jay stopped playing, the man with the hazel eyes said, "Can you play *Skip to my Lou*?"

Jay's eyes were twinkling when he started.

When the man offered me his hand, I took it. I hadn't danced in what felt like forever, but it was easy. It felt. . .nice. Things hadn't been normal since we'd set out a month gone, but without the ever-present mud, without the bone-deep exhaustion from walking, walking, walking, and with wagons full of supplies, I felt. . .optimistic.

It made me smile.

And when someone began singing, "Lost my partner, what shall I do?" I was shocked when John Snyder appeared right next to me and snatched my hand away from the hazel-eyed traveler with a smile.

"Finally," John said. "I've been waiting a month for a chance to dance with you."

My heart flipped over in my chest.

His hand tightened on mine, and he pulled us tighter together with a grin that only I could see in the fading light. It was a surprise, because in the month we'd been traveling together, he hadn't so much as flirted once. When the song ended, he didn't let go of my hand. When I tried to tug it away, he said, "I can't let go. I'm worried you'll dance with that other man again." His intensely blue eyes were holding my gaze.

I swallowed. "Why do you care?"

"I might have to punch him if you do." The side of his mouth turned upward, but just a hair. I couldn't tell whether he was kidding.

"You wouldn't dare punch a stranger."

"Try me." The intensity of his gaze was even more exciting than his good looks. He seemed deadly serious.

I dragged a breath into my tired lungs, and I lifted my chin. "Well, if you don't want me dancing with anyone else, you'll have to give me a reason not to. A reason that makes sense."

He stepped closer, reminding me just how much he towered over me, and he whispered. "I've liked you for quite some time, Mary Ann Graves, but as I'm working for your father right now, I thought I ought to leave you alone."

"And this is leaving it alone?" I arched one eyebrow.

A muscle in his jaw jumped. "Sometimes what I think I *ought* to do and what I *actually* do aren't the same."

"So if I don't dance with that guy, you'll just keep ignoring me?"

He blinked. "Maybe."

"That won't do. I better find him quick."

He laughed then, loud and long. "You're quite a girl, Mary Ann. Quite a girl."

That was when it started. Right there, on the very night we finished our business at St. Joe's, we set out for California and John Snyder took my hand and squeezed. It was the point of no return for a lot of things.

CHAPTER 4

Virginia Reed

By the time we crossed the Platte River on June 8, it had been almost two months since we left home. At first, I was excited to get bacon each morning. We only had it a few days a week back home. Mama preferred eggs and fish at least half of the time. I'd never been much for fish, especially lake trout, which was the easiest thing to come by in Illinois, but after two months of nothing but salted pork every single morning, I was heartily sick of bacon as well. I wasn't alone in being tired of it, but most of the men were too exhausted to try their hands at fishing in the waning light after we made camp each night, so salted pork was all we had.

When Papa suggested that we could swing in a wide loop to look for game now that we saw some open, grassy areas, I heartily agreed. He loaded up his bag and we set out, just the two of us. Eddie's ma needed him to help her with some hauling today, so he wasn't riding out. I suspected his horse might've gotten a little sore, too. There were a lot of rocks, and Trixie was moving slow as we made camp. I loved having a friend who also loved to ride, but I also liked having some time with just my father.

That day, I wasn't unhappy that it was just me and Papa.

At first, we mostly just saw geese—from too far a distance to shoot— and then a few rabbits. Papa wasn't above shooting a rabbit, but today, I could tell he wanted something bigger. He wasn't even taking aim at the little critters. We'd gone about as far away as we could without tiring the horses, I could tell, but that's when we saw them. Three elk. A mother and its baby, which Papa tried not to shoot, and a young buck, with growing but still prominent antlers.

"This is it, darling. Hang back while I bring one home."

I had no problems hanging back. My pony Billy was many things: golden, shining, and brave, for a few. He never shied or fussed about walking through streams or even fording rivers, even though Papa said horses can't tell how deep the water is. He was willing to charge through anthill infested fields, he would plow past piles of old leaves or other detritus, and he never balked at climbing or descending steep hills.

But he didn't much care for gunshot.

Papa was lucky that Glaucus, his grey mare, didn't bat an eye at the loud bangs, or shift and rear when he started to reload, either. In fact, after years with Papa, she almost took over while he was busy, and once she saw the elk, I could tell she knew what Papa wanted. She skirted the small bluff with a thicket to provide some cover, and then when they reached the edge, she froze, holding entirely still.

That's when Papa took his shot. The buck shuddered, and then he went down. It was one of the easiest kills I'd seen Papa make, and he had made a lot. He was right handy with a rifle, but he also knew how to use a handgun—his favorite was the Allen & Thurber pepperbox. I wasn't sure if he'd brought it today, its range not being nearly as good as the rifle, but I knew he could manage one.

"Darling, head on over and take her." He meant Glaucus, of course.

Because now, our biggest problem was going to be transporting the majority of the elk back to camp with just two horses. I knew what Papa would need first—a rope to hang the elk and drain a lot of the blood, and then help with the horses while he quartered it. That wasn't a part of hunting that I particularly enjoyed, so Papa handed me Glaucus's reins and I took the horses to be watered and graze for a bit while Papa worked.

Once the horses were grazing happily, I wandered back to see what progress Papa had made. He'd already drained the blood, and he was nearly done field dressing it, which is a messy business. I was sure he'd wash in the nearby stream, but Mama and Eliza would still have quite a lot of work cleaning the blood out of his sleeves.

He wiped his brow with his shoulder, and a smear of red covered his forehead. I laughed, which is how he knew I was near, and that's also how I was caught. "Come on over and help me hold this steady."

I sighed heavily, but I knew he'd need my help to quarter it properly.

"It's a shame I can't take the head back. For a young buck, he's got a proper rack." Papa was happy to provide meat, but he also enjoyed being regaled by the other travelers for his hunting prowess. I knew it would bother him to leave his trophy behind, but the meat was too valuable to sacrifice, and we only had two horses to take it.

"Do you think we'll rejoin the trail around where the wagons are?"

Papa sighed. "I hope so."

We'd have to walk alongside the horses on the way back, since it was unfair to ask them to carry both us and the elk, but it would be worth it. I was hardly salivating while looking at all the disgusting gore in front of me, but I would be soon enough, I knew. Elk meat was good eating. It wasn't as fatty as the salted pork, but in many ways, it was more delicious.

It took us another hour and a half to get the meat prepped, and Papa and I both cringed a little when we lashed it to our beautiful saddles— cleaning them up would be a long process—but the meat would hold up much better if we didn't drag it such a long way.

"It's a lot of work to bring back meat for the wagon train," I said. "We could maybe salt it and keep it all ourselves."

Papa rolled his eyes. "It's much better fresh, and besides, that takes time we don't have. We need to keep moving. There will be more elk, darling. Don't you worry about that."

There were always more elk, especially when your papa was as great a hunter as mine. "I know."

"Plus, game always tastes better when it's shared."

Sometimes it annoyed me that we were always the ones doing all the sharing, but it never upset Papa, so I tried to be glad, too. When we got back, we were hailed as returning conquerors, and I understood his desire to help the others on the trail a little more. He even let me pass out sections to the families we were traveling with.

George Donner clapped Papa on the shoulder and beamed. "You always shoot the best elk, Reed. Thanks."

George's younger brother was much, much smaller, and he always looked a little ill to me, but he was just as happy for the meat. "Many thanks, my friend." Jacob Donner waved his wife over, and she was practically beaming. "It's a welcome change from the salted pork."

I wasn't the only one sick of it, clearly.

That night, we all feasted, and there was even a little dancing. Eddie Breen surprised me, dancing a little jig on the back of their wagon tongue when his pa played a fiddle.

"That little boy can dance," Papa said with bright eyes.

It was a good day, if an exhausting one. Mama insisted on doing all the washing, and then Baylis, who was very excited for the meat, insisted on cleaning up both our saddles! I hadn't expected that. Maybe that's why, the next afternoon, when we were scouting out a decent place to stop for the night, Papa was so upset.

"Reed!" William Russell was the leader of the wagon train we'd been following, and I rarely saw him smiling so broadly. Usually, I saw him at night, and the Kentuckian was almost always taking a swig from his silver flask. "You'll never guess what we did today." He slapped his knee.

Papa frowned, slowing Glaucus to a stop. "What?"

"You sure thought you were the hero yesterday, sharing out those small portions of elk, didn't you?" Russell's eyes were wild, his chin lifted. "That piece you gave us was small enough. Well, well. I guess you're not the star today, not anymore."

The furrow in Papa's brow deepened. "What do you mean?"

"What do I mean? Joseph shot a buffalo! We just dragged it back. It puts that tiny elk of yours to shame."

As they moved on, I noticed that one of the men I didn't know had lashed a large hairy carcass to an oxen team. He was dragging it along behind them with two sturdy ropes. Papa's eyes narrowed as they passed.

"Looks like you'll have to relinquish your crown, Reed," the bearded man said, spitting on the ground. "You greenhorn *sucker*."

Papa almost never got angry. When I made a mistake and ruined the finish on our dining table, when Patty knocked a nice glass bottle over and it broke, when Mama burned dinner, or when Thomas soiled Papa's favorite trousers with a carelessly spilled bowl of stew, my father would just smile or shrug and say, "Life happens. It's a memory."

Mama had more bad days than good most months, leaving a lot of her chores to me and Papa, but he never got mad about that either. He would just shrug, smile his sideways smile, and say, "Life isn't always fun."

But not that day. That day, he was *mad*. His mouth trembled. His hands tightened into bright, white fists around Glaucus' reins. And once the men had ambled past, Papa spun around, holding Glaucus still until he had chosen our direction, and then he shouted, "Hiyah."

I had to kick Billy hard to keep up.

It took him nearly an hour, but we rode up and down the lines of the wagons until Papa found three men willing to go with him on a hunting party the next day.

"I mean to kill some buffalo," Papa muttered as we reached our campsite, finally. "Not one. Not two. At least three." He nodded. "I'll tell Milt to have our oxen team ready to come and get them when I do."

Our family friend was just as upset as Papa when he heard what the men had said, but he had to drive the family wagon, so he couldn't go. "I'll have the oxen ready when you show them." Milt spat on the ground. "You're no sucker."

George Donner and one of his teamsters, a man even larger than Mr. Donner, named Hiram Miller, were both coming, too. Hiram Miller was also friends with my father, and he'd come by the house a time or two before we left. He was supposed to be a good shot, too. They were nearly as riled up as Papa and Milt had been.

I hadn't realized what an insult calling someone a sucker was, I guess, but the men all knew. The next morning, they had barely drunk their coffee and grabbed biscuits before Papa was swinging up into his saddle. I had to scramble to finish getting Billy ready and hop on.

Papa pointed. "Russell said the buffalo herd was that way."

We had to cross the Platte River a few times. It reminded me a little bit of a braid, winding back and forth with wider and deeper parts here and there. It took a little time, but we always found some shallower spots to wade through. It was warm enough that getting a little wet didn't upset me much.

But I worried about how we'd get all the buffalo he shot back, if we ever found them at all. Milt might have the oxen ready, but they were there, and we were here, and he had no way of knowing where to bring them.

When I finally swung up in the saddle, I asked, "How's Milt going to know where to bring all the oxen?"

Papa and Hiram Miller both laughed then, like I'd made a funny joke.

"Once we've shot the buffalo," Papa said. "That'll be your job, darling. You'll head back to the wagons, and you'll let everyone know where to find us."

"Oh."

"Why else did you think we let a little girl come along?" George Donner had five daughters, two of them from his first wife, and the oldest was my age. We'd been friends at school, but she never came riding. Unlike Papa, George encouraged his girls to do 'female things.' I was glad I hadn't gotten stuck with George Donner as my papa.

I began to worry that we might not even find any buffalo, much less kill any. Papa didn't seem nervous at all, though. Once someone else had done something, he was sure he could do it too, and better than they did. After a lot of years of watching him, I had learned not to stress much when he was sure of something.

"Are you scared at all?" Hiram asked. "They do say that buffalo can stampede. And you've never shot one before, so—"

Papa waved him off before he could even finish. "With Glaucus, it won't matter. No buffalo could possibly catch us, and trust me. She won't balk. Not when it matters."

George Donner shot Hiram a nervous look.

Just then, a rider joined us from the direction we'd just traveled. It was a man Papa liked, William Eddy.

He was also the man I had talked to the most, and I was glad to see he was coming along. He was like Papa—he loved to talk. He built carriages before he decided to move west, and he was young, with a pretty wife and two small children. He had longish, very straight brown hair, which was almost boring, but he took a lot of care with his clothing. Even that day, he had a nice little folded necktie, which was a little silly when it was so warm.

But when he joined the group, he waved at the men and smiled at me. "Nice to have a little beauty on our side." His smile was kind, just like his wife.

Eleanor Eddy had her hands full with their three-year-old son and one-year-old daughter, so I was surprised he came. "Who's driving your wagon?" I asked.

"You know, my wife said she could do it for a day," Mr. Eddy said. "She didn't get any last night, and she was jealous."

Papa and Mr. Eddy and some of the others had refused to eat the buffalo the men brought back yesterday on principle. "Don't worry," Papa said. "We'll bring back plenty today."

But almost an hour later, as sweat began to roll down my back, we hadn't seen a single buffalo. I could tell the other men were starting to get a little cranky.

"Didn't they say they were this direction?" George Donner asked. "A huge herd—can't miss them."

Papa grunted.

"Do you think they'd lie to us?" Hiram asked.

"They do move around," George Donner said. "A massive herd of cattle like that could cover quite a bit of land."

"Or they exaggerated how many there were," Mr. Eddy said. "It would be just like that Herman to do that."

George Donner wiped a sleeve across his brow. He looked a little pale.

"Are you alright?" I asked. "We could take a break and water the horses."

"I'm fine." Mr. Donner squared his shoulders and scowled.

"My mama gets headaches, you know," I said. "I know some days can be hard."

"My brother Jacob gets headaches, but I'm fine," George said. "I never got the ague. I'm just hot and tired."

I'd heard of the Illinois shakes, and it wasn't something I wanted to deal with. I felt sorry for poor Jacob Donner, and I was glad his brother didn't get sick too. Having fevers and shakes that came and went would make anyone miserable. "I'm sorry to hear your brother's sick a lot," I said.

"At least he didn't get cholera," George said. "That would have been far worse."

"Mr. Donner." Hiram glanced my way, like George had said something untoward.

"What?" I looked toward Papa. "What's wrong with cholera?"

"Other than the fact that it kills people, where the ague just makes them miserable?" Mr. Eddy asked.

"Has Ma ever told you about how she and I met?" Papa asked, slowing Glaucus a little, so he could watch my face.

I shook my head.

"Well, you're thirteen. That's old enough to know." Papa nodded slowly, easing Glaucus to a walk so she would fall into step beside Billy. "Your Ma was quite a sight, back in the day."

"Was it love at first sight?" I asked.

Papa laughed. "Of course it was, for me, but she caught the eye of someone else, someone she fancied more."

My jaw dropped. "What? How?"

"Your Ma would ride bareback all around town, her bonnet dangling back from her neck by its strings. Her body would be crouched low over her horse, and she won every race she entered. I'd never seen a finer horsewoman."

I could barely believe his words. How could he be describing my mother? "Mama?"

He laughed. "She was a sight to behold—she didn't get headaches, not then. And one of the richest men in the entire county had asked her to marry him. She said yes."

"Was that my other Pa?" I asked.

He shook his head. "Not yet. Let me tell the story, darlin'."

The other men slowed down, too, all of them listening as intently as I was. It looked like maybe George was the only one who had heard this before.

"Your ma was all set to marry the richest man in town, when his very own groomsman stole her away, right out from under that old, rich man's nose."

My eyes widened. "Really?"

Papa nodded. "Your mother and your father were quite the pair, and they were truly in love. I was jealous—I won't lie. But then." Papa's nostrils flared. "Cholera."

"What's cholera?" I asked. "I mean, I know it's a sickness, and I know it can make you die. But how?" I winced, trying to prepare myself.

"You get a very angry, very upset stomach, and your belly and legs cramp something fierce, and it pulls all the water right out of you. Some people die within hours." Papa was looking off into the distance, like he was thinking about how my father died.

"Were you friends with him too? My other father, I mean?" I couldn't bring myself to call him my papa. I only have one papa, and he's right here.

"I knew him," Papa said. "But I'm not sure we were friends." He chuckled, dispelling the misery that had slunk in around us. "But I was engaged to your aunt."

"My—" I spluttered. "My what?" I tilted my head. "Stop, Papa. I know Mama was Grandma Keyes' only daughter."

His voice was sad, soft. "Your Aunt Elizabeth died in the same cholera epidemic, before I could marry her. Before she died, she begged me to do one thing—take care of her sister."

George practically bellowed. "You sure did that."

"Married her a year and a month later, on her sick bed, even." Hiram was smiling.

"You didn't," I said. "You're kidding."

Papa shook his head. "My Elizabeth had begged me to care for your ma, and I fell in love with Margaret quickly, but I didn't propose until it was almost a year after my fiancée and your mother's husband had passed." Papa scowled at George. "But we'd set the wedding date, and then your mother got sick. It wasn't cholera. It was something else. I told her I was willing to wait, but Margaret didn't want to."

"Your ma was lying in bed the day they were married," George said. "I heard."

"And you were sitting right next to her," Papa said to me. "You loved all the flowers."

Before I had time to reply, Hiram whooped.

We'd just crested a hill, and down below were the buffalo. They stretched out before us like a great, shaggy brown sea, milling around, jostling for position on the plain below. There had to have been over a hundred, or maybe even closer to two hundred of them.

The other men started to mill around, murmuring, but not my papa. He shouted, and he and Glaucus took off, like a shining white knight, off to save the princess. He had his rifle out and ready, and I saw he had his Allen and Thurber pepperbox at his belt, too.

"Let's go," Hiram Miller said, but when he took off, it was at a trot. Mr. Eddy followed at a brisk trot as well, a beat behind, but George Donner hung back.

"Why aren't you going?" I asked.

George gestured. "Look at all those buffalo. They could stampede. They say that's the biggest danger."

Before I could encourage him to go, I realized that it was too late for him to help. Papa had just struck the big bunch of buffalo, like an arrow piercing the side of a great, foggy landscape. Buffalo flew outward and away from the bright shaft of white he and Glaucus made, barreling away from him in all directions like an explosion.

Mr. Eddy had slowed up, but Hiram Miller had somehow fallen even farther behind, though he started out after Papa first. No one was even remotely close, but apparently Papa didn't care.

Bang.

He'd fired his rifle.

Bang. Bang.

He'd fired his handgun, too.

It took him some time to reload, but the buffalo clearly didn't know that. They were running away from my father so quickly that he wasn't in the least bit of danger. When George Donner finally tried to force his horse down the hill toward the retreating buffalo, it balked.

Perhaps that's what held up Mr. Eddy and Hiram, too.

Glaucus, though, she was as unfazed as ever. Before the others even got their horses started toward the hill where Papa and Glaucus were resting, Papa had reloaded his gun, wheeled that mare around again and taken off. He managed to shoot two more that were trailing the herd a bit. Papa killed five buffalo alone—four huge ones and a smaller calf, and no one else had even closed with the herd. The men set out to butcher the animals and field dress them, and I turned back to intercept the wagons. I was so proud, on my way back to the trail, that I couldn't help smiling the whole way.

"Where are you coming from so winded?" Mr. Russell asked, eyeing my pony. He'd noticed me and knew who my father was, I was sure.

"I'm going for oxen," I said. "My father shot five buffalo all by himself." I narrowed my eyes. "Which is five times better than your friend." I lifted my chin. "His very first time to ever clap eyes on a buffalo." I smiled, and it wasn't forced at all.

"You're lying," Mr. Russell said.

I just shrugged and kept right on riding. He'd see soon enough.

When I reached the Donner wagons, I didn't expect *them* to argue with me, too. "I mean it," I said. "My father shot five."

It took a lot of convincing, but the Donners finally sent two oxen, Mama sent two, with Milt to drive them, and so did Eleanor Eddy.

"Will I get my buffalo steak, then?" She was smiling.

I nodded. "And then some."

"Tell your pa I said *Huzzah*!"

"I will," I said.

"I can't wait to tell everyone else," Eleanor Eddy said. "And I'm not sharing a single bite of buffalo with any of those folks from yesterday."

"Papa will share," I said. "I'm sure."

She shook her head. "That's what they get for calling such a great man a sucker."

After the men returned with five buffalo? No one ever called Papa a sucker again.

CHAPTER 5
Peggy Breen

My husband wasn't fond of James Reed.

I thought they might become friends—we were all Irish, after all. But aside from the sin of being Protestant, James was also someone who liked to be admired.

"But now you rejoice in your boastings," my husband Patrick said. "All such rejoicing is evil." My husband was fond of quoting scripture, but this one I already knew. James, chapter four, verse sixteen.

Patrick held people to very high standards. Very few people held up. Sometimes, I didn't feel like I was even among the lucky few.

Every night, after the chores were done, after we were all fed, the cookware was cleaned, and the sun was setting, Patrick would gather us all together to read the Bible. He always read, and we listened, but that night Isabella wouldn't settle, perhaps from a touch of colic.

About the third time she started fussing loudly enough that the children couldn't hear, I could tell Patrick was irritated. "I'll just. . ." I tossed my head toward a tree between our wagon and the next one over. "It'll give you some space."

He bobbed his head, and I did my best to ignore my flash of irritation. He surely knew that I couldn't control the baby's mood. I knew that he wanted to make sure we were giving at least part of each day to God, and I loved him for that devotion, but sometimes it felt like it was all he cared about.

A wife likes to be high on her husband's list of concerns.

As irritating as it might have been to be banished from my own family for a moment, Isabella liked the shade tree. The cooler night air began to steal over us both as I sat down and leaned against the base of the trunk, and she finally settled into nursing without whimpering and fussing. She was starting to doze off when I heard something.

"I'm tired," a small voice I couldn't quite place said. "I don't want to. Not tonight."

"You're always trying to get out of it." I recognized that snide voice. If my husband didn't adore James Reed, his irritation was nothing to how I felt about Lewis Keseberg. The German immigrant took great pains to ensure that everyone knew he spoke four languages and had received an impressive formal education, but clearly no one had taught him the things that mattered: manners, generosity, and godly kindness.

He was the worst with his own family. I'm assuming the soft, sweet voice was that of his young, pretty wife, Philippine. She ducked out of their tent and was walking away—I could make out her silhouette, even in the dying light—when Lewis stormed out behind her. It was easy to recognize her from her profile. She was heavily pregnant, due any day. She had told me only last week how much she looked forward to having this baby. With the amount of walking we had to do every day, being so pregnant in this kind of heat had to be vexing indeed.

But none of it was really any of my business.

The good Lord had consecrated their marriage, and what went on between a husband and wife was no one else's business. It wasn't right for me to interfere. Even so, it made my skin crawl, watching him grab her arm. "You will come back, right now. Ada's finally asleep, and you have certain duties to perform as a wife, duties you've been shamefully neglecting."

"I'm too tired." She tore her arm away, and I heard rather than saw the sharp crack when he struck her.

I bit my lip, forcibly reminding myself that it was not my fight.

But someone other than me also saw it.

Small, bright, kind-hearted little Virginia Reed cried out a bit too loudly. "Sir, you shouldn't *ever* hit your wife. It even says that in the Bible. Don't you know that much? Or do they not teach proper manners and godliness in Germany?"

I wanted to cheer.

But even in the fading light, I could see Keseberg's rage over her interference. "You shouldn't be here, you little mick. Has anyone ever told you that you don't resemble your father at all?"

"Of course I don't, because my papa's not my father."

Lewis moved toward her, and I started to rise to my feet. I wouldn't have interfered in how he treated his wife, but I couldn't stand by and let him accost a little girl.

"You admit that you're a whore's daughter?"

Virginia Reed moved closer to him, her head tilted up, the set of her lip defiant, her eyes flashing. "You may think you can treat me badly because I'm smaller than you, but I'm not like your wife. I'll cut out your tongue and feed it to Cash if you say nasty things like that one more time." Beside her, a very small dog with fluffy brown and white fur growled lower than I expected.

"Your dog can't help you, little girl, and there's no world in which you could harm me." Lewis balled his hands into fists at his side, then he took a step toward her.

Virginia Reed didn't so much as flinch. "I feel very sorry for your wife. You're rotten all the way through."

Lewis raised his hand to strike Virginia, and I started toward them.

"What's going on?" James Reed strode up behind his little girl before I could, and I saw his eyes flashing, even in the nearly nonexistent light.

"Keseberg was threatening your daughter," I said, loudly enough to be heard. "I was nursing my daughter under the tree."

"I did nothing of the kind." Lewis fell back. "She came here and began attacking *me*."

"Because you were beating your wife again," I said.

Reed, to his credit, did not back down, and he didn't question a word I said. "*Again?*" Reed tugged Virginia behind him with one arm, and then angled his body so that he stood between Keseberg and me as well. "I'd heard rumors that you beat that poor girl you're married to, but I'd hoped they were malicious lies."

"He kept telling his wife that she had to do her duties, and then he hit her face," Virginia said. "I heard the crack from over there." She pointed at the edge of the stream. "Eliza couldn't hear Mama asking her for water, so I came to get it."

Now that she'd pointed it out, I could make out the shape of a bucket lying on its side at the edge of the creek.

In the amount of time it took me to see the bucket, Reed had already taken action. He shoved Keseberg back and slammed him up against another tree, one that was not three feet away from the one I'd been leaning against. Poor Isabella, my baby, whimpered a bit, but I shushed her.

But Reed wasn't done. "If I ever hear of you demanding any kind of *duties* from that wife of yours, or if *anyone* at all, including a five-year-old child, sees you beating her, or if I so much as notice a dark spot on her wrist, I will string you up by your toes and let the crows feast on your flesh. Do you hear me?"

Keseberg was making a strange noise, but it took me a few seconds to realize he was choking. Was Reed going to kill him right here, in front of his own young daughter?

James Reed stepped closer still, his face pressed right up next to Lewis Keseberg's. "You may have a fancy degree, and you may speak several languages, and you definitely look down your nose on people like me. But I've fought in a war, and I've killed before. I'm not at all afraid to do it again if someone deserves it. If you ever so much as *speak* to my daughter again, I'll slit your throat and leave you to rot. That's not a threat—it's a bloody promise." James Reed dropped him, spun on his heel, and walked away. Virginia and her little dog veered off course to grab the bucket, and then trotted off behind him, disappearing entirely into the dark of the newly fallen night.

Thanks to their lantern, I could see that Philippine didn't go to her husband. She didn't take his arm or help him back to their tent, either. She turned around and ducked into their tent herself. That wasn't the behavior of a woman who was concerned that her husband had been mistreated or unfairly judged. We'd been right—he had beaten his pregnant wife after trying to force her into his bedroll.

My husband and I don't often disagree, but this time, we do. I quite like James Reed, boastful or not. After what I just saw, I honestly think that even God would be on his side. Reed was the closest thing to an avenging angel I'd ever seen in the flesh, and I was glad he was with us on this trek.

CHAPTER 6

Peggy Breen

Christmas day should be the most celebrated day of the year. It is the day our Lord and Savior was born, after all. To most of the heathens we were traveling with, the Glorious Fourth was even more exciting. I was beginning to feel like we were falling dangerously far behind on the trail with all our small delays, but no one was moving today, not a single wagon in any party.

As another volley of shots were fired for no reason at all, my husband shook his head. Traveling wasn't safe in these conditions even if we'd wanted to keep moving. We might have been accidentally shot.

"You'd think those idiots didn't know that we're traveling into a war." Patrick wasn't really a grump, even though sometimes he sounded like one. He was just pragmatic. "Not that I expect the war will change much for people like us." His pragmatism was one of the things I loved most about him.

"I don't speak Spanish," Patrick Dolan said. He and my husband Patrick had been friends for years and years, bonding over their shared Irish heritage, and when we announced we were moving to California, he'd come along with us.

"Neither do I," Patrick said. "Wasting ammunition for no reason won't help matters, though."

"The people in this wagon train may be headed for Mexico," I said, "but they're all proud Americans. I can't blame them for celebrating our independence." I picked up my favorite hen and shifted her behind the wagon where there was a large rock. I managed to pry it up, and then I watched with a grin as Omega snatched up the grubs, one by one. When I returned to the center of the camp, Omega followed, clucking softly.

"That hen's nearly as dumb as all the people wasting ammunition to celebrate," Patrick said, "instead of walking at least another ten miles today."

"My feet are glad of the break," Mr. Dolan said, collapsing on a split log beside the fire. "Don't tell me yours aren't aching by the end of every day. You're more than fifteen years older than me."

"I think all our feet hurt," Patrick said. "If we stopped for that, we'd never get there."

"It might be good that we'll be arriving a bit late," I said. "California's part of Mexico now, but perhaps not for much longer. If we can miss the war, that's all the better."

"If President Polk has his way, it'll be part of America very soon," Mr. Dolan said.

Patrick sighed as he began to arrange buffalo chips Simon and James had gathered earlier into a small dome to build a fire. "I just hope we don't get dragged into that fight. I don't much care what the flag looks like where we live."

We'd already both emigrated from Ireland to Canada and then came together on down to Iowa, so I reckoned he meant it.

Virginia Reed barreled around the corner of our wagon just then, only narrowly managing to stop herself before knocking over Patrick's carefully arranged pile. Her little brown and white dog, Cash, jogged along at her side, as always.

She and our second son Eddie had been as thick as thieves for quite some time, but she'd been even friendlier to me ever since the night before Philippine Keseberg had her baby boy—the night James Reed almost killed Lewis Keseberg. She must've seen me standing up to defend her before her father showed up.

"My papa shot another buffalo just a few minutes ago." Her sides were heaving. "I thought I'd see if your family would like some?" Her bright eyes lightened even more when she smiled. "Mama and Eliza are determined to make a pot pie with it." Her laughter was high and easy, as usual. "They're pretending it's chicken."

Omega clucked, as if she disapproved. You'd think she'd be eager for anything to take the place of chicken.

"Your chicken's a smart one, huh?" she asked. "She's pretty, too."

Omega was a lovely shade of bright, orangey red. "My mother gave me a hen when I was much younger, and I managed to bring her to America when I came. That chicken hatched out chicks, and those chicks hatched out chicks, and then those hatched out chicks. Each time, I took my favorite hen, and kept one of her chicks. This chick was the one I kept from that last nest." I couldn't help my smile.

"So she's a gift from your mother, and that makes her special." She stepped closer and ran one hand down Omega's back. Omega clucked and then jabbered at her as if she agreed. "She *is* a smart one." Virginia's little dog was entirely focused on my hen, but the girl clucked. "Ah, ah, Cash. You will be polite and leave that sweet chicken alone. No chasing at all." She crouched and patted his head lightly, and he leaned into her hand.

One of the things I liked most about Virginia Reed, other than her bravery and verve, was her genuine joy. No setback ever seemed to bring her down, at least, not for long. Before Patrick could say something dour —he was being a real pain about the additional delay—I said, "We'd love to have some of your buffalo, if you have any to spare."

"Of course we do, and it's ready now," Virginia said. "Papa drove this one right into camp. He got sick of having to haul them back, so he resolved to make this one run to us, and then he shot it not ten yards from our wagon." She clapped her hands, her eyes sparkling. "Mama's eyeballs nearly burst from their sockets when it came careening toward us."

I could actually imagine James Reed and his now-famous grey mare chasing the buffalo right into the camp, and even more clear was the image of his very pale, very reserved wife, her eyes wide, her hands pressed against her cheeks, as he shot the poor beast and it dropped dead at her feet. I couldn't help chuckling a little at the whole idea of it. "I wish I'd seen it," I confessed.

"It was a sight to behold," Virginia said. "I wish you had, too." When she sighed, her dog sat down and dropped his head on his paws, like he was just a reflection of his owner.

Patrick jumped in, then. "I'm sure you would have been just as shocked and horrified as Virginia's mother was, Peggy." Patrick dropped an entire armful of buffalo chips, scattering the ones he'd already neatly stacked. "Don't encourage bad behavior."

"It was smart behavior, if you ask me," I said. "Those buffalos are great, shaggy beasts, and hauling the meat back tires out all the animals. That Reed is quite the horseman."

"Oh, he is, but Mama was shouting and hollering right along with Walt and Milt. You should've seen Baylis, too, screaming like a little girl from inside the wagon. He thought the buffalo was going to plow right into him, exploding the whole wagon into bits." Her grin was incorrigible.

"Should I follow you over to bring back our share?" I asked.

"I'll just find Eddie," she said. "You have so many sons that they should at least be useful, or that's what Mama says."

"They're off playing some sort of games," Patrick grumbled.

"Oh, the rope pulling?" Virginia's eyes lit up. "Are they good at that? I couldn't find anyone to make a team with. Patty and my brothers are all too small." Her face fell.

"I'll go with you," I said. "If we can find them, you can join their team."

"I made Mama promise to save you a whole haunch," Virginia said, "but we better hurry. A lot of people always show up when Papa brings home buffalo, and they all saw this one coming." As she turned, Cash's little brown face turned upward, and then he shot up like a bolt, jogging along on his tiny legs more quickly than I expected. He had no trouble keeping pace with her.

I didn't doubt her claim that others would show up quickly, asking for the meat. I'd seen them do that myself. "I saw the boys running toward the wide part in the stream. Quite a few children had gathered there—I told them they could stay until dinner."

As we drew closer, I heard the rowdy shouts and hollers from the group of gathered young men. There were a few girlish squeals as well.

"Oh, look. There's Eddie." Virginia waved, and when he didn't see her, she began to leap up in the air, both arms waving back and forth over her head. "Edward Breen!"

He finally turned, and his face lit up when he saw her. If I told Patrick his son had an eye for the Reed girl, well, he'd probably throw another kidney stone out of disgust. I rather thought Eddie would be lucky to have a girl like her, but we were too late for her to join their team. In fact, with all her waving and his grinning like an idiot, Eddie's grip slipped.

His team lost.

John was clearly annoyed. "We were going to win that elk steak and the little cake," he said, pointing. "Now what will we take back to Ma and Pa?" His eyes shifted a little, taking in my presence. His mouth opened slightly, in the shape of a small letter o.

"Well, I'm coming with news of something even better, so there." Virginia dropped her hands on her hips, and her little dog yipped as if to punctuate her irritation. "My Papa just shot a buffalo, and if you hurry, you'll get a whole haunch. And if that's not better than a stupid elk steak, I don't know what is." Without waiting for an apology or offering a hair of one herself, she spun on her heel and flounced off, leaving Eddie and John where they stood.

Both boys' mouths gaped open, and they watched her for several seconds in complete shock.

"Aren't you going after her?" I laughed. "If you don't, I wouldn't be surprised if she gave our buffalo haunch to someone else."

They shot off, Patty and Simon trailing them like baby ducks.

"Hurry back," I shouted. "Pa and I already started the fire."

True to her word, Virginia sent them back with a fine haunch, and Patrick's mood improved dramatically. He was laughing and smiling as we all ate dinner, and he even broke out the small snifters his mother sent with him from Ireland so Mr. Dolan, Patrick, and I could each drink a glass of brandy.

As if on cue, almost a hundred guns fired off to the west in quick succession, and I thought about something Virginia had told me last week. Her father had apparently made plans to turn to the east at the same time that all his friends turned to the west. That was how, even though he left, they'd share a drink together.

"Would we have left," I asked softly, "if we had been surrounded by friends back in Keokuk?"

"What?" Patrick turned to face me, the shadows on his face shifting like clouds being blown across the sky.

"If you had lots of friends—if we'd been surrounded by other Catholics like us, and if our business was prospering, would we have stayed? Or would we still be here, on this trail on the way to California?"

"Does it matter?" Patrick was a simple man. He didn't get caught up on 'what ifs' or bogged down with regret. I usually liked that about him, but sometimes I felt a little nostalgic. It irritated me that he never did.

"If you two hadn't left, I wouldn't be here," Mr. Dolan said. "Like you, I don't have many friends. I don't see it as a bad thing. I really like the ones I do have."

"I suppose that's a good point," I said.

Patrick upended the last swallow of his brandy. "To California and making new friends, but keeping the ones we have."

While everyone else was celebrating, and whooping, and hawing, we gathered as always, read a few verses in the failing light, and then prayed together. I could tell that the boys loved and respected their father, but they were also a little like me. They glanced back at the fires of the other travelers, and they too longed for a few more friends.

CHAPTER 7

Mary Ann Graves

The Glorious Fourth was notably less glorious on the trail to California. Yes, men had guns, and they fired them as much as the rest of us could bear. And yes, there was food—someone had killed an elk—but if you're pooping in a hole you've dug in the dirt on the side of a trail, not even halfway through your trip, life can't be *that grand.*

Even so, after we'd fed the mob of Graves children, and after the sun had begun to set, Jay got out his fiddle, and lots of people began to gather around.

One of my closest friends on the trail was a woman named Mary Jane. She had one of the finest fathers I'd seen—Pa loved Colonel Ritchie—and she had one of the handsomest husbands, too. In all, if I could take advice from anyone on the trail, it would be Mary Jane. So when she ambled over to our campfire with an apple pie she'd made, I welcomed her with open arms and a growling stomach.

"I hope there will be dancing over here," Mary Jane Stark said. "Because on the Southern side over there, no one's even singing. The men just keep drinking and shooting."

"Where did you say these men were?" John Schull Stark, her husband, had a large, impressive beard, and might look scary to someone who didn't know him. In this case, his broad smile made it clear he was only teasing her. He sank down on a log with a sigh.

She slapped his enormous shoulder now that it was within reach. "You know just where they are. Be off with you, if that's the kind of night you want."

He grabbed her by the waist and pulled her down on his lap. "I always want to be wherever you are."

"And I'd say it's about time for some livelier music." John Snyder clapped my brother-in-law Jay on the back. "Don't you agree?"

Before Jay could even voice an opinion, John Snyder whipped his harmonica out of his pocket and began playing one of my favorites —*Teardrops in my Heart*. It's not the easiest song to dance to, but I'm not sure that's why he played it.

While Mary Jane, my sister Sarah, and John Stark helped us pull two wagon tailboards off and shove them together on a flat spot near the fire for dancing, John Snyder glanced my way several times. It's hard to smile while you're playing a harmonica, but not impossible. As more people showed up, we all shoved over to make room, but I noticed that when John stopped playing so he could dance, he was standing right next to me.

He grabbed my hand and dragged me up beside him, and pretty soon we were both laughing and dancing while Jay and another man I'd never met played the harmonica. John's smile was bright, and in the low light, I doubt anyone even noticed that his hand brushed against the lower part of my back a few times.

But *I* noticed.

A shiver went up my spine every time he did. A dozen songs or more later, I finally begged off. "I've got to take a break and get something to drink," I said.

John sighed. "Me too. I hate to stop while the music's still going, but I need to catch my breath."

One of the Ritchie girls followed us. "You were right. I need a break, too." She was grinning at John, practically batting her eyes.

"Ah, but all my things are that direction," John said. "And yours are surely over there." He pointed toward the Ritchie wagons.

"You can't share some water?" She looked up at him with definite interest.

"I already promised Mary Ann." He didn't say he liked me, but he'd made it clear he wasn't into her.

It felt nice.

Still, as we both scooped water from a bucket on the side of the wagon and gulped it down, I didn't expect him to say much more. Things didn't have any reason to move quickly between us. We had a long journey ahead yet.

When I lowered my cup, John was closer. Much closer. He looked down on me from only a few feet away. "You looked brighter than the stars tonight, Mary Ann."

I blinked.

"You look brighter than the stars every night. I've never met another girl that even compares."

I liked John.

Clearly I found him attractive.

But those kind of corny lines annoyed me.

It's not that I thought I was unattractive. I think it was actually the opposite. I'd heard my entire life that I was lovely. I wanted someone who noticed something *other than* my face. I wanted someone who thought I was funny or smart or clever.

Probably because *I* worried I wasn't any of those things.

"You're pretty handsome yourself," I said.

But as I tried to duck under the edge of the wagon and his arm, he caught my wrist. "Mary Ann." His head dropped lower, closer, and slowly, his mouth was moving toward mine. I realized what he meant to do—he was about to kiss me.

I could have ducked away.

I could have shoved him backward.

I could have squawked and any number of people would have come.

But I wanted to know what it would feel like. I was nineteen years old, and no one other than my mother and my sister had ever pressed their mouth against mine. John's was warm, and his arms, as they slid from my wrist and the side of the wagon upward to grasp my upper arms, were strong. When his mouth moved over mine. . .

I liked it.

I liked him.

It might not have been as dramatic as the Lady of Shallot falling for Lancelot, or the Little Mermaid falling for her human prince, but John Snyder was strong, he was handsome, and he was *here*.

"Mary Ann." He murmured my name against my own mouth, and it was exciting.

I wanted to hear it again. "John."

"Marry me," he whispered.

I stumbled backward, the bucket of water tipping when my back slammed into it, and water tumbled down, drenching my back and skirts. "Oooh," I whimpered.

"What's going on?" Sarah and Jay shot around the corner of the wagon, Jay's eyes casting around for anything untoward.

"A spider," I said, my voice a little too high. "I saw a spider, and then I shot backward, and I hit the water bucket." I spun around so they could see my back.

It was dark, but thanks to the moon and the stars, and the fact that our eyes had adjusted, they could see enough.

"Oh, no," Sarah said.

"It's not that big of a deal," I said, though the night was getting chilly.

"I don't care about your back. A little water will hardly hurt you," she said in typical Sarah fashion. "But now one of us is going to have to walk down to the stream to refill the bucket, or Ma will surely scold us all tomorrow."

"I'll go," John said nobly. "I'm the one who failed to kill the spider."

"How considerate of you," Jay said. "I suppose I should at least offer."

"It's fine," John said. "I really don't mind."

"Alright, if you insist." Jay steered Sarah around us and they disappeared into the back of their wagon. I had an inkling they had more celebrating yet to do.

"You know what?" I tossed my head. "I'll come with you. We should give them some space." Space was hard to come by on the trail.

"Smart call," he said.

We hadn't gone a dozen yards down the path to the stream when he reached for my hand.

"Whoa," I said.

"You didn't answer me." He stopped, lifting his chin a bit, which cast the features of his face in moonlight. "Marry me, Mary Ann. We'd be the most beautiful couple in California."

What an absurd thing to say—and who even cares about that?

Maybe that's why I said no.

Or maybe it just didn't feel *quite* right.

"I can't," I finally said. "I really like you, but I don't know you well enough." And then, after rejecting him, I pretended to step on a rock and went back to the wagon alone, leaving him to carry the water bucket himself.

The next morning, I was milking our cows with Sarah when Lovina and Eleanor finally left to gather bison chips for the fire. "Sarah."

"Finally." She leaned closer, her hands still moving rhythmically. "What happened last night? He was watching you like Ollie watches Ma slicing the bacon."

Our dog, Ollie, was obsessed with the salted pork. Sometimes he stared at it from the ground as we all walked down the trail. He just walked along, staring at the pork hunk swaying. The idea of John Snyder watching me with that kind of longing, a longing to *eat* me, well, it was a funny parallel. "It wasn't like that."

"But clearly something happened by the water bucket." She leaned closer. "Did he kiss you?"

For some reason, I didn't want to talk about that. "He proposed."

Sarah's hands stopped moving as her mouth dangled open.

It was fairly satisfying.

Finally, after blinking a few times, she spluttered, and then she spoke. "Well, what did you say?"

I shrugged. "I turned him down."

"You didn't." She leaned closer. "How could you? He's the handsomest man on the trail. The two of you could pose for a painting or be the models for a Greek statue or something."

I twisted one of the udders and squeezed, spraying Sarah in the face.

"Hey." She sprayed me back just as fast, and we were both laughing when someone's shouting distracted us.

A young girl jogged into our campsite, her eyes casting around frantically. "Is Mrs. Graves here?" She glanced at us, but then clearly ruled us out, her nostrils puffing, and her eyes still scanning. "Mrs. Wattling said I should come this way—she said Mrs. Graves is nigh unto a midwife?"

Sarah cast a sidelong glance my way, but it wouldn't do any good to stay quiet. Ma would hear her.

"She's not a midwife." I stood. "But she's had eight children, and she's helped with a lot of births over the years."

"My ma's having a baby, only, something's wrong." The girl's voice was sharp, and it was clear she was putting all her hope on our ma.

We'd just admitted she found the right place. Before we could say anything more, Ma walked up the rise from the river, her arms straining from the weight of the two buckets she was lugging. "What's the fuss about?"

"I'm Hattie Pershing," the girl said. "And my ma's having a baby. Something's not right. Mrs. Wattling said you might be able to help."

Ma set the buckets down and nodded. "Of course. I'll do whatever I can."

We stayed behind to get breakfast ready and help Pa and Billy gather in all the animals. We knew as well as anyone that the wagon train wouldn't wait. We'd have to move out, and Ma would catch up.

"Should I saddle up Luna?" Billy asked. "I could stay with her until she's ready to ride."

"You need to drive the wagon," I said. "I'll saddle Luna and Smoky and wait with her."

Billy didn't grumble, which was good of him. I knew he hated having to drive the wagon and keep an eye on Frankie, Johnny, and Nancy, but Sarah had already taken baby Elizabeth, so he could hardly complain.

"Frankie can ride with me if he likes," I said.

That made Billy smile. Frankie got pretty annoying around the fifth mile of the day most every day. I mean, I got it. When you're five, and you have to walk as far as you can before getting in the wagon, you learn to complain early on so you can ride more. Ma would manage him pretty well, making him walk a bit more than he wanted each day, but then she'd let him get in. Billy didn't have the patience for it. Since I was going to have Luna and Smoky saddled anyway, Frankie may as well ride with us.

Thankfully, the problem was one Ma knew how to handle. An actual midwife had shown her how to flip a baby inside the stomach, and so it came out head first after all. But by the time the baby was delivered, Ma was exhausted.

"Were you nervous?" I whispered as Ma washed her hands in the river.

"I'm always nervous when the baby's facing the wrong way," she said. "Feet first isn't safe for mother or babe, but blessedly, it was alright. God was with us. Mother and child are exhausted, but she has a wagon, so at least they can ride today."

It could easily have gone the other way.

I'd heard of lots of things going wrong in childbirth over the years. As we got cleaned up and mounted our horses, I couldn't help thinking about how that poor woman now had to travel fifteen miles with a baby lying next to her on the wagon. And she was lucky.

Some people don't have wagons.

If you don't keep moving, you fall behind, and that's even worse. When we finally caught up to our wagons, I tried waving, but Sarah didn't even see me. She was plodding along, her eyes on the ground, her lips compressed flat. When we stopped for lunch, I took Smoky's saddle off and found him a place near the sweet grass to graze while we ate. Luna— Ma's horse—was right behind him. The two of them were nearly inseparable.

Glancing behind me, I saw Sarah pass little Elizabeth off to Ma, her tiny arms reaching all shaky and excited for Ma's neck. Elizabeth had plenty of siblings to play with, plenty of love, but nothing was quite like your own ma. There was even a nice, broad tree for Ma to nurse her under.

I was checking the bucket hung from the side of the wagon and covered with a cheesecloth to see whether it had been churned sufficiently to have butter yet when Sarah walked up behind me, tapping me on the back.

I squealed, which was a little embarrassing.

We'd been startling each other like that since we were quite young, and normally it was a game we quite enjoyed, but not today. Today, when I turned back toward her, smiling and a little annoyed, Sarah's face was ashen grey.

"Sorry," she mumbled.

"Since when do you apologize for scaring me? What's wrong?"

She swallowed slowly and leaned against the side of the wagon, and it made me think about how sullen she'd looked earlier. "I—"

"What?" I was actually concerned now. Was something wrong?

Before I had time to fret more, she spoke. "I'm late."

"Late for. . ." It hit me then—she hadn't started her period last week when I did. I'd have seen her, like me, down by the river, scrubbing and scrubbing. Every single month, it's the worst week of all. You're tired, aching, and you're still stuck walking and cooking and cleaning and walking more.

But then I thought about the girl who came this morning asking for Ma's help, and about how quiet Sarah had been when Ma left to lend a hand. Sarah's newly married—a baby would normally be happy news, but not now. Not here.

Not on the trail.

It's too much walking, too many chores, and no rest of any kind.

We immediately start working as soon as we wake—all our normal chores have to be done from the back of a wagon, rummaging around for all the things we need, and once we're done, we can't take a break. No, after all our normal work, that's when we walk fifteen or twenty miles. And then we get up and do it again, day after day, across unsteady and uneven terrain. We ford streams and scrabble down and across rocky scree. We harangue the other animals, like sheep, pigs, and other cows to keep up. We harass oxen to keep going. We keep an eye out for the small children we love, to keep them safe from snakes, dangerous pests, gopher holes, and wagon wheels.

None of it slows for poor weather, sickness, or injury. We're barely a third of the way through the journey, and for her to be pregnant now, well. It didn't feel like great news. Ma was sick a lot when she was pregnant, and if Sarah's anything like she was. . .

"I'm glad I turned him down," I said. "And I'm sorry to hear you're late. I'm happy for you, but I'm also sorry."

Sarah's face was still pale, but she took my hand and squeezed it. That's all the time we had. We went back to work, preparing our luncheon of beans, bread and butter, and leftover hunks of bacon. Then we helped water the animals, taking our turn at the nearby river. Once that was done, it was time to clean up.

Ma couldn't help me, because she was nursing and changing little Elizabeth. Which is exactly what Sarah had to look forward to, probably.

"At least we'll be in California by then," I whispered. "What does Jay think?"

Sarah shook her head. "He doesn't know."

I blinked.

"I don't want to say anything until I'm sure."

I nodded.

But I thought about it most of the day. She could ride, at least in the beginning. If she alternated horses, it wouldn't make any of them more likely to go lame. She could certainly use my horse, Smoky, as often as she wanted. I was about to tell her that when Ma waved me over.

"Your Pa isn't feeling well. Can you ride Jerry up ahead with Billy? He wants you to find us a place to make camp."

I didn't argue. It's not like I had a reason not to go. "Sure," I said. "Of course." Jerry was Pa's horse, because he was green. He was a lot to handle, but I knew Billy would trade with me if he got to be too much. I could ride Billy's horse Ranger into the middle of a storm without trouble.

We hadn't gone very far when an Indian party fell in beside us. Almost all the natives we saw along the trail here were Sioux, Pa had said. Usually they passed by us, barely acknowledging we were there, but this time, they didn't pass on.

They circled around.

"We're looking for a good place to stop for the night," I said. "And then we'll go—not stay."

The eight of them were all male, and they were all shirtless. Several had feathers and marks on their bodies, and they were all riding horses. Grey, paint, black, and brown, their horses were all different colors, much like the men riding them.

"We're going this way." Billy pointed. "Please let us through." He pointed behind us. "Many more of us are coming."

The men continued to circle us slowly, and Jerry did *not* like it. He began to toss his head and shift forward, his trot big and bounding. I checked him by pulling back softly, and then I released his face, not wanting to irritate him so badly that he took off, plowing his way through these somewhat hostile men.

One of them leapt from the back of his horse and pressed his hand against Jerry's nose. My traitorous horse settled down immediately. The man blew on his face, and Jerry tossed his head once and then lowered it. The native man smiled, his teeth bright against his black hair and dark face. "Yes, I like."

Plenty of the natives we encountered spoke some English, so I shouldn't have been surprised, but they hadn't said a word up until now. "Good horse." He tilted his head up toward me and smiled again. "Better woman." He turned to look at Billy. "I want."

Was he saying. . .he wanted *me*?

Billy shook his head. "They're not for sale."

The natives circling us laughed, speaking rapidly among themselves. Then the man in front of me pulled something off his belt. "Much money. Great warrior."

"I'm sure you are," Billy said. "And you're quite smart, to have learned our language so well, but she isn't for sale."

"I want." The man stepped closer, and Jerry lowered his head, as if he agreed with the Indian man. When he reached for my reins, I yanked them back, startling Jerry.

He reared back, and I very nearly fell off.

Thanks to God's grace or pure luck, I managed to hold on, and when Jerry's hooves hit the ground, the Indian had moved backward to avoid being struck. I kicked Jerry in the ribs, and he lunged forward. Unfortunately, the men around us were not having it. Two of them wheeled around and blocked our progress. Jerry bucked then, tossed his head, and screamed.

My heart was racing.

I could tell Billy was as scared as I was.

"I take her." The man shook the pouch resting on his extended palm at Billy. "This good trade."

Billy was only seventeen, but he looked like a man. He was over six feet tall, and he had some muscle already. Even so, he was young. I was proud of him when he shook his head again. "No trade. My sister stays with me." It had to be terrifying to have eight full grown men all staring us down.

"Sister?" The warrior looked back at his companions and they began talking again, quickly.

But when the warrior reached for my reins a second time, someone burst through the trees behind us on a large, grey horse—John Snyder. He was waving a pistol, and he shouted. "Back up. She's not available."

When I turned to look at the warrior in front of me, Billy had pulled out his rifle in the distraction and had it trained on the man's face. "Don't make me shoot you," Billy said, his hand trembling slightly. "Because I'll do it."

The warrior leaned a bit closer, smiled his grim smile, and then leapt sideways, back onto the side of his sleek black horse. Then he yipped twice, and the whole of them took off, pounding their way off and away from us.

The second they were gone, I nearly collapsed in the saddle, my fingers barely holding onto Jerry's reins. John had dismounted and was at my side, tapping my leg. "Come on. Hop down, now. You're safe."

When I slid into his arms, my head resting against his shoulder, I whispered the words. "Yes. I'll marry you."

His grin was a sight to behold, as brilliant as the sunrise.

"But not until we reach California, and you have to keep it a secret."

He blinked twice, but he nodded, and he never breathed a word of it out loud, not to anyone in my family or beyond, as far as I knew. Pregnancy might be dangerous, but there were worse things here on the plains. Without a man to keep you safe, well, your prospects out here could be pretty lousy.

John might be a little corny, and he might like me for the wrong reasons right now, but we had time, and he had proven himself to be a good man in a pinch. Maybe it wasn't romantic, and maybe it wasn't exciting, but it was still true. When the wagons finally caught up, Sarah was beaming.

Her period had finally come.

It was good news all around, even if my family didn't know the whole of it.

CHAPTER 8

Virginia Reed

The Parting of the Ways had been all anyone talked about for at least a week, so when it turned out to be no more than a simple fork in the long and dusty road we'd been traveling for so long, I was a little disappointed. Most of the wagons that had been traveling with us for the past two or more months turned their oxen to the north, but we headed south.

Why did our party turn south?

I blamed Lansford Hastings. He wrote a book that said that California was far better than Oregon, and in the book, he shared a new path to get there, a path that would be much, much faster. Looking at the map, it was pretty clear. It should save us a third of the distance if not more.

Papa's dear friends the Donners, as well as my good friend Eddie and the Breen family, all made the turn south, thankfully. I was honestly a little disappointed to see that poor Philippine Keseberg and her pushy husband did, too. Levinah Murphy was a widow who didn't look any older than Mama, and she was the leader of her family. It was rare to see a woman leading the family, but she had two big sons-in-law along with her, and that had to help. I was happy they turned south, because her oldest daughters were nice women. Their babies were cute, too.

That night, along the banks of the Little Sandy River, the wagons that had decided to take the southern route gathered and took a vote.

Although Papa's good friend William Eddy voted for my father to be the new leader, the others voted for George Donner. Papa didn't mind. He loved George.

We all did.

But I thought, after we took that Southern path, that the decision to take Hasting's shortcut had been made. After all, every wagon was California bound. We had a leader. Our leader knew we were behind, and he wanted to make up for lost time.

Apparently, I was wrong.

George Donner's wife didn't agree, and there was one more place we could have turned north and rejoined the others, and we had just reached it—Fort Bridger. If we went north, we'd rejoin the path to Fort Hall. If we kept moving south, we'd be leaping off on Lansford Hasting's untried path.

"I think it's a mistake," Tamzene Donner said. "I've said it before, and I'll say it again. This isn't a path that people have taken, and I don't want to be the first."

She didn't usually argue, not with us, and not with anyone that I'd noticed. I really liked Tamzene. She was a good ten years or more younger than her large, gruff, hard-working husband George, but the school-teacher in her made her his match, I always thought. Her grey eyes were steady and calm and usually very kind.

In that moment, they were flashing lightning in a storm.

"But we're behind, and there's no denying that," George said. "If we take the established route, there's no way to catch up. And if we hit the mountains too late. . ."

He didn't even finish his sentence. We all knew that reaching the tallest mountains in the country would be terrible if winter storms hit first.

"Clyman said it was a terrible trail," Tamzene continued. "You heard him—you fought beside the man, James. He's reliable, and he said this isn't the path for families and wagons."

"But he had just taken the path himself," Papa said. "He thought it was awful, but *he made it through*. After every baby, Margaret insisted she'd never have another." His smile, directed at Mama, was fond. "There are plenty of things that are hard, but once we get through them, they're valuable. Everyone knows we're behind. We may have to suffer through some bad days or even long weeks if we want to catch up, but I think this is the way to do it."

Mama rolled her eyes when he talked about babies, but she didn't argue. She'd go anywhere he asked. She'd already proven that by leaving Illinois and all our friends and her brothers.

"We don't want to go to Oregon," Jacob Donner said. He rarely said much, except to agree with his brother. "I don't see the merit in going to Oregon first, and then having to head further south when we're all California bound. I agree with Reed. We should go south."

"It's an unknown trail," Tamzene pressed. She was really riled up.

"Every trail is unknown until people pioneer it," Papa said. "I'm not afraid to be one of the first. Never have been."

"But your friend—what was his name?" George snapped his fingers. "The newspaperman."

"Edwin Bryant." Papa nodded. "He went ahead and said he'd write me and tell me how the path was." He stood and crossed the room to talk to the proprietors of the small fort.

Calling this little building a 'fort' was really a bit of a stretch. It was more of a poorly-stocked supply post. Even so, the men who ran it seemed to be nice. Papa was talking to them long enough that George stood and followed him over. I decided to trot along behind him.

None of the other men allowed their daughters to sit around, listening to the adults, but Papa has always been different. He always wanted me around. He never minded when I listened, because he wanted me to learn from him. "Did Mr. Bryant leave you a letter?" I peered around his shoulder. I liked Mr. Bryant. He had great stories, and he was as patient and calm as Papa.

"No letter. I suppose Edwin got too busy, or perhaps he forgot, but Mr. Vasquez here did see him. Mr. Bryant traded his wagon for mules, loaded them up, and headed on South about a week past."

Mr. Vasquez smiled and nodded. "Sure did. He traded his wagon for mules. And if you'd like to talk more about trading any of your animals, this is the last place you can do it between here and California."

"There's no other forts?" I asked.

Mr. Vasquez shook his head. "Not until you reach Sutter's fort in California."

Mr. Bridger, the owner of the fort, stepped closer. "Don't forget about Johnson's Ranch," he said. "It's about twenty or thirty miles closer."

"Still, it's on the other side of the Sierra Nevada mountains, in California," Mr. Vasquez said.

"But," Papa said, "Louis said that Lansford Hastings himself is only a few days ahead of us with a much larger party. If we make haste, we could catch them and follow the man who discovered this cutoff and has taken it before. Right?"

Both Mr. Bridger and Mr. Vasquez nodded.

"And he's the man who literally wrote the book on it," George said with a smile.

"Exactly." Papa said.

"And you don't need to worry," Mr. Vasquez said. "The Hastings shortcut has plenty of grass like what you see here, and enough streams and rivers to keep your cattle well-watered without trouble."

"Except for that desert," I said.

"Except for that," Mr. Vasquez said. "But did I show you the nice, thick barrels we have for sale?"

Mr. Bridger and Mr. Vasquez were pretty friendly, and they did give us a discount on the supplies we bought. Papa even bought me a new pair of shoes, moccasins this time, so my feet wouldn't feel the heat of the desert through the thin treads of my old shoes.

We rested one more day, letting the oxen eat their fill of the thick, rich green grass and drink as much as they wanted from the good, clear water of the Black Fork River. We'd all felt nearly ragged when we finally cleared the South Pass, so it felt nice to take a small break. We all knew we were behind though, so it couldn't be long.

By the time we readied our wagons to go, we had been joined by another family—the McCutchens. The woman, Amanda, was quite young indeed, and very pretty. She had the cutest little daughter, Harriet, who had just learned to walk the very day before they arrived. The man, though, William, was the tallest, largest man I had ever met. He made even Hiram Miller look small by comparison. He towered over Papa, and next to his little wife, well. He looked like her Pa almost, when he was holding her hand.

"How wonderful to have another strong, braw family along," Mama said. "And what a darling little baby girl, too."

"How about those boys George picked up?" Papa shook his head.

He had thought about bringing one along, but we didn't need more help, and Papa was worried about space in the wagons as it was. Still, I felt bad for the poor young man with the terrible cough—Luke, I think was his name.

"I heard him tell Tamzene he thought the weather in California would heal him," Mama said.

Papa shook his head. "If he lives to see California, it'll be a miracle."

"Eddie says miracles do happen sometimes," I said.

Mama and Papa exchanged a glance, but they didn't argue with me.

"Eddie said he's seen them happen."

Papa's nostrils flared, but he just went to help round up the oxen.

Mama looked just as uncomfortable talking about miracles, so I decided not to press the issue. It might have been my favorite thing that Eddie talked about, so I wasn't sure why they looked so sour.

"Mama, I'm going to saddle up Billy," I finally said.

She didn't argue, so I took that as permission. She had Eliza to help her finish cleaning up breakfast, after all.

I skipped off, rope in hand, but when I slipped the lead around Billy's head, I quickly realized that something was wrong. He was hobbling—it took me almost five minutes of patient coaxing to get him back to the side of the wagon where his saddle was kept.

"Papa!" I called and waved. "I think Billy lost a shoe or something."

My father came over right away, but when he lifted Billy's feet, he had all his shoes.

As Papa examined Billy's legs and hooves, I prayed silently the entire time. *Please, God, please let him be alright. Please let Billy be okay.*

"No swelling," Papa finally said. "And I can't feel his pulse—no real heat anywhere." He asked Billy to walk, and he hobbled again, and Papa grimaced.

"We can just put a new shoe on, right?" I could feel tears welling up in my eyes. "I mean, I know that one's still on, but maybe a nail's bad or something."

"He hasn't lost a shoe. It might be something as simple as an abscess," Papa said, his eyes wide. "But we can't wait for him, and it's clear he can't walk, not like this." He shook his head slowly.

"Can he ride in a wagon?" I asked. "He's not that big. Or maybe—"

"Ginny."

I started to cry. "We can wait a day or two, right? We could catch up with the others. Or maybe we can tie him to the back of the wagon? I don't need to ride. I can walk until he's better. I will."

"There's no way he can keep up, and it's unlikely he'd recover quickly and be able to catch up," Papa said. "It could be an abscess, a bruise, or something else entirely. But darling." He crouched a little, brushing his hand against my face. "We can't wait to find out. We don't have time."

Tears were already streaming down my face. "I can't." I shook my head. "Don't ask me to leave him."

Papa's eyes were sad, but he didn't delay. A few moments later, he had spoken to Mr. Bridger, and he was leading a shiny sorrel mare my direction. Her body was a deep red, but her mane and tail were nearly white, just like Billy's. "Her name is Buttons," Papa said. "Mr. Bridger says she's calm and steady. He said he'd put his daughter on her, if he had one."

I hated her.

I'm sure she was nice enough, but she wasn't Billy. I saw Mr. Bridger leading poor, hobbling Billy slowly into a small paddock by his miserable little fort. Papa held out the reins, but I just shook my head. I climbed numbly into the back of the supply wagon, and I watched through my tears as we pulled away. Billy tossed his head and called out for me, his nostrils flaring, but I couldn't do a thing about it.

Cash heard me bawling, and he hopped up into the back of the wagon. Mama said the dogs couldn't ride, but I decided that today was an exception. As I hugged my sweet little dog against my chest, burying my face in his fluff, I realized that even having him didn't fix it. My darling Billy was gone, and I'd never see him again.

It was the worst moment of my entire life.

CHAPTER 9

Mary Ann Graves

Now that I was engaged, I spent a little more time thinking about what would happen when we reached California. John owned almost nothing—which was part of the reason he'd decided to move west. By all accounts, acquiring land in California was easy, and the land there was the highest quality.

Before she left, Sarah and Jay received a handful of wedding gifts, mostly from their families, but Jay had also saved quite a bit of money, and they managed to buy most of the things they'd need to set up a new home in St. Joe, and Ma and Pa gave them a wagon in which to keep their belongings.

I had no such luck, and like John, I had very little money saved.

"Thirty-one dollars," I said.

"I have nearly a hundred," John told me. "It's not a lot, but once we reach California, I'll take any work I can find. If we can find land for cheap, I doubt it'll be too long before we can put together a decent homestead."

Since agreeing to marry him, he'd become even more attentive, helping me carry water as soon as he'd finished with the animals in the morning, lugging the clothing and blankets over to the river to be washed. Sitting and talking with me while I washed them.

"We each have a horse, assuming they make the journey, and that's not nothing either." John was smiling at me, and I didn't regret my decision at all. I felt even better about it.

But as our wagons headed up the steep South Pass en route to Fort Bridger, many of the other settlers began to struggle. There wasn't nearly as much grass as there had been, and there were plenty of animals looking for it. No pasture can really handle a never-ending column of animals that want to graze on it, and this area hasn't gotten the same kind of rainfall as the places behind us. Without enough grass to eat, the oxen pulling some of the wagons ahead were failing. We were passing more and more oxen that had been abandoned, hobbling around, looking for food and water on their own. Pa and Ma talked about trying to take one or two with us, but we couldn't afford to stop while they recovered any more than the people who left them, which made them useless to us.

"I'll ride out," I said. "I'm sure Billy and I can find a place to stop that has grass." It took us some time, but we did it. We found a lovely spot that had long, waving blades of grass, and it was only a twenty-minute walk off the wagon path, with a nice stream branching away from the main river for the oxen and other cattle to drink their fill.

When we got back to tell the others about it, John waved me over. "Look what I found." He gestured behind him, at the supply wagon he drove. "People are dumping this stuff."

It was a dutch oven, a pile of plates and utensils, and a cast iron cooking pan. It would have cost us more than twenty dollars back in Missouri, and even more at a supply post here.

"They're just *dumping it?*" I had trouble believing they'd abandon perfectly serviceable things like that.

"They're lightening their loads so they don't overtax their oxen." John shrugged. "Their loss. . .our gain."

"But what about our oxen?" I glanced ahead at where our three oxen teams plodded along. "We don't want to overwork them."

"You found them a great place to rest today." He smiled. "They're doing fine."

It felt true—we had planned, and we were being careful. If we could keep our oxen safe and plan for our future at the same time, well. It made sense. It was exciting, honestly. That night, as the animals were being watered and staked, before I milked our cow, which wasn't making much milk anymore, given the poor grass she'd been having and the age of her calf, I stashed our newly pilfered goods among the edge of the other supplies.

It felt. . .thrilling and also nice. Planning for my own home, finally. John and I were working together to try and make a future. It was one I wanted. One I looked forward to. After that, we both kept our eyes out for things here and there. A bolt of muslin, only slightly soiled. A teacup and saucer, along with a rolling pin. A hammer for John, as well as a nice box full of nails of various sizes. I saw lots of furniture items I'd have loved to take, like rocking chairs, a lovely chest of drawers, and several tables, but they were too large to risk. I did find a Bible without a name in the front and several other classic books. I only owned two books myself, so growing that number to eleven was pretty exciting. The list in my head lengthened as our stash grew in the wagon.

But eventually we reached the South Pass, and I fretted. "Will they be alright?" I whispered.

"Who?" John's face really was beautiful, even when he frowned in confusion.

"The oxen," I hissed. "Look at those hills." I worried more, because it was so dry that increasingly, even going on ranging, looping passes, I wasn't finding them anything substantial to eat. "What if the extra weight—"

John turned toward me, smiled his cocky smile and said, "They'll be fine. I may not be rich, but I know my boys here." He clicked and called, and they struggled forward, responding just as he said they would to the sound of his voice.

But on that last, long climb, Andre strained while Angus grunted, and Ulysses and Homer stalled out for a moment or two. Titan and Zeus, though, they were our lead team, and they never faltered. Titan was the largest ox I had ever seen, and he bellowed a time or two, and the other five all stepped up, straining against their yokes until they reached the top.

It wasn't long after we reached the summit that we began to find better grass and thicker streams. Blessedly, all the Graves oxen had made it, and so had all our horses and cows. Ma had us bake pies to celebrate, because not everyone had been so lucky. We all sent up prayers of thanks as we baked a small feast. That night, our friends the Tuckers, the Ritchies, and the Starks ambled their way over to our campfire. As they arrived, Pa stood, barefoot and happy, in his element in all ways, raising his hand to welcome them.

I realized that he had invited them.

Ma passed around the pies, and they quickly disappeared with so many eager mouths. Then they all sat down, and I realized they had come with a purpose.

"I'm heading for California," Pa announced. "It's a shorter path, and we're all late."

"But the Oregon route is a known path," Reason Tucker said. "Thousands of wagons have passed that way."

Pa folded his arms. "Exactly. Just as you've seen here, there won't be enough grass. And the later in the season, the less rain, the worse it is for us."

"I do like the idea of going a direction not everyone else has already traveled," John Stark said, his wife nodding at his side. "Our oxen are practically starved. A few days rest will help, but I'd rather not throw away anything else." It looked personal to his wife. I wondered whether we'd picked up anything they cast off.

Colonel Ritchie frowned. "There's safety in numbers out here, like it or not, and almost everyone we spoke to is going north. You can always move on down to California later."

"I'm not scared of being on a less-trodden path," Pa insisted.

"Even if you have to go farther and work harder to find water?" Reason Tucker looked skeptical.

"You can't live your life in fear," Pa said. "That's no way to live."

"But you're going south because you're afraid we're late," Reason said. "If we'd been early, you'd be following us."

"Maybe," Pa said. "I've heard the Sierra Nevadas aren't welcoming to those who are late."

"Not at all," Reason said. "But if we push a little harder, we can make up some lost time."

"I agree. We'll be going north, up to Fort Hall," Colonel Ritchie said. "It's the established route, the one we know is safe and solid."

"Unless," John Stark started.

But his father-in-law shook his head. "No, we've decided. Haven't we?" Colonel Ritchie looked at Reason Tucker, who nodded.

"Well, then this is where we'll part paths," Pa said. "Tomorrow, at the Parting of the Ways, we'll head south." He smiled. "And we'll get first pick of the land in California. Maybe we'll try and save you something half-decent."

When the men went back to their camp, I was sad, but everyone else seemed in high spirits. If anything, Pa seemed to feel reassured that our path would be one without quite so many hungry mouths to snatch at the grass around us.

I wasn't really worried. Pa was always right.

With a name like the *Parting of the Ways*, I expected something dramatic. I thought there would be, well, a grand sign, or a large and lovely copse of trees, but no. There was simply a wide, dusty, flat path headed to the right, and a smaller, brush strewn, overgrown path that branched to the left.

We took the overgrown one.

I was surprised how my heart wrenched, knowing Mary Jane and her husband were no longer right in front of us. Now we were well and truly alone—none of our friends had opted to go this direction. We had heard there was another party ahead of us, rather large, that had taken the Hastings shortcut as well, and we hoped to catch them.

"Let's try and make good time," Pa said as our wagons creaked along. "So we can catch that other group. The Reed party, I think."

"No," Ma said. "I heard they voted, and it's the Donner party."

"That's a lucky sounding name," Pa said.

And as we made our way to Fort Bridger, we truly felt lucky. The grass was green and plentiful. The streams were easy to find, and no trouble to ford, and on July 28, as we finally rolled into Fort Bridger, my dear little sister Eleanor turned fifteen. Ma was making her a cake when Pa came jogging down the path.

"Good news!" His bare feet were slapping happily against the dirt, and his hat was bunched up in his hand as he slid to a stop. It was Pa in his most natural state. "The men up at the fort said that Donner party had some kind of minor issue, and they're likely no more than three days ahead of us. We could catch them quite easily, I think."

Ma wiped her flour-sprinkled hands across her apron and smiled. "That's the best birthday news ever."

Eleanor smiled. "I hope they have lots of men in their party." As birthday wishes went, it was a good one.

John caught my eye and winked. It really felt, for all the world, like we were on the perfect path, and our future was bright in all the ways that mattered.

CHAPTER 10

Virginia Reed

There's apparently a limit to how much crying a human can do.

I hadn't discovered that before, but I did on the day we left Billy behind. Eventually, no matter how much I longed to sob, I had no tears left.

The next morning, when I woke up, Mama and Eliza had completed almost all of the chores, and Papa was waiting for me. After I was dressed and ready for the day, my new moccasins on, Papa waved me over, and he handed me the reins on Glaucus.

"What?" My eyebrows rose.

"I'm not giving her to you, but I decided I should ride Buttons first, just to make sure she's good enough for my girl." Papa was smiling, and he looked happy enough, but I knew it physically pained him to be separated from Glaucus.

It was quite the olive branch, from my father. He never shared Glaucus. Never.

I knew better than to say no. "Thanks, Papa."

"And Eddie Breen will be riding out today. I thought you two could scout for us together." Papa's smile was tentative, as if he hoped that might improve my spirits. No one in the wagon train got me quite like Eddie did.

"Thanks, Papa."

Once Eddie and I set out, no adults even trailing us, my spirits rose.

Billy was the perfect pony, and I would always miss him, but there were other amazing mounts out there. Glaucus was proof enough of that. Her stride was smooth, and it never faltered. She was sure-footed, calm, and she listened perfectly to anything I asked.

"How far can we go?" Eddie asked. "I mean, the ground's good, so they could make, what? Fifteen miles today? Twenty?"

We had barely made five miles when we trotted into a beautiful clearing—and we decided to race. It was something I hadn't done in a long time. On the long climb up the South Pass, the animals were too tired, and I missed it. Most of all, I knew it would raise my spirits. Papa would approve. And on Glaucus, I was sure to win.

"First to the copse of trees?"

Eddie's eyes flashed, and he grinned. "But what's the prize?"

"Whoever loses hauls the other one's water."

He grimaced. "Gathers firewood."

I snorted. "Fine. Firewood. But for a whole week."

Eddie's smile came back, and it lightened my spirits. Normally, he looked a little too much like his stern father, but when he smiled, he looked like a completely different person. Actually, I realized, he reminded me more of his mother when he was smiling. "Hyah!" He kicked his mare, Trixie, and they shot forward.

Glaucus didn't even have to be asked. She threw her head out and took off, eager to prove that Trixie couldn't beat her. We were only halfway through the clearing when I noticed the prairie dogs to our right. "Hey, watch out for them." I threw my head sideways.

"Right, yes, I'll be very careful." Eddie rolled his eyes.

"I mean it," I said. "Prairie dogs mean prairie dog *holes*." We should probably have stopped, but neither of us wanted to. We were more than halfway through the field.

Only, that's when a flock of pheasants on our right side burst upward and into the air, clearly startled by the two huge beasts pounding toward them. Glaucus simply turned her head, but Trixie spooked, veering sharply to the left. And then, from the corner of my eye, I saw it.

Trixie's leg sank into a prairie dog hole, and she went down. Eddie flew over her head, slamming into the hard-packed prairie ground with an ominous crack.

I hauled on Glaucus' face, and then I wheeled her around. Trixie bolted, but by the time I got to where Eddie was lying on the ground she had slowed and was coming back, the reins dragging on the ground beside her. I leapt from Glaucus' back and dropped beside my dear friend. "Can you stand?"

Eddie groaned and pushed himself up, grimacing. "There's something wrong with my leg."

I closed my eyes, sighing heavily. "Oh, no." When I opened them again, he met my eyes, and his expression was grim. "You're going to have to go for help."

"I don't want to leave you here." My voice sounded small.

"Why not?" Eddie lifted his chin, his eyes brightening. "Afraid I won't be able to keep myself safe if the army of prairie dogs comes to attack?"

I giggled, and then I clapped my hand over my mouth. Not the right time to be laughing. "I'm sorry."

"It's fine," he said, his face still tight. I'd seen enough people in pain to know what it looked like.

After that, we tried to get him back on Trixie, but his leg hurt too much. And frankly, I could see bones pressing against the skin, which probably meant he shouldn't ride even if he could. The sight of the edge of a bone poking against his skin almost made me lose my breakfast. It was all I could do to help him hobble over to the copse of trees so he could rest in the shade, and his face was so pale by the time we got there, I worried we'd done more harm than good.

Eddie bumped my arm. "Go get my Pa. He'll know what to do."

I hobbled Trixie so she couldn't wander far, but she could still graze, and then I raced Glaucus back as fast as I could. I was grateful not to be on a horse I didn't know. Glaucus didn't so much as spook the entire ride back to the wagons, even though she was alone, and even when a deer burst out from behind a huge boulder and bolted away from us. I did finally cross paths with Papa, who was happy to tell me how well Buttons was behaving. . .until he heard my news.

When Papa and I reached the wagons, no one was happy to hear what I had to say. Eventually, Papa and Eddie's pa, Patrick, decided to ride back to Fort Bridger in the hopes that there might be someone there with enough medical knowledge to help. Luckily, Mr. Breen wasn't having trouble with his stomach pains that day. Having little rocks that form in your body must be terrible, and to hear Eddie talk about how his dad reacted, it was bad for the whole family.

I took Glaucus back to where Eddie was waiting with John in tow, Eddie's older brother. "You were very smart and level-headed, hobbling Trixie like that and coming for help all on your own." John smiled. "I'm glad Eddie had you with him."

"Maybe we should've taken one of our fathers," I said.

"Or maybe *not* raced." But John's mouth is curved up on one end, like he knows that it was a silly thing to suggest. There weren't a lot of fun things to do on the long overland journey from Missouri to California. None of us would have happily given up the occasional race.

"What does my brother owe you for losing?" John asked.

I startled. "What?"

"Well, I'd say you beat him. What's he supposed to do?"

I stared at John blankly.

"I'll do it for him," John said. "Since he may not be doing much for a while."

"Oh, it's fine," I said. There was no way John would be hauling my family's firewood. Not after this disaster. But just then, I saw the trees and pointed. "Look. He's just over there."

"You do have a fine mind for direction, especially for a girl," John said. "I'm impressed."

We waited there for what felt like forever, but it was probably only four or five hours. Eventually, Papa and Mr. Breen arrived. To my surprise, Mrs. Breen was also with them. I wondered whether Ma and Eliza were watching her baby.

There was another man with them, a man I'd never seen before. He had a shaggy beard, partially red, partially grey, but none of the grey was on his chin at all. It didn't even look red there—it was all dark brown. He was also large. He almost looked too large for the bedraggled little roan pony he was riding. He swung off and walked toward Eddie.

Eddie's pa hadn't even said anything yet, and no one stopped the man.

"Who are you?" I asked, before he could poke or prod Eddie.

The man turned slowly, his eyes boring into mine. "Name's Howard," he said, and then he spit. Brown juice spewed out of his mouth and some of it dripped down his chin. He didn't bother wiping it away, and I could see exactly why his beard was that strange color on his chin. Blech. "And who are you, little lady? You the one what caused this mess?"

I blinked back tears. "Me—I—my name's Virginia."

"She didn't cause it." Eddie straightened, his eyes dark and angry. "It was my idea to race, and my horse spooked."

"It's no one's fault," Mr. Breen said. "But can you please take a look and see what can be done?"

The man crouched near Eddie, spitting again right near him, and then he started poking. With one solid poke to the swollen area, Eddie cried out, sharp and high.

"Yep." The man spit again. "Broken. Snapped in two, looks like. Only way to keep him alive is to remove it." He stood and walked to his knobby, shaggy pony, and he pulled a long, dirty bundle from the side of his saddlebag.

I shuddered when I realized what it was.

Remove it.

As he unrolled the bundle, Eddie realized what he meant, too. "Is that —is that a saw?"

It was a long, nasty, serrated dagger, and next to it, a bone saw. I'd seen one before, when our neighbor had an infection that kept getting worse. I had hoped to never see one again.

"No." Eddie shouted, his eyes wild. "No, you can't cut off my leg."

"We can't set it." The man spit again. "You're going to have to be in a wagon, boy. And with all that jostling and bumping, there's no way this bone can heal proper. That means you're going to be in constant pain, and then you'll wind up with an infection. You know what that means?"

Eddie shook his head.

"It means you die." He drew a hand sideways about an inch below his throat, and it was even more terrifying, because he was holding a dagger in that hand. "So what'll it be? Want to lose that broken leg? Or your life?"

Mr. Breen's mouth was grim, but he nodded.

When I was about eleven, we had a dog that caught rabies. It completely flipped out, and Papa had to shoot it. Before it died, it was snarling and thrashing and baring its teeth at everything that moved.

Eddie looked a lot like that dog as Mr. Howard approached.

"No," my friend shouted. "You can't remove it. You can't. I'll sit real still. I'll be quiet, and I don't mind the pain."

"Boy, they have wooden legs," Mr. Howard insisted. "This is below the knee. You'll be able to walk."

"No!" Eddie wasn't pale, and he wasn't calm. He continued to thrash and shout and argue, until finally, even his father's quiet resolve gave out.

"We'll set it," Mr. Breen said.

Mr. Howard spit on the ground in front of Mr. Breen. "You're too weak to do what's needful, so you'll watch your boy die." He was chuckling as he walked back to his horse.

Mrs. Breen pulled coins from her saddlebag and offered it to the man. He took the money—which looked like about five dollars—and turned to leave. It was quite the operation, getting poor Eddie back to the wagons, and then we all sat for more than an hour while they found the largest, straightest sticks they could and set his bone between them with strips of muslin tied tight. Every single shout and scream felt like nails digging long furrows down my back.

Their family may not blame me, and Eddie may not either, but it felt like it was all my fault. I should never have raced—I knew better. Glaucus kept me safe, but not everyone has Glaucus.

In a small mercy, we didn't go much farther that day, but the next five days were absolutely horrible. I gathered wood every single day and took it to the Breen wagons, and it gave me an excuse to check on Eddie. He looked pale—terrible, really, and I fretted.

"Don't worry too much," Eddie said. "You know I'm not the best person, but my ma is great, and God loves her. She's been praying for me every single day."

I thought he was kidding at first, but then I realized he wasn't. "You think praying will keep your leg safe?" I was a little incredulous, because I'd been watching since he told me about the miracles, and I hadn't seen a single one yet.

"I do," Eddie said. "My ma believes it, and I believe her."

"Can she teach me how to pray?" I asked.

"I don't see why not," Eddie said.

And then he asked her to.

It was remarkably simple, really. "You talk to God in much the same way you talk to your ma," Mrs. Breen said. "You speak respectfully, and you speak clearly and politely, and you thank Him for all He's done. Then you ask for what you need."

Things were not looking great for poor Eddie. The past six days had been brutal—we all heard him crying out and grunting, sighing and moaning. The next week or two was not likely to be any better. In fact, it looked like it would only get worse. We could all see the Wasatch mountains looming ahead of us, and climbing up and over mountains, with their rocky inclines and scree-filled declines, was not smooth going.

I prayed that night, for the first time I could really remember, that the passage would be smooth so that Eddie's leg would heal. I begged and pleaded with God that he wouldn't get an infection. Praying should have been a waste of time and energy. Papa certainly didn't put much stock in it, but it felt good. I felt. . .happy after doing it. If Mrs. Breen, who really was a good woman, thought God was listening, maybe He was. As if to reinforce my belief, that night, Papa found a note, tacked to a sagebrush.

It could've easily blown away, or been rained on, or just fallen and disappeared. But Papa saw it, and the note was from Lansford Hastings himself. Unfortunately, the note told us not to go any farther. Mr. Hastings said, in his messy scrawl, that the path they were on was no good for wagons, and that we should wait. He said he'd circle back and let us know what path to take instead.

No one was keen on waiting, though I thought it was a bit of luck that we had the chance to take a break, at least, for Eddie's sake. In fact, if I were talking to Mrs. Breen or Eddie, I'd say the respite almost felt like an answer to prayer. But the adults had quite a meeting to decide what to do about that note.

Some of them argued to sit and wait. Some of them wanted to plow on. But finally, Papa suggested something that everyone agreed upon.

As usual.

"How about I ride out ahead and find Hastings? I can ask him directly what route to take, and we won't have to wait quite so long?"

Once everyone had agreed upon that, they decided Papa shouldn't go alone. I'm sure Eddie's misfortune had something to do with it. "I'll go with him," Mr. Charles Stanton said. He was a small man, always scribbling in a little notebook, and usually smiling. I liked him, and so did Papa. He nodded, pleased to have Mr. Stanton along.

"And I'll go, too," Mr. William Pike said.

His wife, Harriet, paled noticeably when he volunteered. She did, after all, have two very small children, but she didn't argue. The three of them saddled up and left while the sun was yet low in the sky, eager to make as much time as they could while they could see. With Hastings just ahead, none of us wanted to risk losing him.

Days passed, and while it was wonderful to see Eddie rest, all of us became a little nervous. The grazing wasn't excellent here, so we ranged a little far, trying to find decent enough food for our poor cows and oxen.

On the fourth day after Papa left, another family rolled up to meet us—they said they were the Graves family, and they were quite large, like the Murphys and the Breens. They had three wagons, and one of the daughters was married to a thin gentleman named Jay. They also had with them just one drover—a very handsome young man named John Snyder. His blond hair gleamed, his bright, deep blue eyes sparkled, and his smile was broad.

And when we got ready for dinner and Mama asked me to take their family a pie she'd made of dried apples and raisins, they were very gracious and excited. When I went to leave, Mr. Snyder caught my eye—and winked.

For weeks, I had thought John Breen was the handsomest man in our wagon train, with his brother Eddie a close second. But now, they were clearly no longer at the top. Mama was pleased to have a new family in the group, but not as pleased as I was. John Snyder was the most exciting thing that had happened on this trip, no question. And as if on cue, Papa rode into camp the next morning, and the biggest shock of all was that he wasn't riding Glaucus.

She was fine—she was actually trotting along behind him—but the great Lansford Hastings had loaned Papa another horse, a boring, dark bay with sad eyes, because poor Glaucus was almost done in with the constant searching and riding up and down to reach Hastings and come back to us. Luckily, she always revived fast.

Because Papa had word.

He had met Hastings, and while the man didn't have great directions about where to go as he had promised he would, Papa had found and marked an old Indian train he thought we could take through the Wasatch mountains. It wasn't really the news we all wanted, but at least we would be on the move again. It was beginning to feel like this shortcut wasn't quite as short as we'd been led to believe.

CHAPTER 11

Peggy Breen

Two new families have joined us since we decided to go south, following the elusive Lansford Hastings. It was reassuring at first, knowing that there were others who made the same decision and were in fact behind us and just barely catching up.

Or at least, at first it was.

But when Hastings left us a note, telling us the way was *impassible*?

I wanted to turn back.

"We can't turn back now," Patrick said. "It's too late for that. We've come a week down the trail, and frankly, maybe this was God's will." My husband lowered his voice. "Maybe this happened to give Eddie's leg time to set."

I had the same thought, but I wasn't sure God worked that way. "There are almost ninety people in our party," I said. "Do you really think He'd delay all of them, just so our boy's leg could set?"

"He's the good shepherd. Of course He would do things for one lost sheep."

I wasn't sure.

And when Reed returned and we began to wend our way over the great Wasatch mountains, my feeble hopes that this was all part of His plan broke down even more. On the first day, our wagons jerked and lurched across large, flat boulders, sliding and scrabbling to find purchase.

The oxen strained and lowed. Poor John could barely manage our second wagon, and I nearly despaired with the third. Edward had been helping me with the children while I drove the oxen, but now he was resting in the back, and with every bump and jostle he paled further.

My heart quailed. Surely any benefit the break had been was lost.

"Ma," he whispered while the lead wagons searched for a way through yet another impassable section. "Don't worry about me. Just think about the oxen and the path ahead. I've been praying. God will save me."

He was that kind of child—always had been. Faithful. Calm. Considerate. I hated that he was laid up in the back of a wagon, but even more, I hated that our wagons were too cumbersome to make it through any of the paths they found. The trail that James Reed had sent us down, when Hastings dismissively pointed in this direction, was an Indian path. It was narrow, it was not flat, and it wound sharply and confusingly through dense pine and scrub trees.

Every few dozen yards, we had to stop again to cut even more trees.

"It's good for Eddie," Patrick said again, after another back-breaking day of work for him and John. "I still think—"

"If you say God's plan one more time," I said. "I'll sleep in the wagon tonight instead of the tent."

Patrick grimaced.

At least the addition of the massive McCutchen man and the Graves family, with their strong drover John Snyder, and Mr. Graves himself, not to mention their tall boy Billy, made the tree-cutting a quicker job. They all worked hard, and they seemed exactly the kind of people we wanted to add to our group.

But they didn't have a son with a broken leg, and they didn't see this path as a blessed one in any way. "How did we wind up having to clear this path?" Mr. Graves asked on the third night. "It's ridiculous that Hastings didn't have a better route for wagons. He wrote a book about this."

"The Harlan-Young party made it through, but their route was rough," James Reed said. "Even with mules and horses instead of wagons, as they all had, they barely made it." He was frowning, like he too was unimpressed with our absent and silent leader. "But I'm sure once we get through this patch, we'll be clear. After this, we'll circle the Great Salt Lake, which is flat going, and then we'll pass through a desert. It's a rough two days of travel through that bit, but we'll make good time, which will help make up for the time we've wasted sawing and cutting."

As if his words proved prophetic, we spent the next few days doing even more sawing and cutting, and then we had to cross the same creek over and over. As the wagon approached the blasted creek *yet again*, I gritted my teeth. Poor Eddie poked his head out. "What's wrong?"

I sighed. "We're crossing again."

Eddie groaned. "It's the thirteenth time," he muttered. "An unlucky number for an unlucky leg of this stupid trip."

He had hardly been positive lately, but I couldn't really blame him. When the oxen forded the creek, the wheels had to roll over the rocky bottom, and the whole wagon lurched and groaned and rocked. It couldn't have been comfortable in any circumstance, but the last time, water had poured through one end, forcing Eddie to do his best to keep our dwindling supplies dry. He had gotten soaked thoroughly in the process.

"Why do we keep having to cross?" Eddie asked, his eyes strained.

"It's the only path through the mountains," I said. "The creek bed's rocky, but it's the only place that's even somewhat flat."

He nodded and retreated back into the wagon.

But then, even our slow progress stopped entirely. Virginia came trotting up, apparently getting along well enough with her new sorrel, Buttons. "How's he doing?" she whispered, gesturing at the wagon.

I shrugged.

"Can I chat with him while they decide what to do?"

I nodded slowly, and I took a chance to water my oxen. With Patrick dealing with a particularly miserable kidney stone, I was stuck handling one set of oxen while poor Patty junior tried to manage the third himself. It was the smallest wagon by far, but he was only nine years old. It's not something he should ever have been doing. He had his father in the wagon with him, lending a hand, and our dear friend Patrick Dolan was behind us, supporting our movement as best he could.

"We're going to have to make camp," George Donner finally announced. "The good news is, we really only have one day's journey ahead of us, but the bad part is that the trees are so dense, and the mountain so steep." He sighed. "We'll have to use the trees we cut to make a passable road."

His words proved true—to Eddie's relief and the rest of camp's great dismay, we were at that work for nearly three full days, and that fourth day was one of the worst we'd endured. Even once we reached the top of the biggest mountain and managed to survive to come down on the other side, we were greeted with yet another canyon, this one so overgrown, I almost gave up hope.

It would have taken us *weeks* to cut down enough trees to forge a path through the dense forest in that canyon. The only way we would ever get through was by circling around the edge and climbing over and then descending the terrifyingly steep side. When Reed suggested it, I thought my husband's eyes were going to pop right out of his head.

"We'll have to share our oxen," Reed said. At least he was the first to unhitch his teams and offer them to others. He wasn't a perfect man, but he always put his actions where his mouth went, and he followed through.

"I want to see you try it first," Lewis Keseberg insisted. "If you can get that monstrosity over, then I'll try it with my wagon." Lewis hated Reed's family wagon and mocked or derided it any chance he could.

But miracle of miracles, Reed actually got all three of his wagons up and over the edge of the canyon. It took nearly forty oxen to get them over, but he did it. I had never seen anything like it, and Reed assembled a team of drovers and experts who knew their various teams in a way that impressed even Patrick.

"This whole mess may be his fault," Patrick said, "but at least he's not miles and miles ahead, forging through with mules. He's really thrown himself into helping everyone survive."

I thought the wagon with Eddie in it was going to pitch over and dump our belongings and my beloved son right out into the valley below, but with one last heave, it made it over too. It was nigh a miracle that we all survived. Only then did we see the Great Salt Lake, and it was like something out of a ghost story.

"It's so beautiful." John's eyes were wide, and his expression rapt. "It's so large. It looks like the ocean itself."

He hadn't seen the ocean, but I supposed this was close enough to it.

At first, like my dear son John, I was excited to see the massive lake—it was beautiful and vast. It meant we had finally conquered the Wasatch mountains. But as we drew closer, it looked quite strange, with great white mounds all around the edge, where the water met the land. Those great white mounds weren't snow or anything we'd seen before and could make sense of.

No, they were great piles of salt.

The water was entirely undrinkable, and there was nothing growing inside the lake or on any part of the land surrounding it. No plants, no fish, no trees. Not even grass. It was especially strange because usually water meant life. Water that spawned nothing but death was counterintuitive and felt. . .wrong.

We did refill our salt supplies, which was something.

"I'm going to take all this salt with me to California," Virginia said, beaming as she filled several jars. "I'll tell everyone I got it on our trip through the Hastings' cutoff."

"Weren't you afraid going over the canyon?" Eddie asked, when she brought him a jar.

Sweet Virginia shook her head. "Papa said we'd make it just fine, so I knew we would."

I wish I had the faith of a child, but I knew too much for that.

Another thing I knew, but that I didn't bother explaining to the children, was that it was now August twenty-second. Crossing the Wasatch mountains had taken us more than two weeks, time we didn't have. I was beginning to panic—our shortcut was taking far longer than it should have. Longer even than the established route should have.

And the snowy storms of winter would not wait for us. So if this wasn't all part of God's plan, then we were doomed.

CHAPTER 12

Virginia Reed

A few days after we conquered the Wasatch mountains, Luke Halloran, the sickly young man the Donners had taken in back at Fort Bridger, died.

He had been hoping the weather in California would heal him, but he only seemed to get worse as we traveled closer. His cough was just terrible to hear, and Patty would nearly break into tears every time she heard him hacking.

I think it reminded her of Grandma Keyes.

George Donner probably wouldn't have taken him in, had he known what was coming, but his wife Tamzene had lost her husband and children from her first marriage to some epidemic years before, and she was too kind for her own good sometimes. I thought she knew he wasn't going to make it, and she let him ride with them anyway. Though we'd known him for a very short time, she still prepared him for burial herself, and she looked very broken up about all of it.

We couldn't spare enough time for a truly correct burial, but the men did take time to dig a proper grave, and while they were doing that, Tamzene Donner, who had escaped to cry someplace by herself, came running back.

"I found. . ." She swiped at her tears and dragged in a ragged breath. "I found something." She crouched low to the ground and dropped a handful of shredded paper in a pile. "I think it's another message from that cursed Hastings man."

The paper was the same kind of brownish-cream that the last note had been, and the few words I could make out were written with a similar scrawl. It took us some fifteen minutes, but we put the shredded pieces back together.

2 days and 2 nights hard driving. Cross desert, reach water.

"He must have gone through the desert and come back to leave us this note," Papa said. "Bless his soul for preparing us at what must have been great cost to himself."

But when Papa and the Donners started sharing out the news to the others, no one seemed very grateful.

"Two days and nights without stopping?" Franklin Graves frowned. "That's terrible news."

"But at least we're prepared now," Papa said. "We know to plan for a long haul and to bring as much water as we can."

"We already knew we'd be crossing a desert," Franklin Graves said. "We would have stocked up as much water as we could."

Clearly some people were less forgiving of Hastings than Mr. Reed. The biggest problem was, water weighed a lot, and we didn't have that many barrels. Up until now, we'd always been able to get water somewhere along the way. We'd mostly traveled along the paths made by rivers and streams as they wound their way through the land.

"We'll need wood for fires too," Mama said, "and grass for the oxen as well, won't we?"

Papa nodded. But the wagons were already heavy, and the oxen were tired. Between the long run of travel in the mountains, where not much grass grew, and the terrible climb down from that canyon, the humans and the oxen were both already exhausted. And to make matters worse, there wasn't much grass here at all. Barely enough for them to eat, much less save for a two-day haul.

"It'll only be two days," Papa said. "We can do anything for two days, right?" He patted Glaucus on the neck and smiled.

When Papa set his mind to it, he really could do anything. I did worry about Mrs. Breen with her tiny baby, and the others, too. Mrs. Graves had a nursing babe as well, and so did Amanda McCutchen, whom I really liked. Poor Philippine Keseberg's baby boy could barely hold his head up on his own, and they had just the one wagon to load with all the water and grass they would need to get their animals and babies across the desert. The Pikes and the Fosters had tiny children, and they'd have a hard time as well.

We spent hours and hours encouraging the animals to graze on the last patches of grass and filling every barrel, bucket, and bin we could find with water, and then we headed for the edge of the desert.

We only had to survive for two days.

Just two days.

But as we actually looked over the desert from the last crest, we could see it from relatively close for the first time, and it sure looked like it was more than the forty miles Lansford Hastings said it would be.

"How far do you reckon that is?" William Eddy asked my father up ahead. Mr. Eddy was pretty good at anything to do with wagons, animals, and travel. The concern in his voice didn't give me confidence.

Papa squinted, blocking the sun with his hand. "Hard to tell."

"But more than forty miles, don't you think?"

My father usually had words for everything, but this time, he just grunted.

"Do you think Lansford came back to leave that note?" Eddy asked. "Or made an assumption and left it on his way out?"

Papa looked like he was concerned it might be the second one.

At least we could see one spring, right at the edge of the desert, and when we reached it, we planned to refill our water one more time. It might not help that much, but even half a day's water felt precious, now that we knew it was possibly even more than forty miles.

To our great dismay, when we reached the spring, it stank. When we tried to drink the water in spite of the smell, it was disgusting. Not suitable for man or beast. No one wanted to backtrack—we had already filled everything we had, and even if we backtracked, we'd have to come the same distance again, and we'd need water for that trip. Our animals had already eaten almost all of the meager grass the land near the end of the little stream behind us provided, so the animals would be hungry on the way back too. We might have rationed the water a bit better had we known the spring was bad, but it was too late for misgivings.

We had to push on.

I wasn't the only one repeating the mantra, *it's just two days*, when we set out. All of us were nervous, but we could do sixty miles in two days if we walked day and night. We'd done twenty before on regular days, and we hadn't walked through the night. Papa was in fine spirits, and that helped me.

The Graves' wagons were rolling along right behind ours, and I was walking alongside Buttons—I was worried about her. After losing Billy, I couldn't bring myself to even contemplate losing another animal. I rubbed her nose as we walked, and she bumped my hand, hoping for a treat at first, and as the night wore on, hoping, like the rest of us, for water. Patty and my little brothers, James Junior and Tommy, had crawled into the back of the family wagon and gone to sleep.

I didn't want to add to the weight for our poor animals, so I kept on walking. Mama and Papa were near the front of the wagons, chatting with Milt. I worried about Mama, but she was doing better every day with this trip. Her headaches had lessened, and she looked alive and happy.

John Snyder was leading the first of the Graves' wagons, and so he was out front, walking just behind me. "It's a terrible kind of beauty, to be sure, but it *is* beautiful."

Beautiful? I looked around at the white salt of the desert, which was almost glowing in the moonlight. "I suppose so." The ground beneath our feet was a little boggy, but it was at least soft. The rays of the sun weren't beating down on us, and I'd rather travel through a chill than a blistering heat. "I guess things could be worse."

"It's getting colder," John said, "but I prefer that to sweating."

"So do I." I smiled at him in the moonlight. "The more we walk, the warmer I stay, too."

"Exactly." He looked even more handsome in the moonlight—his broad shoulders and his fine features almost glowed. "Once we get through this desert, we're nearly there. To California, I mean."

"Why did you decide to come?" I asked. "To California instead of Oregon, I mean."

John's voice was deep, and he talked to me like I was an adult, just like Papa did. Like he valued my opinion. "There wasn't anything for me back in Missouri," he said. "California, with its limitless land and opportunity, felt like a promise."

"A promise?" I frowned, my moccasined feet sticking more in this section of the stupid, boggy ground. "What does that mean?"

"Land, work, and a place that'll be my own." In the moonlight, he looked like a work of art. He looked. . .surreal. "I also had a feeling that the woman I was destined to meet—I would meet her on this journey."

Did he—was he talking about me?

My heart skipped a beat.

Then it skipped another.

He smiled, then, and I knew. He *was* talking about me. Or at least, he was implying that I was the girl he was supposed to meet. Right? It would be better to make sure I wasn't misconstruing his words.

"And have you met her yet?"

"I think I have, now." He winked at me then, and something inside of me thrilled. Chatting with Eddie Breen was fun, and he was a good friend, but this, this was something entirely different. This was. . .exhilarating. He was exactly the kind of man I always hoped I'd find. Someone dashing and strong, hard-working, and exciting, like Papa.

"Do you want to farm when you reach California?" I asked.

"I hear they need ranchers there," John said. "I like cows, and they like me." He glanced at the oxen. "I'll just need to work long enough to come up with some starting capital."

"Unless the woman you marry has a father with money squirreled away for just that." I knew Papa had quite a lot of money—he'd always done well in business. Everyone knew he was the richest person in the wagon train. The Donners did well, but even they didn't do as well as Papa.

"Yes." John smiled. "Unless my future father-in-law decides to help my new family with a little boost. Then I could marry and find land and cattle right away."

"There's a war there right now," I said. "Papa said he knows some of the people who are running it. He's a war hero already, you know, and he'll make us connections and get us even more money if it's still going when we arrive."

"Knowing a man like your father would be a real boon," John said. "That's for sure."

The rest of the night passed quickly, chatting with John, imagining a future in California that was more exciting than any I'd contemplated before. But when the sun came up, we got to experience heat far worse even than the prior day.

"See?" John's smile wasn't nearly as bright. "This is what I meant about preferring cold to heat."

I understood quite well.

Mama and Papa had convinced Patty and James Junior to walk for a while, trying to lighten the oxen's load any way they could, but the two of them whined something fierce.

"My feet hurt," Patty said.

"My mouth is dry," James Junior whined.

"I'm sick of this," little Tommy wailed from his coveted place in the back of the wagon. "I want to find a stream and stop to eat."

"There's nothing *to* eat," I said. "Nothing but hard tack, which we already gave you."

"But Mama said," Patty said, "that we'd stop for a break soon."

We were all too hot to contemplate lighting a fire, and I knew we didn't have the time to spare to stop and cook until we got through this cursed desert. It was hard tack and tiny sips of water while Mama and Papa and the drovers gave the cattle and the horses grass and water, too.

My favorite oxen, the smallest of the Durhams who pulled our family wagon, was almost all brown, with just a few white speckles on his rump. Patty and I named him Brutus, and he would bump me with his nose any time he saw me. At the end of that first day, I could already tell Brutus was tired.

He didn't bump me. He didn't even *try* to bump me, he just stood there, heaving, his nostrils flaring. I scratched his great head, and his mouth, which was always slobbery, was dry.

Nearly bone dry.

His tongue was foamy.

But his neck wasn't even sweating, which I took as a bad sign. Hot things should sweat, right?

"It's not much farther," I lied to him, hoping he'd understand some part of what I was saying. "I swear, Brutus. It's not much farther." But I found Papa, and I asked him something I'd been thinking about. "I think we should get rid of some of our stuff. The wagon's too heavy for Brutus and Caesar and the others. They look bad."

Papa didn't argue. He stared at me for a moment, and he nodded. "I've been thinking the same thing. What should we leave behind?"

While the others rested, Papa and I used a hammer to remove the heaviest parts of the stove we'd had built into that fine family car for Grandma Keyes. Then we carefully took her bags of clothing, which Mama had not been able to part with, and all our extra cooking pans, and we set them to the side of the wagon.

"Those are brand new." Mama had noticed what we were doing. "I wanted to use them for the first time in California." She looked forlorn, and I hated seeing it.

"But we do want to make it to California," I said. "I'm worried about Brutus." I looked his way. "He's tired. They all are."

Mama didn't argue more. She helped. We had an entire cooking stove that was also brand new that we carefully unloaded and left on the ground. It hurt, but it would hurt more if the oxen gave out. By the time we started walking again, the family wagon was quite a bit lighter.

I rode Buttons for a bit, just to reach the Breen family up ahead and see how Eddie was doing. Buttons was usually pretty frisky, almost too fast for me, honestly, but not now. I could barely get her to move fast enough to pass the families ahead to reach the Breens, who were at the front.

"Eddie," I called.

His head poked out of the wagon cover, and he smiled. "Virginia."

I hated that he broke his leg, but at least right now, he had one benefit. We were all heartily tired of walking. "Well, I guess no one can make you walk."

Eddie didn't smile, though. "I feel horrible. Our oxen are so tired. Everyone is—everyone but me."

I rolled my eyes. "No one blames you, idiot."

"I do," he muttered.

"The ground is terrible," I said. "That's the worst part. It's almost sticky—hard for the oxen to walk in, too."

"I heard," Eddie said. "I tried to tell Papa that I could walk, but—"

"Edward Breen. You will do nothing of the kind," I said. "You are in enough danger as it is."

"I hate feeling helpless," he said. "And worse, I'm a drain on the oxen and my family."

"You're not," I said. "Your family's way up here, whereas we're behind everyone but the Graves. In fact, John Snyder—"

"You're back by him?" Eddie asked sharply. "I hope you're not talking to him—I don't like him at all."

"What a silly thing to say," I said. I couldn't have my best friend disliking my beau. "He's been a perfect gentleman, and he's handsome, and strong, and polite." If I hadn't been riding Buttons, I'd have folded my arms and huffed. As it was, I had to settle for glaring.

"He's none of those things," Eddie said. "You should be careful around him."

I rolled my eyes, and then I wheeled Buttons around. "I'd better head back. I'm sure Papa's worried that I'm not close by." I wanted to wheel Buttons around and kick dust up in his face. But I didn't want my poor sweet mare to have to walk any farther than she had to, so my moment of indignation was ruined. I had to wait, standing still while the other families passed me.

It was a little underwhelming.

By the time my family finally struggled their way to where I was standing, Buttons was already puffing, so I slid off her back and took off her saddle. I was less annoyed by then. Eddie was probably just jealous, after all. When you're a boy of thirteen, it's normal to be jealous of an older man, especially one that clearly likes someone you admire. I might need to have an awkward conversation with Eddie at some point, when John Snyder finally proposed, but I'd deal with that when it happened.

Papa looked truly weary, and he was walking alongside Glaucus, like I was doing with Buttons. Even our dogs were trotting along at his side, having been kicked out of the supply wagon they usually spent half a day or so riding in. "When we stop next," Papa said, "we should thin out the load on the other wagons. Brutus and Ceasar aren't the only oxen who are struggling."

It was a sobering thought, that we'd have to leave even more of our precious belongings here, in the middle of a desert, when we were so close to reaching our destination. But if Papa was suggesting it, it was probably necessary.

As we stopped for a miserable lunch on our second day, I realized I wasn't the only one who was worried. Papa and Mama were working with Milt and our other drovers, Walt Herron and James Smith, to jettison everything we didn't strictly need to keep. Everyone up ahead was doing the same thing, though not quite to the same degree.

As the Graves wagons prepared to pass ours, John stopped for a moment. "The miserable desert's not as beautiful anymore, is it?" John Snyder's face, even sweaty and exhausted, brought a smile to mine.

"It's dreadful," I said. "The whole place feels like the hand of death is just pressing down on us, doesn't it?"

"You're poetic," John said. "You're quite a girl."

"A woman." I squared my shoulders. "There's no other woman in camp who can ride as well as me, and none who can shoot as well, either. Papa taught me well."

"I believe he did." John met my eye. "You're quite a *woman*, Virginia Reed. When I think about this time in the desert, you'll be the only bloom that I'll remember fondly."

That made me smile, even if my throat was so dry it was practically burning. But when night fell again, even with the lightened loads, our family had fallen even farther behind. The other families in the wagon train were so far ahead that I couldn't see them anymore, and Pilot Peak, the towering, sloped mountain we were heading for the base of, looked nearly as far away as it ever had.

Mama and Papa both looked nervous. "Just a few more steps," I whispered to Buttons, but I think both of us knew it was a lie. She kept coughing and wheezing, and I was worried, as worried as I'd ever been. I felt silly for worrying about leaving new pots and a stove behind, and a bag of clothing that reminded me of my grandmother. But what if. . .

What if we don't make it?

What if our oxen give out?

What if *we die in the desert?*

I saw all those questions running through Papa's mind when the sun slowly set after our second full day of miserable walking in the never-ending, sand-crusted wasteland. "We have to have made it at least sixty miles," Papa whispered to Milt.

But I heard him.

"What do you want to do?" Milt asked.

"I think I need to go for water," Papa said. "If I take the horses, we can make better time, and we can bring back buckets for the others." He glanced back at the heavy oxen. "But if things get worse. . ."

Milt grimaced. "If they refuse to move?"

Papa nodded. "Unhitch the wagons, and bring just the cattle."

It was as bad as I thought. Or. . .maybe worse.

How could this cursed place be so massive? How could it just stretch and stretch and stretch? Every single footstep felt like a misery as I realized that we couldn't stop. We had been walking for two nights and two days, and we had to keep going.

I hadn't slept.

I'd barely eaten.

Neither had the oxen, and neither had the horses.

My mouth felt drier than paper, my tongue rasping over my cracked, dry lips. But that's when I saw it. Up ahead, not very far at all, was a lush, green hill. Where there's grass. . . "Papa!" I grabbed Button's lead line and lurched forward. "Look!" I pointed.

Papa and Milt's heads turned.

I broke into a jog, desperate to get Buttons to some grass, at least. Her mouth, surely at least as dry as mine, would be so refreshed with a few mouthfuls of that green, green grass. If I'd had any water left in me, I'm sure my mouth would be watering at the idea of finding a stream.

Even a gross, stinky, alkali stream would be a huge blessing. I would gulp that disgusting, vile water down with a smile on my face.

Buttons shied back then, refusing to jog alongside me. She was heaving, and her mouth was flecked with dried foam. "Don't you see it girl?" I muttered. "It's just over that tiny hill. The grass!" I tugged sharply, trying to get her to follow.

"Virginia," Papa called. "You're going the wrong way. We have to keep on toward Pilot's Peak."

I shook my head. "No, look! You just have to see it!"

A moment later, Papa grabbed my arm, his eyes searching the horizon. "There's nothing there, darling. Nothing at all but more salt and sand."

I shook my head.

"You're seeing things that aren't there. Walter started yesterday—it's happened to me twice now."

I shook my head again, this time doggedly. "No, it's definitely there. The grass is a bright, beautiful green."

Papa pulled me against his chest and hugged me tightly. "I'm going to go ahead with the horses, and you need to stay with the wagons and help your ma. I'll come back with water soon, I promise."

I wanted to cry, but no tears would come.

We walked along for another hour. Two? It ran together a bit, but I was stumbling along next to Walter Herron's wagon when it happened. The left oxen in the lead team of oxen stumbled. He was a great, almost white beast, and his feet gave out, and the other oxen yoked next to him collapsed too, lowing loudly while the oxen behind him bellowed.

It was like watching reeds bend in the strong wind, because after the first pair fell, the strain on the other oxen proved too much, and they all tumbled to the earth. The lowing of the oxen was unnatural, too, their dry throats unable to make the sound properly.

"We'll have to unhitch them," Walt told Mama. "They can't keep pulling the wagons. If I whip them to make them keep going, they'll lie down and die."

"We don't even have any water to offer them," Milt said. "The last barrel's completely empty."

Patty began to cry then, great, heaving sobs that distressed little Tommy. "I can't go any more." Patty sat down on the ground, and began to bellow.

Tommy collapsed beside her, his arms and legs kicking feebly. "I'm too tiiiiireed." He began coughing then, and it broke my heart to see his little body shake.

Mama looked at least as wrecked as Patty and Tommy, but she didn't have the luxury of collapsing. James Junior was hugging her, his head tucked into the top of her skirts. "You'll unhitch the oxen, and drive them forward, along with the other cows. They need water, more even than we do, poor beasts. That they've been laboring this long was almost a miracle already."

"How much farther do you think it is?" Walt asked softly.

"At least ten more miles, I reckon." James Smith didn't say much, but when he spoke, he was usually right. That truth—ten more miles—stung. I wasn't sure any of us could make it ten more miles.

"We'll stay here with the wagons," Mama said, as if she could read my mind. "You take the animals. We'll wait for James to return."

The men exchanged worried glances, but they didn't argue.

Mama tried to encourage Cash, Tracker, Trailer, Barney, and Tyler, our dogs, to go with the men. "They might help keep the cattle moving," Mama said. But it was pointless.

The poor dogs whined and circled, unwilling to leave us.

In the end, we all climbed into the family wagon, grateful for the strong, heavy walls to block the terrible cold of the wind. After being awake for more than three days, Ma and I slept soundly, or at least, as soundly as you can when you're so parched that every breath cuts like a knife.

The bright light of dawn woke us, and we climbed out of the wagon slowly.

We peered carefully against the blinding white that surrounded us, but other than Pilot Peak, we couldn't make out a thing. No lush green hills, no travelers with buckets of water—nothing at all.

"Papa!" Tommy whined.

"I want water," James Junior begged. "Please. Just one sip."

Mama's hand trembled as she stroked his head. "I'm so sorry, sweetheart, but we don't have any." Her voice cracked on have, and I wanted to cry again.

But I couldn't waste any moisture, not even on crying.

"Your papa will come," Mama said.

I hoped it was true.

Less than ten minutes later, as if my mother's words had summoned him, Papa appeared on the horizon, moving toward us from Glaucus' back—Buttons and Mama's horse, Peony, were both trailing behind him, and both of them were loaded down with buckets.

My heart soared, and when he finally reached us, he shared out the water with a smile. He didn't let us drink as much as we wanted, but the four or five solid swallows helped me a lot.

"Why are these buckets empty?" Mama asked.

"I passed the oxen not quite ten miles from the spring—and some of them looked pretty bad. I shared out what I thought they needed to make it the rest of the way," Papa said. "But don't worry. They weren't far behind me."

We even gave the dogs a few swallows each, though their wide tongues sloshed some over the edge, and I think we all cringed when they did. But we waited in the heat all day, and by nightfall, the drivers still hadn't returned.

"Where are Milt and Walt and James?" Mama whispered.

I could tell that Patty heard her quiet plea, too.

"I'm not sure," Papa said. "I know you don't want to leave the wagons, but we don't have much choice. If we don't make it to the spring. . ." He glanced at the horses, who looked as if they had revived nicely when I saw them this morning, but without any food and with limited water, they looked much less fresh.

"I think we'll have to head on without the wagons," Papa said. "Maybe the oxen were too tired to return. We may need to rest them for a day or two before we come back for the wagons."

We drank the last of our water, sharing it out between the six of us, the dogs, and the horses sip by sip, and then we left. It broke my heart, looking back at our beautiful wagons, standing alone in the middle of the desert.

"It's okay," Papa said. "I know it hurts to leave your looking glass, and your clothing, and all our nice things." He sighed. "We'll come back for them. We will."

Mama nodded, but she didn't look comforted by his promises. I'm not sure why, but it made me nervous as well.

At the outset, Papa put Tommy on Peony, and James Junior on Buttons. "Glaucus carried me all the way back," he said. "I don't want to overtax her." But we hadn't gone too far, maybe five miles, when Peony and Buttons began to stumble.

"The weight's too much," Papa whispered. "We'll have to carry the boys."

Mama couldn't carry either of them, so I took little Tommy, and Papa took James Junior. We hadn't gone far when I realized I couldn't carry a boy, even a three-year-old one. I was too tired from days of travel with little sleep, food, or water.

"I can walk, Papa," James Junior said. "You can put me down."

Papa took Tommy, and I stumbled forward, my legs aching, my mouth burning, and my whole body so exhausted I wanted to just quit trying.

"How much farther?" Mama asked, her voice cracking.

"Just a few more steps," I said. "I always just think about how I need to take a few more steps, and then when those are past, I think it again. Just a few more."

Mama looked so sad that she might burst into tears, the moonlight betraying her distress, but we kept plodding along. As the moon rose in the sky, I really thought my feet would give out, but one step at a time, I trudged forward. Whenever my mind rebelled at the thought of one more step, I saw little James Junior, his face screwed up and his hands in fists, moving his small feet, and I kept going.

But then, when I felt I might collapse like the oxen, falling on my face in the sand, a terrible rushing sound came from up ahead. "What's that?" I croaked.

"I'm not sure," Papa said.

A steer burst into view ahead of us—Brutus! My favorite. He didn't look like the Brutus I knew, though. His eyes were wild, his expression crazed, his tongue lolling out sideways, as he raced toward us.

"Is he—is he attacking?" Beside me, Cash and Tracker growled, their hackles up.

Papa shifted Tommy to the side and pulled out his pistol, but at the last minute, Brutus changed direction and pounded away from us, disappearing into the night. "What was that?"

None of us knew quite how to answer.

"He looked like he hadn't found water," Mama said.

The idea broke me—Brutus had left to go ahead with all the others. My poor, dear, sweet Brutus. Had he really not gotten water? In all this time? No wonder he was half-crazed.

I thought about the Breens, and I offered up a silent prayer that the other cows had found water, and that Brutus would, by some miracle, change course and reach the spring. "Please, God, protect our best and nicest ox. I'm sure you want him to return to you, but we need him here. Yours respectfully, Amen."

I'm not sure how much farther we made it, but eventually, after what felt like a million more miles, we collapsed just short of the sight of Jacob Donner's family wagon. His wife, Betsy, brought us water in a small bucket, and we all drank a few swallows before passing out in a pile.

I'm not sure how late it was, or how long I slept, but the keen howling of the wind woke us. It was the first night I'd spent without a wagon or tent, and the wind cut like a knife.

"This isn't a normal wind," Papa said. "It's like a hurricane of cold air."

"I'm not sure what more we can do for them," Mama murmured. "Our backs barely block any wind at all."

"The dogs," Papa whispered.

My parents carefully, quietly, called the dogs over and arranged them around my brothers, Patty, and me, their furry bodies the only thing that kept us from freezing to death. It was a long, miserable night, and I have no idea how Mama and Papa made it. Poor Cash was the smallest of the dogs, but his furry little body kept my side warm in one spot, and it helped.

When we woke, we faced an even more depressing prospect.

"I talked to Milt. He said all our cattle are missing," Papa said.

CHAPTER 13

Mary Ann Graves

I actually really liked Virginia Reed.

The first time we met, I wanted to dislike her. Her family was nothing like mine—wealthy, refined, and small. Her father may not have been the official leader of the wagon company, but clearly he ran all the things that mattered. He picked where we stopped every day, and everyone listened to his opinions. It was probably rather a bad thing lately, because the Wasatch mountains and the desert were both awful.

He got blamed a lot for both.

But Virginia Reed was an excellent rider, she was kind, she was funny, and she was beautiful in a fresh-faced, very-young-and-eager kind of way. She never balked at difficult tasks in spite of her pampered background, she kept her head in emergencies, and she never whined.

That was probably why I wanted to hate her as much as I did.

John Snyder started *watching* her from the time we joined up with the Donner party, and he spent far more time than I liked chatting with her, smiling, and *flirting*.

It was my fault that we had kept our engagement a secret. He was willing to announce it to everyone. If we had, he couldn't have walked around, smiling and chatting and flirting with Virginia Reed. But I hadn't told anyone, not even Sarah, so he was free to do whatever he wanted. I shouldn't have been surprised to see him do that. He was a man, after all.

The day the Reed family emerged from the desert, I felt nothing but sympathy for poor Virginia and her family. Crossing the Great Salt Lake desert had been an utter nightmare for everyone. It was cold at night—intolerably, brutally frigid, really—and it was blisteringly hot during the day. We didn't have near enough water, and the animals struggled badly.

But the Reeds. . .

They didn't have enough buckets, and they didn't cut enough grass, or perhaps their animals had been more exhausted at the outset from hauling larger and heavier wagons. Either way, their animals gave out sooner than everyone else's, and their drovers couldn't get them to the water in time. They scattered, and then when we all took a few days, nearly a week actually, to search for them, we managed to find. . .

One cow whose milk had all but dried up, and one ox. One single ox when last week they had twenty. Virginia had been tending their two remaining cows like they were babies, her small lapdog Cash never more than a few feet away from her as she did it.

"Oh, Brutus." Virginia was petting the ox's lowered head. "I'm so sorry." He had pretty coloring for an ox, even if he was a little malnourished, but he had a nasty gash on his rear that contributed to the general theory that the oxen hadn't just run away. What on earth could have gashed him in the middle of the desert? There wasn't a tree, stick, or even a stump.

"It had to be Indians," Pa said. "Those Paiutes must've seen them, cattle thundering their direction, ripe for the taking."

Mr. Reed spit on the ground in disgust, something no one could have done a few days ago, on our drive across the desert. No one had the moisture to spare back then. After spending the past few days huddled around the spring at the base of Pilot's Peak, recuperating as best we could, and searching in parties for the Reeds' lost cattle, we were all doing a little better.

Except the Reeds.

They went from the wealthiest family in the wagon train to the poorest. . .overnight. Poor Virginia Reed. Poor James Reed.

Mostly, though, I felt sorry for Margaret Reed. She'd apparently been ill her whole life, and she still had three drovers, two household helpers, and four children to feed and care for between here and California, with no real way to accomplish that.

"I need to put together enough of a team for at least one wagon," Mr. Reed was saying. "Can you spare a pair? I'll pay you handsomely, and you can have first pick of any of my things I can't fit in my one wagon."

At least Mr. Reed had money left and items with which to barter, but oxen were in short supply just now, and with nowhere to find more, he didn't have many options.

Pa grimaced. "My teams are already tired, and I'm worried that if I sell any, we won't be able to pull our wagons either."

"Just one beast?" Mr. Reed asked. "I'll pay double."

Pa shook his head. "I can't sell one, but I can loan you one, at least until the mountains."

Mr. Reed didn't look too pleased, but he didn't have a choice. Mr. Breen and Levinah Murphy's son-in-law, William Pike, loaned them an animal each as well. With his one ox, they made two teams. Four oxen could pull a wagon, but only if it was light.

The rest of us watched as the Reeds took their two teams out to the desert to choose which of all their worldly possessions to load into their one wagon. Everything else would be abandoned to the desert— depressing in the extreme. Our situation was not quite so dire, but we had been forced to jettison all the things that John and I had collected by the side of the road, and now Ma and Pa forced us to go through our remaining wagons to lighten the load yet again.

The Reeds had arrived with their one wagon, sad faces on all the little children, when Ma asked me to make a decision. I could keep either the muslin I was saving for a future wedding dress—a beautiful, creamy white —or the quilt I made with Sarah last year. It was the quilt I always planned to use for my bed when I wed.

I went looking for John, hoping he might help me make what felt like an impossible decision. But when I found him, he was already busy. With the trickling of the spring behind me, he hadn't even noticed my approach.

"Things are bad," John said. "But you're hardly alone out here. Someone like your father—surely he has money set aside, and he has friends. He knows how to make more."

"Oh, he's already penning letters," Virginia said. "My Papa has nothing if not lots of friends and family ready to help."

John smiled. "And of course, you have me." He took her hand. "We haven't really talked about this, but when we reach California, I think we should get married."

My heart stopped beating for a moment, and then it hammered back to life. There was a strange roaring sound in my ears.

Get married.

Virginia Reed was barely thirteen years old.

"Oh, I don't know," Virginia was saying. "I'm young yet, to make big decisions like that."

"There's no rush," Snyder said, "but I'm positive I'll convince you by the time we reach California."

I'd had friends marry as young as twelve, but John Snyder already *had* a fiancée. Me. He had no business asking someone six years younger than me to marry him.

That's when I realized—she was a step up.

Supporting the Reed family now, when they were in dire straits, might be the only way he could get someone like James Reed to accept someone like him as a son-in-law. John Snyder was many things but above all else, he'd always been an opportunist. If he could entice Virginia to marry him, in one fell swoop, he'd have a much richer father-in-law, and the connections that came with someone like that. It's not as if Virginia Reed was bad to look at, and she was clearly both healthy and malleable.

Fury pulsed through me at the betrayal, sharp and hot.

I considered shouting at him. Exposing him. I wanted to ruin all his plans before he could discard me. But it would simply be my word against his, and for all my good opinion of Virginia Reed, she barely knew me. I would look like a lunatic, because I'd kept our plans secret.

Snyder was a snake, and I realized it too late to do anything about it.

I jogged back to our family wagons and realized I'd missed something. "What's going on?"

Ma was counting something in one wagon, and Pa was counting in the other.

"Hush." Ma went back to counting.

Sarah was poring over things in her wagon, too.

"What on earth is going on?" I asked. "Why's everyone counting things?"

Sarah's head whipped toward me. "Reed came around a few moments ago to dole out some of the provisions he had left and couldn't fit in his wagon. He said his family barely has enough food to make it to California, and they can't fit everything in their last wagon. He wanted us to check and see how everyone else was set."

I blinked.

Worrying about the level of our supplies was something Ma did—and I suppose Sarah did it for her and Jay. "And?"

"We only have enough for a week or two, if we stretch it."

"How can it be that bad?"

"We should have been there already," Sarah said.

By the time everyone reported back to Mr. Reed on how much in the way of supplies they had, he announced that the outlook wasn't great. We all gathered in a large circle to hear the news.

"We don't have enough supplies, any way you look at it." Mr. Reed's expression was grim. "No one does."

"And whose fault is that?" the sour-faced Lewis Keseberg asked.

"Lansford Hastings," William Eddy said. "He lied to us, clearly."

"But who thought we should listen to him?" Lewis Keseberg wasn't letting it go.

"Five of my oxen died," George Donner said. "I've had to collapse down to two wagons, and I could be complaining and angry. That helps no one, however. What matters now is what we're going to do about it. We have a problem, so let's come up with a solution."

"Agreed," Jacob Donner said. "At least Reed has been out and around, sharing whatever extra provisions he had. We need to evaluate our options and choose between them."

"We only have one good option. Men on horseback make much better time," Mr. Reed said. "That's why Mr. Hastings and his party far outstripped us. It's also why the paths they took didn't work for our wagon train. If we send a few men ahead to California, they can ask Mr. Sutter to send us some supplies—supplies I'll vouch to repay him for."

"Mr. Sutter?" Mr. Breen frowned. "Why would he help?"

"He runs Sutter's Fort," George Donner said. "It's the largest settlement in California. He's Lansford Hasting's partner, isn't he? He bears some responsibility for the mess we're in."

"Reed should go, since he insisted we take this route." Lewis Keseberg was clearly angry—he'd lost four oxen and a wagon, too, and he placed all the blame on Reed.

"Donner's the leader," William Eddy said. "Why's everyone going on about Reed?" He looked around, frowning. "He can't go—he's lost all his animals. If you'd lost all your worldly belongings, would you leave your family behind with nothing?" His baleful glares at Keseberg didn't even seem to faze the angry German.

"I'll go," Mr. Stanton said. He didn't talk much, and he was always scribbling in a little notebook. That's really all I knew about Mr. Stanton. He seemed a surprising person to make the offer of help. He had no other family in the wagon train, and he had no reason to fetch supplies and return. "I just need a horse."

Pa was immediately suspicious. "Would you have any reason to return?"

Mr. Stanton straightened his shoulders. "I'll give my word." He looked affronted, like Pa's allegation that he might borrow a horse, get to safety, and never come back was ridiculous.

"I'll go with him." William McCutchen, a massive man from Kentucky, glanced back at his wife and infant daughter, Harriet. "But only if you'll all *vow* to keep my family safe in my absence." He glanced around the circle, eyeing each of the men in turn.

Mr. Reed was the first to step forward. "I'll vow to keep your wife and daughter safe—on my honor and my life."

It was a little ironic that the man least able to protect his own family was the first to swear to help another. But he wasn't the last, thankfully. Even my pa agreed to keep an eye on Amanda McCutchen and her small baby.

"Can someone lend me a horse?" Mr. Stanton was quite small, and as far as I knew, he had walked the entirety of the way so far, living quite simply. As a relatively new member of the party, I wasn't sure whether he even had any belongings other than his pack.

"He can ride my mule," Mr. McCutchen said, "but someone else will have to take in Amanda and Harriet. She can't carry the baby the entire way if I take our horse."

I waited for someone else to offer an animal, but no one did. As our wagon train loaded up to move, I watched Mr. Stanton swing up onto a saddle on McCutchen's big-eared mule, and then the massive mountain man, McCutchen, mounted his own horse. The two of them riding off looked like some kind of joke-in-the-making. What do you get when you have a tiny man on a mule, and a massive mountain man on a stallion?

Not that his horse was a stallion, but it would be a better start to a joke. I really, really hoped that there wasn't a punchline to this setup. If those two men couldn't reach California and bring back supplies, our little party was at high risk of starving to death.

Once we were under way, Snyder lining our teams up to follow right after the Reed family's one wagon, I couldn't help thinking about what I'd seen earlier. Watching him smiling at Virginia and making jokes made me sick, so I moved to the back of our party, walking behind our last wagon. I was sure he'd come to talk to me and break things off, and I needed time to gather my wits so I could handle it with some modicum of grace.

The Breens were positioned just behind us, Mrs. Breen walking alongside her oldest son whose name was John.

"It's good to be moving again." Mrs. Breen glanced out at the sky, as if our tardiness was something she could somehow see. "We need to travel as fast as we can, certainly."

"I doubt that'll happen," I said, "with the Reeds all in one wagon with just four oxen."

Mrs. Breen sighed and shook her head. "A terrible business all around."

"Are you worried about lending them an ox?" I asked. "I know Pa was."

"I didn't feel we had any other choice," Mrs. Breen said.

"I should hope not," Eddie Breen said, and I realized he was riding on one of their horses—the sorrel mare that threw him, I think.

"You're walking again?" I asked. "What wonderful news." I'd only ever seen him staring at me from the back of their wagon, or hobbling with one arm slung over someone's shoulder as he went to the edge of camp to relieve himself.

"Not walking yet," Mrs. Breen said. "But we thought it might be good for him to get his circulation moving at least." She smiled. "It is good to see him up again. How do you feel?"

Eddie's nostrils flared. "Fit as a fiddle. And if Ma and Pa had refused to give my best friend an ox, I'd have climbed out of the wagon and run after them in protest."

He was a cute kid. He'd be a much better match for little Virginia

Reed—and I didn't think it because I wanted John for myself. I no longer wanted anything to do with him. I just felt sorry for Virginia. She, unlike me, had no idea what kind of person he was. Someone who would toss someone over the very second he identified a better option.

But that night, after we stopped to make camp, I forced myself to be out in the open. When John Snyder finished his work for the teams, after he finished the small dinner we were all rationing, I met his eye and forced a smile.

He brushed my hand gently and said, "I'm tired. Let's talk more tomorrow."

Like nothing was wrong.

I'd never wanted to strangle a man more in my life, but I didn't want to cause a scene, so I went to my bedroll and went to sleep. The next morning, when I woke, I was ready to chase him down and bawl him out, whether he admitted what he was doing or not. But when I emerged from the tent, my breath making puffs of steam in the cool morning air, I saw it. It completely knocked me off my plan.

Around the top of Pilot's Peak, plain as the sun in the sky, was a thick white band.

It had snowed.

CHAPTER 14

Virginia Reed

It was funny how the worst week of my life suddenly became the best with one simple phrase: we should get married.

John Snyder was tall, handsome, smart, hard-working, and most importantly, kind. And for some inexplicable reason, he liked *me*. I hadn't told Mama or Papa yet, because I wasn't sure how they'd react, given our present circumstances. Papa was stressed, and I understood why. But having another man to lend a hand would only help, right?

Sure, John had to help the Graves family too—he'd made them a commitment, after all. But surely they'd understand if he lent a hand when we needed it, and he said he was a crack hunter. Papa would really admire that.

Papa was just swinging up into Glaucus' saddle, his eyes still trained on the snow on Pilot's Peak, like it might slide right off and come attack us. I wasn't sure why everyone was so nervous about that. It wasn't snowing down here, and we weren't even going to Pilot's Peak. We were moving beyond it as fast as we could.

"Are you going hunting?" Because if he was, I'd suggest that John might go with him. Nothing impressed Papa more about a man than when he could handle a horse and shoot well. He could borrow Buttons if he wanted to spare his horse.

"Not today, darling. Today we're going to make as quick time as we can, and I aim to make sure we're taking the best route and resting with plenty of grass. Though you never know when you might get lucky." His smile was forced, but it was better than nothing.

"Maybe you could take Mr. Snyder with you," I said. "I hear he has a great horse—it's that dark bay with the star you said you liked."

Papa frowned. "Why would I take him with me?" He pointed behind us. "He's got a job to do, and it's not riding around with me."

I supposed he was right. "Nevermind," I said. "It was just an idea."

After I finished helping Ma get the children ready to walk, and cleaned up after breakfast, I went looking for John. If he couldn't ride out with Papa, I wasn't sure how they'd spend any time together. I knew I couldn't tell him yes until I knew whether Papa liked him. But when I found John behind the furthest Graves wagon, he was already busy talking to someone else.

Mary Ann Graves was the prettiest woman in the entire wagon train, hands down. Everyone said so, even Papa when he didn't know I was listening. She was old enough to have curves, and young enough to still have all her teeth. But on top of all of that, she had a beautiful smile, shining hair that fell in dark curls around her shoulders when she hadn't tied it back or tucked it up under a bonnet, and she had big, dark, expressive eyes.

I hated that John was talking to her. There were enough rumors about her and John as it was. It made sense, and he had told me how silly they were himself. She was beautiful and he was handsome, and people just assumed. It was nonsense, and I knew that, but it still stung a little to see them having such a heated exchange. I knew I should go back to camp and let John and Mary Ann finish their chat without eavesdropping, but I couldn't quite bring myself to do it.

"You can't marry that little girl," Mary Ann was saying. "Have you lost your mind?"

I didn't love being called a little girl. I might not have the curves she had, but I was a woman. I'd seen her already, down by the stream, cleaning her garments alongside mine.

"Have you lost yours?" John's smile was strange, his lip curling up. "Did you really think I'd be dumb enough not to take the chance when it came?"

What chance? What did that mean?

"The sad part is that I'm not even surprised. When I overheard the two of you—" She inhaled sharply, her lip trembling, and then she shook her head. "You're not a man, Mister Snyder. You're a snake." She threw something on the ground—something I couldn't quite make out. "I can't believe I thought this meant something."

She stomped past him and disappeared, and John crouched over for a moment, but didn't pick anything up. He straightened and turned, looking right at the place I'd been standing.

I barely ducked in time.

After I heard the sound of his boots move around the front of the wagon, I breathed a sigh of relief. I should run back to Mama and Papa, but I had to know. What did he mean when he said he'd be dumb not to take the chance? What did she throw on the ground when she called him a snake? All of it felt. . .loaded. Like maybe there was something in the rumors that had been circulating since the Graves family joined us.

The wagon had started to move when I crept over and looked at the object on the ground.

It was tiny.

It took me a little searching even to find it. But when I did, it made my heart race. I bent over and picked up the tiny wooden ring carefully. It was small—just about the right size for my finger. Someone had carved it, and my guess was John.

That small ring meant something.

As I walked all day that day, I thought of a lot of things that might have explained their interchange, but none of them made nearly as much sense as the two of them being engaged, and me being 'the chance' he couldn't pass up.

But we'd lost all our animals and most of our belongings. Sure, our family still had some money. Papa had a gold watch. He had his Mason medal. We had friends and family who would send us more money, and Papa had other valuables, but surely we were no better off than the Graves family, and I knew I was no match for Mary Ann as far as appearances went.

So why was I a 'chance'?

Was it because the Graves family was poor? Is that why John preferred me? Was it possible that Mary Ann, fair of face, was *defending* me? Not angry at him for liking me, not up there trying to break us up, but advocating *for me*, because of her dislike of John Snyder and the way he was treating us?

It wasn't a comfortable thought, but it made the most sense.

When John came by that night, offering me a pheasant he'd shot, I thought about turning him down. Then I thought about how much Patty and Thomas and little James Junior would like having that for dinner, and I accepted it with a smile. "I'd be stupid to turn down this chance," I said, turning before he could say anything else.

I thought about it as we roasted and ate his gift. As we cleaned up. While lying on my bedroll under the stars—our tent didn't fit in the one wagon we had left. The next morning, I decided I wanted to confirm my suspicions. I took Glaucus and Buttons and walked them to the stream nearby for water, just as I saw John Snyder crossing with a team of oxen.

"Virginia." He smiled that smile that I thought was just for me.

It sent a thrill up my spine, like it always did. I squished it down this time, though. "How long were you engaged to Mary Ann Graves, and why did you break it off?"

He dropped the lead he was holding, but luckily, the oxen were already fixated on the water and didn't misbehave.

"I'm just asking because I want to know how big of a jerk you are."

"You're such a spitfire," he said, his smile returning. "But it's not like you think. I don't know what you heard, but Mary Ann and me, we weren't serious, not like I am about you. And of course, my feelings for you showed up right after we met. From that moment forward—"

I tossed a ring at him. The little wooden ring. "So you carved her this ring before or after you met me?" I tilted my head.

John's eyes widened. "No, I mean—"

"I knew I liked you for a reason." Mary Ann was walking another pair of oxen over, and she was smiling. "You're smart, Virginia Reed. Too smart for him."

"Too smart?" Papa had come up behind Mary Ann, and none of us realized it. "Why is Virginia too smart for. . ." His eyes met John's and he froze. "My beautiful, beloved daughter Virginia is barely thirteen years old. How old are you, Mr. Snyder?" His eyes were as hard as I'd ever seen them.

Like flint.

"I'm twenty-five, sir," John said. "But you've misunderstood something."

"Oh, I don't think he has," Mary Ann said. "But just in case, I'll explain. I was engaged to Mr. Snyder here, but I asked him to keep it a secret. It never occurred to me that he'd take that to mean he could woo anyone he wanted, including your young but bright daughter." She coughed. "Which he did do."

My father looked apoplectic.

Before he murdered anyone, I decided to take action. I shoved the lead line for Glaucus into his hand. "Well, the horses have drunk plenty. Time to go."

I managed to distract him most of that day, and by the time we broke for lunch, it had become clear that we had to lighten the load on our wagon yet again. Brutus and the borrowed oxen were all straining. That didn't improve Papa's mood. Not at all. When we were about to get underway again, I saw him turn and head behind us—he was making a beeline right for Mr. Snyder.

I grabbed his arm. "Papa, please don't. It's better if we just leave it alone."

"He's worse than that Keseberg," Papa said. "It's predatory for him to pursue a girl who's barely thirteen."

I rolled my eyes. "Half the women in camp were married at thirteen or fourteen. Harriet Pike—"

Papa's eyes flashed. "She was fourteen. I heard that straight from her mother."

I sighed. "Fine, but Papa, listen, the Graves family likes him, all but Mary Ann. Actually, everyone likes him."

That stopped him, because he heard what I didn't say. Everyone liked John Snyder, and right now, given our current mess, not many people really liked my father. It wasn't fair, and it wasn't all his fault, but they had to blame someone. Picking a fight with a man when we could just walk away was a bad idea.

Luckily, my father was smart enough to drop it.

At least, until the next day.

I was riding, which was rare for me. Papa had wanted me ahead, I suppose, far away from John Snyder and the Graves family. Since Eddie was riding his horse Trixie again, we rode together. For a moment, it even felt like the start of our trip. Eddie and me, riding, smiling, laughing. Before we lost all our oxen. Before the man I liked turned out to be a jerk. Before Eddie broke his leg.

"It's nice that we're finally making good time," I said. "More than twenty miles a day."

"It makes sense to hurry here," Eddie said. "Dry valleys are bad all around."

The valley we were traveling through wasn't a desert—there was some grass—but there wasn't a stream. According to the maps provided by Hastings, which we now didn't entirely trust, on the other side of the Ruby Mountains, we'd rejoin the Humboldt River, and then we'd have a clear shot until the base of the Sierra Nevada mountains. Well, except for another desert, but anyone on this path had to cross that. It was much smaller than the one that had ruined my family's situation, and then we'd be free of the cursed Hastings cutoff, at least.

"Do you regret coming?" Eddie asked.

"Coming—do you mean leaving Springfield?"

Eddie nodded. "Your family had money in Illinois. You were comfortable."

"Do you regret leaving?" I asked.

He shrugged. "Some days." He grunted. "Most days."

"I'm sorry about your leg," I said. "I'm sure the pain was terrible."

He frowned. "It wasn't good, but that's not what I meant. I'm worried."

"About your leg still?" I stared at it, but he didn't seem to be favoring it. Trixie was listening to him as well as she ever did, I thought. "Or about the supplies?"

"Everyone's running out of supplies, and my father said the snow's coming soon."

"But think about what we've already done," I said. "Rainstorms. The desert. Indians. All of it. We can do whatever we need to do—and we will."

"You think that because your dad's healthy and strong," Eddie muttered.

"Is your dad not doing well?"

He sighed. "It's been really hard," he said. "And I worry about my ma. She always looks tired, and she has the baby."

"Babies are hard," I said.

"She always wanted a girl, and now she has one, but it's made the whole trip really, really long for her."

I could imagine. "But we're so close to the end," I said again. "I think all the bad stuff is behind us."

The next few days I stayed clear of John Snyder, and we made decent progress. We cleared the Ruby Mountains and rejoined the Humboldt, even though it wasn't quite the river we'd hoped to find. The dry heat that had been baking us reduced the Humboldt to a dusty river bed in many places, but we could always find a section with enough water for our animals, even if the grass was sparse and crunchy.

We hadn't long escaped the Hastings cutoff when we met our first Shoshone Indians. A pair of them came into camp to trade, which was a welcome surprise, honestly. Increasingly, the heavy things we had dragged all the way from Illinois felt less like treasure and more like shackles. Papa actually traded a fine hammer for a bowl full of strange, small berries. Mama made a pie with them, and I was glad he'd traded the hammer. Even if it was worth far, far more than a bowl of berries anywhere else.

But the next morning, two of the Graves' oxen were gone.

I suppose we shouldn't have been surprised when Mr. Graves came around, asking for his ox back. He and Papa argued for a while, but in the end, Papa had to surrender the animal. It wasn't ours.

It broke my heart a little when Papa and Milt hooked up our poor milk cow into the space vacated by the Graves ox. There just wasn't another way. We carried on like that, barely managing to haul our meager supplies for *just* one more day, for quite some time. It felt like my walk across the desert.

But ultimately, it was doomed. I think we all knew that.

We fell behind even further, which was frustrating for Papa. His best friends, the Donner brothers, were at least two days ahead of us by now. We had been the finest, strongest family, and now we struggled on, near the back each day.

When we reached an area known as Pauta Pass, the biggest hill that we'd seen for some time, we realized that we had a problem. Normally, we'd simply unhook our oxen from one wagon and 'double team' each wagon, using six teams to get each wagon over. But now, we didn't have a team with which to double. In fact, we were operating on just a two-thirds team as it was.

In front of us, nearly every family had found the pass problematic. The Murphys had shared oxen with the Pikes and the Fosters to get all their wagons over—which made sense. Levinah Murphy was mother-in-law to William Pike and William Foster, who in addition to being married to Murphy sisters were also best friends who had worked together for years. The Breens had three wagons and six teams of oxen apiece, so they had spent over an hour getting all of theirs over earlier this morning. They were waiting for us on the other side of the pass.

The Kesebergs and the Wolfinger family had made a plan to join forces to drag their wagons over, but they were one of the few families behind us. After stopping for a lunch break, Jay Fosdick and his wife Sarah, Mary Ann Graves' sister, worked with their father, Mr. Graves, to hook five teams of oxen to each wagon to get them over the pass. It took long enough that the sun was high in the sky by the time their first wagon had finally crossed.

Papa had been out hunting with William Eddy that morning, but when they got back, they immediately saw the trouble.

"I know you're struggling and heaven knows we're all sorry for it," Mr. Eddy said, "but there's no way either of us will get over this pass alone." He glanced back at where our poor cow was struggling in the yoke. "I'd be willing to double team our wagon over second, once we get yours through, but I'd like the help from your teamsters to get mine past."

Papa agreed readily. "Of course they can help you. They're much better with the oxen than I am." He clapped a hand on Mr. Eddy's shoulder.

"Better than me, too." Mr. Eddy was smiling. "I've always been more useful with a gun in my hand."

Not everyone in the company had lost their minds, at least. We still had some friends. Papa and Mr. Eddy left the wagons to the teamsters and started cleaning the deer they'd shot. I was hanging back with them, eager for any excuse to avoid John Snyder, when there was a commotion up ahead. Apparently Mr. Snyder, right ahead of our wagon, had felt confident that his normal three teams of oxen would be enough to get their last wagon over.

"Why didn't you double team?" James Smith, one of our teamsters, was shouting.

Milt was encouraging our oxen, linked to Mr. Eddy's borrowed oxen up the hill, but it looked like Mr. Snyder's oxen had floundered, and their wagon was sliding backward, right into our poor animals.

"You should've waited to climb until I was done." Snyder wasn't happy to be criticized, clearly.

"You like telling people what to do, don't you?" Milt said. "You're the kind of man who wants a wife he can push around, because you're the kind of person who likes to push *everyone* around."

My head whipped around so I could glare at Papa. Clearly he'd told Milt what had happened.

Papa stood, dropping the half-skinned deer on the ground. "Virginia, go and get Glaucus some water," he said, clearly trying to get rid of me.

"Not a chance," I said. "You never should have said anything to Milt."

But while I argued with Papa, Mama was taking matters into her own hands. She had stood and jogged over near Milt. "Stop yelling and get your animals under control," she snapped, her eyes glaring at John Snyder. "And if you can't do it, you need to tell us. We're halfway up the hill, and I won't have you injuring our remaining animals because of your incompetence."

Mama knew, too. Half of me wanted to groan, and the other half wanted to scream. How many people had Papa told?

"I know how to manage oxen, and I know how to manage women," Snyder said, "which is more than I can say for Reed on both counts. He hires men to handle his oxen. What does he do for his wife and daughter, I wonder?"

Mama's eyes widened, and Milt's face twisted into a grimace. He stepped away from the oxen and toward John Snyder. "Why, you—"

But Mama wouldn't allow it. She jogged into the space between the two men, her hands flung outward. "No, you're not going to fight. Do you hear me? We have more important things to deal with right now."

Snyder's eyes had been fixed on Milt's—he didn't see Mama. He had pulled out his bull whip, already at hand to move the oxen up the hill, and he reacted to Mama's movement. Or perhaps he was just getting a woman under control. Either way, the edge of his whip struck Mama, leaving a bright red welt on the side of her face and her neck.

I could see it easily, because she crumpled like a dry weed, her shocked face turned toward me.

Papa shot past me like a furious bear, his hand already tightening around the belt knife he'd been using to skin the deer. "How dare you touch her," he bellowed. "You need to stop trying to manage things that don't belong to you."

But Milt was much closer. Milt was just as angry as Papa—we'd known him for years, and he called my mother 'ma.' He reached for John, clearly intending to yank his bull whip right out of his hands. Again, Mr. Snyder was distracted by the devil he saw, and he ignored the bigger threat.

Papa.

This time, Mr. Snyder brought the butt of the whip down toward Milt's head, but Papa dove forward to deal with him and spare Milt. When John's whip handle cracked down on Papa's head, it did some real damage.

Blood spurted. Papa cried out. Milt shouted. Everything else happened so fast that I couldn't see the majority of it, but I knew the most vital part: Papa stabbed John Snyder.

John reeled backward from the attack, and poor Billy Graves, who had been helping with directing the oxen for the last wagon, reached out and caught him. Mary Ann cried out from where she stood—not far behind Billy—as John Snyder, jig dancer, flirt, and Graves drover bled out in messy spurts on the rocky sand below us.

None of us knew quite what to do.

Mary Ann and Billy tried to help. Mama and Papa were both bleeding, but still I went to John Snyder's side to try and help. Pressure on the wound didn't stop the blood spewing out. It was clear that something major had been struck, but without a doctor or any knowledge of medicine, we were lost for ideas.

Papa seemed frozen in place.

I knew he'd learned about fighting in the Black Hawk War, but this was a very different circumstance. Milt and Mr. Eddy looked as stunned as Papa did while we watched John Snyder bleed and thrash and spasm. James Smith, our other teamster who was in camp, carefully calmed the oxen and brought them back down from the climb.

Billy went to bring their oxen down. By the time all the urgent tasks had been completed, I realized that no one had seen to Papa's head wound. The front of his shirt was stained bright red, so I dipped a cup of water from the bucket on our wagon and used a rag to try and clean his face.

The gash on his forehead was bad, but it was difficult to do much about it, with John Snyder gasping and moaning not twenty feet away. Papa let me clean the blood and gore from his face and head a bit, but then he broke away and crouched by Snyder. With a rattle, John tried to sit up, saying something—what, I couldn't tell.

"I know," Papa said. Something Snyder said must have made sense to him. "I'm so sorry."

And then John Snyder fell back, exhaling loudly.

It took a few more minutes, but then he was gone. I'm not sure anyone knew quite what to say, but some people weren't waiting for words. Lewis Keseberg pulled the wagon tongue from the innards of his wagon, making sure he had his oxen staked, and propped the long, solid piece of wood upright, leaving it to protrude almost ten feet from the ground.

It was a chilling sight—he was calling for Papa to be hanged.

"He was defending Mama," I said. "It was an accident."

But no one met my eye. They began to murmur, breaking into groups. William Eddy and his wife came to our side immediately, eagerly defending Papa. Our drovers, too, Milt and James, came to stand beside us, their hands on the guns on their belts.

Philippine Keseberg wouldn't meet my eye, but Mr. Wolfinger and his young wife were clearly in agreement that Papa should be punished. Augustus Spitzer and Mr. Charles Burger also murmured and nodded behind Keseberg. They were all milling around, and within a moment, things got really nasty.

Lewis Keseberg spoke up. "Snyder might have used coarse language, and he might have had a firm hand around women, but that didn't justify James Reed *murdering* him. I demand that we take a vote. I want Reed hanged for what he did."

Mama gasped and collapsed backward against the earth.

"Come now." James Smith, our determined teamster, lifted a rifle. "Surely you can't be suggesting something that insane. A man has a right to defend his family and his property."

Lewis Keseberg eyed James' rifle with a scowl. "Those aren't even his oxen, you know. He borrowed them. Your master's as poor as he is arrogant."

"If you want to talk about arrogance—" Milt started.

Papa dropped a hand on his arm. "I think—"

"We don't care what you think," Lewis Keseberg snapped.

"Yeah, we don't care about the opinions of murderers," Mr. Wolfinger said. "Or their friends." He scowled at William Eddy.

Just then, I caught sight of the rest of the Graves family making their way down the hill, Mr. Breen and his wife just behind them. That's when everything really descended into chaos. Everyone had an explanation of what happened, but no one agreed.

Lewis Keseberg insisted that Papa stabbed Mr. Snyder because he had been rough on the cattle and used a swear word in front of me. Mr. Wolfinger said that Papa had gone mad, as a result of some insult from Snyder about Papa's oxen.

That was about as stupid as anything I'd heard, so I stood up, ready to set the record straight. "None of them were even standing close enough to know," I said. "They had no idea what happened."

Mary Ann's expression was panicked, and I wondered whether her family knew she was engaged to John Snyder, or that the engagement had been called off. I stumbled for a moment, unsure what to say. Thankfully, Milt rushed to my rescue.

"Snyder didn't double team his oxen, and they were sliding back into ours." Milt gestured. "We only have four, and two of them are borrowed."

"And then?" Mr. Breen asked, one eyebrow raised. "Then what?"

"Then Mr. Snyder attacked Ma and Pa," I said, "using his bull whip. Look, you can see they're both bleeding."

"Your mother's fine," Keseberg said. "That's just blood from her husband, and he got what was coming to him."

I couldn't believe that he was lying so much. "But—"

"I want to hear what my daughter saw," Mr. Graves said. "Mary Ann, what happened?"

Mary Ann's eyes were sad. "Mr. Reed was defending himself."

"And did he kill John Snyder?" Mr. Graves asked.

It was slow in coming, but eventually Mary Ann nodded. "He did."

"He can't stay," Mr. Breen said. "No one who has slain a fellow traveler can stay with us."

Mrs. Breen caught at his arm, but he shook her off. "All in favor of casting James Reed out of our company with nothing but his horse—no food, no gun, and no ammunition with which to do harm, say aye."

Mama, Milt Elliot, and James Smith, along with William Eddy, all disagreed, loudly, but the ayes carried. To my great frustration, I couldn't hear whether Mary Ann voted. I like to think she voted for Papa to stay.

But that very moment, Papa had to grab Glaucus, surrender his gun and his ammunition, and ride away. He must have looked back a hundred times, and for the first time in my life, I saw a tear glistening in my fearless father's eye.

Some people insisted he was crying out of fear.

No food—no weapons. Dumped into a land teeming with wild animals, hostile Indians, and an uncertain path. . .I'm sure most men would have cried and cried. But not my pa. No, I knew he was crying because he was forced to leave his family alone, with just an oxen, a cow, two horses, and two borrowed beasts, to struggle their way toward the Sierra Nevada mountains late in the season with almost no food stores.

That night, after darkness fell, I saddled up Buttons, and I rode out with all the supplies Mama would allow me to take. A handful of crackers, a bit of hard tack, and a few beans. A bag of dried beef strips.

I also took Papa his rifle and his pistol, along with all the ammunition he had left. I lashed his bedroll to Button's saddle, too. He might not be able to take anything else, but I was determined he'd at least be able to defend himself and poor Glaucus, and he'd have a blanket against the increasingly chilly nights. It took two hours of stumbling around in the dark alone, which was terrifying, but eventually I found him.

Papa cried out and leapt to his feet when he saw me, and when I showed him what I'd brought, he slid off his horse and hugged me tightly. "You shouldn't have come," he said. "It was too dangerous."

"Buttons isn't the same as Billy." Thinking about my angel still made me teary-eyed. "But she's a good mare, and she'll get me back to Mama and the wagons. Don't worry about me."

"Thank you." Papa's eyes were still sad. "Thank you for caring enough to bring me this."

"Please make it to California," I begged. "Please make it safely. I love you."

"I'll make it there, and faster than you. Those idiots left me Glaucus," he said.

His grey mare had wandered over to us, and she bumped me with her nose. I rubbed her softly. "Take care of my Pa." She tossed her head like she was nodding in agreement. It brightened my soul.

Papa had been looking through the food I brought, and he took the crackers and pressed the rest back into my saddle bag. "I won't take any of that. You have barely anything left as it is. Keep it."

"But—"

I could barely see it in the moonlight, but he shook his head. "You're one of the brightest blessings in my life," Papa said. "You make me very proud, darling."

"I just try to be the person you taught me to be."

"I'll be just fine—I always am. Now you promise me that you'll never let those small people dim your light. You hear me? Don't let them. And you keep an eye on your ma and those three young 'uns. Promise me."

I promised with a heavy heart. I longed to keep right on riding with him, just Papa and me with Buttons and Glaucus. In the end, I knew Mama and the others needed me, so I climbed back up on Buttons' and asked her to head back.

"I will come for you," Papa called. "No matter what, just like we took out those buffalo, even when I don't know what to do, I'll find a way."

As I rode toward where the wagons were camped at the base of Pauta Pass, I couldn't help smiling through my tears. Papa had to go, but he was alive, and I knew him. I knew he'd fight his way to California, and if we were still in trouble, he'd save us. That's just who he was.

When I reached the camp, I expected everyone to be asleep. I found my way back quicker than I went, but it was a long ride both ways. Mary Ann, however, was still waiting up for me, and when I reached camp, she stood.

"You found him?"

I frowned. "I did. Are you going to report me?"

"You took him a gun?"

I nodded.

She exhaled. "Thank goodness."

I slid off Buttons, and Mary Ann approached.

"I know it's partially my fault." She hung her head.

"How?" I began to unsaddle Buttons. "None of this was anyone's fault. It was an accident."

Mary Ann watched me quietly, and then she brought me a bucket with water in it. "For your horse."

As Buttons drank, Mary Ann whispered, "Mrs. Breen also waited for a bit. Her family was up at the top, beyond the pass, but she wanted me to tell you that she and Eddie were praying for your safety, and for your Pa."

For some reason, that made me cry even harder than I did on my way back. Sometimes, even when you're suddenly bereft, it helps to feel like you aren't *totally* alone.

I might not have a father here with me anymore, but it felt for the first time like I might have a real friend.

CHAPTER 15

Peggy Breen

The first time I ever met Mr. Hardcoop, we were camping near the Platte River, and he was sautéing mussels in a pan.

"What are you doing?" my husband Patrick had asked.

"The one thing I have missed the most from Antwerp, other than my children," he had with a thick Belgian accent, "is mussels and chips." He sighed heartily, and then he offered me some.

I declined, because the idea of taking something he clearly savored so much wasn't appealing to me. I left him to enjoy his memories to the utmost.

Lewis Keseberg had convinced the old man to come with him to California to 'see the world' before returning home to his children. All of it had been explained to poor Mister Hardcoop as a grand adventure. It was just another reason I had come to detest Keseberg and nearly everything about him. I should have guessed what would happen, when I heard that Lewis Keseberg had lost enough oxen that he was now down to one wagon.

He didn't need Hardcoop to drive the second wagon any more.

Which meant. . .he didn't need Hardcoop at all.

But when I discovered Lewis Keseberg had kicked Hardcoop out of his remaining wagon, I was still shocked. The old man had deteriorated in the past few weeks and couldn't walk. It would have been like us telling

116

Eddie he had to hobble along on his broken leg or be left behind. It was unconscionable.

"Mrs. Breen!" I heard the shouting loud and clear. I dropped a hand on Patrick's arm.

He shook his head. "We can't help him."

"The man can't walk," I whispered.

"He's Keseberg's problem," Patrick insisted. "Our family can't save everyone else, and he's Keseberg's employee and friend." My usually-kind husband kept going, refusing to even look back. I couldn't help turning his way, and what I saw disturbed me. Poor Mr. Hardcoop was hobbling along, clearly not in any state to walk fifteen or twenty miles.

"We're all walking," Patrick said. "Even James, and he's five."

He wasn't wrong. I was carrying Isabella most of the way each day, our one-year-old infant, and we took turns putting sweet little Peter, our two-year-old son, on my paint pony, Boots, while I walked alongside him, or on his father's shoulders. The only one who got to ride regularly was Eddie, and that's only because his leg couldn't take much more than a mile or two before it began throbbing mercilessly.

But by nightfall, Lewis Keseberg had still not relented, and poor Mr. Hardcoop was nowhere to be found.

Mr. William Eddy, the carriage-maker who was such fine friends with the now-absent Mr. Reed circled around on his horse, his eyes intense. "I'm riding out to look for him." He glanced at Patrick. "Can you or one of your sons come along? More sets of eyes would make finding him faster."

Patrick shook his head. "You shouldn't even be doing this. He's Keseberg's responsibility. If we take care of him, Keseberg wins."

"Keseberg *wins*?" Eddy froze. "Do you even hear yourself, man? What about seeking the lost sheep? Isn't that your whole thing? Aren't you Catholic? You read the Bible every day, right?"

Patrick flinched as if he'd been struck. "My duty, first and foremost, is to my family. If I ride out after this man, the man Keseberg has abandoned, and my horse dies or goes lame, what then? If I put him in my wagon and it's too much for them, if I lose my wagons and have no way to take care of my family, who will care for my children?"

William Eddy glared for a moment.

Patrick's smile was diabolical. "I didn't see you giving Hardcoop a spot in your one wagon."

Mr. Eddy flinched. "My oxen are already pulling my two children, and they barely make it into camp each night." Mr. Eddy circled around one more time and then he finally rode off. I heard, less than an hour later, when he returned. Blessedly, Mr. Hardcoop had been found.

But the next day, the old man came to our wagon again.

"Please, Mr. Breen," Mr. Hardcoop begged.

When I emerged from our tent, I saw his feet. They were swollen and red. I'm not sure whether his shoes had given out, or whether his feet had become too large for them to fit, but he was barefoot, and with the Humboldt banks being more dry than wet, it was almost like we were struggling through a never-ending desert again.

I could already tell he wasn't going to make it through another day like yesterday, at least, not without help. "Patrick," I whispered. "Perhaps just a day—"

My husband stood. "There's just no room for you in our wagons. I'm sorry." His face was like granite—hard and unyielding.

As Mr. Hardcoop turned to leave, Patrick and John began readying our wagons. Eddie helped hook up the teams too, riding now from a perch he and John had made at the top of the third wagon.

"Are you sure," I began, preparing to ask Patrick one more time to allow poor Mr. Hardcoop to ride with us.

"We have seven children, Peggy." Patrick's voice was pained. "Which would you be willing to sacrifice to save that old man?"

I couldn't argue with him.

But I had to watch as sweet, brave Mr. Eddy had the same argument with his wife, but in the other direction. He thought they could spare the space, but Eleanor reminded him they'd almost lost their oxen and their own lives in the last desert.

In the end, we all started off again, and Mr. Hardcoop was left to fend for himself. As we rolled out, I couldn't help looking back, watching him struggle along until he disappeared. It weighed on my mind all day long, as the heat from the sun above beat down on us. As Isabella cried, and the oxen lowed, and our feet blistered from the heat of the hard-packed dirt, I worried about poor Mr. Hardcoop, with no shoes, and no one around to even hear his complaints or offer encouragement.

He wasn't the only one struggling, however.

Milt Elliot was driving the one remaining Reed wagon, and precisely because it was so finely made, larger than the normal farm wagons most of us had, it was heavy. Even with the borrowed oxen, Milt had a hard time keeping them moving. The Reeds had systematically emptied out more and more of their belongings, keeping barely more than bedrolls, a few clothes, and their meager amounts of remaining food. On top of that, their two small boys and younger girl, Patty, had all been walking nearly constantly. Not many three- and five-year-old boys can manage to cover miles and miles a day, but those boys did their best. When they looked ready to fall over, Virginia would sling one or the other of them up on her mare Buttons' back and walk alongside them. Her mother and Patty took turns on their other horse when they couldn't move another step, but it wasn't looking very good either.

That day, while I fretted over poor Mr. Hardcoop's plight, I also had to watch as Milt Elliott and Margaret Reed made a hard decision. "The four beasts just can't keep up," Milt hissed. "I know you don't want to leave the wagon, but. . ."

"You're saying that we're better off loading Brutus with our belongings and keeping him and Dove alive."

Milt nodded. "Not only that, but I've noticed the Breens and the Pikes watching."

"They want their oxen back." Margaret Reed's mouth was a flat line.

He nodded.

I stepped out from behind the scrub that was blocking me from view. "You can keep ours," I said quickly. "Don't worry over that, please. If we are watching, it's been from concern and a wish that we could do more, I assure you."

Before I could say anything else, Mr. Graves, who was apparently also lurking, walked toward Mrs. Reed slowly. "It's time to leave your wagon behind." His face was grim, and I felt a little sick, watching. The Reeds had been a bit arrogant, sure, but for any family to endure what they had, all in the space of two weeks. . .Mrs. Reed's efforts had been Herculean, really. She was all that stood between her poor children and death out here on the trail thanks to the exile of her husband.

"I want to offer you one of our wagons." Mr. Graves inhaled slowly, and then exhaled. "We have so few supplies that we can collapse into two, and I think you'll need to leave yours here. Ours are much lighter—simpler, farm wagons."

"But I can't even pay you for it." Mrs. Reed's hand flew up to her mouth. "What little we have, I need to use to buy food. We're probably better off trying to load up our animals."

"They've never carried loads like that," Mr. Graves said. "They'll fight it, and they'll rub against trees, and you'll lose more valuable energy and time." He stepped closer, and then he looked down at his feet. "Take the wagon. We'd be leaving it behind anyway, whether you take it or not."

I watched as Margaret Reed, the proud but sickly woman who had barely left her wagon in the first few weeks of our trip, with the help of James Smith and Milt Elliot, transferred their few belongings to an even smaller and humbler wagon, silently crying the entire time. It said something about her as an employer and friend that all her employees—Milt, James, Eliza, and the elusive Baylis, all followed her without question, even after the Reeds had lost everything.

That night, William Eddy came around again, this time without a horse. "Can I borrow one of your horses to search for Hardcoop?" he asked.

Patrick frowned. "Where's yours?"

Mr. Eddy sighed. "Mine's too sore to go. He's resting. But—"

My husband cut him off. "And you'd like mine to go lame as well? Why do you think I refused before? All that gallivanting around did your horse no favors."

"But surely when a man's life is in danger—"

Patrick turned and walked away.

Mr. Eddy approached Mr. Graves as well, and he was told the same thing with even more frustration. Mr. Graves actually shouted at him, which made it easy to hear. "I've already given away a wagon and loaned out an ox. Should I now throw away a perfectly good horse on a dead man?"

A dead man.

The words were harsh, but they might nevertheless be true.

Tensions were running high, and I couldn't blame any of them. William Eddy seemed almost desperate to try and save *someone*. I couldn't fault him for the sentiment, after watching too many bad things happen lately. Losing Mr. Reed had been quite hard on him, but watching poor

Margaret Reed struggle on with borrowed oxen and four children must have been harder still.

I'm sure every man could imagine the same happening to their wife.

The next day, I overheard the Donners talking, and I discovered that the Reed's teamster, Walter Herron, had been with the Donners when Reed happened by. The two of them had set out together, intent on locating more supplies and returning. With our quickly dwindling larder and no sign of Stanton or McCutchen, I couldn't fault that goal in the slightest.

I did think it a point of possible irony that the man we kicked out might be the one to save us, should we face further difficulty. That was just the sort of thing James Reed would love, if I understood him at all. Being run off under controversy, and then returning as the conquering hero would make him quite happy, I thought.

But I couldn't help feeling like, if he was the hero, we were the villains. That night, I had my first nightmare about Mr. Hardcoop. Only, this time, it wasn't Hardcoop begging for a spot on our wagon—the beggar was me. No matter how I pled and sobbed, Patrick's face remained hard and cold. "We have no room. Struggle along alone."

I had to stand and watch as my family pulled away and left me.

When I woke with a start, I was terribly relieved to find it was merely a dream. Later that day, as we made camp yet again, like we had every day before, and like we would for what felt like all the days to come, Patrick whispered something I never expected to hear. "I may have been wrong."

"About?"

His brow was furrowed, his eyes troubled. "We left that man to die. I wonder what God will think about my decision to leave poor Mr. Hardcoop behind. Even a godless heathen like Mr. Eddy wanted to save him."

I had clearly wondered the same thing, but it was too late to do much about it now. We would have to settle up before the judgment bar, sooner or later. I just hoped God might understand our difficulty and be a bit forgiving.

It felt like nothing had been simple, not in a very long time.

CHAPTER 16

Mary Ann Graves

On October 9th, our wagon got stuck in a bog.

"I don't know what to do," Pa said.

"We keep digging until we free the wheels," Jay Fosdick said. "There's nothing else *to* do."

Jay was right. We dug, and we cut small trees, and we braced the wheels, and we used whatever we could find to lay a path, and we double teamed our oxen, and finally, we got that stupid wagon out, just before dawn. It was almost time for breakfast when we realized it was October tenth—mother's forty-sixth birthday. In our wildest dreams, none of us thought we'd still be traveling today. We all assumed we'd be celebrating in California. When Pa wished her a happy birthday, she laughed, and I was worried she might begin to cry.

"What can we give her?" Eleanor asked, nearly frantic. "I forgot it was coming, and I didn't even make her anything."

"A cake!" Lovina suggested. "Mary Ann and I can make a cake."

"With what?" Sarah asked. "All we have left is a little flour and some dried beef."

When moments later a Paiute brave appeared, offering to trade, Pa didn't run him off. I think we all needed something good, something hopeful, some kind of celebration. It wasn't just about Ma—we all needed to smile. Unfortunately, while Pa was visiting with the brave, one of the

122

Indian's friends managed to make off with something of greater value than any of us imagined possible. When the first brave left, all four of our remaining horses were gone.

It took all of five minutes.

"How could that have happened?" Billy asked. "We were talking to him the entire time."

"He was a distraction." He swore under his breath, using words I'd never even heard before. Pa had never sounded so disgusted before, not ever. "We were stupid for not running him off right away."

He was right. We were idiots.

And now we were idiots without horses.

The Humboldt River had all but disappeared. We were clearly traveling through a hard land, and it had to be a miserable place to live for any of the natives who made this their home. I shouldn't have been surprised to find that they were a hard people. That night we set guards. The theft of our horses had been a warning, Pa said. We had to be ready.

But in spite of the guards we set, in spite of circling our wagons, the Indians came back. They employed the same tactic as they had earlier with our horses, but on a larger scale. Several braves distracted the guards on one side, and when James Smith, Billy, John, Mr. Pike, and Mr. Keseberg rushed over to see what was going on, another larger group of Indians rounded up the cattle on the far end. The shouting when I awoke put the loss of our horses into perspective.

They'd made off with *nineteen* cattle.

"I hate to sound like a ghoul," Billy said quietly as we were hitching our wagons, "but I'm glad they weren't ours."

I couldn't argue with him, but I felt awful for the Donner families and for the Wolfingers, who had lost nearly half of all their animals. Mrs. Reed looked sick. More than anyone else, I suppose she knew just what losing so many of their animals felt like.

After such a significant loss, George Donner set up a rotating guard duty with rules, and we all took it seriously. Even so, less than a day later, as the night guards were coming in, while they were taking a few gulps of coffee to wake themselves up for the day, the Paiutes struck again.

This time, they got *twenty-one* cattle.

The poor Eddy family lost everything they had, save one lone ox. The Wolfingers found themselves in the exact same situation.

"Is it strange?" I asked.

"What?" Sarah asked.

"The Reeds lost all their oxen, except the one Virginia loved, Brutus."

"Okay." Sarah frowned.

Jay's head snapped my direction. "Yes, and now the Wolfingers and the Eddys have had the exact same thing happen." Jay's brow furrowed. "Why do they each manage to keep only one?"

"Would zero have been better?" Pa asked, hooking up our teams.

I shook my head. No one knew quite what to say, but like Billy the day before, I was relieved we hadn't lost our cattle.

As we readied ourselves for the day, two main things struck me. First, I found myself unable to watch as the Eddys drove their one cow out and in front of them. Mr. Eddy slung their three-year-old son James up on his shoulders, and loaded a few loaves of sugar into a bag.

"That's all they have left," Ma said. "They can't carry anything else."

Mrs. Eddy looked tired already as she picked up her one-year-old daughter.

The saddest thing we had to face was the next leg of our trip. Just as we had done not many weeks in the past, we had to cross yet another desert. This time, however, we were all in far worse shape at the start. The Eddys and the Wolfingers had no wagon at all. The Reeds had gone from three to one, and a small, humble one. The Donners had each lost a wagon, and several of our party were no longer with us.

"We should have helped Mr. Hardcoop," Pa said. "God's cursing me." His voice dropped to a whisper. "And we deserve it."

"Perhaps," Ma said, "but we're not the only ones who ignored him."

"That's hardly encouraging," Pa said. "Are you saying we're all doomed?"

I wondered, though. The Breen family had refused to help Mr. Hardcoop too, and they still had all their oxen and wagons. Poor Mr. Eddy had done more than anyone else to try and help Hardcoop, and he had just lost almost everything.

If I had to hazard a guess, I'd say the most likely truth is that any God who may have existed had long since given up on all of us. As we started out once again to cross a terrible desert, it felt an awful lot like we'd already all been consigned to hell.

CHAPTER 17

Peggy Breen

The last desert we crossed had been brutal.

This one looked even worse, at least, from the outset. Humboldt Lake, which was supposed to be quite grand, was nothing but a dry bowl of clay that looked barren and desolate in every imaginable way. The ground had cracks so large opened up in its surface that we had to move slowly with the animals. Entire oxen hooves, wagon wheels, and children's feet could disappear within the cracks the earth had allowed to gape open.

When she saw the barren landscape, poor Isabella burst into tears.

At least near the outer edge of the badly misnamed Humboldt Lake, we found a long earthen berm, and behind it, a small slough, the water dark and shallow but drinkable. We all took turns that afternoon, filling everything we could manage. The Eddys, without much of anything at all, were not in great shape. I watched as Mr. and Mrs. Eddy removed their boots, filling them with water, and tying the laces to sling over their shoulders.

It made my mother's heart quake.

The Great Salt Lake desert had been bad enough, but going into this long trek without any barrels or buckets of water at all?

The last time, my poor son Eddie was stuck in the wagon, along with all the water and grass we'd been able to lay up, but the desert had gone on

125

and on and on. It had been a few weeks since we'd survived that struggle, but it felt like we'd only just staggered out of it. I wish there was some way to explain to our poor oxen that this misery would be shorter, and that if we hurried, we'd all be better off.

But there was no way to tell them anything.

I worried that they'd despair and give up.

Like before, we decided the best idea was to start out at night, to try and avoid struggling through the heat of the day in the middle of the desert if at all possible. By all reckoning, this stretch was supposed to be just forty miles, with a small spring somewhere in the middle, but forty miles without rest is still two very long days of travel across sand without water or grass, and I fretted.

At least my sweet Eddie could ride this time, though his Trixie had been moving slowly. Patrick and I were both worried that she might give out. My paint pony, Boots, had been carrying James and Peter, and I was worried about her, too. At least we still had Earl, Patrick's black horse, and we kept him tied to the back of the family wagon, just in case one of the others couldn't keep up.

The possibility of leaving one of our dear horses behind saddened me, but I knew it was likely. Everyone else had lost horses before now. We had been extremely lucky, and luck like that can't hold forever. Patrick may have seen it as the grace of God, but I knew God loved all his children, not just those of us who believed as we did.

"I don't want to walk anymore," eight-year-old Simon whined. "We already walked almost all day. I'm tired."

But we knew we were running out of time. The dark clouds that had been gathering up ahead had us all worried. "We can't spare another day to rest," I said. "I'm sorry—we're all tired, but we have to keep going." I handed him a piece of dried meat, some of our last, and hoped it would perk him up a bit.

"Will this be like last time?" Patrick Junior's eyes were wide and pained.

"No." I stroked his hair. "Not that bad, I promise."

But as we trudged along, I felt the lie. This desert felt just the same, or possibly worse. At intervals, we'd hear hissing and see an eruption of steam from the ground. Our feet sank into the miserable sand and it was harder to walk than it had been, even in the dry lakebed.

And the oxen. . .they struggled.

We stopped almost every mile to give them a small handful of water each, and a bite or two of dry, brown grass clumps, hoping to keep them moving.

Not everyone fared as well as we had.

The Donners lost another ox that night.

The Graves family lost one as well. Now, even getting rid of one wagon, their two wagons were down to just three yoke apiece.

Keseberg lost a pair. They dropped and would not get back up, no matter how he swore or whipped them. Patrick went back to see if he could help, and when he returned, his face was dark. "Dead. They both just *dropped dead*."

But around four in the morning, we reached the spring we'd been told was nearly halfway in between.

It reeked of sulfur and belched up steam regularly, and the children were afraid. "Are we in hell?" Simon asked.

I patted his head and shook mine. "No, sweetheart. It's quite the opposite." Though the water was boiling hot and stank, when we ladled it up and let it cool, it was drinkable. We wasted no time refilling our buckets, bottles, and casks, and I took a small metal cup and handed it to Mrs. Eddy.

I couldn't bear to see them drinking from their boots.

Her eyes welled with tears, and she clasped my hand. "Thank you."

"You shouldn't be doing things like that," Patrick chided me when I returned to our wagons. "Now they'll think of you with every trouble they face."

But as I watched the Donners give the poor Eddys some coffee, I couldn't regret sharing. They'd lost everything but what they could personally carry, and with two small children to lug, that wasn't much. If watching Hardcoop fall back and die had been a mistake, how much worse would it be to abandon someone like Mr. Eddy, who had helped everyone he could?

I blamed myself only for doing no more than giving them a cup.

We set out again as soon as our water caskets and buckets and glasses were filled, and I couldn't help glancing back and watching as the Eddys hung their sloshing boots, picked up their two children, and struggled forward again.

Around midday, the Murphys lost an ox—left his great body behind to rot, I suppose—bringing the total oxen lost up to six for this desert crossing. Not an hour later, our sweet Trixie refused to walk. We'd moved Eddie to Earl, Patrick's black quarter horse in the middle of the night, but even carrying nothing, Trixie wouldn't take another step.

We tried giving her an entire bucket of water to drink, but that was a waste. Even after drinking, she couldn't move. I watched as my brave son cried—leaving behind the horse that had allowed him to be less of a burden, a horse he had helped break himself, must have hurt him more than any other.

But we carried on.

Not an hour later, Mr. Eddy stumbled toward our wagons, alone. He must have left his wife and children somewhere behind us. I couldn't help thinking of our tears for Trixie and thinking how much worse it would be to lose more *humans*.

"Water." Mr. Eddy gasped. "Please. Just a pint?" He held up a boot. "My children—my wife. They can't go on. Please."

Patrick turned his face away and shook his head. "I have seven children I must put first."

With oxen dropping all around us, part of me understood. But I knew that I would never have peaceful sleep again, not unless we gave them a whole bucket. We could do no less for humans we'd traveled months with than we did for an ailing horse.

Before I could insist that we would share, Mr. Eddy unslung his rifle and pointed it at my husband. "You will give me water." He stumbled forward, the end of his rifle dipping slightly.

I doubted the gun was even loaded, but it showed how truly desperate Mr. Eddy had become. I darted forward and grabbed a small cask, holding it out for him.

Mr. Eddy snatched it from my hands, lowering his rifle in the process, and then turned and lurched away from us.

Patrick said nothing.

The boys looked at me with questions in their eyes, but I shook my head and started walking again. Our poor cattle sighed and lowed and groaned, but they too continued to move. We stumbled and staggered and limped our way forward the rest of that day and into the night. I didn't see Mr. Eddy or his wife at all, but I prayed for their welfare.

Sometime after midnight—perhaps as late as three in the morning—when we had been traveling for some two days without rest, when I felt that myself, my children, and all our animals might drop to the ground and never move again, we came to a tall, sandy rise, moving ever upward.

Perhaps it was because I was so exhausted.

Perhaps it was my stress or my fear for our future.

But the rise looked painfully like the miserably steep hill on which Mr. Snyder and Mr. Reed had fought. It quickly became clear that we wouldn't be able to get our oxen past the hill without double teaming them. No one was nearby ahead of us, and I couldn't see anyone behind us. Otherwise, I'd have made Patrick share our oxen with whoever was near.

I fretted for the Eddys.

I worried for the Reeds. I wasn't sure how Mrs. Reed could possibly summit this hill without more than her four miserable beasts, even now that Mr. Graves had again loaned her an ox to replace her pitiful cow.

But in that moment, all my concern turned to my own family.

It felt like the place in time, just before bringing a child into the world, when you're utterly exhausted. In that moment, your body's spent, and you know you need to make one last push or the baby won't ever come. You're not sure how it can happen, but you do it.

And that's what we did.

We pushed forward—climbing, staggering, one foot in front of the other. . .one miserable, exhausted step at a time, until finally, we cleared the top of that stupid sandy hill with our wagons and all our beasts. Or, you know, almost all of them.

We'd lost Trixie, and we had loaned one of our oxen to Mrs. Reed, but otherwise we had all our oxen, two of our horses, and John had managed to keep all seven of our cows with us. As we slid and slipped our way down the incline, we could see it, far up ahead, a gorgeous sight.

The Truckee River.

Cottonwood and willow trees lined the sides of it, and looking at that spot of *life* gave us a renewed surge of energy. "Let's get some water," Patrick shouted.

The children slid off the backs of their horses, and the oxen straightened. All of us moved forward quickly then, and within an hour, we had reached it. We set up camp right away, drinking and drinking the cool, clear water, all our animals happily munching the tall blades of still-green grass.

The Graves and Murphy families were already there, and the Donners reached us not long after. It was a sign of our utter exhaustion that by the time other families began to arrive, my children had already fallen asleep in our wagons. Our dog, Towser, always greeted new wagons that arrived nearby with a bark and wag of his tail, but he too was sound asleep.

"The Reeds?" I inquired.

Tamzene Donner shook her head. "Not sure. They fell behind."

My heart sank.

I finally gave way and prepared to sleep myself. Just as I was drifting off, I heard barking. Quite a lot of barking. I sat up, and peered out the back of the wagon.

To my great delight, I saw Mrs. Reed and her borrowed wagon lurch into camp, her five dogs frolicking and barking as sweet little Virginia jogged toward us. "It's a miracle," she cried out, tears streaking her cheeks. "Look how beautiful it is." Apparently she could see the same paradise we did, even by moonlight.

The Reeds' cook, Eliza Williams, looked even more exhausted than Virginia, but her brother Baylis looked wrung out, like a ratty old rag. Traveling as an albino was always hard, but after spending another horrible day in the desert. . . He was as red as a radish, and the skin on his face was peeling. He darted off toward the river immediately.

My eyes followed him, hoping that he would at least get some relief with the cool water. But as I climbed out of the wagon to greet the rest of them, my son Eddie had already managed to dart ahead of me, his eyes and arms both wide. "You made it." He must've been waiting up too, worrying about his friend.

Virginia smiled as she embraced him. "It was a miracle," she said. "There was no way our wagon was going to make it to the top, but then Milt suggested we hook Buttons and Dove and Mama's horse up too. We didn't even have a proper yoke for them—we just had rope. We knew they wouldn't be enough." She paused, and then she smiled. "But they were. We got the wagon over, and we're here!" That sweet little girl danced around in a circle, and my poor, limping son followed right alongside her, dancing with no music. "Is that the Truckee River?" She sighed then, and my heart swelled.

They'd made it.

Eddie walked with Virginia past our wagon, and I heard her whisper. "I think it's because Mama let the Eddys tuck their babies into our wagon. That's how we earned our miracle."

I didn't tell her that wasn't how miracles worked like Patrick would have. For all I knew, it was.

Mr. and Mrs. Eddy shuffled their way into camp a few moments after the Reeds. I climbed out of the wagon again, and I grabbed a handful of hard tack. We were down to nearly nothing, but that meant this tiny amount wouldn't make much of a difference. With Patrick asleep, there was no one to object when I handed it to Mr. Eddy.

His face fell. "I'm so sorry for earlier." He shook his head. "I didn't—I wasn't in my right mind."

I tilted my head to the side and tried to look as sincere as I could manage. "The fault was ours. I'm so glad you've made it."

His wife cried when he passed the hard tack back to her.

And then a strange sort of rustling sound drew his attention.

"Go," his wife said. "I'll feed James and Maggie." She turned to me. "They haven't eaten in more than two days."

A loud crack rang out, and then another.

Not a single person in my family woke at the sound of Mr. Eddy's gunshot—Eddie and I were the only ones awake.

But by the time Mrs. Eddy roused the small children, lifting them carefully from the back of the Reed wagon where little James Reed also slept, her husband was striding back, a goose in each hand. "One for you." He held the goose out to Mrs. Reed. "And one for us." His smile was tired. "Can you clean and cook it?" He glanced back. "I'd like to try for more."

Mrs. Eddy nodded.

"I'll help," I said.

In the next forty minutes or so, Mr. Eddy shot *seven* more geese, and he insisted on giving us one as well. "Please tell your husband that I'm sorry," he said.

"The one who feels the most sorry is me. I mean it."

"Even so, we insist," Mrs. Eddy said.

When the Kesebergs rolled in, they had terrible news. Joseph Reinhardt and Augustus Spitzer, two single men traveling with the Kesebergs, reported that the Paiute Indians had killed Mr. Wolfinger as he tried to bury his belongings. He was reportedly quite wealthy, so presumably they had shot him when he resisted giving up his money.

Mrs. Wolfinger was now a widow. I felt terrible thinking it, but at least they had no children. Nothing was worse than trying to care for a young child without the help of anyone else at all, especially out here.

Once everyone had suitably recovered—slept, eaten, drunk their fill of water—and the company was readying itself to leave, George Donner came around with questions about our supplies. I couldn't help thinking about how Mr. Reed had done this the last time.

We'd still had no word from Mr. Stanton or big Bill McCutchen, and things weren't looking good. We had mere days of supplies remaining, and many others, like the Eddy family, were already entirely without.

"I think we'll have to send more men to cross as quickly as possible and return with supplies," George said.

But his brother Jacob was sick, and my darling Patrick was battling yet another terrible kidney stone. I was unwilling to send John, who was not yet fifteen. There weren't many options.

In the end, Levinah Murphy's two sons-in-law offered to go. I felt bad about that, as they'd have no drivers for their oxen and she was already a widow. But the two men were able-bodied, they each had a horse, and they both were decent shots, making them good choices to hunt as they went.

We were discussing what supplies they might be able to procure, and George Donner was writing a letter that William Pike and William Foster could take to Mr. Sutter, when there was a loud crack. Someone had fired a gun.

I glanced around, wondering whether Eddy had found more geese.

But a cry went up, loudly, and when I went to investigate what had happened. . .the news was grim. Mr. Foster's weapon had misfired, hitting Mr. Pike in the spine. Guns misfired often, but it was rare the blow would do any permanent damage. Usually it hit a tree, an animal, or dealt a glancing blow. Not this time. Mr. Pike was writhing in agony, crying out loudly and miserably. I couldn't just stand and watch as he died—it felt ghoulish—but I couldn't walk away either. At least, mercifully, it was a quick death.

In the aftermath of that tragedy, no one was quite sure what to do. We were all discussing our options when a true miracle occurred. Off in the distance, we saw him, a man walking along, leading a train of mules. As he drew nearer, we recognized the small figure.

It was Charles Stanton.

Several of us ran out to meet him.

"My husband?" Poor Amanda McCutchen looked frantic, her hands at her throat, her eyes wide. "Is he. . ."

"He's alive." Charles Stanton nodded. "He was just too sick to come back with me."

She collapsed on the ground, sobbing.

The rest of us were very nearly as emotional—supplies we badly needed had come. The seven mules he had with him—McCutchen's poor beast, as well as six of Mr. Sutter's mules—were loaded down with flour, beans, dried beef, and even a few apples.

George Donner and William Pike worked with me and Mr. Graves to divide up the supplies as evenly as possible. There was great rejoicing, and the smell of biscuits in dutch ovens filled the air. Amanda McCutchen was also relieved to have her mule back and food to lash to it.

John, Eddie, and I were carrying our share back to the wagons when little Virginia held out her hand for a bag of beans. "Thank you," she said.

"Oh," Charles Stanton froze. "I have other news as well." He beamed. "On my way up and over the mountains, in Bear Valley, the western foothills of the Sierra Nevadas, I ran into two exhausted travelers."

Virginia blinked. "You. . .who was it?"

"I saw your father there, tired and hungry, but otherwise healthy." Mr. Stanton's face was kind. "He wanted me to tell you and your mother that he was on his way to Sutter's Fort as well, and that he would come back with help very soon."

Virginia started to cry then, and I couldn't fault her. My dear Eddie set down some of our supplies, which John then picked up, and I shooed him over to help her.

Poor Virginia nodded, wiped her tears, and hefted the bag of beans again. "By chance. . .did he have a grey mare with him?"

"Of course he did," Mr. Stanton said. "You know, he told me that Walter Herron wanted to eat her—things had gotten quite bad for a while. They found five beans that had been dropped on the road and argued over them. Your father took two, and Walt took three. They also tried to eat the tallow from the bottom of an old, discarded bucket. It made your father quite ill, but no matter how bad things were, your father refused to even consider shooting and eating Glaucus."

Of course he had—that man was mad for that horse.

Virginia's face had gone as white as a wagon cover. "He was. . .starving?"

"They had been able to shoot some kind of waterfowl before they met me, and they were making their way down when we passed. I think it's safe to say they'll be just fine."

She closed her eyes and nodded slowly. "Thank you," she whispered, like she was praying. I said a little prayer as well. It was about time we all got some happy news.

Too bad it couldn't last.

CHAPTER 18

Peggy Breen

The next days were miserable in new ways.

A cloud, constantly visible, around the mountains up ahead made everyone jumpy and stressed. We'd all been told at least a dozen times that leaving too late would put us in danger—if the Sierra Nevada mountains became impassible, we knew we'd be trapped. All of us had been on edge for quite a while, being the last party we knew of headed for California.

We were now nearly two months late.

The Truckee River was blessedly clear and clean compared to the alkali water we'd been forced to endure for weeks, but it was also cold. The days had all grown chilly, and most of us were lamenting the lack of the clothes we jettisoned when our oxen were failing on the two miserable desert crossings. None of us were worse off than poor Doris Wolfinger and the Eddy family. The Reeds had gone from the most to the least, but at least they had asked quite a few of us to take things for them. We had two small boxes with clothing and blankets for the Reed family that they couldn't quite fit into their one remaining wagon, but hadn't wanted to lose, including two brand new pairs of shoes. My own shoes were falling apart, so looking at those shiny black shoes every day reminded me that we were all suffering in our own ways.

The only path wagons could take from where we were to the base of the Sierra Nevada mountains took us back and forth across the Truckee River, and in some sections, the boulders we had to cross were almost as large as our wagons. Fording rivers was always dangerous, and it was exhausting from the very first week, but now, with our travel-worn animals and on half-rations for several weeks while we waited for Stanton's return, we were all suffering more than we knew possible at the outset of this journey.

I was sick and tired of being hungry.

It was also shocking how many things we desperately prayed for that became a curse not long after. No one prayed harder for the Truckee River than I did on that last desert crossing, but now it had become its own kind of torture.

"How many times do we have to do this?" Eddie complained as we stared, once again, at the massive boulder-lined river blocking our path.

"At least one more," John said with a half-grin. One of his last remaining sources of joy was taunting his slightly younger brother. "At least you're able to help, finally."

Eddie's leg was almost back to normal, though he walked with a noticeable limp. Maybe he always would. The two boys managed one of our wagons, while Patrick and I each managed another.

My husband Patrick's long-time best friend, Patrick Dolan, had spent several days near the front of the wagon train, but he had fallen back behind us to help me with my wagon on the multiple river fordings.

"Finally through." I sighed a little too dramatically when we made it over the stupid Truckee River for what I hoped heartily would be the last time. Mr. Dolan, just behind me, had seven of the eight oxen he set out with left. They looked like the plentiful grass and water on this side of the desert crossing had been doing them some good, and his three cows tied to the back of the wagon look much improved as well. All of our animals looked much less emaciated than they appeared ten days ago, which was a blessing, though I could still see ribs on all of them.

"I won't be sad if we never cross that river again," Patrick said.

I reminded myself that I'd take multiple river crossings over another desert trek any day of the week and twice on Sunday. As the other wagons in our company slowly but surely appeared on our side of the river, I noticed that one was still missing.

Mrs. Reed and her two drovers were still noticeably absent. I wondered whether Baylis, who had been having a hard time after the last misery in the desert, had finally been unable to travel farther. I said a silent prayer that they were all okay.

Nearly an hour passed before I saw Milt Elliot trudge into camp, dragging two oxen who were still yoked, but with supplies strapped to the yoke in an awkward way.

"Oh, no." I started walking toward him to see whether there was any help I could offer.

Mrs. Reed wasn't crying, but it looked like she had been recently. Her face was streaked with dirt in clear, straight lines, which is what happened on the trail when someone cried. Dirt and dust stuck to any kind of moisture, tattling on you to anyone who sees your face.

"What happened?" I asked softly.

The wagon the Graves family loaned to the Reeds was their oldest wagon, and it also had a wheel that had been repaired twice already. It wasn't in the best of shape. It had already traveled the better part of two thousand miles, much of it through rivers, streams, bog, and desert, and the already-old wood had further weathered and worn.

Which is why I wasn't surprised at Mrs. Reed's explanation.

"We were fording the river and. . .the axle snapped." Her voice sounded broken.

To go from three massive, brand new, custom-made wagons, full of supplies, precious and fine clothing, beautiful cookware and equipment, and the nicest furniture I'd ever seen, including a full-length looking-glass brought over from Europe. . .to this?

My heart ached for the Reed family.

But there was nothing to do but soldier on. I convinced my husband and his friend Patrick to store a few more containers with their food and valuables. After all, our oxen were recovering nicely now there was some grass to eat. The Reeds had already lost nearly everything.

Their two boys finally made it into camp, one on Buttons, who was walking with a pronounced limp, and one on Peony, Mrs. Reed's little brown mare. It wasn't encouraging that the horses could each only carry one small boy.

We were all using the end of our reserves of strength as we finally reached Truckee Meadows on October twentieth. It was a tremendous blessing that we found a valley full of lush, rich grass this late in the season.

We let our oxen and other animals eat as much as they could in that time —not having seen any Indians for quite some time. We knew the poor beasts would need all the nourishment they could possibly get as we attempted the impending assault on the massive Sierra Nevada mountains looking behind us.

None of us talked about the fact that they were already snow-capped or that black clouds obscured the very top. After all, we'd be crossing in the passes, the lowest points we could find, and we had guides who had just made the trek—Charles Stanton and his two Miwok Indian guides, Salvador and Luis.

Surely with their help, and a little Providence, we'd be fine.

We had very little time to delay, but knowing the mountains would offer no food for our cattle, we rested two days. We let the cattle eat all they could, and we cut and laid up as much grass as we could, or at least, those of us with wagons did. After no more than a few days' rest, we were moving again. Unfortunately, that also meant separating, because almost as soon as we set out again, poor George Donner's wagon wheel broke. Unlike the Reeds, at least the Donners had tools yet with which to repair it. While they stopped to work on the wheel, the rest of us struggled onward.

"Where's Mr. Smith?" I asked Mrs. Reed, when I walked back to check on them.

"He's quite handy with tools and has repaired three wheels for us already on this trip," she said. "George asked if he could stay and help." Mrs. Reed shrugged. "John must have thought it was quite the trade up. After all, it's not as if we have any wagons for him to drive." Her eyes weren't even especially sad. She was clearly resigned to their desolate circumstances. "Maybe John can stay with George for the last leg of the trip. He knows we have precious little to eat, and even less for him to do."

At least she'd soon be reunited with her husband on the other side of the massive mountains ahead of us. I noticed, then, that Buttons wasn't with them. Virginia was leading her mother's horse Peony, at least, burdened down with as many things as they could strap to her. "Where's Buttons?"

Margaret Reed's face paled. "Her limp worsened. She—couldn't go on."

My heart sank at the words. With her small children, she was now left with just one ox, one cow, and one horse? She had returned the ox she had borrowed from us when the wagon gave out. I'm sure she returned the ones she borrowed to the Pike and Graves families as well.

"Oh, Margaret, I'm so sorry."

She shook her head. "Stanton offered to let Patty, Jimmy, and Thomas ride on his mules. "We've been blessed with very good friends."

Her family had been good friends to a great many of us. It was the least we could do. I also felt guilty that we hadn't tried harder to support James Reed. That left us at least a little bit culpable for her being here alone. As we struggled down into Dog Valley, and then up the steep climb of another, unnamed pass, I couldn't help feeling that life had been monstrously unfair to poor Margaret Reed. First, she lost her mother, and then she lost her wagons and most all of her belongings. As if that wasn't bad enough, she also lost her husband.

The Eddys, the Wolfingers, and also the Kesebergs had been hit hard with trials during the desert travel, but none had as much to lose or as many children to care for as the Reeds. When we finally climbed down from the second pass, Truckee Lake, into which Truckee River dumped, finally became visible. It was just as clean, crisp, and blue as the river that fed it, and although it was still five or six miles away, we could see the base of the famed Sierra Nevada mountains at last.

They were even more imposing than people said, soaring high into the deep blue sky. Birds cried from high above us, and the wind whistled ominously in the distance, whipping around their craggy tops.

That night, I had trouble sleeping. I woke over and over to the nightmare that I was Hardcoop and my family was refusing to help me. Only, the last nightmare I had was different, and it was even worse. When I went to sleep in the wee hours, I dreamt that not only was I refused entry to my family wagons, but as they rode away, a figure in a dark cloak turned back toward me and laughed and laughed.

"It's no more than you deserve," the figure said, his voice low and ominous. "You must pay for your sins."

When I woke, I already felt ragged deep down in my soul, but I knew that today would be the day we finally started the hardest part of our journey. Today, we'd walk the five or six miles to Truckee Lake, and then on All Hallows Eve, we'd start our trek over the massive mountains, the wall of imposing granite that seemed to be taunting us.

We walked for hours, drawing ever nearer, but the closer we drew, the more impassible it seemed. Everywhere I looked, there was nothing but sheer rock walls, and although there was a small spot on the far southern end that Stanton had told us to look for, something else made even that tried and true path look terribly dangerous.

Large, fluffy flakes of snow began to fall.

Under normal conditions, a little snow would be a minor nuisance. But under normal conditions, such as when we began our journey, we all still had shoes, warm coats, and thick wool skirts and trousers. Over the past two thousand and some odd miles, most of our shoes had worn down. Eddie's were in the best shape by far, because he had been confined to the wagon for such long stretches. But poor John had lost the use of his boots entirely. One of them had lost a sole, and the other was so riddled with holes that it was pointless to even lace it up. His feet had hardened enough that under normal conditions, like small rocks or hard-packed dirt, it was alright. Navigating larger rocks was a misery, but I had seen him grit his teeth and endure.

But with snow, his feet ached, and he slipped repeatedly.

My shoes had three holes on the right and one hole on the left into which snow squished and intruded. My toes went numb first, and then my heels began to ache.

Patrick's shoes were barely better than John's, in spite of how often he went barefoot. As the snowfall worsened, we took a small break to tie strips of muslin around his darned and re-darned socks and the remains of his boots, and we all did our best. Worse even than the pain and suffering of snow with worn and ripped shoes was our fear about what snow on the lower regions of the mountains meant for the upper ones. High up on the mountains, where the only visible part of the Sierra Nevada range was sheer, rocky faces, the cliff walls were already visibly laden with drifts of white.

We tried to carry on, pushing ahead, whipping and shouting for the oxen to continue, but the snow was up to their chests, and they flailed and lowed and grunted in vain. After trying for more than two hours, but making virtually no headway, we finally gave up and fell back. Stanton and his mules had fallen behind us. We hoped that tomorrow, with their aid, we could make more progress.

Patrick had made note of a small cabin on our way toward the southern end, and he set our course back straight for it. No one else had taken shelter in it when we reached it, so we hobbled the animals and gave them their night's grass. When I went to unload our belongings, I noticed something terrible, at least, to me.

"Omega died," I whispered. "Omega and Flurry."

Our last two chickens.

Omega was the one descended from my mother's flock in Ireland.

"Oh good," John said. "Chicken for dinner."

The kids were all excited—they hadn't had chicken in months. But as John and Eddie roasted our last two chickens and we all feasted, our bellies full for the first time in weeks, I worried more than I ever had. As the snow fell all around our tiny cabin, I feared that we might already be too late.

We might be stuck, and if that was the case, things were about to get unimaginably bad, for all of us.

CHAPTER 19

Virginia Reed

The Breens were a full day ahead of us, and we hoped they'd already started into the mountains, leaving a path we could all follow. When we finally reached the edge of Truckee Lake an hour after dawn, Mama was terribly disheartened to discover the whole area already blanketed with snow, and the Breens tucked into a small cabin.

"What happened?" she asked.

Mrs. Breen's children still huddled in the cabin, while she was cooking something in a dutch oven, their clothes extended over the fire by a makeshift wooden rack. "There was too much snow," she said. "We were cold and wet and miserable, and no matter what we tried, we couldn't get the cattle to move ahead."

"We don't have a wagon," Mama said. "Maybe for the first time, that'll work in our favor."

The Graves family was just behind us, and Mr. Graves had grown up around mountains. "The snow appears to be melting," Mr. Graves said. "I think it's warming right now, and that means conditions may be as good as they'll ever be for us to travel over. It's the fluffy snow that becomes totally impassible. We should go again right now."

"What a terrible birthday," Mrs. Graves said.

"Whose birthday is it?" I asked. "Yours?"

Mrs. Graves shook her head. "No, my poor Mary Ann's. She's twenty today."

"All Hallows Day was a wonderful day back home," I said. "But I suppose we aren't back home."

No one smiled, not even Mary Ann.

We didn't have the energy to waste on things like celebrating. No cake. No singing. No celebration for her at all. Instead, we all shouldered our loads and continued forward. Mr. Stanton, who had generously shared the use of his mules with us for the past few days, looked as grim as anyone else.

"I'm sorry," he said to my ma, "but we'll need the mules to try and break a path."

Mama nodded forlornly and began helping the smaller three down. Once again, we were on our own.

"When you came through the pass before, was there snow?" I asked.

He didn't answer at first. I thought maybe he hadn't heard me. But when he finally spoke, his voice was soft. "No. There was no snow either time I made the journey."

There certainly was plenty of snow now. Even worse, as we reached the base of the pass, it was snowing ever more furiously from above. The flakes fell all around us, adding their mass to the weight and shape of the substantial existing piles.

All that snow was not melted in the slightest, disproving Mr. Graves' hope that perhaps slush on the lower levels meant it would be melting at the pass. My mom's horse Peony carried the two boys, but she didn't have much luck either, churning and floundering, rolling her eyes, and crying out in distress. It was my job to lead Patty, Peony and the boys over, but Mama, Milt, Eliza, and Baylis were struggling with another issue. Our poor cow balked over and over, and my darling ox Brutus was worst of all, thrashing around furiously as Milt and Eliza tried to encourage him forward, dumping all the supplies we'd lashed on and around him repeatedly.

Lewis Keseberg had injured his foot some weeks back, and he was still unable to walk at all. He was riding his horse, whose name I couldn't recall, but even as an accomplished rider with a firm grip on the reins, he failed to make much headway.

I watched as the Graves family, who had bundled most of their supplies into one wagon, and lashed others onto the backs of their oxen, struggled in much the same way. One of their oxen even rubbed itself against a nearby pine tree, dislodging the packs that had been so carefully tied to it.

It was chaos all around as we neared the rocky, craggy pass, but our going slowed with each step, because the higher we went, the higher the snow became. If little Thomas and James Junior hadn't been on Peony, the snow would already be over their heads. It came clear up to Patty's armpits as it was.

People began to argue about what to do.

Mr. Graves and Mr. Stanton agreed at least that we should go forward, but they seemed to be the only ones. Mr. Keseberg and Levinah Murphy called for us to stop and turn around.

"We can wait for better weather," Lewis Keseberg said. "Even in winter, it won't snow every day."

"The snow must melt at some point," Levinah Murphy said. "It isn't even snowing now."

But Mr. Graves was from the mountains of Vermont, and he was adamant. "We can't stop," Mr. Graves said. "We're at the beginning of winter, which means we'll only get more and more snow up there." He pointed.

"I agree," Mr. Stanton said. "We can't stop, even if it starts to storm. The only way we'll survive is to go before it worsens." He took his mules in hand and urged Luis and Salvador to follow his lead, finding the path toward the summit of the pass.

"But snow doesn't fall all winter," Mr. Breen said. "It comes in waves. If we wait a few days, this snow will melt and condense down. Then we'll be able to cross over it much more easily. We should rest the animals and try again."

"How long do you think we'll have the luxury of waiting?" Mr. Graves asked. "A month? Two? How long will it be until there's a break in the weather? We're in the mountains already."

Graves and Stanton prevailed, and we continued onward, urging the animals to move, carrying the small children, and with great effort, we gained a few yards, and later, a few feet with each push. But then we came to a rock wall.

Literally.

"What's going on?" Mr. Breen asked sharply. "Why have we stopped?" He plowed his way forward, but after passing us, he saw what we already had.

A large, high slab of stone rose out of the snow with no way to go around it.

"I think we've lost track of the cart path," Mr. Stanton confessed.

Mr. Breen wasn't the only one groaning, but at least he wasn't swearing or shouting. I suppose good Catholics didn't take the Lord's name in vain as a general rule, no matter how frustrated they became. Others did.

"Give us a minute to find the path again," Mr. Stanton said. He and one of the Miwok Indians, Luis, walked off.

Patrick Dolan, a good friend to Mr. Breen, argued with Mr. Graves while we waited. "Look here, now." Mr. Dolan said. "The snow's starting again. All these flurries are going to bury us while our oxen flail around. What good is it to carry on? Do you fancy disappearing under an avalanche of snow? Because that's what's like to happen."

"Things will only worsen," Mr. Graves said doggedly. "We have to continue onward."

They went back and forth like that for some time, but in the end, it was nature that settled the dispute. Well, nature and Mr. Foster and Mr. Eddy, who had set fire to a pitch pine to settle their squalling children.

I didn't blame the small ones for crying.

It was bitterly cold, and we were all exhausted. The harder we struggled, the more we sweated, and the more we sweated, the wetter we became. As the wind howled and the snow gusted in whirling eddies, our clothing froze to our bodies.

None of us were dressed for this weather. In fact, when we left Springfield, the weather had already warmed, and what winter clothing we had, most of us had thrown on the side of our trail in either the desert, or the long, hard miles leading up to the South Pass before it.

We knew that California was warm with almost no winter to speak of, and our oxen had been dying from the weight. None of us had kept much in the way of blankets and warm woolens. What we had kept had been worn badly.

The snow intensified while we waited for Mr. Stanton, and the pitch pine fire blazed, enticing us to surround it and then sit down. I think that by the time we could barely see our own hands in front of our faces, we had already decided that we couldn't go farther that day. We all fell into a sort-of makeshift camp, each family with a wagon crawling inside it.

Those of us without covered ourselves with whatever we could find and passed out, right there wherever we were on our path up the angry mountain. Thomas, Patty, James, Eliza, Baylis, Milt, Mama, and I all huddled under a tarp together, with our five dogs lying down and snuggling in all around us. Beside us, blocking the wind from one side, our cow, Brutus the ox, and Mama's horse Peony bunched together as if they were best friends.

It was probably the most miserable night I had ever passed, though the nights in the screaming wind of the desert were awfully close, at least, until I drifted off to sleep. My sleep was deep and soundless.

When I woke, it was to terrible screaming.

Mr. Keseberg had woken up, and he was bent on waking everyone else. Once he realized we weren't all dead, just covered in snow, he calmed down considerably.

The idiot.

Unfortunately, I wasn't the only one he spooked. Daisy, Brutus, and Peony startled, and Daisy ran away. We chased after her, but she wasn't the only one who took off. We searched for nearly two hours, but never did find her. We were left with only Peony and Brutus.

The Murphys lost two cattle, both oxen, and Mr. Dolan lost a steer. The Breens, like us, lost a cow, and the Kesebergs lost their last goat.

Mr. Stanton was going on about how the pass was not much farther, and it was wide and a straight shot downward from there, but we were all too exhausted, too cold, and too miserable to listen. Babies screamed and sobbed. Mothers could barely stand. Animals stamped and lowed.

We couldn't attempt to cross the pass, not after the trials and exhaustion from yesterday. The snow had slacked a little, although not much, but the piles of snow were only growing in size, and we already knew our remaining animals couldn't pass them.

"We fall back," Mr. Graves finally called.

Mr. Stanton disagreed, but he wasn't in charge.

In fact, our leader George Donner was still seven or eight miles away, down near Alder Creek where we hoped he had finally repaired his wheel. There was no one to force us to listen to Mr. Stanton and his Miwok

Indian guides, so we turned around and headed back down the mountain to make some sort of shelter in which to withstand the seemingly never-ending snow falling. We decided to wait for better weather before we set out again.

The Breens and their friend Mr. Dolan and his friend made on this journey, Antonio, reclaimed the tiny cabin they'd taken two nights before. None of us could really disagree, as they'd already spent some time cutting and repairing pine branches for the formerly-collapsed roof. The rest of us had nowhere to take shelter, which meant it was time to make something.

Without any tools, and with only Milt to help us, we weren't in a good spot.

"What will we do?" I asked.

Mama squared her shoulders, and she started talking to people, beginning with the Breens. It was a big ask, but we'd grown almost accustomed to begging by this point. Mama's pride had shrunk until it was practically nonexistent.

"Our cabin's already so small," Mrs. Breen said with clear regret. "And while we wish we had room, I fear it would do no favors to you or to us to bring in so many people." She looked back at the small windowless cabin with dirt floors.

It felt strange to be coveting something so dirty and small.

She wasn't at all wrong about its size. It looked to be about twelve by fourteen feet, which was smaller than my bedroom back home had been, in Springfield. That hundred and sixty square feet was already housing Mr. and Mrs. Breen and their seven children, as well as Mr. Dolan and Antonio.

"I have tools you can use," Mr. Breen offered, which was actually quite helpful. "An axe. A chisel. A saw." It was generous of him too, because tools broke, and if we lost his, he could be in trouble later.

At least we had Milt Elliot, who had never built a cabin, but he was able-bodied and willing. I was ready to help, and so was Baylis Williams. He was sickly and nearly blind thanks to some kind of childhood illness, but he was at least eager to lend a hand wherever he could.

James Smith was presumably helping the Donners construct some kind of shelter back near Alder Creek. Mr. Graves and Mr. Dolan both seemed certain that he'd stay with them, at least until this storm had passed.

Levinah Murphy and her family, including Mrs. Pike and her two children, and the Fosters and their son, had staked their claim to a large, flat boulder. "We'll only need to construct three sides of our cabin, you see," Mr. Foster said. "And no fire's flames will be at risk of burning that down."

It was smart, and Mr. Eddy had offered to lend a hand if they were willing to allow him and his wife and two small children to stay there as well. No matter how large they could make the rest, with one end limited to the size of the boulder, it wasn't practical for us to stay with them, too. With Baylis and Eliza Williams and Milt Elliot, plus myself and my three siblings, there were eight of us.

We were a large group, and our options were shrinking fast.

"It doesn't appear that Mr. Keseberg has worked out a plan yet," Mama said.

I'd almost rather die than bunk down with Mr. Keseberg for an unknown length of time. Papa and I had never told Mama about the kind of person he was, but she knew he'd called for Papa to be hung that day. I would have thought that would be enough to rule him out, but I suppose when things go badly wrong, your morals get a little. . .flexible.

"What are your plans?" I asked Sarah Graves Fosdick, as she passed by with one of their last remaining cows. It had been close to Mr. Keseberg, and he had lashed it to his horse when we all headed back. She'd come to retrieve it, or we might not have seen anyone from their group at all.

"Uh, well." She paused, her expression a little cagey.

"Come and let's ask Pa." Mary Ann walked up next to her sister. "There are three men working together on our shelter, if you include Billy, and we have plenty of tools. If Milt and Baylis can lend a hand, I'm sure Pa will be able to help you when we're done."

Sarah looked significantly less sure, but with some bit of hope, Mama turned away from her plan to ask Mr. Keseberg, and that was enough to satisfy me.

Unfortunately, their camp was nearly half a mile from the site where the Breen cabin was. Mr. Keseberg was building a lean-to behind the Breen's cabin when we left, and the Murphys and Eddys were building the cabin on the large boulder not twenty yards from there. Mama was getting nervous as we trudged so far through the deepening snow, I knew, but I still thought asking the Graves for help was our best remaining option.

"Pa," Mary Ann called, as we walked toward him where he was notching a log while Billy watched carefully. "The Reeds. . .well. You know they have no one to help them build a shelter." She stared at him pointedly.

He frowned. "They have their hired man, Milt."

"Who has never built a cabin in his life." She arched an eyebrow. "You've built quite a few, and we don't need ours to be that long." She tossed her head at the exceedingly long pine log in front of him.

"What are you asking?" He frowned. "They caused the whole ruckus with John." He stood up, his axe still in his hand. "Or had you forgotten?"

"John Snyder struck Mrs. Reed, and Mr. Reed was defending his wife. I've told you that before. It all happened quickly, but I'm quite sure he didn't mean to kill him." Mary Ann dropped her hands on her hips. "You weren't there to see it, so you'll have to trust my word. If someone had cause to be the most upset, it was me, and I'm the one asking you to help them."

I'd never felt quite such a burden in my life, but Mr. Graves, after sighing for a moment and leaning on his axe, groaned. "Fine. We'll split the cabin into a double cabin, and they can take the smaller end."

He might not have been very happy about it, but he was willing to help. It was the best offer we'd get. Mr. Graves taught Baylis to notch the ends of the logs, which Baylis wasn't very good at, but it was work he could do half-blind with the small axe we'd borrowed from Mr. Breen.

Milt helped cut and haul the logs, in spite of his aching hands.

Patty and I joined the Graves children in gathering up pine boughs. "We'll use as many tarps and hides as we have," Mr. Graves said, "but these pine boughs will provide insulation and trust me. We'll want that."

We went out in batches, after huddling under blankets near a small fire, and gathered up as many pine branches as we could before coming back. It was exhausting work, with my hands alternately freezing and stinging, depending on what I was doing. It snowed all day, worsening that night.

Patty and the younger kids got the easiest jobs, picking up the boughs that Milt and Mr. Graves and Jay Fosdick cut off while preparing the cabins. Mary Ann and Sarah and I ranged farther, looking not only for pine branches for the roof and to fill cracks between logs, but also gathering them for the animals. The oxen and horses and mules didn't want to eat pine needles, but thanks to the snow, it was all there was. My arms were nearly full when I heard something.

"Missus Reed," a voice asked. When I turned, it was Charles Stanton.

"Yes?" I asked.

"We have nowhere to stay." He gestured behind him, where Luis and Salvador stood, their heads bowed in the cold. "We'll be happy to help build—if we can stay with you?"

We already had eight people in our small side of the cabin, but I knew exactly how it felt to have nowhere to go. I turned to where Mama was bundling Jimmy and Thomas under blankets, and she nodded.

"Of course you can stay with us," I said.

Mama smiled then, and I knew we'd done a good thing. Her smile was the thing I loved best about her, and Papa said it was his favorite thing too. Even in the midst of all this, at least that hadn't changed.

With Charles Stanton, Luis, and Salvador, all of whom were quite handy with saws and axes, the work proceeded much faster. The Indians even showed us a smarter way to build an area inside the cabin for a fire, and Salvador came up with the idea of cutting a small opening between the two cabins so we could still preserve whatever privacy we might possibly have, but we could also sit and talk in relative warmth from our respective sides.

We still had two logs yet to go all the way around when Mr. Eddy showed up. "Need something?" Mr. Graves asked.

Mr. Eddy shook his head. "I thought you might need a hand. We're finished already."

He had come just for that—to lend a hand.

Just when I thought every man was out for himself, people like Mr. Eddy showed me that it wasn't true. Mr. Eddy worked for hours with us, and then he stayed around to help Mr. Stanton and Milt cut firewood for our side of the cabin.

"The best thing you can do for the roof, if this horrible snow ever stops," Mr. Eddy said, "is to cover it with animal hides. They'll keep water from constantly dripping through the pine boughs." He gestured to where there were already muddy spots forming on the earthen floor.

Once the cabin was finished, and there was at least a temporary roof in place, the small fire began warming the room. It was still cold, all the time, and our thin blankets weren't even close to enough to keep us warm, but we gathered more pine branches to make beds, and with all the dogs gathered around, I would sometimes stop shivering for as much as half an hour.

The next day, I was sitting on the ground near the hole cut between our side and the Graves side, chatting with Eddie, when I overheard Mr. Graves say something that brought tears to my eyes. "We're going to have to slaughter the oxen. Better to do it now, before they've starved even further."

Brutus' beautiful face filled my mind's eye. How could we eat him after what we'd been through together? He felt like a member of the family.

But then I had another thought. A more terrifying thought.

The Graves had lost most of their cows and all their horses, but they at least had most of their oxen, starved though their fifteen oxen might be. But the supplies Mr. Stanton had brought on his mules were nearly gone, which meant that we had enough food for a week, or if we stretched it, maybe three.

And we had Brutus.

That was it.

With eleven mouths to feed, one small, starved ox whose death would be terribly, terribly depressing felt like. . .almost nothing.

It was the first time I realized that we might all starve here.

I had been worried in the desert that we might be stuck, left to die. I worried Indians might shoot us for Buttons and Peony, or even for Brutus and Daisy. I had worried as we spent that night in the snow that we might freeze. But until that very moment, I had never worried we might starve to death.

Mama wasn't the kind of person to give up, however. That very night, as if the same thought had also just occurred to her, she gathered up all of our valuables, including Papa's Masonic medal and his gold watch, and she walked the half mile to the Breen cabin and begged to purchase some of their starved, emaciated oxen.

She started with the Breens, because they had more than a dozen left, if you included their two remaining cows. I don't know quite what she said or what she paid, but when she came back, she'd managed to convince them to sell her a yoke—two oxen. "You were right about Mrs. Breen," Mama murmured. "She's as kind as her sweet boy, Eddie."

I'd never been more grateful for our friendship than I was that night.

We just gone from one ox to three.

The Murphys, with as many mouths to feed as us, had only five cattle, all told. The Eddys, who were staying with them, had only one. I heard Mr. Eddy next door, arguing with Mr. Graves.

"What will you do?" Mr. Graves asked. "Pull a gun on me?" His laugh was bitter. "Oh, you can't. I hear your rifle finally broke."

Mr. Eddy made a strangled sound.

"You can buy the ox that died this afternoon," Mrs. Graves offered. "We can't offer you more than that."

Mr. Eddy looked pained, or at least, I thought he did. It was very hard to see anything through the small square opening we'd cut, especially in the low light. But he nodded, and the deal was struck.

I didn't have a lot of hope for Mama when she went next door the next morning, but Mr. Graves seemed to expect her. "I know you have a large group to feed, but I'll only sell you two," he said. "Don't ask for more."

The Breens had apparently taken all that Mama had left, so she promised to pay double for the oxen when we reached California. Mr. Graves knew she was good for it, with Papa already on the other side. And that's how we found ourselves with five oxen.

"And a horse," Mama said, with terribly sad eyes.

I gasped. "We can't kill Peony." I stood up and shook my head. "Mama, we can't. She's all we have left."

"We don't have much choice," she said. "I'm not sure how to butcher the animals, either." She sighed. "To be honest, I'm not even sure I can kill one of the cows, much less my darling mare." She began to cry then, and I wanted to crumple into a pile and never think about any of this again.

"We'll do it for you, Ma. Don't worry." Milt wrapped an arm around her shoulders.

"We'll also lend a hand," Mr. Stanton said.

Luis and Salvador nodded.

"Won't the meat spoil?" I asked.

"If the weather warms up, we'll need to smoke it," Mr. Stanton said. "But for now, the snow that's keeping us stuck in here will keep it from going bad."

I went outside to say goodbye to Brutus, but after the men came out with knives, I ran away like a coward. I went inside and closed my eyes tight, blocking my ears and saying 'lalalalala,' over and over. It didn't really help. I still heard the gargling struggle as he died.

I dreamt of poor, sweet, loyal Brutus dying every night for several weeks. Each time, he was looking right at me as they killed him. I asked Mama not to tell me which of the piles of meat we stashed in the snow embankment near our cabin came from him.

That might have been stupid, because as hungry as I was, every single bite I ate tasted like it must have been Brutus. As we had our first meal made from our beloved oxen, I realized something else. I knew we were nearly out of everything. I knew we would have nothing but poor beef, as everyone was calling it, due to the lousy quality and health the oxen were in after this terrible journey. But after my first bite, I was reminded of something that felt fairly important.

When we lost our last wagon, we left the heavy jars of salt I'd scooped up at the Salt Lake. That meant that while we had a big pile of beef now, we still had no salt.

Every bite of Brutus tasted like nothing but desperation and regret.

CHAPTER 20

Mary Ann Graves

Poor Mr. Eddy had only two oxen, the one they had left and the dead one he bought from Pa. He was determined to supplement that in any way he could, which we could hardly fault him for. The hangup was that his rifle had broken, and all he had left was some ammunition.

"Egads, but it's a long, cold walk all the way over here," Mr. Eddy said, shaking snow off himself before stepping into our tiny, dimly lit cabin. "Why did you have to build this so far away from the Breen and Murphy cabins?"

Pa frowned.

"My father grew up in the mountains of Vermont," I said. "He knows exactly how many logs we'll have to cut if we're here for very long this winter, and he didn't want to be so close to the others that we were fighting for firewood."

"And this area is sheltered from wind and storms thanks to the slope," Pa said.

"I suppose those are good reasons," Mr. Eddy said. "But the reason I walked all the way over here was because I have plenty of ammunition, but no functioning rifle."

"I already sold you an ox," Pa said, shaking his head. "I can't loan you my rifle. What if it breaks, too?"

"I know how to handle a rifle. Mine only stopped working when it fell from my wagon and was rolled over by the wheels on rocky ground. If I hadn't been focused on my oxen, it never would have happened."

"But it did happen," Pa said.

"If I shoot anything, I'll share." Mr. Eddy looked almost pained saying that. He had proven himself an excellent marksman in the past, and he was using his own bullets. They had so little that I'm sure the idea of sharing what he killed hurt.

"Fine." Pa didn't hand him the old rifle he was teaching Billy to use. He handed over his rifle, the nicest one we had. "Good luck."

Mr. Eddy managed to shoot a coyote that very day, and an owl the next. Pa didn't have the heart to take the portions the poor man offered.

"Keep them for your family." Pa also refused Mr. Eddy's offer to return the rifle. "Keep trying."

Mr. Eddy looked terribly grateful. I thought part of Pa's reticence might be at the prospect of eating an owl and a coyote.

Not that our oxen were much better.

Pa was even rationing out the offal from the oxen to our dog like a miser. He did offer a bit of it to Mrs. Reed, which was nice. Unlike us, she didn't have just one dog.

She had five.

While Mr. Eddy spent almost every day out hunting, without a lot of success most days, Pa spent his time planning our escape.

"Everyone seems content to just sit and wait." He was pacing again. He'd been pacing so much that he'd worn all the pine boughs into a sort of mud-pine fusion, and then wore them down further still, enough that we mostly just walked on hard-packed dirt. "We can't do nothing. If we wait here all winter, we'll all slowly starve. We have to get over that mountain."

"There's no way Johnny, Frankie, or Nancy could make it," Ma said. "Not to mention Elizabeth and I."

My poor mother was already making less milk than little Elizabeth needed. We all heard her cries and cringed through them. We were rationing the meat—and none of us wanted to eat it, but it was all we had, really. Well, other than the one bag of beans Pa had packed as seed crop for when we reached California, a little coffee, a few pickle jars, one jar of jam, and some tobacco. Ma might have a few more bags of coffee beans squirreled away somewhere, but I hadn't found them yet.

Ma was right though—the youngest children had no prayer of making it through the snow-laden pass. That didn't stop Pa from preparing another attempt for the very second the snow stopped. No one else seemed to share his desperate optimism.

"The drifts are over seven feet now," Billy said. "The snow's higher than me, and I can only imagine it's even worse in the mountains."

"And you don't know the way," Ma said. "You need to be talking to Stanton more. Without his help, without his Indians and Sutter's mules, you don't stand a chance."

On November twelfth, the weather finally improved, with the snow stopping entirely, and the wind dying down some as well. But what mattered more was that it had warmed up.

"I think the sun may have melted the snow," Pa said.

Which meant that if it froze hard tonight, we might be able to walk across a crust on top tomorrow, instead of struggling through feet and feet of powdery fluff. Going even a few yards in the snow as it was then felt like trying to walk through piles of frozen corn in a silo.

It wore you out fast.

"You should go," Ma said. "I'll keep Billy to help me cut wood. Mary Ann, and Sarah, and Jay can go with you."

So it was decided. Pa and I, Sarah and her husband Jay, along with the Donner teamsters, the Reed teamsters, William Eddy, William Foster, Mr. Stanton, and his two Miwoks would all try again to cross the mountain.

We'd lower the number of mouths to feed here in the meantime, and we'd alert the settlers in California to the dire straits in which our whole party found itself. Watching our small piles of meat dwindle was disheartening at best, terrifying at worst.

We all knew we didn't have enough to last until spring. We'd starve long before then.

Ma insisted that we layer the very best and warmest clothing we had. We put on woolen shirts, and flannel jackets, and then we wrapped what bits of fabric we had available around our necks and heads to try and preserve our heat. Ironically, it wasn't the cold that caused us the most problems. As we circled the lake, the snow became deeper and deeper, and there wasn't enough of a crust to walk on top at all. What had packed down to only a few feet near us, thanks to the sunny day, was more than ten feet deep at the far end of the lake, near the base of the mountains.

Each step forward felt like an almost impossible feat. We had to either plow forward, parting the snow upward and to either side of us as we went, which was all the mules could do, or we had to lift our feet up, out of the snow as far as we could, and then leap forward as best we could. Then we'd sink down past our shoulders again, a foot or two ahead of where we started.

At times, I even forgot we were shoving our way through snow. My hands were entirely numb, but the rest of my body was burning with heat. The biggest problem was that, thanks to our meager rations, we were all so very tired. A few leaps forward felt like an entire day's work. What would have been quite a feat even in normal times felt nigh impossible without the energy to do much of anything.

We didn't even make it past the lake. We turned around and slogged our way back, retracing our steps obsessively to try and make it home easier than we'd come.

It was an exhausting day, and Pa was in a terrible mood when William Eddy shot a squirrel not half a mile from the first cabins.

"I want my rifle back," Pa said.

Mr. Eddy, the squirrel in one hand, frowned. "But why?"

"What can you do with that? Will it even feed your family for a single meal?"

Mr. Eddy just blinked.

"Give it back. I can't risk losing it when there's no game left to be had."

By the time we reached the Murphy cabin where Mr. Eddy was staying, I overheard Mr. Eddy and Mr. Foster chatting about the whole thing. "Even a squirrel's better than nothing," Mr. Foster said. "You can borrow my rifle instead."

Pa spent the next day or two obsessing over a new idea: snowshoes.

Billy and I had to help him dig one of our wagons out of the snow and carefully remove the oxbow for the oxen. "I think, if I'm careful, I can split this in two and make it into a set of snow-shoes," Pa said. "Then we can carry on, even when the snow's too high to plow through."

It wasn't a bad idea, but the oxbows were very large, and we didn't have the best tools with which to split them evenly. "What would you use for the mesh between?" I asked.

We were talking through various options when there was a loud commotion outside.

"Mister Graves!"

Pa stood up slowly, the weight of his fifty-one years more obvious thanks to the terrible cold we'd all been enduring.

"Mister Graves!"

Mr. Eddy crashed his way down the path to our home, and by the time he was close, we had opened the door. "What is it?" Pa looked more annoyed than concerned.

"I've done it." Mr. Eddy shifted, and the light from outside suddenly made him quite a bit more visible. The front of the poor man was covered in reddish staining. His woolen jacket, his dark pants, all of them looked to be covered in. . .well, it looked an awful lot like blood.

"What did you do, exactly?" Pa asked. "Please tell me you haven't killed anyone."

"Not just anyone," Mr. Eddy said, leaning closer. "I killed a grizzly bear."

"Bollocks," Pa said. "You couldn't possibly have done that. They'd be hibernating by now, for one, but for another, you had, what? One shot? That wouldn't kill a grizzly. It would just make him mad."

"Oh, when I hit him with that first shot, he was plenty mad." Mr. Eddy was practically shaking. "He came charging at me. I had an extra ball in my mouth, and my hands were shaking so badly that I nearly dropped it. I barely managed to load Foster's rifle in time, and when the bear reached me, I slammed that rifle into his chest and fired."

"Did you miss?" Sarah asked, eyes wide.

I knew her well enough to know she was kidding, but poor Mr. Eddy looked like he might scream. "Of course not."

"Go on," I said. "Did that kill him? Is that why you're covered in blood?"

"It didn't help him, but he was definitely not dead yet, and the force of the shot knocked me back on my rump." He shook his head, his eyes still wide. "But I happened to fall on something hard—a large stick, almost like a club. I grabbed it, and as that bear roared and came at me again, I slammed him in the head." He sighed heavily and his shoulders drooped. "It killed him, blessed be, and now I just have to figure out how to get the carcass back here where we can eat it."

"Which is why you're here." Pa frowned.

"Patrick Breen said you have two oxen left you haven't yet butchered."

Pa sighed. "They're in terrible shape. I'm not at all sure they can drag something here, and if they die in the process, then we'll have even more meat we'd have to somehow drag back."

"I'll share it," Mr. Eddy said. "I have to share with the Murphys and Reeds, because Mr. Foster loaned me his gun, and I vowed to help Mrs. Reed—without her husband, you understand, she's all alone. But this bear is huge. Five or six hundred pounds. Even split four ways, there will be a lot more than nothing."

Pa sighed, but the prospect of fresh meat was quite the lure. "Fine," he said. "I'll help." He grabbed his coat. "Billy."

My brother hopped up quickly. "Yes, Pa."

"Help me get the oxen in the yokes we just dug out."

They didn't come back until after the sun had set—Ma was fretting—but when they did, it was with a large hunk of bear meat. Pa and Billy were exhausted, so Jay, Sarah, and I skinned it and got the meat put into the snow bank.

"What about Mrs. Reed?" I asked. "Should we help her?"

"She has Stanton and the Indians," Pa said, "not to mention Milt. She'll be fine."

I was so tired, I didn't even argue with him. I went to check the next morning, and Virginia and her mother were quite optimistic with the addition of some extra bear meat.

"My papa knows we're here," Virginia said. "It may only buy us another week or two, but I bet that's enough. He'll come for us. I'm sure of it."

Her mother looked less sure, but she didn't argue with Virginia.

Pa put absolutely no hope in the prospect of salvation from the outside. "We have to get out of here ourselves. There's no way someone else is going to save us—not in this weather. Not in time."

He set out to walk around most days, at least for an hour or two, and on the twentieth, he came back bright-eyed. "The snow's melting in large patches near the lake. Bare ground's visible, even."

"Do you think it's melted on the mountain?" I asked.

"Whether it has or not, we have to try again," Pa said, and then he lowered his voice. "Staying here is certain death."

He had slaughtered our last two oxen last night, and they were so thin and emaciated, it had been terribly disheartening. We rallied the other strong, self-sufficient members of the party and we set off again. This time, instead of just fourteen people, we set out with twenty-two. It was most of the original party, but with the addition of three Murphy children, Mrs. Reed's house help, Eliza Williams, Mr. Spitzer, Mrs. Wolfinger, Mr. Dolan, and Antonio.

This time, like before, Mr. Stanton took the lead, using the seven mules he'd borrowed from Mr. Sutter to break a path in the snow. They made better time this round thanks to the combination of melted drifts and colder nights. There was a fine, thick layer of ice on top of the snow that allowed us to walk quite well without sinking up to our armpits with each step.

Even the Murphy children did fairly well. In fact, we made it over the pass on the very day we set out. When we camped that night, near the summit that had defeated us on All Hallows Day, I finally felt like we might make it. Pa was in even higher spirits, humming a tune as we held our hands over the tiny fire we had made to warm some water for coffee.

Thanks to the Donners, we had enough coffee for one cup each.

But the next morning, the sun, which had been shining brilliantly, worked against us. The crust on the top of the snow began to melt, and while we could still pass reasonably well, Sutter's mules were heavier.

They flailed and sank.

"We're going to have to leave the mules," Mr. Eddy said.

Pa nodded, because we had all realized it. They were too large. We could only make it across the mountains without them. They had admirably broken a path for us on the first day, but to keep them with us would prove our defeat.

"Absolutely not," Mr. Stanton said, his face flinty. "I promised Sutter I'd return with them."

"But you've seen it yourself—they can't move," Mr. Eddy said. "They're too heavy. We need to make good time while we can. The weather never holds for too long." He pointed. "We've passed the summit. We have, what? Four more days to go? Five?"

Mr. Stanton was scowling now. "I won't go back to Sutter without his mules."

"Think about it," Mr. Eddy said. "If we butcher them, we'll have plenty of food to get us safely back to Sutter's fort."

"*Butcher* them?" Mr. Stanton's eyes nearly bulged out of his head. "I gave Mr. Sutter my *word* that I would bring these mules back. Do you know what that means, you ridiculous man? He sent us supplies without which you'd already have starved."

"But surely no mules are worth our lives," Mr. Eddy said. "I can pay Sutter back myself—I'll tell him you argued for sparing the mules, but that I made the decision to kill them."

"We aren't killing them." Mr. Stanton's jaw was set, and his eyes were flinty.

"You must know we can't travel without you, Stanton," Pa said. "You're the only one who has been through the mountains. We don't have to kill the mules. We can just leave them. With all this snow, they're likely to follow the same path they followed here back to the camp."

"Are you listening to yourself?" Stanton spluttered. "You think these seven mules will just amble their way back to our camp? They'll die here in the mountains whether we butcher them or set them loose. I vowed not to let that happen. Property may not mean anything to you, but if we stop caring about property and vows, we're no better than beasts ourselves."

"We're all starving back there." Eddy stepped closer to Mr. Stanton, and I was very aware of how large Mr. Eddy was by comparison to the very small Mr. Stanton. Even I had a few inches on Stanton, in fact.

"We will set out again," Mr. Stanton said, "but we cannot continue today."

"Following Mr. Stanton's not our only option," Jay said. My brother-in-law wasn't a big talker, and he was never contrary. He almost never argued with anyone, but he was right.

"Luis and Salvador have been over the pass, too," Sarah said. "Even if you insist on returning with the mules, Mr. Stanton, surely your two Indian guides can forge ahead, showing us the path. We can ask Mr. Sutter for more help once we make it through, and then we can return with supplies. You can safeguard the mules, and we'll carry on while we can."

But Mr. Stanton's jaw jutted out even farther, and his eyes flashed.

This time, he wasn't talking to us. He was addressing the Miwoks. "If you return to Sutter without these mules, he'll hang you."

Mr. Stanton faced off with Luis and Salvador for one heartbeat and then another, but eventually, the two Indians nodded. They wouldn't go against Mr. Stanton's idiocy, either. Without any guides, we were just wandering around blind.

Pa gnashed his teeth.

Everyone grumbled and complained.

But when Stanton and his Indians turned the mules around and headed back over the summit to the pass, we drooped. Eventually, even Mr. Eddy, hurling curse words and chunks of pine branches at the side of the mountain, followed them back out. It took us just one day to retrace the steps that had been so difficult to traverse the last two times.

We had only just returned to our tiny, dim, depressing cabin, when Pa began planning another attempt. "Those cursed mules," he kept muttering, over and over. But by the time he had worked out a plan for the mules —a bizarre compilation of boards he thought they might be able to hammer together, carry, and then shift in rounds to allow the mules to spread their weight out across a larger area—a storm hit.

Just in time for Thanksgiving.

I wasn't feeling very thankful, to be honest, but when the storm finally let up, and we realized that the very mules who had cost us our success had run off and disappeared in the storm, along with five cows and three horses, I wanted to shoot Mr. Stanton in the face.

We couldn't even locate the corpses of the stupid creatures, because they were buried under the seven feet of snow this latest blizzard had dumped.

"You know, we might have all died in the mountains," Sarah said. "That blizzard hit just two days after we returned."

"One day returning." Pa held up one finger. "Two more days." He shook his head and spat, right on the dirty, smelly, dank floor of our miserable cabin. "We could have gotten through by then, and we might all have survived this."

His implication that now we wouldn't was a little terrifying.

But I couldn't argue with him. No one could. Even rationing carefully, one month after we camped out here, it was clear that we were starving. Part of our misery came from the cold, of course, and the close quarters. When the weather allowed it, we all traveled outside to eliminate our waste. But with the frequent storms, we'd taken to using chamber pots, especially for the younger children. You could only defecate in a pot for so long before your life stopped feeling valuable. The foul smell of excrement, urine, sweat, and filth vied with the lice and the miserable, bone-cracking cold for the most miserable part of our day-to-day life here.

Even so, I think most of us would have listed the ache in our bellies and the pounding in our heads as the worst of the misery. The only thing more awful than the misery of our current predicament was watching the people I loved fade away right in front of my eyes.

Our joints ached.

Our teeth grew loose.

Our hair fell out.

Each time we stood, we'd wobble or see spots in front of our eyes.

The signs were all around us, and there was nothing we could do about it.

Eight-year-old Nancy cried about her aching joints constantly. "My knees," she'd moan at night. "They hurt." Tears would leave sideways streaks down through the grime covering her face where she lay, huddled on a battered and stale pile of pine boughs.

The lice were what bothered poor Johnny the most. The second day of the blizzard that followed our return, Ma used my makeshift scarf to tie his hands together so he couldn't scratch any more welts into the side of his face and arms.

Sarah hated how dry our skin was. "You look like a snake," she said, pointing at my hand. "And it itches. It always itches, but when I scratch, it burns." My sister wasn't one to whine, but we'd all become a version of ourselves that we hated.

What bothered *me* the most was watching as my beloved family members' beautiful faces tightened, shrinking so they no longer had round cheeks or full chins. In fact, sometimes, when I was startled awake, when I looked around the cabin, none of the people I saw even looked familiar.

My family had all been replaced by walking skeletons.

"I've worked it out," Pa said, as he ducked back into the cabin on a particularly dark and depressing morning.

"What?" Ma asked. "I could use some good news."

He lifted his arms and shook the large, cumbersome things back and forth. "They're heavy, and they're not very elegant, but they work." He was beaming, his teeth shockingly bright against the tight skin of his face. "Snowshoes."

I should have known.

As obsessed as I'd become with somehow stretching our food, Pa was even more obsessed with getting us across that cursed mountain. With another seven feet added to the ten or twelve feet of snow already on the mountain, snow shoes were our only hope. I feared that even that was not going to work, but we clung to his hope just the same.

It was all we had left.

CHAPTER 21

Peggy Breen

It was Margaret Reed who had the idea, the day after the mountaineers returned. I'd heard that necessity was the mother of invention, and it was a desperate mother who came up with a way to eat something we'd never before considered as viable food.

Margaret Reed had come to our door to beg, really. Her family was out of meat—even the unexpected bear meat—and she hoped we had some we could sell. "I know everyone's struggling," she said. "But we have nothing at all."

I glanced at Patrick with sad eyes. Surely we could spare a bit of our meat? But he shook his head without hesitation. I couldn't fault him. He had to think about our own seven children. Poor Isabella had taken to wailing for over an hour before she went to sleep. She was too young for meat, and I simply couldn't make enough milk for her.

"I didn't hold out much hope of you having meat to spare," she said. "But I had another reason for coming."

My husband scowled preemptively, tired of everyone asking us for help constantly. "What?"

"Without any meat left, we got a little creative," she said. "I decided to try using one of our hides to feed my family. It was that or start eating our dogs," she whispered.

"The hides?" I asked, incredulous. "Surely you can't just gnaw on it like the dogs do."

We'd been feeding scraps of hide to our dog for two weeks. Now I'm supposed to consider our roofing material—dog food—as viable food for us?

"That's ridiculous," Patrick said. "What's your game?"

"It's not a game." Mrs. Reed sounded so matter-of-fact, I had to listen.

"What do you do, then?" I asked. "How do you eat it?"

"I cut off a largish piece," she said, "and I press it into the fire until the fur's been burned off." She grimaced, as if even the memory of the experience was distasteful. "Then I cut it into strips and drop it into a pot with water in it, and I cook it for a long time."

"Okay," I said. "And then?"

She pulled something out from under her cloak. "Then, if you boil it long enough, you wind up with this." She held the small bowl out toward me. "I told the Murphys already. They're not quite as bad off as us, but they're close."

I eyed the goopy, grey concoction with skepticism. "You can eat that?" My lip curled.

"Well, once you cook it down long enough you can." She sighed. "Some of the kids have more trouble keeping it down than others."

"That's glue," Patrick said. "They cook animal hides and use the byproduct to stick things together."

"Well, it staves off the hunger pangs," Margaret Reed said. "If you get hungry enough, you'll thank me."

"It's vile," Patrick said. "We won't do that."

"It's not delicious," I said, lifting the spoon up again. "But she says it *is* edible." I handed the bowl back to her. "Thank you, Margaret. I appreciate your sharing. I wish we could do more."

She bowed her head, and I barely heard her murmured, "I understand." A bare moment later, she turned and headed back out into the miserable cold.

"With the mountaineers failing," Patrick said, "how much longer will their food last?" He had been so adamant about his refusal when Mrs. Reed asked for help that I was surprised to see him worry about them. Sometimes I forgot his heart of stone was borne of his desire to protect our family.

"We didn't have to fail." Patrick Dolan, my husband's friend who had gone with the others, was standing near the door, slammed his hand against the doorframe. The whole cabin shook.

"What do you mean?" my husband asked.

"We got all the way past the summit," Mr. Dolan said. "We could move across the snow just fine, but stupid Stanton refused to leave those blasted mules."

"It was really a shame he was so stubborn about animals he lost a few days later."

He rounded on us, his eyes flashing. "Yes. We could have been in California already, over the mountains and on our way to help and food and safety, but *Stanton* ruined it."

My husband closed his eyes and dropped his head in his hands. "No way to change the past."

The very next day, another visitor came asking for meat. This time, it was Charles Stanton. There weren't many people in camp who had a greater claim to people's donations. After all, he had not a single family member or even any close friends in our company, and he crossed the mountains and returned to bring us all supplies.

Nevertheless, a lot of people were angry about the mules, and with our supplies dwindling, Patrick sent him away as well. Mere hours later, there was some kind of altercation on the other side of our cabin wall. Mr. Keseberg, detestable human that he was, had built a lean to off the back wall of our cabin. Patrick couldn't really complain, given that we had lucked into this cabin, but it hadn't been comfortable, having them share our back wall. We could hear every time he yelled at his sweet wife, and every time he and Charles Burger or Augustus Spitzer got into a fight.

That was why we weren't surprised when, after another round of yelling, we heard a strange sort of shuffling noise, and then, a few moments later, there was a loud thumping and a concerning sliding sound. Then, finally, a knock at our door.

John answered the door, but my husband was standing just behind him, his rifle close. "Who is it?"

We all peered at the doorway. Thanks to the monumental amounts of snow, you could no longer just walk into our cabin. We had carved crude steps, but our weight had made them hard and somewhat slippery. Anyone who came to visit had to climb down from ten or so feet up to reach our small cabin door. It was strange, but the buildup of snow had made our torturously cold cabin a little warmer. At least the wind no longer bothered us.

"It's. . ." John peered, and we all snuck closer.

"Augustus Spitzer," the man mumbled. "That bastard Keseberg won't give me a single bite of food, and one of the oxen he killed was mine." He was clutching his head and moaning.

"Does your head hurt?" James asked.

Spitzer froze then, and turned to look up at us. "Yes, it does," he muttered. "All the time. And standing makes me dizzy."

He was just a little farther down the same path we were all on—the path to starvation.

"You can't stay—" my husband began.

"It's fine," I said. "In fact, we just discovered a new way to stretch our food." Patrick stared at me, gape mouthed, as I bundled up and headed past Mr. Spitzer and up the stairs.

To cut my first strip of ox hide.

I may not have beef to spare for Mr. Spitzer, but we had plenty of hides, and so far, we hadn't eaten a single one. It took a shockingly long time to burn the hair off, and the stench of it was overpowering. James, Simon, Peter, and Isabella were all crying by the time I finished. Slicing it into strips was also hard—I nearly gashed my hand. That's when John took the task from me. My vision had been going increasingly dark.

Our poor roommate, Antonio, about whom we all knew quite little, moved ever closer as we worked, clearly hoping that unlike the beef, we would share our meal of ox hide. When it was finally ready, share we readily did. In fact, most of my children refused to eat any of it, leaving even more for the ailing men.

Augustus Spitzer, Antonio, and surprisingly, my husband, slurped it down without much complaint. A few grimaces, a few groans, and the entire pot of ox hide goo was entirely gone. Mr. Spitzer and Antonio each crouched in the corner, flopping backward with pronounced sighs.

It might not have been good, but our stomachs had stopped caring about quality of food and begun demanding literally anything. Also, the hides didn't have *much* fat, coming as they did from such emaciated beasts, but they had *more* fat than the poor beef we'd been eating. I thought that might have helped a bit, too. At least, I felt almost better after drinking the hide concoction than I had from choking down small bits of cooked beef.

The blizzard that hit the next day was miserable and lasted right through Thanksgiving without any concern for the date. It was very, very hard for us to think of anything to be grateful for, but our dear friend Patrick Dolan managed it admirably. "I could have stayed back home—I'm sure all of us are thinking about that right now." His chuckle was a little forced, but genuine nonetheless. "But at least I'm here with some of the finest people I've ever met. People who love God, people who have a good perspective. People who are making hard decisions but doing their best to help others whenever they can, even in these circumstances."

On a steady diet of hide goo, Mr. Spitzer had perked up, and he was listening eagerly. Antonio looked better too, which was heartening. Our wood pile had grown quite small, thanks to the blizzard, but with my husband, Mr. Dolan, Antonio, and hopefully Mr. Spitzer's help soon, when the storm let up, it would soon be replenished, or so I hoped.

I decided that I should show my children that even in hard things, there were blessings. "You know. If we hadn't had Mr. Dolan and Antonio here, we might not have had enough firewood to withstand this storm. Helping others often helps you as well."

My oldest, John, straightened. "I'd have cut all you needed, Ma."

I smiled, but I continued. "Sometimes God shows us the right path through adversity, and it's up to us to travel it as gracefully and faithfully as possible. I hope that we can all learn a bit more about God's love and his forbearance with us, even when we've made mistakes. Perhaps this is a good time to read from the Bible for the day."

Everyone else smiled as Patrick pulled out our worn Bible and inched close enough to the fire to read. But Mr. Spitzer, who never seemed very excited when we read, looked almost ill.

"Are you alright?" I asked.

He shook his head and retreated into the corner. But late that night, after the children were in bed, he gathered up his very meager belongings, which he had dragged into our cabin in a small blanket, tied in knots, and he moved toward the door.

"What are you doing?" I asked. "It's still storming out there."

"I can't stay here," he said, his face grim.

"Why ever not?" Antonio asked. "You're getting your share of the hides. You can't really expect them to give you their beef. It's almost gone."

Mr. Spitzer shook his head. "I never believed in God, you know, and that doesn't excuse it, but." He closed his eyes and sighed. "I can't stay here. I just can't."

"Why?" my husband pressed. "Have we done something?" I knew Patrick struggled still, because of his decision to leave Hardcoop behind. And because, when Mr. Reed was in trouble after the awful Snyder incident, he didn't speak out. Patrick had blamed himself ever since for the Reed family's precarious state.

Mr. Spitzer shook his head. "No, but when Wolfinger. . ."

Wolfinger, the man who was killed by the cursed Paiutes while caching his worldly goods, after losing all his oxen. . . "When Wolfinger died?"

"He didn't die," Augustus Spitzer whispered. "He. . . Burger and I killed him and took his money." He whipped toward the door then, moving faster than I thought he could, and before any of us knew quite what to say, he was gone.

"Where will he go?" I asked.

Patrick shrugged.

Mr. Dolan shook his head.

I found that I didn't much care. We'd been nursing a murderer. I knew that God loved all his children, but I wasn't God. I found it harder to love a man when I knew he had taken another man's life.

When the cursed blizzard finally stopped, Mr. Graves came by *again*, looking for another round of volunteers to cross the mountains with him. "It'll be different this time," he said.

"Yes," Patrick grumbled. "You won't even have mules to break a path."

"We'll have snowshoes," Mr. Graves said. "And if you'll help me dig out your oxbows, I can make quite a few more."

It took nearly a day to locate two sets of ours, but we donated them to the cause, and we began to make preparations. This time, my husband wanted to join them. He hadn't gone the first few times, but with the snowshoe plan, he felt that the idea finally had merit. "They've come back twice now," he said. "Perhaps this time, the third time, will be the one that works."

But after they finally finished the last of the snowshoes they could make, and as they prepared to go, a terrible kidney stone struck. "These cursed stones," Patrick groaned. "Why did God afflict me so?"

I could tell he was spiraling again, blaming himself for our circumstances. "Pull out the Bible and let's read," I said. "That always helps."

But when Mr. Graves came around, announcing that it was time to go, Patrick looked even more upset. "If I went, there would be one less person to eat our food," he said. "I can try to push through." But then with an agonized cry, he dropped to the pine bough bed he was lying on.

"I'll go," our son John said.

"No," Patrick said. "Your ma needs you to cut wood when I can't."

Antonio and Mr. Patrick Dolan stood up. "We can both go. It will be fewer mouths to feed, and with John, you'll have enough wood."

I reached for Mr. Dolan's wrist. "But you have enough food. You've already tried twice. Stay here." As one of the only single men who had five oxen of his own and one cow when we got stuck, he was probably the only person who could survive the winter without even resorting to eating hides.

"I want you to have my meat," he said. "Give half to the Reeds, and a bit to poor Amanda McCutchen, and you take the rest." His eyes were kind. "We'll go and get help and return."

My husband, for the first time in a very long time, began to quietly cry. It broke my heart, but it was yet another blessing, having a friend like Patrick Dolan. He was always ready to help and always willing to sacrifice. When Graves came back, we had helped Antonio and Mr. Dolan pack bags. They thought the trip would take some five or six days, and we packed them the provisions we could spare.

"You can't give me more." Patrick Dolan refused any additional food. "One of the main reasons we're going, other than looking for help, is to make sure you have enough."

Nevertheless, I fretted as they took off, their homemade and improvised snow shoes clearly both heavy and cumbersome. What if the snow delayed their crossing? What if another storm hit? Would six days of half-rations be enough for people who were walking and climbing every day?

Were we sending them off to die out there?

"What if he doesn't make it?" I asked no one in particular. "What if we never see him again?"

"It'd still be better than slowly starving in this stinking dark hole, eaten by lice and stewing in our own filth." My husband, instead of being filled with the gratitude I felt, was clearly consumed with something else. "We're all going to die anyway. We're being punished, and rightly so." He turned, shifted into the corner, and collapsed.

I wanted to argue with him, but my short-lived optimism wasn't great enough for that. And besides, I had hide to burn and boil. The stench of boiling ox-hide goo did nothing to improve our mood. Even so, I offered up a prayer to a God I sometimes wondered about, that Mr. Dolan's noble sacrifice wouldn't be in vain.

CHAPTER 22

Mary Ann Graves

This was our third attempt. The first two tries were total failures. I think because of that, volunteers were a little harder to come by this time around. Mostly, Pa managed to roust the same group of people that had attempted to cross the past two times. It wasn't even that we felt like we would surely make it this time.

But my father was desperate.

Baylis Williams, who had been weakening for weeks, had died yesterday.

The combination of terrible cold and never-enough-food had finally gotten to him. It was, possibly, the most depressing funeral I'd ever witnessed. His sister sobbed uncontrollably, but the rest of the Reeds watched with an almost macabre calm.

They all knew it could be them next. So when the weather finally cooperated—after days of snow, we had a few warm days, and then a solid freeze, leaving the snow with a nice hard crust on top—we all knew it was time.

"I've been over it and over it," Pa whispered the night before we left. Billy, Sarah, Jay, Amanda McCutchen, and Ma were the only ones still awake in our side of the cabin, and clearly, he wanted to keep it that way. "I know everyone thinks I'm crazy for trying this again, especially with the way the last two attempts have gone. If anything, the snow's deeper and harder to cross now, but we're running out of time."

"Surely Mr. Reed will come to the rescue any time," Ma said. "That's what Mrs. Reed believes."

"There's no way that my husband, now that he's recovered from his illness, won't come back for me and Harriet too," Amanda said. Her husband hadn't been heard from since Charles Stanton returned with those cursed mules and told us Bill had stayed behind because he fell ill.

"You're both entitled to that hope," Pa said. "In fact, I would say both of you probably *need* that hope. I think all of us could do with a little hope. But looked at impartially, it's likely that neither Mr. Reed nor your husband has any idea how dire our situation really is. When James Reed left, we had seventy-five more animals than we wound up having. Between the cows, mules, and horses that ran away during that blizzard, and the animals stolen by the Paiutes, we have far, far less meat than anyone would have imagined possible."

"But even if they think we have more to eat than we do, won't they come?" I asked. "Surely they must know we're stuck. Even if we aren't dying, we're going to be cold and miserable. They know we threw most of our clothing out in the desert crossings."

"Not necessarily," Pa said. "You have to assume the snow's just as bad on the other side of the mountains, and they'll have as much trouble getting through it as we do. But think about this—if you were Reed, would you have allowed the group to make camp here, at the base of the mountains for the whole winter?"

"We didn't plan to stay here all winter," Ma said, clearly affronted on Pa's behalf.

"We didn't, but now we're stuck. Most of the people here couldn't even travel from here to Truckee Meadows, but if we had made camp there, we might not have had to slaughter all the cattle. They might have had grass yet to eat, and a more temperate climate in which to fatten up. In any case, Mr. Reed also has *no* idea where we are."

I'd never thought of that. The rescuers that Virginia and her mother were staking all their hopes on. . .might not even know that we needed them. They might, in fact, be *waiting* on better weather intentionally.

"Some of us *have* to get back through and tell them about our situation," Pa said. "Because any way I look at it, there isn't enough food for our family, and we're the best off of the bunch, other than maybe the Breens. With a winter this severe, we could be looking at April or May before the snow really melts. In fact, I think it's likely. We have perhaps ten *days'* worth of actual meat left, and then what?" He shook his head.

"We have the hides," Ma said, but even she couldn't suppress her grimace.

"We do," Pa nodded. "But you know some of us have trouble tolerating them."

He was being nice. It was Ma, Nancy, and Franklin Junior who couldn't seem to keep the goo down. They took forever even to bring themselves to eat it. Without a little bit of beef to pair with it. . .I wasn't sure how long Frankie would keep eating at all.

None of us wanted to eat gelatinous, melted remains that had been stolen from the discarded parts of our oxen or if it gets bad enough, our very roof. Not a single one of us.

"But even with those. . ." Pa shook his head. "We have maybe a month or two left before we all starve. As it is, Billy." Pa's face was deadly earnest when he looked my sweet little brother in the eye. "Next week, or the one after at the very latest, you'll have to kill Ollie and eat him."

Billy's face looked stricken. Our sweet family dog, Ollie, having heard his name, stood up and walked toward Pa. He bumped his hand with his nose.

"But he eats the hides," Billy said. "Why do we have to kill him?"

"The Reeds ate two of their dogs last week," I said. "It was horrible—Virginia cried all day. But they had nothing to feed them, and they didn't want to watch them suffer."

"And most important of all, Ollie eats the *hides*," Pa said, his eyes intent, waiting for Billy to get it.

All of us thought about his words for a moment, immeasurably depressed that we couldn't keep our dog because keeping him alive meant he'd keep consuming the rawhide that we ourselves needed to eat to survive.

It was sickening.

I did understand a bit why Pa didn't want to stay and watch it happen.

"What about the Donners?" Sarah asked. "How many people from Alder Creek are coming this time?"

Pa's shoulders drooped. "The last time I went to Alder Creek, things were so bad there, they were boiling bones and drinking the broth or gnawing on them. They lost whole strings of animals when that first blizzard hit, the one where Stanton lost the mules."

Ma whimpered, and I could relate.

"I wish there was something we could do for them," Pa said. "But no one there was in great shape, and I can't imagine anything has improved. George Donner's hand was gashed fixing their wagon wheel weeks ago, and now it's infected. He can't even sit up."

"So our group will be made up mostly from people here," Jay said.

Pa nodded. "You, me, Sarah, Mary Ann. Billy, you'll stay here and watch Ma and the little ones again."

No one even bothered arguing. There wasn't any point.

"I'm going too," Amanda McCutchen said.

"But your baby," Ma said.

A tear rolled down Amanda's cheek slowly. "Can you watch her for me?"

Amanda's milk had dried up weeks ago. Her baby was not doing well. She cried or she lay listless, nothing in between. She looked like a skeleton doll. Ma still had a bit of milk. . . And I realized that Amanda was asking Ma to share what little she could make.

Ma and Amanda exchanged a glance, and then Ma nodded slowly. "I'll do everything I can for her."

And if poor little Harriet died, her mother, like Pa, wouldn't be here to suffer through something she couldn't have stopped in any case.

"We'll leave in the morning," Pa said.

The next morning, we gathered with our meager packs outside the Breen cabin. Mr. Breen read a scripture. "John sixteen, verse thirty-three reads, 'These things I have spoken unto you, that in me, ye might have peace. In the world ye shall have tribulation, but be of good cheer; I have overcome the world.'"

Then Mrs. Breen offered up a prayer. "Oh, Dearest God, we have tried to make a long journey, and here at the end, we were stopped. These brave members of our party have gathered, in an attempt to make it through to civilization and seek help. Please bless their efforts and support them in their desperate trip. Let them find the path clearly and find help quickly. In our Father's holy name, amen."

We didn't have much in the way of clothing. Our shoes had all been worn badly, and our clothing choices were limited. Sarah and I were each wearing one of Ma's woolen shirts, on top of two of our own threadbare shirts. We each had one coat that we had patched with pieces of Ma's winter coat, leaving Ma with none.

"I'll be fine," she said. "We have blankets and a fire." She forced a smile.

"I'll keep the fire going." Billy's smile was forced too, but their reassurances helped, even knowing it was fake.

We all knew they'd die if we didn't make it through. We each had enough dried meat in our bags for six days—one pound per day. We prayed it would be enough to get us past the mountains, because we all felt horrible taking so much of what little our families had left.

"I'll miss you." Virginia Reed ducked her head.

I stepped closer to her and took her hand. "We will get through, and we'll make sure your father knows you're waiting for him."

She nodded tightly, but I could see her eyes welling with tears. "I'm sorry you have to make this terrible trip," she said. "If only I hadn't gotten sick, I would come with you."

"Are you kidding? I've been wanting to get past that one stupid mountain pass for weeks." My smile wasn't forced. Virginia was a good friend now, and her concern was genuine. Our journey would be terrible, I was sure, but we were doing it for all the right reasons. There was no way she could come—she didn't tolerate the hides well, and it was all they had left. She looked worse every day.

I was making this trip as much for her as I was for my own siblings. She needed her father, and he needed to know how much they were suffering.

"I'll be praying for good weather," Virginia whispered. "Praying and praying."

Mr. Stanton and his two Indians, even without the mules, took the front of the line, and the rest of us fell in. I only looked back one time. Ma and little Virginia Reed were still standing out in the snow and wind, and Virginia raised her hand when she saw me look back. I waved, and then I turned around, resolved to focus only on the trip ahead.

We called ourselves the Snowshoe Party, because this time, our third attempt, we mostly all had snowshoes.

I walked just behind Mr. Stanton, alongside Pa, dear Sarah, her husband Jay, and Amanda McCutchen. It's funny how much closer you grow to someone, just by living in the same hovel as them. I'd seen Amanda poop in a pot. There wasn't much about her that could ever startle me again.

"I'm already cold." Amanda shivered.

It made me laugh.

I hadn't been warm in so long I'd forgotten what it felt like.

Behind us, William and Sarah Foster walked hand-in-hand. Like Amanda, they had left their two-year-old son, George, behind. Poor Harriet Pike walked just beside them, and I felt like she had the hardest lot of all. Unlike Amanda McCutchen, she wasn't leaving her two daughters to *retrieve* their father. No, she had to leave her three- and two-year-old girls with her mother, hoping they'd survive, because her husband had already died from that gun-misfiring a few months past. The man walking alongside her, her sister's husband, had shot him, inadvertently, but still, it had to be hard.

If Harriet Pike died, there would be no one in the world, other than her widowed mother Levinah Murphy, to watch her little girls. From what I could tell, Mrs. Murphy wasn't doing very well herself.

Stumbling along behind them were Sarah Foster and Harriet Pike's little brothers, thirteen-year-old Lemuel and ten-year-old William Murphy.

It wasn't the best December sixteenth I could remember.

It was by far the worst.

Behind the four Murphy children, William Eddy, a borrowed rifle hanging on his shoulder, trudged along. His wife had made quite a scene when he left, kissing him all over his face and telling him she'd be praying for him every morning and every night. Beside Mr. Eddy, a German man I didn't know very well named Charles Burger, and two men from the Breen cabin who had come along on the last two attempts, Patrick Dolan and Antonio, also joined us.

Patrick Dolan was actually smiling when I glanced back at him.

"You look. . .happy," I said, when we broke for five minutes to eat a few bites of beef-strip jerky at the edge of Truckee Lake. "How can that be?"

"I've lived most of my life outdoors," Mr. Dolan said, "with the sunshine on my face and the wind in my hair. I came to help my good friends, the Breens, but I also came again, this third time, because I didn't think I could spend one more moment in that dimly lit, depressing, frigid hole." He shuddered. "And watching those children shiver and listening to them cry and scream?" He shook his head. "I'm not sure how the lice were in your cabin, but Peter and Isabella couldn't even sleep some nights for scratching."

"I imagine lice will be the least of our troubles," Mr. Stanton said. "Very soon, you'll be missing them."

"I doubt that very much," Mr. Dolan said.

But when we started back toward the base of the mountain again, it was clear that we needed to don our snowshoes. The snow had grown so deep, and so fluffy, that we couldn't plow our way through without great difficulty. Using snowshoes, however, especially clumsy homemade ones, was much harder than I anticipated. We had carefully tied as many strings as we could find across all the split oxbows, but the frames were heavy, and the strings were probably not plentiful or close-enough together.

The overall effect was that with every step, our feet would still sink at least a foot into the snow. When we were ready to move ahead, that meant removing our feet from underneath the pile of snow we'd submerged them in and shaking them off and then heaving them forward again. It was very tiring work. It took a long time to go a short distance, and I was winded quickly.

"At least I'm not cold anymore," Mr. Dolan joked.

He was right about that. Underneath my woolen shirts and my flannel coat, I was sweating. I could see that Jay and Sarah were, too. Notably, no one had anything to say.

We were all too tired for that.

It took us hours, but we were about halfway across Truckee Lake when we paused for another break. Unfortunately, when we set out, we had only fifteen pairs of snowshoes. Charles Burger had decided to come, even though he didn't have a pair of snowshoes. Apparently the Keseberg lean-to wasn't much better than no shelter at all, or so he said. Little William Murphy, the ten-year-old son of Levinah, also had no snowshoes, but he was so small, we hoped he could walk on top of the snow without them. Mr. Burger was having to bludgeon his way through the snow, as wide and short at he was, and William wasn't skipping over the top of the snow. Light or not, he was sinking. Both of them had fallen quite a ways behind the rest of us. We waited more than half an hour for them to reach us, and when they finally did, they both looked utterly exhausted.

As crude as our snowshoes were, and as bad as we were at using them, it was clear—without them, Mr. Burger and little William were not going to be able to keep up.

Pa grunted. "It appears that it's harder to navigate the snow without snowshoes than we had hoped it might be."

"You can't wait for us." Mr. Burger's chest was heaving, and his cheeks were pink. "I understand. I'll take the boy back with me."

"Ma won't be able to take you in," Harriet Pike said. "We have no food left."

Mr. Burger nodded, his eyes sad. "I know. Believe me, I know."

We made slightly better time after they turned back, but not good enough. By the time we needed to make camp—the sun set so horribly early—we were barely past the lake. The last attempt had gone much faster. That wasn't a promising start, but we went about our tasks without much conversation.

Our camp was quite depressing.

We had no idea how deep the snow we were walking across was, but when we first made a fire, it sank and sank until it was essentially gone. No heat, and no benefit to us at all.

"We'll have to make a bed of long green logs," William Eddy said. "Then we can burn the fire on top of that, and even if the snow directly below it melts, the logs will hold the fire up so we get heat."

It was a lot of work, and then it had to be tended, but at least it helped stave off some of the bitterest cold of being out in the open. I hadn't given our miserable cabin enough credit. Spreading a blanket on the snow and lying in the open near a fire was a new level of misery I had not yet contemplated. My fingers were so cold they were numb. I couldn't even feel my feet, other than a vague aching.

At least we didn't have to make dinner. I'd already eaten half of my day's rations, so I only had a few pieces of dried beef left. I gnawed on them, deep in thought.

"You know, a few months ago, I wouldn't have even eaten this." Sarah was glaring at the strip of meat in her hand.

"Oh, fine," Mr. Dolan said. "If you really don't want it." He held out his hand.

We all laughed.

We laughed a lot more than the joke really warranted, and I realized that we were all starved for more than just food. That night, I tossed and turned, never finding a position where I felt less than frozen solid. Another thing I hadn't really credited the dirty, stinking cabin with was the protection I felt from the howling of the wolves.

One more reason to keep our fire going.

Mr. Eddy got up at intervals to slide more green logs underneath the fire and throw more dry pine branches on it. Mr. Foster helped, too. But all too soon, the sun came out and our chance at sleep was gone. That's when I realized that the sweat that had soaked my clothing from the exertions of the prior day had frozen solid on my arm and legs. I couldn't even bend my arms, and my legs were very nearly as bad. My eyes burned as we broke camp, and I couldn't tell whether it was from the blindingly white snow everywhere I looked, or from the lack of any real sleep.

We shared a miserably small pot of coffee, and then ate a few bites apiece of our dried beef, and then we tied our terribly heavy snowshoes on again, and started off. My thigh muscles screamed, and my back ached.

And we were just getting started.

At least, as we moved, the snow and ice that had encased my body began to melt. The wet and soggy clothing left me shivering even while I was warming up. On that second day, we finally confronted the miserable east side of the cursed mountain pass, the one that had defeated us twice and forced us to turn back on the third trip just after we'd finally crossed it.

The first mile or so wasn't too bad, but I could see that the worst parts were coming. Rising like jagged teeth, outcroppings of granite sprang up in front of us. Strange smatterings of snow and ice clung to their smooth sides, like someone had splattered the side of the mountain with white mud. At least I had gotten much better at walking in the snowshoes. In fact, Sarah and I had both gotten good enough that we could almost walk circles around Jay and Pa.

Not that we had the energy.

Because we were lighter, we sank less, and that meant we could take more frequent breaks. I actually felt bad for the nine men in our party. They seemed to be working much harder than the five women. Over the first few hours of the day, the women gradually moved to the front of the snowshoe party. We found that after we had sort of tamped down the snow, it was easier for the men to walk over it. They didn't sink as much.

Occasionally I would slip on a hidden patch of ice, but most times, that was almost fun. Slipping, after all, meant moving without much work, and that was a rare treat for me. About midday, however, I slipped far enough that I slammed into the side of the mountain, wrenching my knee. Between the misery of struggling to breathe the air, which felt thin and hurt to inhale, and the horrible heat and sweat from our exertions, I really didn't need one more way in which to suffer.

After that, I fell to the back of the front-guard. My knee was still shooting pains up my leg when we crossed the worst part of the cursed pass, but I resolved not to let the injury stop me. I carried on—we all did. In spite of my best efforts, however, I began to lag behind. After clearing the pass, I stopped for a moment, and I marveled.

We had been stuck here by the weather that hit this miserable place months ago, and I hadn't spent much time thinking of the beauty. I thought about the words in that scripture Mr. Breen had read.

Be of good cheer.

There had been precious little good cheer in our lives for quite some time.

But to our north, there were now three large peaks visible—they were generously snow-covered, but in their midst, there were pine trees, and the sun glinted off the snow with sparkles and gleaming light. The bright blue of the sky provided an impressive contrast, and I couldn't help feeling like, if things had been different, we could have really appreciated our journey here. If we'd been transporting Norwegian furs, or some other luxury item, outfitted properly and well-fed, this might have been a journey to remember.

That set me to thinking about Mr. Hardcoop, who had only come on this whole trip for the memories he would have been able to bring back to his children. How badly things had gone astray for him—for all of us, really.

When we finally made camp again, too exhausted to even make small talk, I glanced back, gazing at the land we'd passed in the lengthening shadows from the setting sun beyond us. I was shocked to realize that it didn't *look* like we had gone very far.

"How far have we come?" I asked.

We all knew Sutter's fort was a hundred miles from our encampment, give or take. We thought, if we could do fifteen or twenty miles a day, we could cover the distance in five or six days. Johnson's Ranch was maybe ninety miles. If we got lost at all, we'd hopefully find that, at least.

"I doubt we've gone more than ten miles in the two days we've traveled," Charles Stanton said. "I think it's very possible we've gone no more than six."

My heart sank.

All of us wilted a little.

Because if, in two days, we'd traveled only six miles. . .we were going to run out of food long before we reached our destination. And at that point, we hadn't even realized that we were going the wrong way.

CHAPTER 23
Mary Ann Graves

Day three felt a lot like day two, but my knee felt better, for which I was immensely grateful. One thing was worse, though.

Several people in our party went blind, most notably, our guide. Mr. Stanton didn't only go blind. He was also lagging behind. Mr. Eddy stopped beside me, about an hour or two after we set out. "Have you seen Stanton?"

I blinked.

"He pointed out the direction we've been traveling, but then a moment later, he pointed another way."

I felt sick.

"Then he came back and said we should definitely travel this direction." Mr. Eddy shook his head. "But now, I don't even see him."

When I looked behind us, I realized he was right. Sarah and Jay were just ahead of me, keeping pace with Pa. Amanda McCutchen was in front of them. Antonio had been behind me, and Mr. Dolan behind them. The Murphys were lagging a bit, but I could make them each out, a little below and to the east.

The Miwoks were bringing up the rear, but that was all I could see.

Mr. Stanton wasn't visible at all.

"What do we do?" I asked.

Mr. Eddy shook his head.

"We have to keep on going," I said.

He didn't disagree. What else could we do? But when the sun began to set and we had to stop to make camp, Mr. Stanton still hadn't caught up. "Did you see him?" I asked Luis.

The Indian shook his head.

"What about you?" I asked Salvador. "How long since you saw him?"

"Morning," Salvador said.

"Should we go back?" Mr. Eddy asked.

He was always the first person to lead the charge when someone was missing. I remembered how upset he was when no one would lend him a horse to ride back for poor Mr. Hardcoop. But now, when all our lives depend on one person, none of us had the energy to go another ten feet, much less a long haul, scanning for footprints.

"Do you think he got lost?" I asked.

"He was half-blind." Mr. Eddy sighed in disgust. "I should have stayed next to him."

Blessedly, after we'd all built the fire and laid out our meager beds, Mr. Stanton finally staggered into camp. Unfortunately, that was also when it started to snow.

On the fourth day, Mr. Eddy and Pa and I resolved to keep a close watch on Mr. Stanton. Unfortunately, by ten that morning, it was clear that Mr. Stanton wasn't the only one who had gone blind. Mr. Eddy and Pa were as mixed up as our guide. When we stopped for a short break, Mr. Stanton sat down and broke out his pipe. He had precious little tobacco left, but I had noticed that he smoked it to warm up.

"Are you alright?" I asked.

He didn't answer me, just nodded.

"We'll need to get going again soon," I said.

He nodded again.

But when we all stood up, he was still sitting, smoking his pipe.

"Mr. Stanton?" I raised my voice. "We need you. We don't know where we're going."

"That way." He pointed. "This is my last pipe. I mean to enjoy it."

I nodded, but Sarah was calling me up ahead. "Don't wait too long," I said. "You'll fall behind again."

Sarah had cut herself on a pine branch, and I managed to find some fabric in my pack to wrap it. By the time we finished, we'd fallen behind Pa and Jay, and we hurried to catch up to them. Pa had taken a wrong turn and was wandering down a path that led to nowhere, so I redirected him, and then we pushed to catch up with the others. A little while after we rejoined the trail, I saw something almost miraculous.

Another camp.

I shouted, and I screamed, and I jumped up and down, but no one seemed to hear or see me. The smoke from their fire wound its way upward and they had actual walls and a roof on their small cabin. Surely they'd be provisioned for the winter, living up here. My hands shook with excitement.

But when Sarah and Jay caught up to me, and I pointed at the camp, they said *it wasn't there.*

"You must be snow-blind too." I waved my hand in front of Sarah's face, but she caught my wrist. "It's not there, Mary Ann." Her face was drawn, her lips flat. "You're the one who's seeing things wrong."

I argued with her for a moment, but when Amanda McCutchen couldn't see it either, I despaired. In all my excitement about the camp, I somehow lost track of Mr. Stanton. Again. That night, we all waited and waited and waited, but Mr. Stanton never showed up. The second time he lagged behind, he was well and truly lost.

That was the first time I worried that we had gone off course. Luis and Salvador could see relatively well, but they finally admitted on the morning of our sixth day that they didn't know quite where we were.

"Is different with snow," Salvador said.

"Can not find good path," Luis agreed.

But we pressed on. What else could we do? None of us had any food left, and our energy was fading fast. The miserable distances we'd been able to traverse were starting to shrink, and on December twenty-fourth, Christmas Eve, we reached an impassible mountain.

We had to backtrack.

I cried and cried, my tears freezing to my painfully raw cheeks.

Late in that day, as we finally started on what we hoped was a path that would get us around the stupid, steep cliff wall we'd run into, I heard a gunshot. All of us hurried ahead, and discovered that Mr. Eddy had seen a rabbit.

"I missed." He looked close to bawling himself, his eyes squinted up and swollen. "But I know I saw it."

I had no idea whether he'd seen a real rabbit or not. I'd seen a make-believe camp, for heaven's sake. But when he went rummaging around in his pack for more ammunition, he found something else. As if she knew what was coming, Eleanor Eddy had packed a half a pound of bear meat in the bottom of her husband's bag. She included a note, but he was too blind—he couldn't read it. He handed it to me with desperation in his unfocused eyes.

Dear William,

I can't know what your journey will bring, but I doubt it'll be concluded in six days. I wish I had more to give. This is all I saved.

I love you.

Your own dear Eleanor

It made my eyes well with tears.

Mr. Eddy offered all of us some of his paltry amount of bear meat, but none of us could bring ourselves to take it. With fourteen other people to feed, that half a pound would be gone in a flash. One bite apiece would do us no good. I hoped that the extra food would help Mr. Eddy. He wasn't as weak as Mr. Stanton, but he was struggling. He ate a small amount, and then shoved the rest back in his pack. It was time to make camp.

The next morning, on Christmas Day, I woke up like I had every other morning, and cast about for my boots. My right boot had lost its sole the second day, but the straps of the snowshoe held it mostly together. On the third day, a small hole in the toe of my left boot had widened, becoming large enough for snow to pile in. Things only got worse from there. None of the holes and problems with my boots were the worst of my trouble, though. No, the worst part was waking up every morning with my body nearly encased in ice.

That morning, on Christmas, I could barely move.

Sarah and Jay had to pound on my arms and legs to break the ice so I could bend enough to stand again. Tying on my snowshoes was practically impossible.

We traveled onward that day, relying less and less on Salvador and Luis as it became clear that they knew no more than we did. Jay and Pa began to lag behind, and poor Lemuel Murphy moved slower, still. His sisters fretted, but there wasn't much anyone could do for any of us.

Patrick Dolan was the only person who still smiled. In fact, about halfway through the day on Christmas, he began singing carols. "Deck the Halls," he started.

I thought he had lost his mind at first, but then the words Mr. Breen read came back to me.

Be of good cheer.

Singing carols was pretty good cheer, but it felt hard, to be of good cheer. Patrick Dolan had to be just as exhausted as the rest of us. He had to be just as discouraged. We had hoped to make this journey in six days, but now, nine days after we left, we were still stuck somewhere in the mountains, unsure whether we were even going the right direction.

But somehow, his singing lifted my weary and tattered spirits.

So I joined him.

And Sarah joined me.

Then Amanda McCutchen, and Harriet Pike, and Sarah Foster joined as well. We didn't have the lung capacity to sing for very long, but every few hundred yards, Patrick Dolan would start another song. It was the worst Christmas I could possibly imagine. We were starving, freezing, and badly lost. It had been four days since any of us had had a single bite of food. Five for most of us.

We were probably all going to die. Maybe even today.

But we were doing our best to be of good cheer, anyway.

The next day felt less depressing, since it was the day *after* Christmas, but when we all prepared to leave, Pa didn't stand.

Sarah shook him. "Pa. It's time to go."

When his eyes opened, I exhaled a breath I hadn't realized I was holding. "I'm too tired." He shook his head, barely. "We need to rest."

He needed food more than rest. We all did. We hadn't eaten in five or six days, now. But without any game, and without even knowing when we'd pass down and out of the mountains, there was no alternative. "You have to get up," I said, praying silently that he would. "Please, Pa. We need you."

"Think of Mother," Sarah said. "What about little Frankie?" We all suspected Frankie was his favorite.

As if it was true, his eyes fluttered open again. "I ache. Everything hurts."

I knew what he meant. I ached too, soul-deep now. "But if we don't keep going, they'll all die," I whispered.

I realized, in that moment, why Mr. Stanton had simply sat, smoking his pipe. The cold had numbed me so much that I barely felt any pain in my hands and feet any more. That pain had dissolved away days ago. Now I felt nothing more than the pounding in my head.

Mr. Stanton didn't get up, because dying was better than living, and he had no one for whom to suffer through this torturous, never-ending farce of a life. No one was relying on him. No one was waiting on him. He could just *stop*.

I thought about Ma, then, and little Elizabeth. I thought about how my babiest sister laughed when Ma blew on her belly. I thought about how Lizzie had taken her first steps in that miserable cabin, and how a few days before we left, she had stopped walking, too tired to even stand.

I thought about dear Sarah, and the innumerable times we'd stayed up late, chatting and planning and dreaming. She was strong and brave back home, but now I watched a different kind of bravery as she guided her blind, tiring husband through the snow. I thought about little Eleanor, only thirteen, but Sarah's spitting image. I thought about how Ellie tried desperately to be just like Sarah, right down to tying her bonnet strings the same way, and copying phrases our beloved older sister used.

By rights, Lovina ought to have wanted to copy me, since she favored me with her dark hair and eyes and bright smile, but she preferred to read and sit alone. For her, the largest trial of this terrible encampment had been the lack of reading materials and personal space.

Then there was little Nancy. She had been a real pain lately, because of the circumstances and her age, probably. Eight was a difficult age for all the children in our family, but having no toys, no games, and no friends while being plagued with lice and mites and dealing with intolerable living conditions and starvation. . .it would make anyone sour. I tried to think about what she might be like again, if only we could make it over these cursed mountains and get to California.

Poor Jonathan. I thought about how he had trailed after Pa, trying to take an axe of his own to help cut trees. I thought about how he vowed to keep Ma safe when Pa left, in spite of his inability to keep himself safe at the age of seven. And then I thought about little Frankie, who would sing with his lips stuck out, trying to emulate our father's deep voice. I thought about how he would put on Pa's boots and stomp around, yelling for us all to clean up the messes we'd made.

He was only five. He was far too young to die.

And last, I thought about Billy. Other than Sarah, he was my most beloved sibling. He saved me from the Indians. He cut the wood we needed, tirelessly. He forced a smile in the worst of situations. If he were here, he would force Pa to get up and keep going.

But he wasn't here.

Only me, and Sarah, and Jay were here to help Pa. We were the only people who could save the other Graves children stuck back behind Truckee Lake, and Pa was giving up. I could see it in his eyes.

"Ma needs you," I said. "So does Jonathan. Billy. We all do. Please, Pa."

He opened his eyes, and I saw it. A spark. Fire, burning deep down. He groaned, and he exhaled, and he moaned, but he sat up. The ice that had frozen around his clothing cracked and shattered. He flinched, but he cast around for his boots. I crouched and helped him tie them on.

And then we all got going for another horrible, awful, miserable day. About midday, the same man who had been singing carols had an idea.

"We're all going to die out here," Patrick Dolan said. "It's no more than ten or twenty miles through the mountains, and we haven't even made that yet. I'm clumsier every day, and my head pounds so badly that I don't even mind that I can barely see. I just want it all to end."

"We know," William Foster snapped. "We all feel the same way."

"Then you'll agree when I say that we should draw lots," Patrick Dolan said. "All the men—there are nine of us left. Whoever loses, dies. The rest of us can eat him. Or you know, you can eat me, if I'm the unlucky one."

William Eddy lost his mind, yelling and shouting. "How could you? Have you gone mad? You're Catholic! We can't possibly kill someone and eat them."

"Then we'll all die together, one by one," Patrick said simply, continuing to walk.

William Foster sounded as upset as William Eddy. "You must have gone insane to suggest something like that."

Patrick Dolan merely shrugged. But as we reached camp that night, Pa said, "He might be right."

Jay and Sarah froze.

Antonio, Luis, and Salvador turned slowly toward Pa.

"I'll have nothing to do with this," Salvador said. He and Luis walked several yards away, turning their backs on us.

The rest of the men seemed to have formed some kind of consensus in the few hours we'd stumbled along. It had been so long since any of us had eaten that I couldn't even remember what dried beef tasted like. The worst of my hunger pangs were gone, but other problems had begun. My vision was poor, spots covering my eyes often. My joints stopped aching and hurt outright, all the time. Each step was a misery. My head pounded without ceasing. My hands and feet trembled constantly.

"What about me?" Lemuel asked, his eyes far too large in his skeletal face. He didn't even look childish—not with his skin stretched out over his bones like that. "Do I join in?"

"No," Pa said. "We're all here to save our children."

"But you said nine," Lemuel said.

"Franklin Graves, William Eddy, William Foster, Patrick Dolan, Antonio, and me," Jay said. "There are six of us who agree."

Both Sarahs, Amanda, Harriet, and I watched in horror as William Eddy pulled out carefully prepared pine needles. "One of these is short."

"Whoever draws the short straw," Patrick Dolan said, "will die. The rest of us will eat him. No one will oppose it, even the person drawn, because it's the only way that we don't all die."

The men nodded, slowly, silently.

And then they drew.

Pa took a pine needle.

Jay took a pine needle.

They all did, one at a time.

Happy, chipper, friendly Patrick Dolan drew the short straw.

"No." Pa shook his head. Something about seeing the person chosen broke his resolve. "No, we can't do this. It's wrong."

Patrick's face had drained of all color, but he said, "We have to. It was my idea. It makes sense that it should be me." He turned to face me, for some reason. "I have no family. It should be me."

"No," William Eddy agreed. "We can't do it. This was madness."

That night, we all pitched in to make camp without saying another word, but Patrick Dolan moved more slowly than usual. He was clearly deep in thought.

The snow that had been falling haphazardly now for days intensified.

The clouds were gathering, and the wind was screaming across the peaks. It looked like we were about to be hit with a storm. The hungrier I got, I had also noticed, the harder it was for me to keep warm. Now more than ever before, we needed a fire. We spent extra time laying the bed of green pines, none of us eager to wake up in the middle of the night to rejigger it.

By the time we finally had the wide bed of green trees laid, the wind was howling, and the snow was falling in dense, spiraling flurries that were hard to even see past. When Mr. Eddy went to set the fire using component parts of his rifle as he always did, his gunpowder exploded instead of sparking, and it burned his face and hands.

Badly.

We tried to stop him from trying again, but Pa insisted that we needed a fire. He took Mr. Eddy's gunpowder, and he started the fire that Mr. Eddy hadn't been able to spark. It hadn't been burning very long though, with all of us gathered as close to it as we could get, when Antonio's hand fell into it.

"Oh, no," I shouted.

Jay was close to him, and he fumbled forward, dragging his hand out. "Couldn't you feel that?" Jay asked. "Why didn't you move?"

Antonio never answered.

Because he had already died.

I was shaking after that, and I wasn't sure how much of it was from the cold, and how much was from the horror of our situation. Mr. Stanton had never made it to camp. We knew he'd died, but this death happened in front of us. Beside us, really. We all slowly crept closer and closer together, in part as proof against the cold, but also because we wanted to make sure we weren't alone. Sometime around eight or nine, I think, there was a great cracking sound, and the fire. . .disappeared.

The whole central area just dropped down and was gone.

When we leaned closer, we realized what had happened. We had inadvertently made our camp over a stream, and as the fire heated the snow below it, the fire had melted through the ice. . .and the whole thing dropped down into the water below. "We have to move away from it," Patrick Dolan said, clearly panicking.

"But which direction?" William Eddy asked. "How can we be sure we're not above water anywhere around here?"

Pa was shaking, and he didn't seem to be fazed by the whole incident.

That's when I realized how blue he was. I had thought myself cold that very first night in the open.

I didn't know what cold was yet.

Pa looked colder than he ever had. He wasn't moving, and I realized he'd become stiff. "No, Pa," I said. "You have to sit up. Move around."

Sarah and I chafed our hands on his arms and legs, but I started to worry. He had never looked this much like a corpse before.

"I'm fine," Pa said, his teeth not even chattering. His lips were dark blue.

I wanted to believe him, but I had given up on vain hope.

As we sat in the new spot Luis and Salvador had chosen, hopefully not above a stream, hunger gnawed at my belly, like a hammer against an anvil. Strike. Strike. Strike. My head pounded. My vision went dark in waves.

Patrick Dolan was right, I realized.

No matter how much we wanted to save our families stuck back by Truckee Lake, no matter how valiant and brave and stalwart we were, we were all going to die here. For days, I had expected that we'd starve, but I was wrong. It looked like we were going to freeze first. Before it had actually happened to anyone other than Antonio, William Eddy had an idea.

"I read something once," he said. "About a group that survived a blizzard without a fire. They all sat in a circle with their feet in the center. If we hold our blankets up, we can block the wind."

We hadn't been able to start another fire, not after our last one dropped into the stream, but we could follow his suggestion, and none of us had a better idea. After we formed ourselves in a circle, it did get warmer. Mr. Eddy was right about that. But not an hour or two after we made our little dome, Patrick Dolan stood up, disrupting the whole thing. He fell forward on our legs at first, and then he broke away, moving past us and outward, his legs churning the piles of snow beyond our cocoon. Then he did the strangest thing. He stripped off his coat and his extra woolen shirt, and he tossed them at me.

"I don't need these," he said with a glowing smile. "You take them. You always were the most beautiful." Then he ran out into the snow beyond our pitiful blanket circle. . .and disappeared.

"Where did he go?" William Eddy asked, peering out into the swirling white. He and William Foster roused themselves enough to catch him and drag him back inside, but less than an hour later, even though we'd forced his clothing back on, even though we'd held him in the middle of the circle, he died.

It was hard to gauge the passing of time, but it felt like less than an hour after Patrick Dolan died when Pa called for Sarah and me. "Come closer, Sarah. Mary Ann." He was barely speaking loudly enough for us to hear anything at all.

We both slid as close as we could get, the wind howling around us.

"I'm about to die," he whispered through the bluest lips I'd seen.

"No." Sarah grabbed his shoulder and shook him. "Pa, don't give up." Her voice cracked. "We need you."

"I know you do, and that's why I have carried on," he said, a half-smile on his face. "But my body doesn't care. I'm old—" He coughed, his whole body convulsing. Even in the dim light, I could make out the only color other than blue on his face. His lips were cracked and bleeding, but even the blood was so dark, it nearly looked black in the dim light. He cleared his throat, and then he said, "The only ones who can save your mother and your siblings now are you two. I believe in you both. I always have. I'm proud of you."

"No." I couldn't even cry—it was too terrible. "You can't, Pa. You can't die."

"I can't stop it," he whispered. "But before I go, promise me something. You have to." His voice was the barest of whispers now. "Please."

"What?" Sarah asked, leaning closer. She hugged him against her, and I couldn't fault her for that. She was always the oldest, and she was everyone's favorite. I'm sure she was exactly what he wanted. "Anything."

"Mary Ann?" His eyes cut my way.

I nodded, "Me too." As if our promises meant anything. We were all hours away from death at this point. "Whatever you want."

"After I die, you have to eat me," he said. "If you do, you might make it. If you still save them, I won't have died for nothing." Then Pa closed his eyes, and he sighed one last time.

CHAPTER 24

Virginia Reed

When I was small, I refused to eat potatoes. Mama either had Eliza bake or boil them, and either way, they were squishy and flavorless. I would push them around and around on my plate until Mama snapped at me. Then I'd shove one bite in my mouth and let it roll around and around and around.

Finally, I would swallow it.

Then the whole thing would start over until my mother grew too tired of fighting with me. Usually, if Mama got distracted, I could slip little bits of them to Cash, who liked potatoes as much as I hated them. Actually, I suspected he really just liked the butter and cheese Eliza would try to drown them in.

Either way, every time we ate them, I would groan.

But I would have *killed* for a potato in December of 1846. Just thinking about them made my mouth water. In fact, I would probably have made myself sick eating potatoes *raw*, if they magically appeared in front of me.

I'd learned by then how true hatred felt.

For instance, I hated eating the slurry into which we boiled ox hides.

It wasn't a feeling like the one I used to have for potatoes. It was a dislike so deep, and so deep-rooted, that thinking about having to choke down the vile gelatinous chunks made me shudder. The smell of it turned my stomach, which was impressive, because there was almost nothing *in* my stomach to turn.

Unfortunately for me, the leftover hides of the emaciated oxen we'd killed, including my sweet Brutus, with the fur still clinging to one side, were literally the only food we had left. Ma was the first one to seize upon the idea of preparing them so that we could actually swallow them down.

I almost wish we'd just died.

Milt had left our cabin, tasked by Charles Stanton to take a message to George Donner asking for a compass and some tobacco. But right after he left, a storm had hit, and Milt Elliot had been stuck down at Alder Creek. We weren't even sure whether he was alive. Part of me thought he might be lucky if he had died.

I wasn't the only one who was in poor spirits. After her brother died, sweet Eliza kind of gave up. Before that, she had at least woken up most days and tried to lend a hand with whatever chores were waiting. There was precious little to do compared to the months we spent out on the trail. Mostly we'd just dump out increasingly empty chamber pots, sear the hair off of sections of hide, cut them into smaller strips, and boil the strips all day until they broke down into mush. No one in my family much cared for eating the resulting product, which wasn't a surprise.

I had never before considered how our waste was directly tied to our food. When we didn't eat much, of course we didn't really poop much either. Still, dealing with what little waste we made was disgusting. We had to go farther and farther out in the snow to dispose of it, and when it spilled, as it always did, we had to cook down snow to get water to clean ourselves.

After Baylis passed away, Eliza quit doing anything, really. Two days after the snowshoe party left, she started refusing to swallow the hide-goo. I couldn't really blame her. About half the time I tried to eat it, I would puke small amounts of it back up.

That was the only time poor Cash got any food at all.

To my great horror, my family had already eaten all four of our other dogs. At first, I vowed not to eat a single bite of any of our precious animals, but after Mama started cooking the meat. . .the smell was over-powering.

I was just *so* hungry.

We hadn't eaten my sweet little lapdog, Cash. I had no idea how he was still alive. If Mama had seen me giving him any parts of the hides from our oxen, she'd have lost her mind. She was very clear—no food goes to the dogs. We didn't have enough for the people, and I understood that we couldn't prioritize a dog when humans we loved like Baylis were dying.

I understood it, but it still hurt.

But even without food, somehow, Cash survived. I suspected he was eating lice and crickets, but I'd never seen him do it. Who knew for sure? Maybe he was catching mice. However he was staying alive, he was nothing but skin and bones. In spite of that, he managed to be bouncier than any of the rest of us.

Mama came to me though, about four days after the snowshoe party left, and told me we were nearly out of hide. The only hides we had left were part of our roof. We had tried boiling bones, like the Donners were allegedly doing over in Alder Creek, and the bone broth was palatable, but not very nourishing. When we tried to eat the crumbled bones that were left after boiling the bones more than a dozen times, the chalky, crumbly mess was actually even worse than the hides. I also found myself every bit as hungry after choking down brittle chunks of bone as I had before I ate them.

At least the hides quelled the miserable pangs from my belly.

We were now facing a new choice. A worse choice than we'd faced before. We had to eat the very roof over our heads. . .or starve. First, we decided to pull off the hide on the far end, the one that had quite a few pine boughs still on top of it. At first, Mama would simply cut a chunk of it off from the inside, but that became too hard. We were forced outside, and we had to take the snow off, then the pine boughs, then we had to free the hide, and replace what we could with more pine branches.

It started dripping immediately.

We learned to avoid the muddy spot, which was right where my bed used to be. With Stanton, Luis, Salvador, and Milt all gone, there was just me, Mama, and Eliza to do whatever needed doing.

We were praying for the snowshoe party and for Milt every day, but so far God had not responded. I decided, with Christmas coming, I should visit the Breens and ask Eddie why none of my prayers were being answered. It was a long walk to make in the snow, and at first Mama said I should stay put, but I pestered her until she relented. I was finally starting to feel a little better from my long, miserable cold, and I wanted to move. I needed to do *something* other than wreck our roof and boil skin. *Anything.* She made me promise to ask them for meat, as if they'd have any to spare.

When I reached the cabin, Eddie stood straight up, knocking his little brother Peter against the wall by accident.

Peter promptly began to wail.

"Sorry, sorry," Eddie said. "But look! We have a visitor."

Peter quieted down fast, and Mr. and Mrs. Breen were both very happy to see me. "How is everyone? The Graves? Your ma?" Mrs. Breen asked.

"We're. . .well. Mama made me promise to ask for meat, though I know you have no beef to spare."

"Actually," Eddie said. "When Patrick Dolan left with the snowshoe party, he left some of his beef for your family."

I could hardly believe what he was saying. "He. . .what?"

"I've been meaning to take it to you," Mr. Breen said, "but I had a kidney stone attack just before they all left, and I'm finally recovering."

I felt like dancing. "What's funny is that I told Mama she was ridiculous for making me ask. The only reason I came was to ask you about how prayers worked." My eyes welled with tears. "You see, my family doesn't pray much, but I've talked to Eddie about it, and he told me how to pray right. Or, I thought he did."

"That's wonderful," Mrs. Breen said. "Nicely done, Eddie, and also, well done, Virginia."

"Only, I've been praying and praying and not a single thing has come true."

"It's not like making a wish on a star," Mr. Breen said. "Prayers don't *come true.*"

"Well, that's why I came." I sat on a small stool by the door and leaned forward. "I think I need to know more about how prayers work."

"Prayers are talking to God," Eddie said. "You're thanking him for what He's done, and you're asking for what you want and what you need."

"But God's the only one who really knows what we need," Mrs. Breen said.

I frowned. "I really don't think that's true. I definitely know what I need. I know what we all need—food. And someone to come help us."

Eddie laughed.

His mother frowned. "That's part of what you need to learn. God knows what we need, and it's often not what we think we need. The most important, and the hardest, part of prayer is yielding to His will as it is revealed to you."

"It's the listening," Eddie said, dutifully chastened, apparently. "You have to listen after you pray."

"But one of the things I've been praying hard about was finding food to eat. All we have left are the hides that are part of our roof." I shrugged. "And now God gave us Mr. Dolan's beef."

John grunted. "So if we hadn't told you we had beef for you, would God not be God?"

"That's what I want to know," I said.

"God is God," Mr. Breen said, his face stern, "no matter how He answers your prayers."

"I don't like that," I said. "God should love His children and take care of us." I folded my arms. "And if we just have to agree with whatever *He* does, then what's the point of praying?" I couldn't help my scowl. "We may as well just keep quiet."

Mr. Breen opened his mouth to talk, his face stormy, but before he could say a word, Mrs. Breen cut him off. "That's one of the hardest things we have to learn to do, but Jesus Christ already set the perfect example of doing it. He yielded His will to the Father's and died. I can't imagine that He really wanted to do that."

That made no sense. "But isn't God Jesus and Jesus God?"

"We need to take this one step at a time," Mr. Breen said. "She's getting confused."

"God allows bad things to happen sometimes," John said. "And sometimes He spares us. We may not know why, but when we trust in Him, we can find peace through the storm."

Peace through the storm.

I thought about that the entire walk back, my arms full of as much beef as I could carry. Mama could hardly believe it, and we both jogged back as quickly as we could, Eliza in tow, to get the rest. It wasn't a lot, but it was so much more than we had that morning.

It happened *just* in time for Christmas. Mama told me not to tell the children that we had been given extra beef, so when we went to bed, Eliza and I were close to bursting with the excitement of it. For Christmas, we'd finally have full bellies for once!

The next morning, Mama surprised us all with a huge spread. As we all looked at the food in front of us, she said, "Children, I know it's been a hard few months, but for this one day, you can have all you wish."

Mama had somehow saved a bag of beans, a bit of bacon—really, where had that come from!?—and a few dried apples. She had sliced the apples and made them into beautiful, rose-like centerpieces that sat on the large log we used as a table. Above the stove, there was a bean stew, bubbling and boiling, and grilling on spits over the side of the fire were actual chunks of beef, courtesy of the amazing Patrick Dolan's generosity and largesse.

We had hope in our hearts that the members of the snowshoe party might, even now, be meeting with Papa, and that they might be preparing rescuers and supplies to come to our aid. I prayed to God that day, out loud, for my entire family, expressing our gratitude for God's love for us, and for His birthday. Most especially, we thanked God that on Christmas Day, for the first time in nearly two months, we had full bellies. Mama really had let us eat as much as we liked. And then I asked for what we all wanted most: salvation, a reunion with our dear father, and the return of our darling Milt.

He had been gone for ten days, and with Stanton, Salvador, and Luis all gone, we felt his absence even more keenly. After everyone had celebrated, and while Mama and I were cleaning up, she whispered, "You should prepare yourself, Virginia."

"For what?" My hand, where it was scrubbing a blob of snow against the plate, froze. "What do you mean?"

"God gave us a very large blessing, thanks to Mr. Dolan," Mama said. "But Milt left just before that blizzard hit, and it's very unlikely that. . ."

"No." I set the plate down and turned to face her. "No, you have to have faith. That's what I've learned."

Mama sighed and said nothing more, but I could tell she had no faith at all. That's okay. That night, when I prayed, I told God that I had enough faith for both of us.

The next day, Milt Elliot returned! He had been stuck in Alder Creek thanks to the storm, and then once it ended, he took a few days to recover.

He was happier to be back than we were to see him, and that was saying something.

"You can't even imagine how bad things are there." Milt collapsed in the corner on a pile of sagging and smashed pine boughs. "They're in bad shape. They have tiny bits of beef left, but nothing you or I would have eaten before all this. The Donner family lost most of their animals in the same surprise storm that took all the mules and some of the cows here, so they weren't really sharing their beef at all with the drovers."

Which must have been terrible for Milt.

And, I realize that it probably meant he hadn't eaten in nearly ten days. Mama got right to work on boiling a new pot of hide, and I stood up to help.

"How could they not feed them?" Mama asked.

Milt sighed. "They're all starving," he said. "Don't be too hard on them."

"But you're family," I said.

"They don't see it that way," he said. "I was very lucky to be here with you." He collapsed inward, almost like he was trying to shrink. "James Smith is already dead."

Milt Elliot was our knight of the whip. Walter Herron was loyal and true—he went with Papa when he was banished. And on that horrible day when Papa was cast out, James Smith stood beside him, his rifle aimed at anyone who questioned my father's motives. He was stalwart and loyal and kind.

And now he was gone.

"I can't believe it's true," I said. "I—it makes me so angry."

"He's not the only one who died," Milt said. "So did Joseph Reinhardt and Sam Shoemaker." They were the Donner family drovers.

"We never should have let him help them with that stupid broken wheel." I was fuming. I wanted to march over there and yell at all of them, but I realized that it wouldn't help. Nothing could. Because he was already dead. "If things were so bad, why didn't he come here, to us?" I asked.

"I don't think he knew that it was better here. Besides, it's a long trip," Milt said. "Seven miles didn't seem like much when we were walking twenty miles a day, but they were toasting and eating strips of their buffalo skin blankets and coats at the end. It's hard to even know whether they froze to death or starved."

"I thought the Donners were good people," I said. "Mama, didn't you?"

Mama shook her head, numb.

"I think they are good people," Milt said. "They didn't harm anyone intentionally. George was the strong one, and his hand's in terrible shape. He's very, very sick. Miss Tamzene's beside herself, and she's basically caring for all the children herself. Betsy's nice, but not very helpful now that. . ." He sighed. "Jacob Donner's also dead."

It was a blow.

He wasn't a very strong man to begin with, but he was someone I'd known for a very long time. I remembered my papa spending lots of time laughing and joking with both of the Donner brothers, often late into the night when they came to visit.

And now, like Baylis, and like James Smith, he was gone forever.

"The children?" I asked.

"All alive, so far," he said. "But in addition to having very little to eat. . .they don't have proper cabins like we do. They tried to make them, but the storm was terrible, and without George's energy and health, I guess they gave up."

"Where are they living then?" I asked, wide-eyed.

"Have you seen the Keseberg lean-to behind the Breen cabin?"

I nodded.

"It's something like that, only worse. It's wet, all the time, and cold. The wind's bad, though now the accumulated snow has helped some. They have to go outside often during storms, to beat the snow off the tarps that cover their shelters, or even those will collapse."

"They're living in a snow pit, covered only by tarps?" I couldn't even imagine it.

"The children rarely climb out of their beds because they're too cold, leaving the adults to do all the work, but there are fewer and fewer adults capable of doing it." Milt frowned. "I was happy to leave, but I felt guilty when I left. I won't lie."

"Things aren't so great here either," I confessed. "Up until recently, we had nothing but hides, and. . ." I glanced up at the ceiling.

"The only hides we have left are those." Mama looked up, too.

Milt frowned.

"But Patrick Dolan left us some meat," I said. "So things aren't so bad.

God really blessed us. Plus, the snowshoe party already left, and we hope they made it across the mountains already."

"They didn't come back this time?" Milt asked.

I shook my head. "I really think God's helping them."

Mama and Milt exchanged a strange look. I wasn't sure why, but it felt like it was aimed at me. I decided to ignore it. Again, I resolved to have enough faith for all of us.

The next day, Charles Burger, who had tried to set out with the snowshoe party but had come back because he didn't have snowshoes, died. Mr. Keseberg didn't have the energy to do anything but drag him out into the snow.

A few days later, the beef we got from Patrick Dolan was gone, too. That's when Mama said something awful. Something I would never have been ready to hear.

"It's time, sweetheart."

When my head whipped up and our eyes met, I shook my head fiercely. "No. It can't be."

Mama's eyes were sad.

They were as sad as when she told me that I should go outside and ask Billy to come help us, because Baylis had died. And maybe that makes me a bad person, that I was as upset about this as I was about a dear family friend dying.

But it was still true.

"We can't," I whispered. "We aren't even feeding him."

"But we're starving." Mama's voice broke on the word starving, and I realized it was just as hard for her.

Because everyone loved Cash.

"Please," I begged. "Please, not this." A tear rolled down my cheek, and as if that broke something inside of me, I crouched down on the ground bawling. And of course, when I did that, my biggest supporter—my best friend—came running over to lick my face.

Cash.

"We can't do it," I whispered into his fur.

But that night, Mama had me go out to look for firewood, and when I came back, it was already done. I knew she and Milt would try to do it, but not the same day she told me. Even though she'd tried to prepare me, I wasn't ready.

Everyone else ate dinner that night, and I understood.

Of course, I understood.

But I was also angry.

So, so angry—so angry that I didn't eat a bite.

I had been praying, and praying, and praying, and I was being ignored. Tiny miracles here and there, sure, but never *enough*. After that, I don't know what happened, but I couldn't eat a single bite of any sort of meat. I couldn't be positive it wasn't Cash. In fact, I was relatively sure any scraps we had left *were* him.

Suddenly, we were back to where we were before Patrick Dolan's unexpected kindness. Mama was about to have to rob our very roof again in order to feed us, which meant we had some decisions to make. We could try to find more pine boughs and hope that when it warmed up during the day and the snow on top melted, it wouldn't drip down, soaking us all. We could hope that somehow, we'd survive the loss of our roof.

Or, we could go around begging.

Again.

Mama decided she couldn't do it.

"You aren't eating. Eliza's not eating. Milt and I. . .we talked it over," Mama said. "Our only move, our only option—" Mama gasped, like it was hard to say, and I remembered.

This woman, this woman who had been making all the hard decisions was so frail that she was married from her bed. She climbed into the wagon when we first set out with Papa's help. She spent more time lying down in the bed of our family wagon than helping with household chores.

This woman was standing in front of me, holding our whole family together. Maybe the miracles weren't as small as I thought. Maybe it's hard to see them all sometimes when you're part of them, when you're surrounded.

"What is it, Mama? You can tell me."

"I think you and me, Milt and Eliza, I think we have to try and cross the mountains."

I blinked. "But the snowshoe party," I said. "They already went."

"It's been more than three weeks." Her eyes were grim.

I did the math in my head. It had been. . .I tallied it up. It had been just over three weeks. "But maybe it took more than six days for them to get to Sutter's Fort. Maybe it took them two weeks to reach Sutter's Fort," I said. "And maybe Papa will need some time to get a rescue effort put together, and then they need time to cross as well. We just need to be patient."

"We only have two hides left." Mama's voice was soft. "Two hides will last us. . ." She shrugged. "A few weeks, but we won't have a place to stay. Already, that side of the cabin is uninhabitable."

She was right. The place under where we'd removed the hide was constantly wet and we all avoided it. And that was the part of the roof that was the best without the hides.

"But that's all we have," Milt said. "No more meat. Nothing else at all."

Eliza and I couldn't really tolerate the hides well, and when that truth sank in, I realized what Mama was saying. Even if what I said was true, we were going to die before Papa could even get here.

"And we have to face the possibility that. . ." Mama choked. "They may not have made it. Your father might not even know. . ." Milt hugged her and she collapsed against his chest.

"It's okay, Ma," Milt said.

Mama was only four years older than him, but like all of us children, he looked to her to save us. I can't even imagine how stressful that was. And that's when I realized that she meant to leave our two hides here, along with my younger siblings.

"You're going to offer the Graves the hides if they'll keep Patty and James and Thomas."

Mama didn't disagree. "I hope they'll take them. The hides might be enough to keep them alive until your father can come."

I'd heard stories of old people walking off into the wilderness to spare their families the burden of caring for them. That's what we were doing. "You don't think we can make it, do you?"

"We stand the best chance," Milt said. "We'll only get weaker if we wait, and the weather's clear."

So that's what we did.

The Graves would only take little James, so we ripped one of the hides out of the roof and dragged it to the Breens. We convinced them to take Patty and Thomas along with that one hide. They weren't pleased—no one was, us least of all, but they agreed. So on January fourth, Milt, Eliza,

Mama, and I all walked through the snow drifts and along the line of Truckee Lake. When we camped at the base of the mountain, I realized this was going to be harder than I realized.

It was just *so* cold.

And it was so very far.

The snow was so deep that sometimes it came up above my shoulders. I had to thrash and push and claw my way out. I thought about our snow-shoe party, and for the first time, I allowed myself to consider that even with God's help, they might have all died.

Papa really might not even know we were here.

The next morning, Eliza Williams, a woman I'd known since I was three and a half years old, could barely walk. "I can't," she whispered. "I just can't go any farther."

I looked behind us, where we'd forged a trail through the snow. "Backward," I said. "Don't lie down and die. Walk backward. You can do that."

She shook her head. "There's nowhere for me to go. No one will take me in."

"The Breens took in Augustus Spitzer when he fell on their doorstep. The Graves took in Amanda McCutchen." I thought about the Donners, and how they'd kept their teamsters out of their lean-tos and not shared their food.

But surely the Breens, the Graves, and the Murphys wouldn't do that.

Levinah Murphy had as little as we did. But the Breens and the Graves. . .surely one of them would take her in. "Just walk back," I said. "You can do it."

I was a little jealous as I watched her head back.

Unlike her, I had to continue on. We'd already imposed on the Breens and the Graves too many times. The only way for me was forward. We made it to the base of the mountain, and I realized it was the same point where we had tried on All Hallows Day and failed.

It looked so different.

It was almost unrecognizable.

We struggled on, flailing and sinking in the snow, then sliding down and crashing into snowdrifts. Milt and Mama kept me going. If they could go, so too could I.

Until, on the third day, I tried to move and had no energy left.

I couldn't lift my arm.

I couldn't drag my leg out of the terrible weight of the snow into which it was sunk.

I was done.

Like Eliza two days ago, I couldn't go another step. I sank back and closed my eyes.

"Virginia," Mama called.

I was as ready as I was going to be. Mama had as much as told me that we couldn't stay in camp. She knew that coming out here meant dying, but here we were. I had no doubt that our brave snowshoe party was also dead. Maybe they were directly underneath me. We'd have no way to know, because of the cursed snow that wouldn't ever stop.

For all we knew, even Papa might be out here somewhere, frozen. The more I thought about it, the more likely it seemed. Papa wouldn't have given up, but he hadn't come. That had to mean something, right? Maybe he had come, but had died trying.

I heard the howling of wolves in that moment, and I thought it was fitting. I hadn't been able to save Cash or any of our other dogs. Maybe when I died, the wolves would eat me, and then we'd be even. I'd have given back what I stole. It was a low thought, but once I thought it, there was no going back. I was in a low, low place.

I cursed God then, under my breath.

I felt better for a moment, and then I felt much worse.

I felt like I had to explain.

"I prayed, God. I prayed, and I prayed, and here I am. Dying. I hope you're ready for me, because when I do get up there, wherever you are, I have a *lot* of things to say to you, and you may not want to hear them all, but by golly, I'm saying every last one of them."

Just as I thought I was actually dying, Mama wrenched me backward. Milt's hands rubbed and chafed and scratched me so hard I cried out. "Stop!"

"You can't give up," Milt said. "You're not allowed. Your pa would never forgive me."

"I can't," I whispered. "I can't even feel my feet anymore."

Mama's expression, when she glanced at Milt, was bad. "What does that mean?"

He shrugged, and they both pulled until they dragged me up and flat on the snow. They poked and prodded at my feet, which I knew because I could see them, but I couldn't feel any of their movements.

"It's bad, right?" I asked. "They hurt so bad yesterday that every step was agony, but now?" I shook my head, shoving snow right and left. "Nothing."

Mama's shoulders slumped, her raw, red face as defeated as I'd ever seen it. Her lips were cracked and bleeding, and the blood had frozen in a strange, ragged line down her chin. I imagined it hurt her just to talk. "We have to go back."

Milt didn't argue.

I couldn't walk.

Neither of them could carry me.

So I crawled back, one jerky, miserable movement at a time. My feet had no feeling, but my knees—those hurt like they were being stabbed with tiny ice knives. My head ached, and black spots stole my vision, sometimes for ten or fifteen minutes at a time.

I passed out in the snow at least two times that first day.

We had traveled nearly three full days away from camp. Thankfully, because we'd packed the snow down on our way out, what I told Eliza was true. It was much easier to go back to our lake cabins. We were just past the lake when my small reserve of energy gave out.

That's when Milt carried me.

I don't know how he did it. He was as exhausted, as starved, and as miserable as I was. His hands were blackened in some places, and I knew that was bad. Several of my toes looked just like that where my moccasins had shredded and given way to the ice and snow.

Two days after we turned around, we reached the lake cabins. The cabins looked strange after days away—foreign somehow. I saw them for the first time as dirty little holes underneath snow as far as the eye could see.

I could make out places where the tops of trees had been lopped off. And there were other small signs, if you knew what to look for. The places, near each residence, where chamber pots had been dumped. The wood piles.

But when we passed out on the Breen family doorstep, I could dimly hear them arguing. I was not asleep, but I was also not quite awake. We'd been on the brink of starvation when we left. Five days of exertion without food hadn't helped matters, and I feared that if they took us in, we'd just die in front of them by way of thanks.

"Tell Eddie it's okay," I mumbled. "Just put me where the wolves can get me. I owe them that for eating Cash."

In the end, the Breens took us in.

Me, Mama, James, Patty, and little Thomas, whom Milt went and fetched from the Graves. The Graves, after losing James, agreed to keep Eliza. Milt, who longed to stay as near to us as he could, decided to stay with the Murphys. He could cut wood and start fires for them, as well as brush snow off their roof. The Breens gave one of our last two hides to us, but we didn't have the strength to go and fetch the one from the half of the cabin we'd abandoned near the Graves.

One ox hide and a pile of bones were all that stood between us and starvation.

I hadn't died out there in the snow, but I decided that I would stop eating the hide goo entirely so that more would be left for Mama and the little ones.

Instead of recovering, I was moving the other way.

I lay in the corner, sipping water every now and then, but otherwise, not moving. Without eating, I found that I didn't even need to use the bathroom. At all, really. I was peacefully drifting, while Mr. Breen read from the book of Luke. I was almost asleep, and I thought I might never wake up again. They had placed me near the chimney, which was warm, but it was also close enough to the door that I heard Mama and Mrs. Breen talking.

To my surprise, they were talking about me.

"She's such a strong girl," Mama said. "I'm not going to rush her. She'll recover at her own pace."

"That's why I called you out here." I heard a strange sort of shushing sound. "She's not eating, at all, Margaret. I think it's on purpose. She gave her dinner last night to Patty, and I saw her hand her breakfast to Thomas. I think you need to prepare yourself. I doubt she'll make it another day."

Mrs. Breen was too observant. It would have been much easier if she hadn't told Mama. I would have slipped away, and that would have been that. One less mouth to siphon off the last of our remaining food. As it was, Mama began to sob, and I had to hear it, thanks to where I was lying.

I flipped over then, which was hard. Much harder than it should have been. When I did, I came face to face with Eddie. He was staring at me with wide eyes, and I realized that he too had heard.

"Eat this." He had a small plate, laden down with small, minced pieces of meat.

I shook my head. "It's yours."

"You will eat this, Virginia Reed, or I will hold your nose and shove it down your throat." He wasn't crying. He didn't even look sad.

He looked angry.

"Eddie." I closed my eyes, too tired to argue. "Just go away."

"Last week, Augustus Spitzer came back, you know. That terrible man died right there, where you're lying right now. He *died*, Virginia, and you are not going to do the same."

"Eddie, please stop."

He grabbed my arm and squeezed. "You're nothing but bones. We all are, but you're going to eat this, and you're going to live, because your mother and your siblings are dangling by a thread, and you're the strongest Reed. Do you hear me?" He leaned closer. "They need you more than they need an extra helping of boiled ox hide."

"But we're almost out of that," I said. "And it's not just one helping. It's every helping I would eat." I managed to sit up, my eyes sparking, my anger kindled. "What do you know?"

"I know you need to eat this now, before my pa realizes what's going on." He shoved the plate at me one more time, and I smelled it.

That was all it took.

Pride is strong, right up until you're starving, and then your resolve becomes as weak as, well, as mine was in that moment. I gobbled down the bits of beef, and then I collapsed back on the dank pine boughs I now knew had been the last resting place of a recently deceased man.

"Alright God," I prayed as silently as I could. "Here's my one last deal."

He didn't answer. He never did.

"The Breens, the stupid, stubborn, irritating, wholesome, always-right Breens are the best people I've ever met." Tears welled up in my eyes, even though they were squeezed shut. "If you will grant me this last wish, if you will save me, and my mother, and my three siblings, I will pay you with my immortal soul. When we reach California, I'll join the Catholic church and be baptized, and I'll raise all my little babies to be good Catholics, just like the Breens."

When He still said nothing, I opened one eye and looked around.

Mrs. Breen was staring right at me.

"That's my last and final offer, God," I muttered. "Take it or leave it."

"He'll take it," Mrs. Breen said. "Now make sure you eat." She turned and walked out the door again.

The next few days were long ones.

The Breens, at least, had several books, but they read them over and over. Poor Mrs. Breen's throat sounded almost raw from all the reading. Her husband read the Bible, but she read everything else. Two or three days after I made my offer to God, Mrs. Breen caught Eddie bringing me bits of meat.

Both of us froze, unsure how she'd react.

She smiled, and later that day, she handed me a book to read. It had three small pieces of meat pressed inside of it. She winked.

I liked her before, but I loved her then. God may not be real, but the Breens were.

Maybe that was enough.

CHAPTER 25

Mary Ann Graves

Somehow I missed it, but during the interminably long, miserable blizzard, one of the men was cutting a log into pieces and the axe got stuck. In the process of yanking the blade free, the handle broke away from the blade. The head went flying and disappeared into the snow.

Without an axe, we had no way to cut logs.

As if that wasn't bad enough, upon emerging from our storm-induced huddle, we realized that everything not in the center of our blanket circle with us. . .was gone. We spent the next few hours searching and searching for the axe head, our lost packs, our heavy snowshoes, and for many of us, our discarded boots.

It was while we were all getting up and moving that I realized William Foster wasn't. His wife Sarah had been fretting for some time, it seemed, bringing him her blanket and trying to chafe his arms into better circulation.

"What's wrong?" I asked, remembering when we did the same for Pa, without a great result.

"He can't move his arms and legs," Sarah Foster said. "I think he's just stiff from sitting still for so long."

I hoped rather than believed she was right.

He did finally stand, half an hour or so later, and he joined our search.

We found six pairs of snowshoes and one single one, and we found two of the missing pairs of boots. We also found three blankets and two packs, not that they had much in them, but we never found the axe head.

"Without an axe, what are our options?" my sister Sarah asked.

"We'll have to gather pine branches to burn," William Eddy said. "It's the only way we can start a fire."

"But it'll sink," William Foster said. "What good will that do?"

"Maybe we can use a pile of branches to set a tree on fire," Mr. Eddy said.

Lemuel Murphy, eager to do something to help, snapped a dry pine branch off and somehow, the movement dislodged a mouse. The dark little creature darted off and away, but Lemuel was faster. He caught it in his hands, staring at his clasped palms intently. He swallowed slowly, but never looked away from his prize.

"What should we do with it?" William Foster, his brother-in-law, asked.

With wide eyes, Lemuel finally looked around at all of us, and then he shoved the whole, live mouse into his mouth. I could hear it struggling as he chewed and then swallowed.

Aghast, my jaw dangled open.

"Well, I suppose that's one way to eat it," Jay said, clearly as surprised as I was at the whole ordeal.

One thing that no one talked about and all of us avoided even looking at were the dead bodies. Patrick Dolan, Antonio, and my father had all died in the course of that cursed storm. Hypothermia hadn't helped matters, but I suspected that they had died mainly because they didn't have enough energy for their bodies to generate heat.

We'd all gone more than six days without eating.

Well, all of us except Lemuel, anyway.

And, we'd been starving for two solid months before we left, one minute, one hour, and one day at a time. My father had begged us to eat him. Patrick Dolan had suggested that we draw lots and *kill* someone in order to survive as a group. Antonio had participated willingly in the lottery.

Now they were all dead.

We had no idea how far we had yet to go, or how long it would take us to reach Sutter's Fort, but we did have three bodies in front of us. I think if it had been left to Sarah and me, we never would have eaten our father, in spite of his last pleas.

But we weren't alone.

As the sun began to set, William Eddy found a tree that was mostly dead, the branches dry and crumbly in spite of the storm, and the sides of the trunk coated with pine sap. After months of using pitch pine torches in our miserable cabins, we knew what the presence of pine sap meant. We had no axe, but William Eddy, not even healed from the burns on his face and hands from several days before, lit that pine tree on fire.

It only warmed us for a while before it had burned down below the snow level, but it was a welcome warmth while it lasted. It also meant that we'd devised a way to cook the meat, by spearing it and suspending it over the pine tree as it burned down below.

If any of us could butcher the dead, we could cook them.

That night, as we all lay down to sleep, poor Lemuel Murphy, his stomach apparently stimulated by the addition of the mouse, began to shriek in agony. "It hurts, it hurts! My stomach!" He clawed at his belly for a few moments, groaning, and then he stood up.

We'd made a tent of sorts, taking the blankets of the deceased and hanging and draping them around the branches of nearby trees to block the wind. Before Lemuel could dart away from us entirely, his sister, Sarah Foster, who had been so worried about her husband earlier in the day, grabbed him by his arms and dragged him back into the middle of our camp.

He kept screaming, "Give me my bone," and then he started trying to bite poor Sarah. Their sister Harriet and Sarah's husband both stepped in to help, but it was a painfully long time before poor, tortured little Lemuel finally settled down.

Sometime after midnight, when a batch of clouds had passed in front of the stars, blocking out nearly all the light but the flickering of the barely visible parts of the burning pine tree, Lemuel Murphy died.

William Foster dragged his body out by the other three.

We had started out with fifteen people in our snowshoe party, but now we were down to just ten. We still had no idea where we were. But now, at least, we had food.

The next morning, when we woke up, no one said a thing, but

William Eddy went to work, his knife flashing in the sunlight as he butchered the dead members of our party.

I felt like a coward as I hid near the edge of the camp, standing behind our tent to block the bloody, disturbing view. Mostly, I just couldn't stomach the sight of my own father, sliced and diced into something edible.

The thought of it turned my stomach.

Salvador and Luis weren't impressed either. Unlike me, they had the strength and fortitude to stand up and walk away. In fact, they moved so far away that we could barely see them. They took with them a little of Mr. Eddy's gunpowder and nothing else.

But the smell of roasting meat. . .I'm not proud of it. My brother-in-law Jay Fosdick, William Eddy, and William Foster did most of the worst parts, carefully assigning to each man work that had nothing to do with their direct family.

"I'll take Lemuel," William Eddy said, a sick look on his face.

"I'll take Antonio," Jay offered. "And I suppose we can share Patrick Dolan."

"And I'll deal with Mr. Graves," William Foster said.

"If we're all careful, we can be sure that no family members. . ." William Eddy trailed off, and I shuddered.

But that's exactly what they did. Over the next two days, we butchered and ate as much of the men as we could, and then we dried the rest as best we were able. We loaded it into the packs that had not been lost, and after almost a week in the same place, we started moving again.

For the first time in a very long time, my head didn't ache.

My arms and legs had enough energy to move without trembling muscles, and agony in all my joints. My stomach was unsteady and grumbling, but even that felt good after so long without anything in it at all.

That first day moving again, we manage to travel four miles or so.

It felt like a hundred, honestly, after being stuck in the same miserable place for so long, and after losing so many of our dear family and friends. The next day, the last day of the year, we traveled nearly six miles by William Eddy's reckoning.

The last mile was the very hardest. We crossed a gorge so steep that our bodies strained to clear it. In places, we had to grab hold of plants growing from the cracks in the rocks just to pull ourselves up and over. With every second, I expected the winter-ravaged, dead roots to give out, plunging me to my death.

Sometime that day, after clearing the gorge, with enough open space to move in all directions, Luis and Salvador left us. I wondered whether they had been looking for a way to escape for quite some time.

On the first day of the year, we ran out of food again.

We traveled as far as we could each day after that, but on our fifth day without food, we started to eat our own shoelaces. It wasn't like they were doing us any good, really. Our shoes were such a disgrace that the laces were doing us no good anymore.

Most of us now barefoot, we stumbled onward through the snow. But on that day, the day we shared four pairs of shoelaces for dinner, Jay Fosdick, my sister's husband, began to fall behind. Sarah stayed with him, guiding him because now that we were moving again, he had gone entirely blind from the brilliance of the snow.

They didn't reach our camp for several hours after we stopped for the night.

"It's like Stanton," I whispered. "I'm worried."

"But what can we do?" Sarah asked.

Nothing.

There was nothing we could do.

We struggled on.

The next day, Jay fell even farther behind. I was debating whether to fall back and look for my sister and her husband, or continue on like the day before when I heard it.

A gunshot.

I stumbled ahead, desperate to know what had been fired upon. Not a quarter mile ahead, I saw blood-red snow.

"I did it." William Eddy pumped his arm in the air. "I got a deer."

He had already found a pine and lit it on fire, and William Foster was butchering the beast. My mouth began to water just thinking of food, but I had another reason to celebrate.

With renewed vigor, I turned around and headed back, searching in earnest for Sarah. I called her name. I called for Jay, too. But when I found her, my heart sank.

The deer had been found too late.

Jay Fosdick was already dead.

Sarah was nearly insensible, so distraught had she become. She was rocking back and forth where she was standing over him, sobbing and saying words that made no sense.

"Sarah," I said. "Sarah!"

She finally turned toward me, and I pointed. "William Eddy shot a deer."

My dear, sweet sister sat down then, cradled her dead husband's head on her lap, and started to sob, great, heaving tears. "No, no. No. No."

At first, she wouldn't even consider leaving him, but eventually I coaxed her away. By the time we reached the camp, we could smell it. The deer's organs were being roasted on a branch already.

After Sarah had eaten, I broke the news to the others. "Jay is dead."

William Eddy, our hero and savior, looked up, eyes wide. "Can we eat him?"

My jaw dropped. "But you just shot a deer."

"A deer that's already half gone," he said. "Split among seven starving people." He lowered his voice. "You and your sister can have the deer. We'll eat him."

I looked at Sarah, but she acted like she hadn't even heard us. It was one of the hardest things I had ever done, but I forced the words out. "Sarah, can we? Is it okay?"

Sarah dropped her face in her hands, but she didn't say no. The men took that as assent. When, later in the day, they began roasting Jay's organs —liver, heart, kidneys—Sarah stood up and walked away. I chased after her, worried.

"Are you alright?"

She kept walking, only stopping once she had walked quite some distance away. She dropped to her knees and braced her hands a little farther apart than her knees in the snow.

"What is it?" I asked. "What can I do?"

We'd lost too many people I loved—Jay, Pa, Mr. Dolan and Antonio, poor Lemuel. Knowing we ate them, well, it made it worse, but it didn't change the real pain. They were gone. I couldn't lose Sarah too, and I was worried. She loved Jay *so* much, and she'd always been Pa's favorite. How much could one person take before giving up?

When Sarah finally lifted her head, I wasn't at all surprised to see a single tear on her cheek. "I smelled him," she whispered. "I knew it was him, and I wanted nothing to do with it, but. . ." She shook her head. "I had to move away, or, or. . .I would have. . ." She burst into tears then. "What's wrong with me? I'm a monster."

I wrapped my arms around her. "No, you're not. You're starving, and even so, you walked out here and away. I'll bring you more of the deer."

I hugged her for a while, and then I went and got her more to eat. She and I ate away from the others that night, but after the most vital parts were through, we went back to camp. Sarah kept her eyes averted, but she didn't break down again.

Neither of us had the energy for it.

We'd fall apart later, once we reached Sutter's Fort. We'd fall apart once we'd let people know that our families were in danger. We'd fall apart once we saved the others and not a minute before.

Four days later, our meager supply of what we could dry before we started moving again was gone, and once again, we had no food at all. We pressed forward anyway.

The next day, as we struggled, I noticed that Sarah's feet were leaving bloody, red streaks on the ground that was now as much rock as it was snow. I cried out in alarm. "Sarah! Your feet!"

She turned and looked and tilted her head. "Yours have been doing that for two days." She turned around and kept going.

That evening, as the sun began to set, we heard another gunshot. Then there was a second one right after the first. Sarah and I hurried, Amanda McCutchen just behind us.

All of us hoped beyond reason for another deer. Would two be wickedly greedy? But when we reached Eddy, William and Sarah Foster beside him, they weren't looking at a deer.

It was Salvador and Luis, our guides.

They'd left us, it's true, but we had resorted to cannibalism. I couldn't really blame them. Unlike us, they didn't have family trapped by the lake, their lives resting on them for survival. They could afford to take the moral high ground.

But. . .had William Eddy *killed* them? The thought made me ill. My hands began to tremble, and my head began to pound even more than it was.

"They were half dead already," William Foster said. "Both of them were entirely unconscious, their breathing ragged and labored. It was a mercy."

I didn't know whether to believe him or not, but his wife nodded, and William Eddy didn't disagree. Sarah and I hung back, unsure what to do. But when the smell of meat roasting hit our noses. . .

We kept going.

Two days later, when we reached a camp made by Miwok Indians, I remembered that Luis and Salvador were Miwok. Were we walking into their camp with packs full of their family members' remains? The thought horrified me. Thankfully, they asked us no questions, and they didn't investigate any of our belongings.

They simply invited us into their tents, no questions asked. We didn't deserve it. They should have beaten us, or killed us outright, but they didn't know. I should've been riddled with guilt over what we had done, probably, but I wasn't. For the first time in nearly a full month, I lay down on something other than snow and icy rocks, and I fell asleep beside a fire. When I awoke, a woman with kind eyes was cleaning my feet. It felt like she was pouring oil on them and setting them on fire.

I scrambled backward, crying out.

She stopped, but she looked at me with sad eyes from then on. When they offered us bowls of some kind of mash, I glanced around. The women were cracking and rolling acorns into some kind of paste. It reminded me a little of the boiled hides, but I was hungry enough to eat anything. They could have brought me caterpillars, and I would have tried them.

It wasn't delicious, but it was edible.

I ate three bowls.

The next day, after resting for nearly a day and a half, I forced myself back to my feet. That's when I realized that the key to our forward movement was the snow. The ice had numbed my mangled feet enough that I could walk on them.

Now, after recuperating for more than a day, I found that each step, each shift or tiny movement, was agony unlike any I'd felt before. Even so, I had family that were depending on me. They were starving slowly, and if I wanted any hope of saving them, of sparing them the same decisions I'd had to make, I had to keep going.

I could tell Sarah's feet hurt as well, and watching her take one step and then another gave me the strength I needed to do the same. I walked for two days, slowly, at a halting pace, before I collapsed. I couldn't go one more inch.

And I wasn't alone.

Next to me, Amanda McCutchen, Sarah Foster, my sister Sarah, William Foster, and Harriet Pike had all collapsed or stumbled to a halt.

"I can't go on," I said feebly. I didn't even have enough energy to yell.

"I'll go," William Eddy said.

And he did.

While the rest of us collapsed on the ground, spreading blankets and tents where we could, he stumbled onward.

I'm not even sure how long it was before the others came, but we were all still alive when they did show up. Somehow, in the next day or so, William Eddy reached Johnson's Ranch. He told them that there were more of us waiting not twenty miles behind him.

The first thing I asked, after I ate a large hunk of bread, was, "What day is it?" We had long since lost track of the days, but I knew every minute mattered to our family back at Truckee Lake.

"It's January seventeenth," a man said.

When I was finally able to focus on his face, I realized he was someone I knew. Matthew Dill Ritchie was a colonel who had fought with James Reed, Virginia's father, in the Black Hawk War, and he had traveled with us for much of the first part of our trek west.

"Mary Ann Graves." Mr. Ritchie handed me a canteen of water. "Sip this and tell me something. I heard the Reed family was with you—are they yet alive?"

I nodded slowly, too overwhelmed to talk. We hadn't even reached Sutter's Fort. We were almost forty miles away at a place called Johnson's Ranch, and it had taken us *thirty-one* days to find help. Everyone back home must have given up on us by now.

"Miss Graves?" Mr. Ritchie's brow furrowed. "Mr. Eddy was exhausted, but I can go and find him and ask him instead."

"You don't need to do that. They were alive when we left." I forced what I thought was a nice smile. "Thank you," I finally said. "Thank you for caring and helping, and just thank you." I cleared my throat. "Thank you."

Mr. Ritchie patted the top of my head, but I could tell he wasn't sure what to say. I'm sure I sounded at least a little bit crazy. We probably all did.

A moment later, a woman with bright red hair arrived carrying a bucket and a large bundle. She set both down near my bed, and glanced over me, taking in my shredded clothing and my filthy, exposed body. I had hardly even noticed, not having changed my clothing or bathed since we became entrapped.

I'm sure my smell alone was utterly intolerable.

"I brought warm water and soap." She pulled a bar of soap from her pocket and set it near the bucket. "I can stay and help, or I can leave."

"Are those. . ." I eyed the bundle and then looked back at her.

"Clothing," she said. "I'm sure it will be too large, but it's what I had."

She'd brought me her own clothes.

As I finally cleaned off some of the stench and filth that had become a permanent fixture in my life and slid my abused and skeletal arms and legs into new garments, I decided that in some ways, the clothing was more important than the food.

Food keeps you alive, but it's not what makes you human.

Once I dressed, they brought me stew and bread. I had just eaten, however. "I can't possibly eat more," I said. "I just ate."

"That was four hours ago," the woman said with a strange expression. "It's time to eat again, for all of us."

It had been so long since I'd had a regular meal that four hours between feeding times felt almost incomprehensible. Once I had even more food in my belly, my top priority was finding some kind of doctor. The bucket bath I'd had made one thing very clear.

My feet were in very bad shape.

Between frostbite and the lacerations I'd inadvertently acquired from walking a hundred miles without boots, I'd had to be carried the last fifteen miles to Johnson's Ranch. Even now, relatively clean and wearing new clothing, I couldn't stand. Any attempt I made was met with terrible and radiating pain.

The closest thing to a medical professional they could find came and cleaned my feet again, but not the way I had done it. He used a strange sort of rough cloth and scrubbed and scrubbed and scrubbed. After a few moments, the pain became so bad that I passed out, which was a mercy.

When I awoke, my feet were bandaged, but I still couldn't stand. I had to be carried to go to the restroom.

Thankfully, we had been found by the kindest people I'd ever met. They patiently and generously tended to Sarah and me, as well as the others. Amanda McCutchen, Harriet Pike, and Sarah Foster were all given new clothes and bathed. Their feet were bad, but not as terrible as mine. Their boots hadn't disintegrated quite so early.

A few days later, another surprise that I didn't expect showed up. One of my favorite people from the trail before we took the cursed Hastings cutoff came to visit. It was John Stark, my friend Mary Jane Ritchie Stark's husband. The one whose father-in-law had insisted on traveling to Oregon. I probably shouldn't have been surprised, as John Stark's wife was Colonel Ritchie's daughter, and I'd already seen the Colonel.

"You're alive." John exhaled sharply upon seeing me. "Mary Jane will be so pleased. She's asked around about you, you know. We were worried when we found out your party hadn't yet made it across."

I grabbed his hand, which was as huge and beefy as ever. "Did they tell you?"

"That your families are still there, stuck in the mountains?" His face was earnest.

That moment was the first true relief I'd felt since our arrival.

"I heard," he said. "Rest assured that we're preparing a plan to save them. I was enlisted in the war with Mexico—I'm sure you've heard about that, but my daughter Leah's fallen ill, so they gave me leave. As soon as I make sure she's alright, I'll ask for permission to join James Reed on his attempt to cross the mountain."

"Leah's ill?" His oldest was only five or six years old, and she was the sweetest little girl. She had loved playing dolls with my sister Nancy when we were traveling together.

"I'm on my way to check on her now," he said. "But I had to at least stop by. I hope you'll understand why I can't stay long."

"Of course," I said.

He told me how his twin daughters were doing—they were quite naughty and always getting into things they shouldn't—and then described their fat-cheeked baby son. "He's going to be walking soon," he said with pride.

"Thank you," I said. "For reminding me about life before."

He dropped his hand on mine one last time, and then he left, saluting me on his way out.

I fell back in my bed after that and closed my eyes.

It had been the worst month of my entire life in every way I could imagine, but he had confirmed that Mr. Reed was rallying support and would be headed into the mountains soon. We had done it. Help was *finally* on the way.

Pa would be proud.

CHAPTER 26
Peggy Breen

I hadn't done much with math in my life.

When I made biscuits or bread, I knew how much of each ingredient to add by feel. As my family grew, I made more. I didn't use math for anything, really, other than buying supplies. I had to know what things cost, and how much we needed, but most of the purchasing was done by my husband.

Lately, though, everyone's been downright obsessed with math.

The snowshoe party left on December sixteenth. It's now the twenti-eth-first of January. It was supposed to be a six-day trip, even with the snow. Charles Stanton said he crossed the mountains in two and a half days and then spent another two long days traveling from there to Sutter's Fort. Our mountaineers, on which are resting all our hopes, left with enough food for a day or two, under the reckoning of the start of our jour-ney. They were hoping to stretch it to last six days.

If they took longer to reach Sutter's Fort, they would be traveling with nothing to eat.

It has been thirty-seven days.

When we first took the Reed family in, we all hoped and prayed that rescuers would soon arrive to bring food and help us over the cursed mountains. Since that time, with five extra mouths to feed and only one hide and some bones to add to our stores, no one has come. Not a single solitary sparrow. By any reckoning at all, if travelers from the snowshoe party survived, someone should have come to our aid by now.

Even if they took ten days to reach help, and the rescuers had to make preparations but took six days to come back, they should have been here already.

It was starting to look like no one was coming.

"You have to stop sharing," Patrick whispered, though with the wind whipping around our heads out here, there was no way anyone could overhear.

"I'm barely sharing anything at all," I said, "and when I do share, it's only hides."

"Our supply of those is dwindling, too." My husband's face had aged terribly in the months we'd been entrapped. His kidney stones had worsened, which seemed impossible, given that we'd been eating almost nothing.

"What exactly do we have?" he asked.

"Part of one single ox," I said, "and about six hides, including the four covering the roof."

His jaw dropped and he looked utterly sick. "Less than one ox left?"

"We also have a few cups of sugar, a half a bag of coffee beans, and a few handfuls of beans meant for seed."

He closed his eyes, and I knew he was saying a silent prayer. He did that a lot. When he opened them, his expression had not softened. "I forbid you to share another bowl of anything with the Reeds. They are staying in our cabin, and that is already a kindness, but if no one comes, we'll barely survive until April."

I shook my head. "We won't survive until April. Whether we share or not, if no one comes, we'll all starve."

Patrick was adamant—no more sharing.

Which meant I had to do it when he was gathering wood or tending the fire. We'd been through a lot, but one thing I would never do was watch a mother and her four destitute children starve to death under my roof.

One day later, on January twenty-second, another blizzard hit, which was always miserable, but we had wood stockpiled, and we were beyond worrying over the smell in the cabin. We all stank so badly that there was no helping it.

But.

Having everyone locked in one room made it impossible to sneak food to the Reeds.

Virginia and her mother had nothing to eat but boiled bones and the broth from them. They kept the younger children from speaking about the food I'd been sharing, but they couldn't stop them from crying and sobbing in hunger. My heart broke. And the next day, the second day of the blizzard, little Lewis Keseberg Junior, who had been born on the trail, died. Even over the screaming wind, we could hear his poor mother, wailing like, well, like her newborn son had died.

There was nothing we could do but ache for her.

When the storm finally relented, Patrick stood up. "I'm taking John, and we're going over to the Graves cabin." He frowned.

"Why?" Margaret Reed asked.

"You have another hide there," he said. "It's time you recovered it. Your family clearly has need of it."

"Mrs. Graves won't give it back," Margaret Reed said. "We already went over for it, and we'd only cut a small part off when she came over and started yelling."

"It's not her hide," John said. "Let her yell."

The second John and Patrick walked out the door, I leapt to work. The poor Reed children could barely sit up after three days with nothing but bone broth.

"Here," I said, thrusting a bowl at Virginia first. "Eat quickly."

She shook her head. "I'm not even hungry anymore. My stomach stopped hurting yesterday. Let Patty or Mama have it."

I crouched in front of her and cupped the side of her face. "I'm giving them food, too. Now eat it as fast as you can."

Eddie was already walking over to sit beside her—he had tried valiantly to distract Patrick several times over the past few days so we could sneak them something, but my husband had been on high alert. "Quickly, now," he said. "Or Father will find out and be very angry."

Virginia's hands shook as she gulped down her bowl of boiled hide. "I forgot how disgusting it was." But she was smiling as she said it. "And I'm so, so grateful for it." Her eyes welled with tears.

Margaret shifted so her daughter could see her face. "No crying, now.

Patrick could return at any time. He mustn't know we were upset or that anything happened at all."

"He's going to realize that you're giving us food," I said. "Otherwise, we'd have perished within a week or two."

"Augustus Spitzer got almost nothing, especially when he came back," Eddie said. "He lived for weeks and weeks on bone broth, you know."

The first time Mr. Spitzer left, I was relieved. After all, he had confessed that he was a murderer. But when he returned. . .Patrick didn't want to take him in until I reminded him that we had made mistakes as well.

We all had.

I couldn't judge Mr. Spitzer any more than I could judge Patrick. Our job was to minister to those who suffered, and he certainly suffered. I did not give him any of our food, but I did make him bone broth. Watching him gnaw on old, crumbly bones, I felt that he was already being punished for his crime.

It might have been Mr. Wolfinger who was spared, honestly. It felt like all of us were being punished.

Even so, his death was the first my children witnessed up close, and if I had anything to do with it, they would never see the Reeds'. I sat down then and said a prayer that Patrick would at least be able to pry the Reeds' last hide from Mrs. Graves' fingers. They deserved that much.

I knew that Mrs. Graves didn't see it that way, however.

CHAPTER 27

Virginia Reed

Mrs. Graves wouldn't return our hide—Mr. Breen and his son John looked pretty disappointed when they returned.

"It was still there." John kept looking down at his hands. "On the roof, frozen in place, with one end covered in icicles, and she wouldn't let us remove it."

"We did cut two small pieces off before she stopped us." Mr. Breen tossed his head behind him. "We left them in the empty space near our own cache."

"That's a small relief," Mama said. "It's something, at least."

"Ma can use those pieces as a cover," Eddie said, smiling as he whispered to me. "Now, take this quickly." He handed me three small pieces of dried beef.

I shook my head.

"Don't argue," he hissed. "Even Mother might be upset if she saw." Then he hopped up and crossed to the shelf by the fire, grabbing a book after leaving the stolen meat with me. "I'll read."

As January ended, the days were much as they had been. Mrs. Breen snuck us food whenever she could, and we all survived, somehow. Eddie would occasionally share some of his slop or tiny pieces of beef with me, and every single time he did, I felt terribly guilty.

Mama and I had been so sure that Papa would come. It now seemed that the snowshoers must have all died, and that meant Papa didn't even know we were in such trouble. Mrs. Breen and her son had kept us all alive, but not everyone had someone like her to help. I worried the most about Milt Elliott and Eliza, whom we had no way to take care of.

Milt came to visit us as often as he could manage without upsetting the Breens, which worked out to a few times a week, when weather permitted. The Murphy cabin, built into the side of a rock, was quite close, much closer than the Graves. If he had any energy left after gathering and cutting wood for the Murphys, he would walk over to say hello.

On February first, he came over.

"Milt," I said, standing and brushing off my tattered and threadbare skirts. "You haven't come in three days."

Milt's face was gaunt, the bones of his face clearly visible. He looked terrible, with enormous bags under his eyes. After stepping through the door, he almost immediately collapsed to the dirt floor.

"What's wrong?" Mama crossed the room to stand beside him.

The Breens always tried to huddle on the far end when he came to give us privacy, but Mr. Breen was there that day, and he never did that. He just stared at us while we talked.

"The Murphys have been very kind, sharing anything they had with me, but last week, they consumed their last hide." He wasn't even looking at Mama. He was staring at his hands.

"Oh, no." Mama wasn't crying, but her shoulders were shaking, like her tears had all run out, but her body knew how it felt. "Milt. I'm so, so sorry."

"It's the same here," Mr. Breen said. "Mrs. Reed and her children ate their last hide this week, and all they've had was boiled bone soup and crumbly old bones since."

Milt looked up then. "That's the only thing we're eating too, but it's not enough." He shook his head. "Yesterday, Landrum died." His voice was flat—hard, even. Landrum was the oldest Murphy boy, and he had been doing all the hauling and wood-cutting and fire-making, along with Milt. I'm sure they'd become friends, and now a seventeen-year-old boy who had been strong and healthy. . .was just gone.

Mama crouched next to him and wrapped her arms around Milt, and he sobbed on her shoulder. "What can we do, Ma? What can we do?" He sounded entirely broken.

Our knight of the whip. Our genius with the oxen.

Our protector in Papa's absence.

My dear friend.

A flash of anger welled up inside of me, but anger takes energy, and it soon gave way to despair. What good did praying do? What good did anything do? Mrs. Breen really should save their food and stop sharing with us. We had nothing to offer Milt, because the food that was truly keeping us alive was already coming from the largesse of someone else. It hurt, watching Milt leave again that day. I worried I might not ever see him again.

Papa was either dead or he had no idea how bad things were.

Mrs. Breen kept sneaking us little bits of food, but I couldn't always bring myself to eat it. Sometimes I gave it to Patty or Mama, telling them my share was unfairly large.

And every day, it felt like there was more bad news.

The next week was the worst we'd had. First, Amanda McCutchen's babe died. Her mother wasn't even there to hold her. Given the lack of a rescue, we now feared the entire snowshoe party was probably dead. How big Bill McCutchen would hurt, I thought, when he found out. Two days later, William Eddy's baby died, little Maggie.

Eleanor Eddy still had a four-year-old son to care for, so when I heard about Maggie's death, I walked over to visit them. Milt didn't get up to greet me when I arrived, which was strange. He always smiled and stood and hugged me when I came.

He was lying in the corner of the room, almost like he was dead. I had brought a handful of beans for him, a gift from Eddie to me that I had hidden instead of eating, but I couldn't give them to him here, in front of the Murphys and Mrs. Eddy.

"Milt," I said. "Can you stand? Why don't we sit outside for a bit."

Milt turned his head toward me and pointed. Poor Mrs. Murphy was lying down on a stack of pine boughs with her children, but on the floor next to her, Eleanor Eddy was lying utterly still. It took me a moment before I realized why her eyes were open, and her small son was patting her and crying, but she wasn't moving.

She must have also died.

I couldn't take any more.

We'd all be better off dead than just watching all of this. After a moment, Milt shuddered and stood, and I helped him haul poor Mrs. Eddy's body out of the cabin. We didn't have the energy to bury her, so we simply dragged her up, up, and up a little more. Then we collapsed at the top of the entrance to the cabin and laid her on the snow. When I realized why that spot was a bit lower and flat, it made me sick.

It was the same place the Murphys had stored their oxen, and now Amanda McCutchen's baby, Eleanor, and Maggie Eddy were all lying next to one another. I couldn't help thinking about how Eleanor loved to sing, and that she had the most beautiful voice, like a songbird.

"At least poor James won't keep staring at her now," I said.

"And out here in the ice, she won't stink," Milt said.

I offered him the beans, but he refused them.

"You eat them," he said. "Please." He wrapped his hand around mine and squeezed. "I've always thought of you like a little sister, you know. With the Breens, you might actually. . ."

I did know. But I also knew that there was something wrong with Milt that day. His eyes were off. They were flat, and dark, and strange. Like he already looked dead, like he'd resigned himself to it.

"I'm not hungry anymore," Milt said. "You've been praying so much, that I thought I'd give it a go, and that's what I prayed for, that the hunger would go away." He smiled then, but it was macabre, and it made me profoundly sad. "God answered my prayer." He nodded slowly. "The aching, the gnawing hunger. . .it's gone."

I kept thinking about what he'd said, and I wasn't sure it was an answer to prayer. It felt like it was a very bad sign, that Milt wasn't hungry. What kind of starving person refuses food that's offered to them? Isn't that hunger a good thing? It tells us what we need. The more I thought about it, the more uncomfortable I got.

The next morning, I forced myself to walk over again. It was a very short trip, but it took me almost an hour to work up the energy to make it. When I arrived, I cried out. I couldn't help it. I'd never seen anything like this in my entire life. I never imagined I would.

"What happened?"

This time, it wasn't Milt who came to the doorway. It was poor Mrs. Murphy. She was only thirty-six, younger than Mama, but she looked much, much older. Her hair was stringy and thin. Her face had shrunken down to skin stretched over pronounced bones, just like Milt's.

She scared me, honestly.

I realized that the only reason Mama, Eddie, Mrs. Breen, and Mr. Breen and the others didn't scare me was that I saw them every day. When I came yesterday, I'd only seen Mrs. Murphy's back. Seeing her face, and comparing it to the one I knew from before, was terrible.

But the mess in front of their cabin was worse.

When I left their cabin yesterday, none of us had the energy to try and bury Mrs. Eddy, so we'd draped a worn and tattered quilt over her and Maggie to try and show some respect.

The wolves had shredded the quilt, along with one of her arms and most of her insides. The snow was spattered bright red in places, but there was a lot less blood than I would have expected. I stumbled back and tripped. When I righted myself, I realized that I'd tripped on her hand.

If I'd had anything in my stomach, I'd have retched, I was sure.

"Wolves," Mrs. Murphy said, clutching at the doorframe. "Wolves came last night. We heard them, but there was nothing we could do."

"I should have buried her," I said. "I was just so tired."

"We don't even have a shovel," Mrs. Murphy said. "We threw it out in the desert."

I stumbled my way home, sickened and miserable. What more could possibly happen to us?

The next day, Mr. Breen sent John over to bury the McCutchen babe, Maggie, and Mrs. Eddy's remains so no more wolves could eat them. John was gone for quite some time, and I began to worry. What would take him that long? Unlike the Murphys, the Breens were still fairly hale, if not energetic.

When John finally returned, he refused to meet my eye.

"What is it?" Mama asked. "You can tell us."

I braced myself to hear that wolves had dragged away the whole lot of them.

But when John finally looked up, he didn't say anything about wolves. "I buried the Eddys and the McCutchen baby." He swallowed. "And it took me some time, because I tried to bury Milt, too, but I didn't have enough energy." His look was pained, and I thought about how it must be for the Breens, taking on the task of helping everyone and not being able to do enough.

Never enough.

It looked like I was right. The absence of hunger was not a good thing. My dear friend Milt had died, and still no one had come to our aid. The next day, even the Breens began boiling bones to try and make the rest of their hides stretch. I worried that, thanks to their generosity, they might also run out of food before this winter would end.

"I hate it," Patty said after his first bowl of bone broth. "It tastes like water, but worse." Little Patrick Junior scrunched his nose. "I'd rather just have water."

"Wait until you have to eat the crumbly bones that have been boiled too many times." I pulled a face. "It tastes like I always imagined chalk would."

"Chalk?" Patty blinked.

"You know, dummy," Eddie said. "Chalk. The white sticks you used for writing letters at school."

"You've eaten that?" Now the little boy really looked appalled.

"Of course she hasn't," John said. "She said she *imagined* it tasted like that."

"Who imagines what chalk tastes like?" Patrick Junior asked.

Everyone laughed then. It wasn't even that funny, but we were all desperate for something to smile about. Just then, Mr. Breen came inside. He had taken his shovel over to the Murphy cabin to try and finish burying Milt Elliott. He didn't knock the snow off his boots and walk inside like he usually did.

He just stood in the doorway, unmoving.

"What's wrong?" Mrs. Breen stood up.

Mr. Breen blinked. "Mrs. Murphy, Levinah, she says. . ." He swallowed.

Mama stood up, her eyes wide. "What? What did she say?" Her look was pained, and like all of us, she was waiting to hear who else had died. "Have they heard from the Graves? Is everyone alright over there?"

We loved the Breens, and no one could possibly have been kinder, but we also missed the Graves. After spending months next door to them, they also felt like family. After losing Milt, we had to prepare ourselves. Would it be Eliza next? I had to know.

"Who?" I asked. "Just tell us."

He shook his head. "No one else has died that I heard, but Mrs.

Murphy told me not to bury Milt too deep, because. . .she said they're going to *eat* him."

Mama's shoulders drooped.

Mrs. Breen sat down.

John's jaw dropped open.

Eddie shrugged. "Maybe they should. It's better than the wolves getting him, isn't it?"

Mr. Breen's entire face contorted. "Of course it's worse! No God-fearing Christians can consume human flesh. It's an abomination."

"Where in the Bible does it say that?" Eddie asked. "I mean, if you find the verse, then sure, I'll agree with you. But I doubt the Bible really contemplated this situation, and it's not as if anyone killed him."

No one said a word after that, but Mr. Breen went right to the log-stump table and started scritching in his journal. Whenever I looked over his shoulder, he was writing about the weather, but I'd bet today's entry had something about Milt and Mrs. Murphy.

The more I thought about it, though, the more I agreed with Eddie and Mrs. Murphy. I was glad it hadn't come to it, but I didn't think it was worse to eat poor Milt than it had been to eat Cash. Or Brutus, for that matter.

Milt was already dead—he might have even suggested it himself, had he had the idea.

I took comfort as I crouched in the corner of the cabin, in petting the Breen's dog, Towser. He hadn't been eaten yet, and I hoped he wasn't. If people were dying anyway, we should eat them and not sweet little dogs.

After he finished writing in his journal, Mr. Breen spent hours poring over the Bible, and finally, just before bedtime, he slammed his hand down on the trunk next to the good book. "Here, in Second Kings, chapter six, verse twenty-nine, it talks about cannibalism. I knew it was in here somewhere."

Eddie stared at him.

"See," Mr. Breen said. "I told you."

"What does it say?" Eddie asked. "Read it."

"Yes, do," Mrs. Breen said.

"In Second Kings, what's going on?" Mama asked. "So it will make sense."

"Samaria is under siege," John said. "Right? And King Jehoram is wicked. That's Second Kings, right?"

Mr. Breen smiled. "Yes, that's right. Nice work."

"It's not like he had anything else to do in here but read the Bible," Eddie muttered.

"The verse I found is talking about how bad things had gotten," Patrick Breen said. "Here, I'll start with verse twenty-eight." He cleared his throat. "*This woman said unto me, Give thy son, that we may eat him today, and we will eat my son tomorrow. So we boiled my son, and did eat him, and I said unto her on the next day, Give thy son, that we may eat him, and she had hid her son.*" He shut the book. "As I said, it's an abomination."

"But the verse doesn't say that was the sin," Eddie said. "Does it? Isn't it about the women making a deal? They'd both share in eating their children because they were all starving? But then after eating the first child, the second woman reneged."

All of us stared at Eddie, but then we turned back to Mr. Breen.

When his father didn't respond, Eddie leaned over and picked up the Bible slowly, opening, presumably, to Second Kings. He peered at the words, struggling to read from the failing light of the pitch pine torch. After a moment, he looked up. "After that, it doesn't condemn the women. The king whom they were complaining to just walked off and said he wanted to kill the prophet Elisha's son."

Patrick Breen scowled. "Some things are so obvious they don't need to be spelled out. It would hardly be a terrifying story to teach us something if the women weren't doing something wrong."

Eddie frowned, but he stopped arguing.

The more I thought about it, the more I thought that if he had a say, Milt would want the Murphys to eat him. After all, if they didn't, the wolves would. It would be better if those small children took nourishment from him.

I thought God would understand, too, but I was glad we weren't stuck making choices like that. We still had a pile of bones, even if the bone broth was disgusting and not at all filling.

The very next day, though, there was a banging at the door. When Patrick opened it, Elizabeth Graves shoved her way past him. "I want the Reeds to come here and get their hide down."

"That's great news," Mr. Breen said. "John and I can even help them."

Mrs. Graves shook her head, her eyes wild. "No, not for them. I want it right *now*."

Mama straightened and glanced around, clearly wondering if any of the rest of us knew what she was talking about. "You do have it."

"I can't get it down. It's frozen in place. I want you to come and get it down, because you never even paid us for those oxen you took." She stamped her foot. "You never paid us!" She jabbed a finger at Mama. "You *stole* from us, and we're starving."

I stood and stepped in front of Mrs. Graves. "Please don't shout and jab at my mother."

Mrs. Graves acted like she hadn't even heard me, stepping around me to have a clear view of Mama. "Margaret Reed, you're nothing but a thief!" Mrs. Graves' face looked an awful lot like Levinah Murphy's, as if starvation was the best way to make us all look exactly the same. Her hair was wild, pointing up and out in all directions, and her skin was stretched so tightly, I could see her cheekbones. I wondered whether her gorgeous daughter, Mary Ann, had looked like a crazed skeleton before she died.

And then I caught myself.

Was it incontrovertible? Had the snowshoe party died? It was February eleventh, which meant they had left nearly two months before. It must have been true—they must have frozen on the mountain, or been eaten by wolves, or fallen down a gorge.

"We took in James, and then we took in Eliza. . ." She waved her arm through the air. "And now I can't get the hide down you promised me, and I want the meat back, too. We never should have sold you those two oxen." She balled her hands into fists. "I want them back!"

Mr. Breen stood up. "See here, now. You *did* sell them two oxen, same as me. That's the only reason they're still alive, and I'm happy they're alive. The Reeds are good people. They don't owe you anything."

"They never paid me," Mrs. Graves said. "Is that what good people do? They cheat others?" She stepped forward again, advancing on Mama, and the Breens' dog, Towser, growled mightily.

I already loved him, but now I loved him more.

"Get your mongrel away from me," Mrs. Graves said. "You should be as angry as me. Her husband must be dead, and thanks to our decision to share with her, we're all going to die too."

Mama blinked back tears. "I—I want to pay you back, and I would give you back the oxen if I could. I'm so very sorry."

That hurt, watching my mama be attacked and then hearing her apologize for it.

"I'll come with you." I stood up. "I'll help you get the hide down, and I'll help you cook the first parts."

I walked toward the door, and Mrs. Graves followed, her head lowered, her eyes no longer flashing.

"I'll come too," Eddie said. "I'll help."

"And me," John said.

We had walked no more than a few dozen yards when Mrs. Graves began to sob. "I'm sorry." She stopped walking. "I'm sorry." She shook her head.

I wrapped my arms around her, because I realized that she was scared, too. She was a mother, and she couldn't feed her children, and she was afraid. She was rethinking every decision they made, and watching Eliza waste away along with her kids. . .she must have been terrified.

And there was nothing any of us could do.

When we reached her cabin, I did precious little. Eliza came rushing up to me and hugged me tightly. "I've missed you," she rasped. "But I'm not strong enough to walk over."

While I consoled Eliza, John and Eddie managed to extricate the hide from the rooftop. As we rested for the return walk, Mrs. Graves tried to nurse her baby. It clearly wasn't working—little Elizabeth cried and cried.

I wondered whether that was the impetus for her anger. Watching your baby starve had to be very, very hard. When we got up to leave, Mrs. Graves stopped us. "Take part of the hide," she whispered. "Take half of it with you."

Before we left, Mrs. Graves turned toward me. "I'm sorry. I'm very, very sorry."

I nodded. "I know."

When we got back with our half-hide, I thought Mama would be happy. But instead, she was making plans. Plans to leave again.

"It's too late for that nonsense," Eddie said. "We're not the Graves. We're not angry at you, and you have food now." He pointed at the door. "Did you hear what Virginia said? Mrs. Graves relented—she sent us back with half a hide."

"Besides," John said. "If you couldn't climb over the mountain a month gone, you certainly can't do it now."

The part that hurt was that John was right.

That half a hide lasted us almost a week. We'd just eaten the last bowls of it about five days later, when I heard something outside. Something strange.

Voices.

Mrs. Murphy wasn't far, but she never came out anymore, and we never went to her cabin either. Mostly I stopped visiting because if she was eating Milt, I didn't want to see it, and if she wasn't, well, I didn't want to know who else had died. Moments later, someone rapped on our door.

"Hello?" Mr. Breen asked.

"It's Matthew Dill Ritchie," a voice said. "You might remember me as Colonel Ritchie."

Mr. Breen frowned. Clearly he'd never heard the name, but I had. I didn't have the strength to jump up, but I clapped. "He's Papa's friend," I said as loudly as I could. "Open the door!"

"I'd let in the devil himself," Mr. Breen said, "if he had a loaf of bread." He swung the door open, and Mr. Ritchie backed up a step, his back hitting the piled-up snow right outside. He'd clearly descended the stairs to our doorstep, but he wasn't prepared for our living conditions.

I couldn't blame him for that.

A moment later, Colonel Ritchie rallied. "We don't have bread, unfortunately, and we have to ration the supplies for our return trip, but we do have biscuits." He reached into his bag and brought out two handfuls of biscuits, maybe seven or eight in all.

Every set of eyes in the room was on them, and my mouth began to salivate at the very thought. When I rubbed my eyes and blinked, Colonel Ritchie and the biscuits were still there. Thankfully, the Colonel said, "Don't worry. We have more—you can all have one."

Other than our surprise Christmas meal, that biscuit was the single best thing I'd ever eaten. It practically melted in my mouth. And if I huddled in the corner and ate it like a feral dog, well, I wasn't the only one.

After we finished our biscuits, the rescuers passed out strips of dried beef. It was meat that *hadn't* been sitting in a hunk of snow for months. It wasn't a bowl of slurry made from cow skin. It had been smoked properly, and it was *tender* for dried beef, which was really, really good. Most of my teeth were loose, and I was hungry enough that I might not be careful.

I watched Mama suck on her first strip for a long time before she finally chewed and swallowed. She'd lost two teeth in the past two weeks from gnawing on bones. I was worried she might lose more soon, but hopefully food would help the ones she had left stabilize.

The next day, the rescuers continued on to visit Alder Creek, but Colonel Ritchie gave us a warning. "We need to leave the minute we return with everyone who's able to travel. We've cached supplies along the way, but we'll have to travel as fast and as light as we can."

We all knew why.

Blizzards didn't wait, and they never gave warnings. If we had any hope of making it over the mountains, we needed to move fast.

"Wait," Mr. Breen called out as they began to walk away. "What happened to our brave snowshoe party? There were fifteen of them."

Colonel Ritchie paused for only a heartbeat. "They all made it, but it was a long, difficult journey," he said. "They're recovering. Mr. William Eddy made a valiant effort to join us, actually." He grimaced. "But a few days after we reached the snow line, he had to turn back." He shook his head. "That man has a spine of steel."

That night, when I went to sleep, I dreamt of biscuits and Papa. The next day, Mama and I worked our hardest to repair the rips and tears and tatters in our miserable clothing, and we readied the little children to make the assault on the mountain.

God had finally answered my prayers, and I prayed for almost an hour, thanking him. "Now I just need a little more help," I said. "Let Mama and Patty and Jimmy and Tommy survive long enough to reach Papa. Once we do, he'll take it from there."

Of course, at the time, we had no idea that Colonel Ritchie was lying, and we certainly had no idea how hard things were about to get for our little rescue party.

CHAPTER 28

Virginia Reed

We had already been planning to try and leave again, so the rescuers made our decision a simple one. The second they arrived, we knew we'd leave right away.

The Breens struggled a bit.

"We have enough hides to last at least another week," Mr. Breen said. "Not everyone does. Let them take the others out, the ones who are suffering the worst. We'll stay and wait for the next group."

"But you're strong enough," I said. "You have to come now." My eyes pleaded with Eddie.

"I'd like to go," Eddie said. "Can I?"

Mrs. Breen looked torn. "We want to stay together as a family, and Eddie helps a great deal with cutting wood and hauling water."

"He can bring Simon, too," I insisted. Of all their smaller children, Simon was the most stir-crazy. I knew he made his father insane with all his questions. "You should at least send a few of your children now. What if the second group's delayed? You'll have more food if they come with us."

"I want to go." Eddie stood. "They don't have their pa, and it's a long trip."

"Mr. Tucker and Mr. Glover can help them," Mr. Breen said. "The next rescue group is just behind the first. Colonel Ritchie said as much already. We'll all wait together."

"I think you should all come now," I said, stubbornly. "Why wait?"

"Someone has to keep an eye on the children who can't yet travel," Mr. Breen said. "Mrs. Murphy isn't in great shape. They need someone who can keep things together here until the next rescue group comes."

"But Eddie wants to come now," I said. "You're being selfish."

Mr. Breen stood and stepped toward me, but Eddie jumped in front of me. "Father, she's entitled to have thoughts of her own."

"She and her family have taken enough from us," Mr. Breen said, glaring at me. "Now let it go."

The next morning, as we were preparing to leave, I realized how little we really had to take. We each had a few long-sleeved shirts, which we layered, but we only had them because the Breens had stored them in their wagons for us when we left everything behind. We each had a blanket, albeit thin, and we had shoes that were mostly intact.

Other than the half a pound of dried meat apiece that Mr. Tucker and Colonel Ritchie had given those of us who were traveling, we had nothing else.

"It's insanity," I heard Mr. Breen saying as we headed for the door. "They're taking a three-year-old child with them? More than twenty people are going, and there are only seven men to help. It's better to wait for the next group."

"What if Eddie's supposed to go with them and help?" Mrs. Breen asked. "What if that's His plan?"

Mr. Breen froze.

"He's formed a connection with the Reed family, and he's still begging to go."

Mama took my wrist, and I followed her up, still hoping that Eddie might come. As we were waiting for everyone to gather, a miracle happened. Eddie and Simon came out as well, their parents trailing them. "We've decided to send two of our boys with you," Mr. Breen said. "I hope you'll watch over them as carefully as we've sheltered your family."

"Of course I will," Mama said.

Stupid, embarrassing tears slid over my cheeks, but I brushed them away before anyone noticed. "Thank you."

Mr. Breen looked my direction, but made no response. What did I care? Eddie was coming! His dog Towser tried to follow, but it quickly became clear that the poor, emaciated dog couldn't keep up. "You have to go back, boy," Eddie whispered.

Mrs. Breen called for Towser, and reluctantly, his wiry-haired dog slunk back. That poor beast's eyes might have been the saddest of all as the people staying at the cabins saw us off.

As we walked toward the edge of the lake, I looked around at the people traveling with us. Reason P. Tucker was the leader, and his friend Aquilla Glover was helping. Poor Mr. Tucker had agreed to carry Naomi Pike the whole way back, since her mother had left with the snowshoe party, and her father had been shot. Colonel Ritchie was also along, as well as two brothers I'd never before met, Daniel and John Rhoads. I didn't know the names of the others.

"Virginia?" A thin man with a bushy beard was looking at me sideways as we trudged along. "Are you Virginia?"

I blinked.

"Your father's James Reed, right?"

Mama turned toward the man slowly.

"He saved me, back in November. He was trying to come and save you, but the snow was too deep. No matter what he did, he couldn't get over the mountains. He tried everything he could. On his way back, he ran into me."

"And now?" Mama asked. "Where is he now?"

"He was back in California, working to assemble supplies and men to come over the mountains again. I think he wasn't far behind us."

My heart surged. Perhaps we'd run into him on our way. I couldn't stop smiling.

"If he hadn't given me food when he did, I'm not sure what would have happened to me," the man said.

"What's your name?" Mama asked.

"Jotham Curtis, ma'am." He bowed his head a few inches.

"Thank you," Mama said. "For coming all this way, and for risking your life to help us."

He smiled and nodded, but we were all struggling in the snow. Talking made it harder.

Most of the people with us managed reasonably well in the drifts of snow covering everything between our camp and Truckee Lake. But once we reached the lake, it became harder. The snow was higher in some places than others, and the taller drifts made it really difficult to keep moving. Each step grew more difficult than the last, my arms and legs aching, my head pounding, and my breath coming harder.

I watched helplessly as Jimmy scrambled, thrashed, and kicked his way through drift after drift. "I hate snow," he muttered.

Patty and Tommy were doing far worse. In fact, as a family, we'd already fallen to the very back of the group while waiting for them. Eddie was glancing at Tommy and Patty with concern, and I couldn't blame him. We hadn't even reached the edge of the lake yet. We had nearly a hundred miles yet to travel.

"I'll carry Tommy for a while," Eddie said, "and Patty can lean on you."

I thought it sounded like a good plan, even if the idea of Patty leaning on me made me want to whimper.

"You can't." Mr. Glover was bringing up the back, and his expression was quite severe when he said it. "It's hard enough to make this trip when you're not starving. We had five grown men who weren't operating with no reserve turn back as we traveled here, because they were worried they'd die."

I swallowed.

"If they're having trouble already and you carry them, you won't make it either." Mr. Glover's eyes were utterly serious. "They have to go back now, while we're close enough that they can."

Mama looked stricken, her entire face draining of blood. "But I can't leave them, and I can't send Virginia and Jimmy on alone."

"Ma and Pa will take them in," Eddie said. "They can eat my share of the hides, and when the next group comes, they'll be strong enough to come out with them."

The whole group ground to a halt while Mama thought about it.

"I should stay with them." Her brow was furrowed. "I'm their mother." She was squeezing her hands closed over and over. "But if I stay here with nothing to feed them, we're burdening the Breens again. And I'm sending Virginia and Jimmy on alone." She dropped her face in her hands. "I don't know what to do." She looked up at me. "What would James tell me to do?"

"Papa isn't here," I said. "I—he would tell you—" But I didn't know. I had no idea what Papa would do, because we'd never faced decisions like that. Every time I opened my mouth to answer her, I saw little Harriet McCutchen lying on the snow, dead and frozen. Her mother had left her, and she died.

But then again, Eleanor Eddy stayed with Maggie, and they both died. "You should go," I said abruptly. "Tommy will have Patty, and they'll stay with the Breens. More help is coming. Spare them the extra mouth to feed and come with us now."

Mama nodded jerkily, her forehead wrinkling, her mouth a grim line. "Yes." She crouched down in the snow, and little Thomas fell against her. Patty threw herself around Mama's body and hugged her tightly.

We'd gained quite an audience as we deliberated, brief though it was. There wasn't a person here who didn't understand our dilemma and empathize, but we weren't ever sure how long good weather would last.

We couldn't delay without putting everyone at risk.

"I'll take them back," Mr. Glover said, watching Mama and her two exhausted children with kind eyes.

"Mama," Thomas cried, his hands bunching on her dress.

Patty straightened then, and she carefully pried Tommy's hand from Mama's flannel. "It's time for us to go back now," she said. "Mama will go ahead and make sure we have hot bread waiting when we arrive." She forced a smile.

I'd never been prouder of my sister in my life.

"And Mama, if something happens, and we don't see you again." Her lips trembled, but she gulped in air and threw up her chin. "Do the very best you can, and keep Virginia and Jimmy safe for me."

That broke me, her bravery in the face of what must have been abject terror. A soft noise beside me had me turning to find that Mr. Glover was crying. So was Eddie. In fact, almost every face I surveyed had tears glistening on it somewhere.

We stood stock still and watched as Mr. Glover disappeared. He returned quickly, and that made me more certain than ever that, as fast as he traveled the distance, there was no way they'd have been able to continue for the whole trek.

We'd made the right decision.

I said a silent prayer, begging God to look after them and us in our different locations. As we stumbled along, Eddie moved a little ahead, and I decided it was time for another real chat with God.

"Dear God. You haven't answered all my prayers, but you've answered some of them. Papa's alive, and he's coming for us, and help did come. Now if you could just watch over us for the next few days, and keep Patty and Thomas safe, then I'll trust in you forever." The whispered words might have been a complete waste of time, but I felt a little better for saying them.

From a few feet ahead, Eddie turned and said, "That's not really how God works. He doesn't buy our belief."

I pushed as hard as I could to catch up. "I know."

"I'm not sure you do," Eddie said. "Our job here on earth is to have faith."

"Why?" I asked.

"Do you even know what faith is?"

"Of course I do. I've been listening to you all for months. It's charity. God's love."

"Faith is a belief in something you can't see or hear or feel. It's trusting that God knows what's best for us, even if what's best isn't something we want."

"Like Milt dying." I couldn't help my frown.

"Like Milt dying," Eddie agreed. "Because the part that's the hardest is learning how to trust in Him even when He doesn't do what we want. So you can't really condition your faith and your belief in Him on Him getting you through the mountains, because that may not be what He wants for you."

"But it's what *I* want," I said. "And if God wants me to die, then I don't want to believe in Him."

In fact, the more I thought about God and all His stupid rules, the more I wanted to give up. I wanted to stop walking. Stop trying. Stop pushing and pushing and pushing. But in spite of what I wanted, I did keep going. It still might not be quite what Eddie meant, and maybe I didn't really understand God yet. Even so, it kind of felt like He was there with me, and there with Jimmy a little bit too, as we struggled through that miserable snow to the far end of the lake and made camp for the night.

That night, as if he could tell we were all struggling, Mr. Tucker passed out all the remaining beef. "We cached about half our supplies at the Pass," he said. "We gave most of what we kept to all of you, leaving whatever we didn't eat already with those staying behind at the cabins. But we'll make the pass tomorrow, so we can eat all we have." He was smiling as he passed out more than three times as much food as any of us had eaten in weeks and weeks.

Since Christmas, really.

As I chewed on a piece of my dried beef, I thought about what California would be like.

"What kept you going today?" Eddie asked.

Before I could answer, Jimmy did. "I kept thinking, with every single step, with every single footprint, that I got closer to Papa. And closer to loaves and loaves of delicious, fluffy *bread*." His smile was almost maniacal.

I couldn't blame him, though. Just the thought of that biscuit we'd had made my mouth water all over again. "You know what I miss more than bread?" I paused. "Jam. Bread with jam and butter."

Eddie shook his head. "With jam or without, I don't care. I don't miss anything more than bread, and I just left my whole family."

"Hey," Simon said. "Your whole family? What am I?" He shoved Eddie.

"Chopped liver," I said.

"Ooh, I would *love it* if you were chopped liver," Mama said. "That's my favorite."

That made Jimmy laugh.

"I do also want cake," Eddie said. "It's as soft and chewy as bread, but even more delicious."

I closed my eyes and imagined. "Ah, sweet cakes. Mama and Eliza made the best sweet cakes I had ever had."

"With raisins," Simon said.

"I liked cobblers best," Eliza said, her eyes closed where she was lying back on her small, thin blanket. "That's what I want when we make it over the mountains."

"What kind?" Eddie asked, watching Eliza intently.

Eliza's voice was soft. "Baylis loved peaches," she whispered. "I think I want peach first."

"You may have to wait," James said. "It's too cold for peaches."

"Unless someone canned them," Mama said.

After that, we all finally drifted off to sleep. That night I dreamt of biscuits, peach cobbler, and bread. But when I woke up, my belly rumbled, and I wished I hadn't thought so much about food.

We all got ready quite early. After passing out all the food the night before, there wasn't much to do. Mr. Tucker started walking, and the rest of us followed, many of us sucking on bits of dried beef we'd saved.

It was hard the second day—harder even than the day before.

But thanks to Jimmy, I had motivation. Every single step took me closer to Papa and biscuits. Buttery biscuits. Piping hot. In spite of our best efforts, our family fell behind again, bringing up the rear. This time, poor Simon was the one who was really dragging.

That's why we were the last to discover that disaster had struck.

"I don't see how this could have happened." Mr. Tucker's face was bright red, and he was waving his arms around like a windmill. "We cached it properly, just as I was taught."

"It wasn't a bear." Mr. Glover was crouched over shreds of fabric.

"What happened?" I asked.

The men turned toward us slowly, Mr. Glover answering. "All the food we left here's gone."

James started to laugh.

Within a moment, I had joined in. Pretty soon, Eddie, Eliza, and Mama were all laughing with us.

"What am I not understanding?" Mr. Tucker asked. "Our supplies, all our supplies, are *gone*. Something ate them and shredded the blankets we wrapped them in, even though we hung them up high from the branches of a pine tree."

I shook my head.

Eddie explained. "No food is something we understand. We've been training for this." He straightened his shoulder, and he kept on climbing.

"Time for short rations again," Eliza said.

"Not short rations," Mr. Glover said. "No rations."

"That's not true," Mama said. "Most of us didn't finish all our dried meat."

Mr. Tucker's jaw dropped.

But Mama was right. The rescuers had eaten all of their meat, but when we started asking around to the others, Elitha and Leanna Donner,

Billy, Lovina, and Eleanor Graves, as well as all of us had all saved some part of what they'd been given.

"It's second nature for us," Eddie said. "I've been sneaking little bits of food to Virginia for more than a month."

"We can't ask you to share what you kept," Mr. Tucker said.

An awful lot of us insisted, returning the bits we'd saved to Mr. Tucker to redistribute. "Short rations," I said. "That's something we can do."

The next day, though, the first true disaster happened. Mr. Denton, who hadn't been able to see well since the second day, apparently because the snow was too bright for his eyes after living in constant darkness, said he could go no farther. We'd known him since Springfield, and he'd stayed with us part of the first month in the double cabin we shared with the Graves.

At first, Mama tried to convince him to keep coming. Jimmy crouched near him and said, "If you think of biscuits, it helps. Or sweet cakes, if you like those better."

John Denton was too tired, even, to smile. He simply closed his eyes and sighed.

We were much too far away for him to turn around and head back like Patty and Tommy had.

"I'll make you a fire," Mr. Tucker said.

I had no idea where his energy came from, but Mr. Tucker never rested. Colonel Ritchie helped with the fire. The two men's assurances that more help was on the way and would hopefully reach him soon were so convincing that Jimmy wanted to stay.

"I can keep him company." Jimmy sat next to him on the ground. "And if this wood runs low, I can gather more branches."

"No," Mama said. "You can't stay." I could tell she knew that help wouldn't come soon enough. As we continued onward, I couldn't help it —I kept looking back. Mr. Denton looked so toasty by the fire, wrapped in the extra blanket Mr. Tucker had given him from his own pack. I could see why Jimmy wanted to stay too. I knew the truth, though.

We left Mr. Denton, who carved Grandma Keyes' gravestone, to die.

The rest of that day, as we trudged along, I still thought about Papa and biscuits, but I also kept thinking about Mr. Denton, dying all alone in the middle of a snowy mountain. Before we went to sleep, Mr. Tucker passed out the last few pieces of beef, and we all got one piece each. The very small children got one and a *half*.

It wasn't nearly enough, but the next day was worse.

It warmed up, and at first the sun was a welcome addition to our trip, but it became bright enough and warm enough that it started to melt the snow, and when it goes thirty feet deep, soft, slushy snow is very, very bad for anyone traveling over it.

Once, Jimmy dropped so far that I could only see his head and his waving hands.

Eddie leapt to my aid to help drag him out, but without Mr. Rhoads rushing over, we might never have succeeded. Daniel Rhoads knew about siblings—he was on this rescue mission with his brother John. After we got Jimmy clear, Mr. Rhoads helped us brush the ice and snow off him as best we could, and then he stayed close to us as we moved along. Less than an hour later, John Rhoads took Ada Keseberg from Philippine. Little Ada was only three, and she was terribly small, but Philippine was struggling. John carried her the rest of the day, giving her mother a break.

Carrying her wasn't enough, though.

Without food for far too long, little Ada died shortly after we made camp that night. It was too much for her mother. She'd now lost both her children, and she'd left her husband behind at the lake, in the wretched lean-to they'd lived in for more than four months.

She had nothing left.

The sound of her wailing was *terrible*. It sent chills up my spine. She crouched over little Ada's tiny body and refused to move away. All that night, she slept next to her dead daughter, sometimes chanting something I couldn't understand. Even the next morning, when the sun rose and it was time to set out again, she refused to move.

"I can't go," she screamed when Mr. Tucker encouraged her to stand.

"You must." It had to be hard for him to remain calm and reasonable.

It took Mr. Tucker more than twenty minutes, but he finally convinced the distraught Philippine to let him bury little Ada. He did it himself, since none of us had the energy. We all watched, numb, as he dug and dug and dug in the snow.

But when we all started off, Philippine still wouldn't move.

Mama was staring at her almost like Philippine had stared at her daughter's body. I couldn't bear it, so I made my way over to Philippine and sat down beside her.

She turned her head away.

"I know your life hasn't been easy," I said. "And I have no idea what it must feel like to lose two children."

"Three." Her voice was so soft that I almost didn't hear her for the whistling of the wind in the pines.

"What?" Three? What could that mean? I'd seen her children.

"Ada was a twin," she said, still not meeting my eyes. "When I lost her sister, I almost gave up." Her shoulders shook. "My heart broke, but for Ada, I kept going."

And now Lewis Junior and Ada were both gone, too.

I had no idea what to say, but I could see the other travelers becoming restless. They wouldn't wait much longer. I couldn't leave her here like John Denton. Like her daughter. She was alive—she had to keep going.

"I held on for nothing. The more I try, the more misery I endure."

"But you knew her," I said. "If you die, no one who really loved her will be around to remember her." It was the only thing I could think to say.

"I can't leave. She wasn't buried well. She'll be eaten by wolves."

I didn't bother pointing out that if she stayed, the wolves would eat her as well. "Think about the happy times," I said. "What made her smile. Her favorite foods. The way she looked when she slept."

Her head whipped toward me then.

I waited for her to tell me that Mr. Keseberg could remember her, because as I said that she was the only one, I remembered that Ada also had a father who was still alive back at the cabins by the lake.

But Philippine didn't argue—she just stared at me.

A moment later, she stood up, and then she started walking.

When I rejoined Mama and Eddie and Eliza and Jimmy, they were all staring at me.

"What did you say?" Eliza asked. "How did you get her to leave?"

I shrugged. "I have no idea."

That day, when we stopped to take a break, those who had shoelaces toasted and ate them. Mr. Tucker cut the fringe off the bottom of his coat and fed the pieces to all the children. Normally I'd have insisted I wasn't a child. In this case, however, I ate three.

The ache in my belly and the pounding in my head were terrible. Shoelaces and fringe, unsurprisingly, didn't help.

Mr. Tucker, the Rhoads brothers, and Colonel Ritchie kept talking about it. They said they were dizzy. They said their bellies felt like something was clawing their insides. They talked about how hard it was to walk, to climb, and to function.

But for us, all of that was normal.

What was hard was digging my feet out of the snow and putting one foot in front of the other again and again and again. With every step, I had to decide whether I wanted to see Papa and biscuits more than I longed to sit down and stop fighting so hard. I understood John Denton all too well in those moments. The idea of a fire and a nap appealed to me more and more with every passing mile.

But for Mama, for Papa, for Jimmy, and for Patty, Tommy, and the Breens, I struggled onward.

The cold wind bit at my face.

The brightness of the snow made my eyes ache, and it was hard sometimes to make out what I was looking at. The edges of my vision would go dim often, or be so covered in spots I couldn't see my hand in front of my face.

I stumbled a lot.

We all did, far more than we should have, even with the mounds of snow, and even with as tired as we were. Simon and Jimmy fell behind constantly, and Mama had stopped even noticing when they did. She just kept trudging along, her eyes fixed on Eliza's back up ahead of her.

When Eddie or I would notice they'd stopped, we'd fall back to help them. Even our self-appointed savior, Daniel Rhoads, was distracted. His brother had traveled ahead with Mr. Glover to look for the second relief party that was meant to be just behind them, and he was worried, always watching for his brother John.

"If we can just find them, they should have food," Daniel said. "Please, *God*, let them have found food."

"That's not how you ask God for things," Simon said.

I could almost *hear* Mr. Breen saying it in the exact same way.

"It's an expression," Daniel said, one eyebrow raised.

"Then you're using God's name in vain." Simon was really frowning now. "That's a sin."

His pious righteousness made me smile.

Not much had done that lately.

As the sun started to set and we began to look for a place to make camp for the night, I was about to pray again in the somewhat angry fashion I'd been unable to stop, when I saw something up ahead. There were black specks on the horizon that were moving toward us.

I wasn't the only one who saw them.

Mr. Tucker sped up, urging all of us forward. "There's something there."

As we grew closer, we all recognized what it was we saw. There were two men—real, live men—carrying big packs.

"Who are you?" Mr. Tucker called out with a lung capacity I envied. "Did you talk to Aquilla Glover or John Rhoads?"

"Rhoads and Glover sent us." The man's voice was barely audible. "We brought meat."

Eliza cried out beside me, shouting and hollering. Jimmy began to cry. Mama laughed. Eddie growled and pumped his fist in the air. All around us, people celebrated.

When the men reached us, we stopped right where we were for the night. Before even bothering to build the green-log base on which to make a fire, the men opened the packs and shared out handfuls of dried beef.

It wasn't the bread we wanted, but it was damn good.

"You don't know everything," I said to Eddie that night.

"What?" His brother was asleep next to us, so he was whispering.

"God listens, even when your prayers are angry," I proudly proclaimed. "I've been yelling at Him for days, and look. He finally brought us food."

When Eddie went to sleep, he had a smile on his face.

The next morning, all of us were impatient to be off. We'd eaten all the beef in both packs, and our bellies were still rumbling. Mr. Tucker walked over to where we were strapping the blanket roll to the small pack Simon was carrying.

"Mrs. Reed?" Mr. Tucker was frowning.

"Yes?" Mama turned. "Is something wrong?"

He smiled then. "Actually, I think something's right. I wanted to prepare you, but I worried that if I told you last night, you might try to travel in the dark."

Mama went utterly still. "What?"

"The men who brought us meat also brought me some news." He was beaming. "The leader of the relief party that stopped for the night just a short distance away. . .is James Reed."

Mama's eyes widened, and she stopped breathing.

I threw my arms around her.

Jimmy grabbed my leg and clung tightly. "Papa!" he shouted.

That day, our family wasn't at the back of the group. We were the first to leave, barely waiting for Mr. Reason P. Tucker to show us the way. We hadn't gone far, maybe a mile or two, when we saw them. Mama broke into the closest thing to a run any of us could manage, and my heart slammed loudly in my chest, I was so giddy.

Jimmy cried out over and over.

Papa's face, when he saw us, was strange. He didn't look excited or happy at all. He looked. . .agitated. Upset.

But when Mama reached him, she fell to her knees in the snow and began sobbing. He lifted her up carefully, and she pressed her face against his neck. They embraced for a very long time, but when she finally stepped back, Jimmy and I rushed in to hug him too.

It had been five months since we'd seen Papa.

Five long, horrific months.

"I stayed up all night baking sweet cakes over the fire," he said.

I smelled them then. The only thing better than Papa—sweet cakes with raisins. They tasted better even than the biscuit. Papa gave us three each, but when we started to say something, pressed his finger to his mouth. "Shh."

"Don't eat them at once," Mama whispered. "Tuck them into your bag. Eating them all might make you sick."

Papa's eyes widened, and his lip trembled, almost like he was going to cry. He didn't, but I wondered what else had caused that. Before I had time to dwell on it further, Eliza, Eddie, and Simon rushed up.

Papa passed sweet cakes out to everyone, including the rescuers, and then he circled back to where Mama was standing. He pressed one hand against her face. "Tommy and Patty?"

Mama shook her head.

His eyes widened and he opened his mouth.

I realized he thought they had died. "They were too weak to come with us," I blurted. "We had to leave them with the Breens."

He gulped in a breath or two and then nodded. "Then I really can't delay. I'll go and fetch them right away."

"We can wait for you," Mama said.

But Reason P. Tucker was shaking his head. "No, we'll all continue on. There's no way to know when a storm will hit. He'll rejoin you in California soon."

Mama looked like she wanted to argue, but she didn't.

Less than twenty minutes after being reunited with Papa again, we set out in the opposite direction from him.

"Now it's only biscuits to think of," I said softly to James, who was struggling again.

"I have a cake in my bag," he said. "I want to sit down here and eat it."

"But you'll save it for later," I said. "Trust me."

The walking got easier and easier as we headed down the path, and soon we found another cache of supplies, right where Mr. Tucker said they'd be. In fact, he'd left his son and another boy to keep an eye on these things. But the more I ate, and the better I felt, the more I worried for Patty and Thomas.

And Papa.

Grown, well-fed men were worried they'd die. That meant he could too.

As we finally made our way to a place called Johnson's Ranch, a place that looked every bit like the paradise we were promised California would be, we saw it off in the distance.

Another storm was coming.

When I said my prayers that night, they weren't angry. They were desperate. "I know you got me here safely," I said. "And I'm sorry for being so angry and rude about it, but I need one more big thing." I paused. "Actually, it's two very small things. Please help my Papa to save Patty and Thomas. And second, bring them all back to me, *please*."

Maybe Eddie didn't really know everything he thought he did about prayer, because even though I had been angry, it really felt like God was finally listening.

CHAPTER 29

Peggy Breen

With nothing but boiled hides and small scraps of the worst sort of beef for flavoring, like ox tails, you almost forget what real food tastes like. After the small supply of food the first rescue shared was gone, only a day after they left, the hunger hit us even harder than before.

"I don't want that slop," James cried. "I hate it."

My hand rested on his head for a moment, understanding all too well the revulsion, since I did nearly all the singeing and boiling of the hides in order to make the awful sludge. "We *have* to eat well for the next few days, consistently," I said. "We have to be strong enough to walk a hundred miles when the next rescue group comes."

James and Peter continued to argue, as most two- and five-year-old boys do, but eventually they did shovel down every last bite, and the bigger boys didn't fight me at all. I had missed flour more than I could say, and we were all suffering from the glimpse of delicious food, but we had a goal.

At least, everyone but poor Towser did.

Our emaciated family dog lay by the door and whined for more than a day after Eddie left. Even that small effort wore him out, and he eventually stopped whining, but he didn't eat the crumbly bone I gave him. He just nudged it away and closed his eyes with a sigh.

He was Eddie's dog.

I didn't think he was up to making the trip, not without having been given more than a single, boiled and crumbly bone or so a week for so long. I should have let him go with Eddie—he'd have had the best chance at surviving if I had. When Patrick was busy reading the Bible, I tried to sneak him a bowl of ox-hide slurry.

Even that, he refused.

"Why are you bothering? He's a dog." Patrick sniffed. "He's the last dog that's alive in either camp. We should've eaten him long before."

Patrick's disdain notwithstanding, I was beside myself about it, worrying about what Eddie would say when we saw him next. Eventually, I started trying to clean up the abysmal cabin a bit to distract myself from thinking about it. When I went outside with the chamber pot to dump it, I heard a terrible sound near the cabin.

A gunshot.

There had been wolves coming around with increasing frequency, and while we usually only heard them scratching at the door and howling at night, we never knew what they'd do if they got desperate enough.

I raced back. "What happened?" But I could already see. The snow was red, and Patrick was dragging Towser's body behind the side of the cabin.

"We need to be strong enough to travel." He grunted. "He wasn't going to make it, but he can help us in another way."

I made stew like Patrick ordered me to, but I refused to eat a single bite of it myself.

It had been February eighteenth when the rescuers arrived. A few days later, on the twenty-second, two of my beloved boys disappeared with them over the mountain. Reason P. Tucker, the leader of the group, promised me that there was another group coming, just days behind them.

But on the twenty-sixth day of February, four days later, we still hadn't heard anything. The Graves and the Murphys had both heard the gunshot, and both of them had come by asking for a share of the meat from our half-dead dog. They had no idea how meager Towser's body had been, but in any case, Patrick refused to share. I decided to walk to the Murphys and see how Levinah was doing.

When I reached her cabin, I froze.

Outside her door were the remains of what I thought must be Milt Elliot. They had begun to eat him, as they said they would. It couldn't have been wolves. The cuts were precise and even, and someone had removed his head. Wolves don't do that.

I closed my eyes and inhaled and tried to block out the image, but it was too hard. His stomach had been sliced open, the organs removed. His hands and feet were also removed. I'm not sure where they had gone, but both his legs had been carved on.

It almost made me lose the bowl of hide I'd just choked down.

I turned to go, not willing to talk to Levinah while I was so upset, but she called to me. "You had four times as many oxen as me," she said, her voice clear. "You would have done the same, to save your children."

I wasn't sure she was right, but when I turned and faced her, I nodded.

"Mothers do what they have to," she said. "We do what we must."

I said a prayer on my way back to our cabin, thanking God that it hadn't come down to me making that choice for our family. The next day, we ate the very last scraps of our meat, and Patrick started to worry.

"They said it would be a few days." He was pacing. None of us had been energetic enough to pace in months, so at least our concerted effort to choke down more hides was working. "It's been five days. Why hasn't anyone come?" He stopped. "Could they have been lying?" His eyes were desperate.

We were at our strongest right now. If days turned into weeks, and we had nothing more than bone broth, we'd be like the Murphys.

We should have gone with the first group.

"They could be delayed," I said. "There might have been an incident. Or maybe they got lost."

"We should pray," John said.

So we did.

Even poor little Patty Reed, absolutely miserable with a toothache and a swollen jaw, said a prayer. It was sort of a mess, but it was genuine at least. "Dear God," she said, like she was addressing a letter. "Please help my mama and papa to be safe, and please bring strong men with lots of bread and cakes to save us right now."

"That's not how God works." Our Patty, Patrick Junior, was a whole year older than Patty, and he loved to make sure she knew it. "You can't demand things on a timetable."

She frowned. "Then what good is He? Mama said being late is *rude*."

I laughed. Patty was so much like her sister.

My husband Patrick frowned, but I liked to think that God had a sense of humor, and being called rude by this starving, abandoned little urchin struck me as funny. I think God would have seen the humor in it, too.

At least, I hoped He would.

There wasn't a whole lot else to smile about that day. Patty did play with her doll, and she let little Isabella hold it. In spite of how she was feeling, she didn't even screech or yell when Isabella drooled on the little wooden doll's face.

"Mama doesn't know I have this doll," Patty whispered. "Can you not tell her, please?"

I patted the log bench beside me. "Why can't she know?"

"She told us we had to leave everything behind," Patty said. "In the desert, she said to take *nothing* we didn't need to survive." She looked down at her feet. "I was very naughty and hid this in the corner behind a blanket."

I hugged her.

She leaned into me and sighed.

It's hard caring for someone else's children when you're worried about saving your own, but it was easy to love Virginia and Patty Reed. James Junior and Thomas were very sweet, too. The Reed children were all kind, and excitable, and generous, just like their parents.

I hoped Isabella would grow up just like them.

We passed another day with nothing but boiled hide and bone broth to eat, and I began to really worry. "The kids won't eat more than a bowl," I said, "and I'm not sure they should. It's been seven days now, and there's still no sign of another rescue." I lowered my voice. "We have one hide left."

As if it was an answer to prayer, that very day, a native came to our door. Patrick swung it open, and all of us peered at him in shock. He was carrying a very large pack, and he was bundled in a strange combination of animal fur and rough-woven cloth. He also wore snowshoes that appeared to be made largely of bark. While we gawked rudely, the man said something.

Unfortunately, it was unintelligible to us.

I could imagine that Patrick was frowning, but I hoped he remembered his manners and tried to smile. The man offered him something, and when Patrick hesitated, he left several roundish things on the dirty ground in front of our cabin. Then he turned around and walked away without another word.

"Thank you!" Thomas called. Then he crept closer. "What are those? They look like little poops."

I laughed at that, and so did John. He was right. They did.

We all wanted to know what we'd been given. Once washed, they looked a little like onions, so I resolved to cut them up and add them to our boiled hide. We scrubbed them well, and I sliced them up—they had none of the layers of an onion. As they cooked down, they actually smelled quite good.

"It tastes like a sweet potato," Patrick declared, eating the first bite. He insisted that we all wait for at least half an hour after he had a few bites, just to make sure it wasn't something that would make us ill.

When he suffered no bad effects, we all ate some. It brightened the flavor of the hide mush quite a lot. "I don't like the weird little fibers in it," John said. "But it's sweet. Pa was right about that."

I suppose most anything would have tasted sweet after our recent diet. We all sort of hoped the man would return, but the next day was March first. That was the day something much bigger happened, just an hour before sunset. Patty, who had taken to sitting on the top of our cabin, swinging her feet off the edge, started shouting. "Papa!!!"

We all rushed outside, and sure enough, Mr. Reed himself was jogging toward our cabin. He ran to his daughter first, as he should, picked her up, and spun her around. Before little Thomas had even come outside, Mr. Reed pulled a somewhat-smashed sweet cake out of his pocket and handed it to her. "I baked these two days ago, the night before I saw your mama. Sorry they're stale."

Patty didn't mind at all. She wolfed it down so fast, I almost worried that I'd imagined its existence. But when Thomas came out, Mr. Reed gave him a cake, too. He kissed his son on his bony, gaunt cheek, and then Mr. Reed stood up. "I have more." His face was kind as he passed a sweet cake to each of us in turn, including Patrick, who was hanging back a little. "You must take one too, Mr. Breen. I heard from my wife that your family was all that kept them alive."

Patrick took the cake then, nodding gruffly.

Others around us were stirring, and more men were walking past. "We have some limited supplies to distribute—we passed Mr. Tucker on our way here and their cached supplies were eaten by animals, so we shared some with them. They hadn't eaten in days, and some of them had died." Mr. Reed's expression was solemn.

I closed my eyes for a moment, praying silently and frantically. "Was Eddie alright?" I stepped closer, involuntarily reaching for his sleeve. "What about Simon?"

Mr. Reed's eyes were kind. "I'm so sorry—I should have led with that. Your boys and my children and wife were all alive and relatively well." His nostrils flared. "Mr. Denton and tiny Ada Keseberg didn't make it. We passed John Denton's body on the way here." He grimaced. "Nasty business, but we buried the remains when we found them."

After passing out some few supplies, including, blessedly, clothing and new blankets, Reed and his men found places to sleep for the night. Mr. Reed stayed with us, but early the next morning, they all prepared to push on to Alder Creek. I placed most of the few supplies he left on the small shelf that we'd put up in the side of the cabin near the fire, but the cup of sugar he gave me, I tucked into the pocket of the men's trousers of John's that I'd been wearing underneath my skirt. I planned to surprise the children with more sweet cakes, but I had to wait until they went to sleep and bake them outside, or they'd know.

Before he left, Mr. Reed had a request. "Can you help Patty and Thomas clean as best they can and get dressed?" He glanced to the east. I knew time was of the essence if we wanted clear weather.

"Of course," I said. "We'll be ready when you return."

"I would go with you," John said, "but—"

"Don't be silly," Mr. Reed said. "You've done so much here, and so much for my family." He shook his head. "You shouldn't try to walk an extra fourteen miles round trip in one day, not in your condition." He did crouch down by his young daughter and hand her a small bag. Then he whispered something in her ear.

After he left, Patty opened up the bag and walked toward our meager kitchen area near the fire.

"What are you doing?" Patrick asked before I could.

"My papa told me to make bread. If he makes it back tonight, we'll have one special meal before we leave. If he doesn't, the bread will cheer me up."

To our surprise, Patty actually knew, at eight years old, how to make bread. "Eliza taught me on the trail," she said. "I've practiced lots." It might not have been considered the best bread in the world a year ago, but it smelled and looked finer than the nicest cake to all of us. It was practically killing the boys, smelling it and waiting to eat it.

That night, an hour after sunset, Mr. Reed actually returned, big Bill McCutchen with him. "Papa, I made the bread!" Patty was practically bouncing. "And we waited for you to get here to eat it."

It was a near thing. I thought John might have knocked Patty over the head if she had insisted on waiting another moment.

"We should each eat a piece," Mr. Reed said, "and then wrap the rest up in our packs for the trip."

After passing out one piece to each of the people in the cabin, including little Isabella, Patty finally ate one herself. I wasn't sure if my baby would eat bread, but when I put a small piece in her mouth, she nearly swallowed it whole. Her first taste of bread at just over a year. My other babies had been slow to acclimate to new food, but I suppose starvation made everyone less picky.

"And here." Patty handed another piece to Mr. McCutchen. When I saw Patrick Junior open his mouth to complain, I shook my head. Patty had made the bread from flour her dad brought us, and she could pass it out how she liked.

But Bill McCutchen had as keen a sense of justice as Patrick Junior. "I've already had one. I'm bigger, but trust me. You need it more."

Patty shook her head. "Bread makes you feel better, and you must be heartbroken." Her lip trembled.

Bill stared at her with wide eyes.

"Harriet was such a sweet little baby," she said. "I used to hold her sometimes and sing to her, before her ma left." Patty reached her tiny, stick-like arms around his neck and hugged him.

I watched as a massive man, almost six and a half feet tall, bawled like a baby. The men looked away, but I couldn't. He should be able to grieve, and who better to comfort him than someone else who loved his little girl when he wasn't able to?

We left the next morning early, the rescuers taking turns carrying two of Betsy Donner's young children, Isaac and Mary Donner, on their backs as they had the day before. The Donner children's older brother, Solomon Hook, was a child from Betsy's first marriage, and he hovered as close to them as he could, keeping his eye out. He was around Eddie's age, and watching him made me say a silent prayer for my own sons. I hoped Eddie was as attentive to Simon as Solomon was to Mary and Isaac.

In all, seventeen people made ready to leave this time. The three children of Betsy Donner, Patty and Tommy Reed, myself, Patrick, and our five remaining children, as well as Elizabeth Graves and her last four children.

It wasn't a group that was strong and hale—it was mostly children.

We didn't move quickly, even with the rescuers carrying what limited supplies we had left. They, at least, had snowshoes, but the rest of us did not. We had to rely on them to tamp down the snow for us, while we struggled through after them, most of us sinking to our knees with virtually every step. I had Isabella, who was only one, but still tiring to carry. Elizabeth Graves had her newborn as well, little Elizabeth. The smallest children, especially, had a very hard time.

Franklin Junior, only five years old like my James, kept stopping. No one had the strength to carry him, and Mr. Reed was already carrying Tommy. We often paused, but I was nervous he might slow more and more. I could only imagine the fear Mrs. Graves felt all alone with so many small children.

Near the end of the day, as we approached the far end of the lake, the rescuer carrying Mary Donner ground to a halt. "Can you walk for a bit?" he asked. "I'm too tired to carry you."

Mary, who looked to be six or so, stumbled a few steps and stopped. I handed Isabella to Patrick, who was struggling pretty badly himself, and I went to check on her. Her boots looked strange, and I thought that maybe if I could somehow repair the fit, she'd be able to walk for a bit on her own.

"These are far too large," I said.

"They aren't mine," she said. "My shoes got chewed up by the dog."

"Whose are they?"

"My ma's," she said.

"And who put them on you? Maybe we can tighten them up so they don't slosh around so much."

She looked up at me warily. "You can try."

While I worked to untie the laces, brushing snow off of them, I decided to keep her talking. "How old are you, Mary?"

"I'm seven," she said. "Eight soon."

She was very small for her age, and surely the lack of food lately hadn't helped. But when I took her first boot off, one of her toes was poking through her soggy stocking. The travelers ahead of us were moving on without us, and Patrick and Isabella were growing impatient, but I peeled the stocking off anyway. I needed to know what I was dealing with.

I let out an unintentional cry.

Her foot was almost entirely black.

"What?" Mary asked. "Is there nothing you can do about the shoes?"

The poor child's feet were so badly frostbitten, it was a wonder she could even stand—of course she couldn't walk. I wasn't sure what to do. I could barely carry Isabella. "Maybe John can. . ."

Patrick frowned. "What?"

"Can you possibly keep carrying Isabella for a bit?" I asked. "Mary's feet. . ." I carefully slid her stocking on and then tied her boot back up. "She needs someone to carry her."

"You can't save the whole world without risking your own family," Patrick said.

"I'm not trying to save the whole world," I said. "Just this one little girl."

He arched one eyebrow. "And the Reeds. And the dog."

I took Isabella back from Patrick and handed her to John. "Carry your sister. I can carry Mary for an hour or so."

"You'll tire yourself too much," Patrick insisted. "You can't."

"I can." I pointed. "Go."

Patrick didn't listen, still glaring at me.

But when I started walking, he didn't continue to argue. I knew he was miserable right now—I could always tell when he was dealing with a stone, but we didn't have any other options. We couldn't leave a little girl alone out here.

John didn't seem to mind taking Isabella, and unlike the baby, Mary Donner clung to my neck. It was tiring in a different way, but I could manage it for a while. I trudged along for the last forty minutes until we reached the edge of the lake. Once we caught up to the Reeds, I even had a nice distraction to keep me from obsessing about how tired I was.

That Patty had become quite a little chatterbox.

The extra rations had done her a world of good, apparently. "This is much better than last time," she said. "When I tried to leave with Mama before, I kept having spots in front of my eyes. I thought I would just fall down in the snow, and sleep and sleep. That's why I turned back."

I could tell from Patrick Junior's face that he wished she'd sleep now, or at least stop talking. He rolled his eyes almost as much as his father.

But the jabbering made Patty's father, James Reed, *very* happy, and that was worth a lot. He loved his children as much as anyone I'd seen.

The people who disliked James Reed early on in our journey had clearly misjudged him. As he walked the whole day with Tommy on his shoulders, in addition to carrying his pack, I thought about how I'd seen him go to Lewis Keseberg's lean-to after eating Patty's bread, before resting for the night. James Reed had already traveled fourteen miles through snow that day, carrying Isaac Donner much of the way back, and then he had gone around the back of our cabin to check on Lewis Keseberg, who was alone in his lean-to. Thanks to the proximity and our shared wall, I could hear much of their exchange.

Five months ago, Lewis had called for us to hang Mr. Reed.

Now the man he had tried to kill said hello, offered him some supplies, bathed him, and helped him dress in clean clothing that Mr. Reed had carried himself. Then James Reed vowed to come back for Lewis in the next two weeks.

I couldn't even imagine making this journey four times over, much less making it for a man who had tried to end my life.

There weren't many things I wouldn't do for Mr. Reed if I could.

But instead, he continued to do things for us. Once we sat down at the designated campsite, which looked almost the same as everywhere else, with the exception of a small fire, we all collapsed. The rescuers told us to sit still while they cut more logs to keep the fire going, melted water, cooked some of the food into warm soup, and then passed it out in tin cups. When Patty passed around the rest of the bread she'd made, all the pieces halved so everyone could have one, there were a lot of smiles.

The second day went much as the first, although we did make it over the pass that had defeated us back on November first of the prior year.

That was a little exciting, but also depressing, thinking about just how miserable we'd been, and just how naive. At the time, we really thought we'd be able to wait for a bit and make it over later, once the weather had a good run.

On the second day, the rescuers took turns carrying Mary and Isaac again, and this time, when the day drew to a close, Bill McCutchen came and took her. "I heard you carried her yesterday," he said.

I shrugged. "Not for long."

"You shouldn't have had to carry anyone. You'd been carrying your baby all day."

"Not much in our lives is really about justice anymore," I said. "We all do what we can." When he said nothing, I added, "I'm sorry about your baby. She was beautiful, and the world is darker without her."

He didn't cry, but he nodded once.

It was enough.

But the third day. . .it started out alright, but about noon, clouds began to roll past, and Reed began looking at the sky with nervous eyes.

"Do clouds mean there's going to be a storm?" I asked.

Reed's grim expression was my only answer.

I was no mountaineer, but it seemed to me that we were in a very bad spot for bad weather. There were peaks on nearly all sides of us, and the snow underneath our feet was so high that we could barely see the tops of any trees. The ones we saw barely poked past my shoulder.

I very much doubted the blizzard would wait for us to reach a more accommodating place.

Apparently Mr. Reed agreed. "Make camp," Reed called. "Blizzard coming." As if to emphasize his words, the wind picked up, screaming past the pines around us.

I had endured quite a few blizzards in the past months. I'd hated each and every one. The wind whipped in through cracks in the door, and it screamed outside all night long, but at least we had a cabin and the snow around us insulated us from the worst of it.

Now a blizzard while camping on top of thirty feet of snow drift?

Upon consultation, we decided to make a fire and gather around it in a big circle. All of us put our feet toward the center, our backs forming a sort of windbreak. It was a windbreak we needed, because as the wind tore past us, chunks of snow and ice hit us like the scattering of buckshot.

Our children huddled between us, Patrick and I on either end, with John in the center. I held Isabella underneath my clothing, peering in to see whether she was alive from time to time. My milk had dried up entirely around the time I refused to eat Towser, but she still tried furiously to get something to eat whenever I let her. I had prayed for a miracle, that our extra rations would bring my milk back, but so far, nothing.

"Is she okay?" Patrick asked. I could barely hear him over the howling of the wind.

I nodded. Isabella was shivering, so I knew she was alive.

Elizabeth Graves was across from me, her baby also clutched against her, Nancy on one side, and Franklin Junior and Jonathan on the other.

Big Bill McCutchen and James Reed periodically stood up and left, sometimes with Hiram Miller or someone else, to search for more firewood. They went less and less often, and it took them longer each time as the storm went on.

After burning everything close, they began struggling to find more.

In many, many moments, I couldn't tell whether the fire was making any heat at all. The wind gusted so badly that any heat it made was immediately whisked away.

"Where's that Woodworth?" James Reed kept asking Bill. "He said he'd be right behind us."

"Who's Woodworth?" I asked.

"He's a man I met with the Navy, and he's responsible for bringing most of the supplies," Mr. Reed said. "He sent someone up river to say he was stuck, but I got sick of waiting on him. Even so, he was supposed to be *just* behind me. *Where is he?*"

I understood a bit more why he gave away so many supplies at the camps. It wasn't misplaced generosity. Any moment, he expected more supplies and men to appear. After having bread, gruel, and dried beef in small portions intermittently, I should feel better than I had before, but slogging our way through snow and trying to keep warm had taken its toll, and I felt empty.

No, worse than empty.

Hollowed out, like an empty shell.

The ache in my belly was painful and persistent.

My head began to pound constantly. I couldn't feel my fingers. Sometime in the middle of the night I nodded off. During that time, in an effort to warm up, big Bill McCutchen turned his back to the fire and crept closer and closer. He crept so close that his clothing caught fire. I woke up to his screaming, but by the time we got it put out, his four shirts had all burned, and his back was raw and blistered. It hurt just to look at the blackened parts.

I was grateful when he wrapped his blanket around it.

Sometime nearer to dawn, when I dozed off again, a screech from John brought me back. "He's—he's not moving." He was pointing at Isaac Donner, who had slumped face first into the snow. "Someone shake him."

Mr. Reed crawled around his two children, who were both trembling with cold and glassy-eyed, to check. Reed closed his eyes and shook his head.

Little Isaac had died.

He was only five. His mother wasn't here. We were all doing our best, but the storm was doing its worst, and it was too much. How could God have done this to us? How could this be happening?

"Can't we pass out some food?" I snapped.

Mr. Reed's eyes were sad. "I—I pressed on, positive my friend was coming right behind us." He shook his head again. "But it's been almost four days. There's nothing left."

I started wailing then.

It was all too much. As I looked around, everywhere I looked, people were freezing to death. The fire wasn't warm enough. The wind was too strong. The children—there was nothing we could do for any of them.

That's when I noticed poor Mary Donner's feet were *in* the fire.

I was holding Isabella, but I cried out, and Patrick stumbled forward to pull her out. It was too late—on one foot, the sole was melted so thin that I could see her feet beneath. On the other, the sole and her skin had both melted away. I couldn't look at the ruin.

I started to sob then, and I couldn't stop. "You did this to us," I said, shouting irrationally at the man who had come to save us. "You should have waited! At least we had cabins at the death camp."

Reed flinched.

The others murmured and scowled, but Bill McCutchen, his burned back covered only by the blanket he'd wrapped around it like a shawl, shook his head. "You were thanking us earlier. The weather can't be controlled."

I knew he was right, but I couldn't stop sobbing.

Instead, I decided to recite all the prayers I could think of. I started with *Hail Mary,* moved on to *Our Father*, and then did *Act of Contrition*. Mr. Reed tried to say something, but I couldn't stop. My tears were freezing on my cheeks or being whisked away as soon as they fell, but I couldn't stop. Nothing in this world made sense, but prayers were something I knew. As I finished up the *Nicene Creed*, the words hit me.

"I look forward to the resurrection of the dead and the life of the world to come."

I stopped.

I finally stopped praying and sobbing. Isaac Donner was dead, but he had moved on to the life to come. God didn't see as we saw. Isaac was probably eating as much bread as he wanted, and he was surely as warm as a summer's day. As the deep darkness of the miserable night began to lighten, a new day beginning, the storm raged on.

Like night turns to day, we would keep striving. We would keep struggling. Those whose struggle had ended would be with God. I had finally found some measure of peace in all the misery, even if my stomach, after nearly two long, brutally cold days without a single bite of food, screamed and protested.

"No!" Bill McCutchen, more attentive thanks to his recent ordeal, reached and grabbed my son John, catching my oldest child just in time to keep him from pitching forward into the fire.

The very thing that was keeping us alive kept trying to kill us.

Something struck me as terribly funny and sad and also horrifying about that. But as the light grew bright enough for us to really see, I noticed something.

Even though the fire was being kept propped up on a bed of green pine logs that Mr. Reed was working tirelessly to maintain, the whole thing was, nevertheless, sinking. The snow all around the fire was now at least ten feet lower than the drifts farther out all around it. The reason we kept sliding and pitching forward was that we were all sitting on the edge of a sinking pit.

But if we stopped burning the wood, we'd all freeze to death.

CHAPTER 30

Peggy Breen

Even though I prayed almost without ceasing, the storm never stopped. It never even slowed. After claiming Isaac Donner's life, after forcing us to huddle around a sinking fire all night, after screaming at us all day, it still showed no signs of letting up.

The second day of the storm was one of the most miserable days of my life, and I was almost an expert at enduring misery by now.

"The sun's setting again," Bill McCutchen said.

James Reed blinked.

"Hey, Reed," Bill said. "You okay?"

Mr. Reed passed a hand in front of his face. He swallowed slowly. "I. . .can't see."

"I've heard about this," Bill McCutchen said. "Amanda told me about it." His wife. "Almost all of them went snow-blind on the way out back in December."

"Bill and I will have to take over the fire," Hiram Miller said. He had been part of our party at the start, but he joined the mule party that traveled with Lansford Hastings ahead of us. When he heard how we'd been trapped, he was apparently one of the first men to volunteer.

And now he might die for it.

"We need longer logs." Thanks to a fluke of the wind, I heard Hiram

Miller's urgent whisper. "The pit keeps getting deeper and wider, and if we let the fire sink any farther. . ."

"We'll all freeze," Bill McCutchen said.

"How deep do you think that pit is now?" Hiram Miller peered over the edge, trying to see past the flames.

"It was ten feet after one day." Bill sighed. "Fifteen feet now at least."

In the coming hours, the fire guttered out, and Bill McCutchen and Hiram Miller *barely* rekindled it. No sooner had they done it then Mr. Reed tilted sideways. Both men leapt to his side, shaking and rubbing his arms. "Wake up," they screamed. "Reed, wake up! We need you."

They must have been close to giving up when James Reed finally opened his eyes and sat up. Poor little Patty Reed was too cold to even climb out of her meager blankets while she watched them try to revive her father. I couldn't even see Thomas. I hoped he hadn't followed poor Isaac Donner.

After they revived James Reed, I decided to shake all my kids to make sure they were still alive. I started with Patrick Junior, who was not pleased at my prodding.

"What are you doing?" Patrick hissed.

"Making sure they're alive," I said.

"What about Isabella?"

I nodded.

Then I poked James. He growled and moaned. Peter cried for me to hold him. As much as it pained me to keep crawling, I poked John next. He had his eyes closed, and I hated to interrupt any sleep he might be getting, but I had to make sure.

Only, John didn't respond. I shoved and shook him, and still nothing. My oldest son, my strongest son, the one who cut firewood for five months, the one who helped me with every single task when his father was ill, the one who butchered cattle and kept me going. . .was dead.

I closed my eyes.

I said a prayer. A frantic, frenzied prayer. The most desperate prayer I'd ever prayed, offering anything God wanted, *anything* at all, if only He would help me with this one thing. Keep my John alive.

I knew that wasn't how God worked. I'd told Patty and Virginia as much. You couldn't bargain for what you wanted. What was God's will was God's will, but I begged and pleaded and prayed anyway. I was willing to give anything, try anything.

That was when I remembered Lazarus.

"He's only sleeping," I said.

Patrick was shaking him by then too, and John still didn't shift. My husband's eyes were dark. "He's gone."

"He's only sleeping," I insisted.

I remembered something—something I'd utterly forgotten when Mr. Reed gave Patty that bag of flour and set her to baking bread. I remembered the sugar I'd hidden in the pocket of John's trousers. I reached beneath my shirts, beneath my skirts, jostling tiny Isabella until I found it. In the pocket, there was yet a whole cup of sugar. I pulled out a large pinch and pressed it into John's mouth. Then I closed his lips, and I prayed again, with purpose this time.

I practically screamed the words into the howling wind. "God, please revive your humble servant. I know you would welcome him home, but I still need him here. I've endured. I've cared for all my children as best I can, and my one plea is that I die before any of them do. Please, *please* bring him back to us."

A moment later, John's eyes fluttered open.

Patrick sprang to work, rubbing his arms and leg and helping him sit up. Not long after John sat up and began talking again, Nancy Graves began calling for her mother. Elizabeth had been tending the baby, so the two boys had crawled into a pile around their older sister.

Nancy, apparently, felt quite abandoned.

"Ma!" she howled. "Ma, help us too!"

"What do you need?" I asked. "Your mother's exhausted." It looked like Elizabeth was finally sleeping. I could see, barely, her body rising and falling, so I knew she wasn't dead.

"I'm cold," Nancy howled.

I could barely force myself to do it, but I crawled around the rim of the pit and dragged the blanket back over Nancy's side and tucked it under her leg.

Hiram Miller, watching what I was doing as he returned with wood, checked on Elizabeth Graves. "Are you alive? Are you alright? How's your baby?" She didn't answer. She just shook her head.

Then she started to groan.

It wasn't a sound that humans made. It was a groan and a rattle, and then a kind of wheezing keen, almost like the sound the oxen made before they gave up in the desert.

A moment later, she lay entirely still.

Poor little Nancy had been watching as intently as I had, and she knew. I saw her shoulders slump. I saw her expression crumple. Then I saw her crawl over to her mother, the one she'd just been crying out for, and take the baby from her arms. Nancy Graves, the oldest member of her family now in the mountains, held her little sister and stared off into the fire.

Eight years old, and already a surrogate mother.

Dawn came soon after, and with it, the snow began to slack. It was an answer to prayer, two days too late. Mr. Reed, who had nearly died the night before, gathered his two children and roused them as best he could. "We have to get moving," he said. "Woodworth isn't here, so we have no food. Our only hope is to keep moving until we reach someone with provisions."

I leaned against John. "I know you're tired. I know you almost died, but we have to get up. We have to keep moving." I sighed. "He's right."

John struggled to his feet, albeit unsteadily, but my five-year-old son James couldn't even sit up.

My husband Patrick was hardly any better. He shook his head. "We can't go on. Reed said more help was coming—this Woodworth man should be here any day with more supplies."

"Nonsense," I said. "We have no idea whether they'll even pass exactly this way."

"We burned logs on our way in," Hiram Miller said. "And so did Mr. Tucker before us. The path is well marked." He pointed behind us. "You can see one, right back there. They'll come this way."

"See?" Patrick said.

"No." Reed shook his head. "You can't stay. You all must come with us."

"Mary couldn't even walk before." Patrick pointed. "Her feet are even worse now. Who here can carry her?"

The rescuers shifted, all plainly uneasy.

"None of you can," Patrick said. "But you can hurry the other rescuers on when you meet them. You can tell them to come find us as quickly as they can."

While we argued, John had been busy. As the fire burned down, down, down, some of the green logs had fallen in. They now tilted at strange angles from the pit. More of the trees that had lost their tops and been burned as the fire worked its way down were also tilted, hitting one another at cross points.

"Ma!" John yelled. "I've climbed down, and there's dirt down here."

"What?" Patrick perked up. "There won't be wind down there, and if it's melted to the ground, we could burn a fire safely. We could stay warm."

It's relative, of course. None of us had been warm for a very long time —four months at least. But we could be *warmer*, and after two and a half days of nearly freezing to death, that sounded like heaven. Mary was already nodding enthusiastically.

James was struggling to sit up. "Yes, Ma," he said. "Please. Don't make me try and stand. Just carry me down there."

"You can't stay here," James Reed said. "You'll all die."

"Which is no different than if we try to follow you," Patrick said. "But if we stay here, we'll be together. It's better to die warm by a fire than to collapse somewhere on the trail."

James Reed's eyes were wide, his hands clenched at his sides. He shook his head. "I—please don't do this." He turned toward me, his expression desperate. "You saved my family. *Please* come with me."

"You can barely carry Tommy," I said. "You've done all you can for us."

"I'll carry Tommy," Hiram Miller said. "Reed's carrying Patty."

I shook my head. Staying was madness. Traveling was madness. We'd entered a world with no viable options. We watched as James Reed, Bill McCutchan, Hiram Miller and the others cut wood and stacked it near the top of our pit, and then walked away.

Patty Reed must have turned around a dozen times. The rescuers were departing with only three of the people they'd come to save. Patty, Tommy, and Jacob Donner's stepson, fourteen-year-old Solomon Hook, left.

Elizabeth Graves and Isaac Donner were dead, killed by the blizzard.

The rest of us stayed behind.

As they walked away, John helped the children descend into the pit Patrick had just climbed down into. Mary Donner went first, clinging to John's back with a determined look on her face. Patrick Junior climbed down on his own, and I managed to descend with little Isabella, leaving her in her father's arms.

The embers on the ground were flaming back to life with Patrick's help when I passed her off to him.

John and I climbed laboriously back to the top for James and Peter, and then we did the same thing two more times to retrieve the four Graves children. As I started down with little Elizabeth Graves, she cried out and reached for her mother. The bodies of Elizabeth Graves and Isaac Donner lay there, at the edge of our pit, a desperate reminder of what we were hoping without much real hope to avoid.

But I couldn't keep from thinking about Levinah Murphy—that decision I'd thanked God for not needing to make was upon me. Two adults and ten children, and all of us about to starve or freeze. . .in a pit of ice. Rescuers on the way, people who knew we were here.

How far would I go to keep my family alive?

Mary Donner seemed almost chipper, once she warmed up a bit by the fire, but the children had trouble sleeping that night, being so hungry and miserable. After they'd finally fallen asleep, I worked my way over to Patrick's side.

"We're going to starve here."

His head turned toward me slowly. "So be it."

"There's food at the top of the pit."

He shook his head. "No."

"Patrick."

"No." He shook his head again.

The next morning, before anyone had woken up, I took Patrick's knife up to the top of the pit, and started looking for something—anything—to eat. I closed my eyes, and I knelt in the snow, and I begged God to help me. I just needed one small thing—one tiny thing. "Please, God," I prayed. "Just send me something—some kind of sign. Tell me what to do."

In that moment, I heard the rustle of a branch. I didn't think. I didn't wait. I threw my knife, and it whistled through the air, and struck the top of a lopped off pine tree.

Pinning the wing of a bird.

I broke its neck with my bare hands, and then I cut up Isaac Donner's tiny body, and I sliced open the bird, and I carried everything down into the pit, my hands full of feathers and blood.

"I prayed," I announced, "and God sent us food."

Patrick lurched up until he was sitting, and he glared. But when he saw the bird's feathers and beak, he closed his eyes and flopped back against the ground.

I cooked everything I had brought down, and I fed it to all the children. By way of penance, in spite of how good everything smelled, in spite of the pounding of my head, in spite of my cramping belly, I ate a few bites of the bird and nothing more.

"Here," I said, handing my husband some grilled meat. "Eat."

"This is bird," he said, looking me in the eye. "You swear it."

I knew he'd ask. I had put one single bite of that tiny brown bird on top of his food. "It is," I said. "I swear it."

God never sent me another bird, and Patrick never asked me to swear on what I fed him again. I think, in his heart of hearts, he knew. John knew for sure, because he helped me carve steps into the snow so we only had to cross from one side of the pit to the other across a log in one spot.

He helped me butcher and carry down food, and he helped me cook and feed the children. Everyone ate bits of Isaac Donner except for me. I couldn't bring myself to eat a single bite after preparing it. I had pinches of sugar, and I ate pine bark, the pulpy part on the underside, and I ignored the pounding in my head and the cramping of my belly, and I fed the children and Patrick.

Even so, we were quickly out of food again.

A small boy of five who had been starving for four months didn't provide much, and I couldn't really bring a lot down without Patrick realizing there was no way I'd killed so many birds. Frankly, throwing the knife at the one creature had been complete idiocy. By all counts, I should have missed and lost the blade, buried forever under soft, fluffy snow.

I had avoided cannibalizing Mrs. Graves because her four children were down below.

But in spite of my best efforts, her son Franklin Junior died three days after we descended into the pit. I gave him a pinch of sugar after I realized he was gone, but it didn't help. John and I hauled him up to lay next to his mother and what remained of Isaac Donner.

"You have to do it," John said. "If it were you, and you were dead, wouldn't you want us to eat you?"

I thought about how opposed Patrick was, and even so, I nodded.

When I went back down, I was trying to decide how I could explain the existence of more meat when John dropped down next to James on all fours. Ever since the end of the blizzard, my poor son had been struggling. He still couldn't sit up, and now he wasn't moving at all.

I said another prayer, and I put the last pinch of sugar I had left in his mouth, and we waited. At first, all our rubbing and prayers did nothing. But then, miraculously, he too revived.

That night, while everyone slept, John and I crept up and cut up Mrs. Graves as well.

"Why did you wait so long?" John asked me softly. "James almost died."

"I would beg you to eat me," I said. "But your father's *so* opposed. I'm worried that even if you live. . ." I shook my head.

"Dad gave up," John said. "He would rather die than do whatever it takes to live. He's not even trying to protect us. I hate him for it."

"You can't hate him," I said. "He loves God more than anything else, and he thinks this is wrong. He's a man of principles."

"But you love us more," John said.

"I'm a mother."

I was back at the top of the pit, alone, a little before sunset, hunting for branches I could drag back. Our wood was gone, so it fell to John and me to cut and drag everything we needed.

That's the only reason I saw them.

I waved furiously, and I shouted as loudly as I could. The two men walking past froze. They turned slowly, and then they walked toward me. As they drew near enough for me to make out more, I could tell they were young. They were hardy.

I had met them before.

"You're Stone and Cady, right?" I lurched toward them. "It's Peggy Breen. You met me on your way to Alder Creek."

The taller one, Stone I think, frowned. Then he shook his head. "We're headed back."

"Can you take a child with you at least?" I pointed back toward the pit. "There are eleven of us. We've been here since the storm. The fire kept sinking and sinking, and now we're at the bottom of a pit."

Stone shook his head. "We can't carry anyone. We don't want to die ourselves."

"But surely, a small child—"

"What's that?" Cady pointed. The two of them took a few more steps and froze. "You're eating people here, too." His lip was curled. "I heard the Breens hadn't done that. I guess I heard wrong."

"I did it only for the children," I said. "So they wouldn't die."

"You should have let them." Cady turned around and started walking, Stone on his heels.

"You have no idea what we've been through," I said. "And judging by how you're running away, you'd have died in the first tribulation." They ignored me, and a flash of anger bubbled up inside of me. "You're cowards! You came to be heroes, but being a hero is messy. It's painful. It's terrifying. And it was something neither of you could handle. Go ahead and go, but our deaths are on your heads."

Stone turned around for a moment, staring at me.

"When I get to hell," I said. "I'll make sure they're ready for you."

He swallowed slowly, turned and walked away, churning slushy snow as he abandoned us. My fury soon faded, because in my heart, I couldn't even blame them. I hadn't eaten human flesh, but I was the biggest monster of all—feeding a mother to her own children. That was the moment I realized that everything I'd done might have been for nothing. It had been days and days, and still no one had come.

We were all going to die.

I spent the rest of my strength gathering wood. I gathered wood until I couldn't gather another single stick, and then I climbed down into the pit for the very last time. Just as Patrick had said, at least we could all die warm next to a fire instead of alone and frozen on the trail.

Two days passed like that before we ran out of wood.

It was a good idea, really.

Dying warm by a fire. But you can't really control how long your body will cling to life. When you're desperate to live, you can die, like Isaac Donner, Elizabeth Graves, and little Franklin Junior. But even once you've surrendered, sometimes the length of your suffering rests in God's hands.

After the fire guttered, the last embers barely glowing, I surveyed those lying around me in the miserable hole. Without eating more than a few bites here and there, you make a surprisingly small amount of waste. We'd designated one small spot on the far end behind a fallen log for waste, and all of us who could crawl went there.

John and I were the only two who could even stand.

But now, with the fire running low, it fell to me and John to gather more wood, or we'd die in a pit, freezing and starving, while my children cried piteously for things to just end.

The worst death imaginable.

"We have to go back up," I said.

John didn't argue. He just inhaled deeply and dragged himself back upright. Even so, I had to take the first crawling lurches toward our crude stairs before he started to move vertically. We were both too tired to move, but too strong yet to die.

After reaching the top, I was too tired to go on.

John, however, had brought a knife. "We need more, Ma."

I didn't argue with him. While I struggled, crawling on my hands and knees looking for more branches to burn. John carved on poor little Franklin Graves. As I tossed branches down—we'd found a place we could shove them that had a cross-lying log that made them ricochet to the corner without hitting anyone—I worried about what I'd tell Patrick. There were no birds and no squirrels. We had no explanation whatsoever for what John and I were about to bring down.

But when we reached the bottom, rekindled the fire, and began to cook what John had carved off, the concern was taken from me. Patrick wasn't even conscious. Once the meat began to cook, tiny bits John had carved from Franklin's arms and legs, his liver, and his kidneys, almost everyone roused. Their bulging eyes peered at us out of skeletal faces. Their skin was red, scaly, and raw in places, and their hair was matted and filthy, but they were all alive.

And they could smell food.

As I fed the children, I wondered whether I should have simply let everyone freeze. My mouth salivated, and my hands shook, and I have never in my life wanted to eat something as badly as I wanted to eat Franklin Graves Junior.

The only way I could think to punish myself for making such terrible decisions was to deny myself a single bite. After everyone had eaten, they all collapsed back to the ground.

Even John.

But the fire had been burning for a while to cook what we'd brought down. I crawled over to the corner where the branches we had tossed down fell, only to realize that they had gotten stuck. They were two-thirds of the way up the pit, still, thanks to one errant branch. The only way to free them was to climb almost all the way out again.

I climbed up three steps, then shimmied across the log, and then I started up the steps on the far side. My hands were numb from the ice. My eyes only partially worked—yesterday I'd started seeing spots almost every time I moved. My teeth ached. My arms howled with even the slightest exertion, but I pulled upward.

Like those inhuman eyes that stared at me, getting firewood for my children had become a compulsion. I'd do it, or I'd die trying. I was almost to the top when I saw it. The branch that was lodged against an outcropping of ice was close. If I could simply lean to one side, I could kick it free.

But I didn't have the strength to do it.

I started to cry.

Sobbing like a baby, incoherent, I almost didn't hear them. Someone was talking. Then another voice answered.

Was I hearing things? I froze in place. If there really were rescuers, could I face them? We had done nothing to hide the three bodies at the top of the pit. They would see that we had eaten two children and started Franklin's mother. They'd know just what we were—doomed and damned.

I slumped against the side of the pit and began to sob silently.

Why couldn't God just let us die?

But then a head poked over the side of the pit. "Mrs. Breen?" The same voice shouted back toward the others. "Come quickly. You did see smoke—Mrs. Breen is alive yet, anyhow."

"Mrs. Breen?"

I couldn't make out any facial features, so blurred was my vision, but the voice I recognized.

"Mr. Eddy?" My voice shook. "Is that you?"

"Can't you see me?"

I shook my head. "No food for—well. More than a week."

"But you had—"

I heard scuffling around.

"Just for the children," I said. "The children were dying." I shook my head. "And now I fear they're going to die anyway."

"How many are yet alive?" That sounded like Mr. Foster. "Here, let us lift you out."

"How many of you are yet alive?" Mr. Eddy asked.

"Franklin Junior died a few days ago," I said. "Mrs. Graves and Isaac Donner died in the blizzard. Everyone else is alive."

Hands reached down then, seizing my shoulders and lifting me from the pit. They set me gently on the edge. I blinked several times, and then I could make them out.

Hiram Miller I recognized. "You came back?"

"You can see me now?" Mr. Miller smiled. "Indeed, how could I not return?" He sighed. "I could have been stuck here myself."

"But then, did Reed and the others. . .?"

Hiram nodded. "We finally met Woodworth. The coward was just sitting down near the snow line." He practically growled. "You should have heard Reed go after him. They'd raised funds and run the whole rescue together, but when it came time to really help, the man did nothing."

"He got tired from carrying his blanket," Mr. Eddy said. "Foster and I came with virtually nothing, but we're still going."

"We're hoping for a miracle," Mr. Foster said.

"Your sons," I said. "Of course. They were alive when I left."

A few moments later, Mr. Foster and Mr. Eddy and the men they'd paid personally to help rescue their sons left, continuing onward with haste. Hiram Miller was one of them. My heart expanded at the courage he'd shown. He came all the way to our camps, did all he could to keep us safe through a blizzard, carried Tommy Reed out, and then came back to help Mr. Eddy. I said a small prayer for the Eddy and Foster boys and the four brave men trying to save them.

When I opened my eyes again, three of the men were still staring at me. "I can take a child," one man said. A young man. A man I now recognized.

"Mr. Stone." I swallowed.

"You called me a coward." His lips compressed. "You said you'd ready a place for me in hell."

"I—I was angry," I said.

"You were right," he said. "I was a coward, and I didn't like it. So I came back. I'm hoping that place won't be needed."

"We all make bad decisions sometimes," I said. "Fixing them is hard, but it's worth the effort."

He nodded. "I'm sorry for what I said to you, and I'm sorry we left you. I can take a child back. It may not make things right, but it's a start."

"Mary Donner still can't walk or even stand," I said, "but she's still alive. Her father and brother have already died." It hurt to say the words. "She had frostbitten feet, and now they're burned. You'd have to carry her the entire way."

"I'll do it." He climbed down and located her. He wrapped a blanket around her, tying her to his shoulders and waist, and then carried her back out.

"I could take a child as well," the other man said. "My name is Howard Oakley. I'm sorry you've had to go through this."

"Take Jonathan Graves," I said. His sister was in better shape, but she was the only one that baby Elizabeth wanted. I couldn't split those two up.

Howard Oakley went down and got Johnny the same way that Mr. Stone had taken Mary, wrapping a blanket around Jonathan's tiny body and carrying him out on his back. "You probably can't take Nancy and baby Elizabeth," I said to the last man. "If I can convince her to leave the baby with me, maybe you could take Nancy."

"How many of you are there?" The man's eyes were kind. "Including you."

"I have five children," I said. "And my husband isn't conscious, but he's alive too. My oldest boy, John, might be able to walk. Not very fast, but maybe a little."

The man nodded, his face somber. "I'll take John, and I'll take this Nancy. I think I could carry the baby too, if her older sister can keep hold of her."

My heart swelled inside my chest. Poor Eddie and Simon wouldn't be all alone if John survived. "Thank you." My voice broke on you, and I dropped my face in my hands. "Two of my boys went with the first group, with Margaret Reed and her other two children."

Mr. Stark stared at me, silently. "You can walk."

I sighed. "I could walk. I can crawl a little. I—I haven't been eating when the others did. I—I couldn't."

He nodded slowly. "I understand."

"We know we can't survive this," I said. "We're not delusional." That made me smile. "At least, I'm not right this minute, anyway."

Mr. Stark shook his head then. "Actually, I won't leave anyone," he said. "You're all going."

"You'll die on the mountain if you try to take all of us," I said. "Did you hear the other men? That Stone man and another man he was with walked right past us before. They didn't even try to take someone down. If another storm hits—we'll slow you down. You'll surely get caught."

He shrugged, repeating his proclamation. "I won't leave any of you."

I couldn't breathe. "It's suicide."

He crouched down beside me, and he pressed his hand against his chest. "I'm John Schull Stark. From the time I turned fourteen and started growing, do you know what everyone has said to me?"

I shook my head.

"Good God, you're huge, Stark." He snorted. "Or 'you're built like a mountain, kid. What have you been eating?'"

"There are nine of us," I said. "My husband, my fourteen-year-old son. My baby daughter, and three other boys. Nancy Graves, her baby sister, and me." I shook my head. "It's just too many, even if you're large."

"And yet." He stood. "I won't leave without all of you."

I shoved to my feet. "Didn't you hear me? None of us can walk."

"You're standing now," he said. He leaned closer, his voice a whisper. "I have four children, you know. And if they were here, I wouldn't leave any of them either. So go down there and rouse them. I'll set my pack down and lay down a tarp and come down to start carrying them out."

"But the storms can come at any time." I was sure he didn't really understand.

He stopped arguing with me, set his pack on the snow beside me, and began carefully picking up the mutilated corpses and dragging them away until they were hidden behind a copse of hacked-off tree trunks protruding from the snow. Then he came back, rummaged around in his pack and pulled out a thick blanket, laying it out on the ground. Since I hadn't moved, he ignored me.

John Stark climbed down the crude stairs, scrambling across the log with a lot more agility than I expected from a man his size, and used another small blanket to tie Nancy Graves on his back. He carried baby Elizabeth up the whole way in his arms.

Once he reached the top, he handed me the baby. Then he carefully set Nancy Graves on the blanket he'd spread across the snow next to me. "I'll be right back."

He came up the second time with Jonathan Graves on his back in the blanket and Patrick in his arms. My poor, emaciated husband was carried like he was a child by that massive man.

Patrick barely even opened his eyes.

John walked up after John Stark, making eyes at the space where Isaac Donner, Elizabeth, and Franklin Graves Junior's bodies had been. Then he nodded. "We're really being rescued?"

I sighed. "Or we're going to die, freezing on the trail, more like."

"At least we're not huddling down there anymore," John said.

Once John Stark had carried everyone out, he started a fire. He used a tin cup to melt snow, and to each of us, he mixed a little flour and some water into a gruel and fed us in turn. It was the first food I'd had in many days.

He also handed me a strip of dried beef. "Eat this." He did the same to John. "And you."

By the time he was ready to go, John and I could both stand again— it's shocking what a bit of gruel can do. Or maybe it was something else, something we hadn't had in an even longer time.

Hope.

Either way, I carried Isabella, and John carried Elizabeth, who was too exhausted to know whose arms she was in, and we stumbled forward.

"It's ninety-four miles to Sutter's Fort," John Stark said. "We don't have to go that far. There's a cowardly man named Woodworth who's camped out with his men at a place on the edge of the mountains, maybe twenty miles from here."

"Twenty miles?" As I said the words, I realized it might as well be twenty thousand miles.

With every step, John and I sank up to our knees or higher in the snow. As the two of us struggled along, carrying babies who weighed almost nothing, John Stark carried the others, two at a time. He picked up Jonathan and Nancy and carried them twenty or thirty yards and then set them down. Then he'd walk back and pick up James and Patrick Junior. He'd set them down and go back for Patrick and Peter.

By then we'd have pulled ahead.

He'd start all over, moving past us quickly, and then falling behind as he walked back and forth, over and over. We hadn't gone far when I could no longer carry Isabella. I collapsed in the snow, tears welling in my eyes.

My son sat down a few steps ahead, probably as tired as I was.

John Stark ground to a halt not far ahead of us, dropping the two people he was carrying and backtracking like always.

"I can't go any farther," I said. "You keep on. Leave me here."

"You can keep going." John Stark's eyes were steady. "You've already done things that would have broken anyone else I've met. You kept going when you had nothing left. That means God's already with you."

I dropped my face in my hands. "You should let me die. The things I did—"

"You need to let go of all that," John Stark said. "You're a mother, and one of the finest mothers I've ever seen. You did what had to be done. You're strong, and God knows it. He made you strong enough to keep all of them alive."

"I—it's too much."

"It's just one more step," Mr. Stark said. "Think of it that way. Each step you take, you just have to go one more."

"What about when I can't go a single extra step?"

John Stark smiled. "That's when you take a break." He walked back toward his pack, raising his voice. "Let's see if I have any food in my pack."

After another cup of gruel, I discovered that I could stand.

But I wasn't the only one who noticed that Mr. Stark didn't eat a single bite this time either. "You should eat something," Nancy Graves said. "You haven't eaten a thing, and you're carrying all of us."

"When we get out of the snow, I'll eat," he said.

"But there's so much snow," Jonathan Graves said. "You should eat now."

John Stark shook his head. "I hate eating when I'm cold."

"I like eating any time," James said. "And I'll eat almost anything."

"What about pork?" When John Stark pulled out strips of salted pork, everyone squealed with glee.

Even me.

It was exciting enough that John and I both struggled to our feet again.

"I'll give everyone some of this pork the next time we stop. Less than a mile away."

"Don't carry me," my husband Patrick said.

"Can you walk?" John's eyebrows went up. "That's wonderful."

Patrick shook his head, not meeting John's eyes. "Just leave me."

John Stark rolled his eyes. "You must need more food. You're still delusional." He scooped him up and carried him first, not giving him time to argue.

When John Stark showed up with the last two children, two-year-old Peter and Nancy Graves, this time, Nancy was chatting. "I just feel so bad," she said. "I mean, the snow is so deep, and you're having to carry all of us. I'm so sorry."

"You weigh less than birds," John Stark said. "If you ever have to carry five people twelve miles through snow, make sure they've all starved properly first."

Nancy burst out laughing.

"I mean it," he said. "You all weigh so little that if God had simply thought to give me a wider back, I could just carry you all at once."

That night, Mr. Stark made gruel again, but this time, he sprinkled a little sugar into each cup.

"You must have some," I said. "Please."

He shook his head. "Listen, I told you we'd do this, and we will. If things get bad for me, I'll eat. Right now, you all need it much, much more. Trust me to know my own limits."

The second day was better than the first. For the first hour or so, Nancy walked. Her energy was short lived, but it was a huge improvement. On the third day, she managed to walk close to three hours. Patrick walked for an hour, too.

It was while my husband was trudging his way through the snow that a rabbit burst out and took off running.

Mr. Stark practically dumped James and Jonathan on the ground and yanked out his gun. He took aim, and he fired. An hour later, we were all eating rabbit. I'd never had anything so delicious in my life, not even the biscuits of sweet cakes the rescuers brought.

On day four, Patrick walked until close to midday. Nancy walked all day. We covered more ground that day than we had in the previous three. A few hours into the fifth day, John Stark shot another rabbit, and this time, we convinced him to eat a few bites.

All of us cheered.

On the sixth day, we reached Woodworth and the other men as we came down the mountain and reached the Yuba River. Even then, John Schull Stark never left our sides. He had some help carrying us, and once we hit the end of the snow, there were even mules some of us could ride on, but he stayed with us, all the way back to Johnson's Ranch.

When we finally reached Johnson's Ranch, it was long after dark. Even so, someone must have roused Edward and Simon, because as we approached, they rushed out toward us. Not caring that I was filthy, or emaciated, or exhausted, Eddie threw his arms around me. "Ma!"

Simon wrapped himself around my waist as well. "You finally made it. I was so tired of waiting."

"We did," I said, smiling through my tears.

"How did you get here?" Eddie released me. "Mr. Reed said they left you crawling into a pit in the ground. A 'starving pit,' he called it." His face was drawn and tense.

"We thought we were going to die," I admitted. "In fact, I thought I knew that we would die."

"God saved you," Eddie said, as faithful as we'd taught him to be. "I knew he would. We prayed and prayed, Virginia too, every single day."

"We felt those prayers," I said.

"And Mr. Woodworth answered them," Simon said. "Everybody's talking about how he saved you all."

I shook my head, then. "I thank nobody," I said emphatically. "Nobody but God, the Virgin Mary, and John Stark."

No one else could have done what he did.

As far as I was concerned, John Stark was God's hands on that mountain. I'd never believe anything else.

CHAPTER 31

Mary Ann Graves

When I reached Johnson's Ranch, my feet were destroyed. I looked like a filthy hag, and my clothing had been shredded and torn to the point of horrible indecency, not that I had any curves or anything for someone to leer at.

I had arrived more than half-dead.

But the faces I saw in the people who surrounded us looked perfectly welcoming, perfectly healthy. Round, soft, and smiling. I had grown so accustomed to seeing the other wraiths who had traveled with me that their visages didn't disturb me overmuch either.

In the months that followed, the charity of others helped nurse me back to health. My feet slowly healed. My body regained curves and fat, and slowly, slowly, I became human again.

When Virginia Reed showed up, tumbling into Johnson's Ranch with the same energetic fervor she'd always had, I could hardly believe it. She looked like a skeleton, but she still smiled like an angel.

"Mary Ann!" She raced toward me, for all the world nothing like a starved refugee. She threw her arms out to hug me.

"You made it." I still couldn't wear shoes—my feet were better, but not healthy yet. "Now you have a very hard thing to do." I eyed her with my severest face.

"What?" She frowned. "Tell me."

"You must eat everything you possibly can for as long as you can." I broke into a smile then. "Let's get started right away."

"But wait," Virginia said. "Did you hear?"

"That Mother stayed behind?" I nodded. "One of the rescuers already said as much."

Virginia smiled, her thin, scaly lips peeling back to reveal her teeth. "Billy convinced her he could chop lots of wood before he left—he came."

As if her statement summoned him, I spotted my brother, hobbling down the hill. My feet were still sore, but I raced toward him anyway, barefoot. I hadn't seen anyone in my family other than Sarah for two months, and even Virginia's drawn face hadn't prepared me.

Billy was bright, and jovial, and kind. He was healthy and strong, rangy and limber, just like Pa. He could walk for miles, cut firewood, take aim and shoot birds, rabbits, and deer. He rode like the wind, and he kept me safe from the hostile Indians.

Only, the man in front of me looked days away from dead.

It hurt to look at him.

His face looked like Pa's, right before he died. I broke down before he reached me, sobbing. He knew me better than anyone but Sarah, and he understood. He simply stood in front of me while I got myself together, and then he held out his skeletal arms.

I hugged him too tightly, but I couldn't help it. I heard his bones grinding together, but still I squeezed. Thankfully, I'd watched the women we were staying with making several loaves of bread just that morning. I ushered him toward the kitchen, and I sat him down next to Virginia and watched as the women fed them both.

Small portions, always small portions.

But I planned to feed them *a lot* of small portions over the next weeks. Billy would not feel hungry again, not any time soon, not if I had anything to say about it. I helped the people who reached Johnson's Ranch as much as I could once I could walk again, sticking around in part to provide a friendly face to the survivors who made it over the mountain, and in part because I wanted to be there if any of my family survived. It helped too that Sarah, Billy, and I had nowhere else to go. The Johnson family blessedly welcomed us, as long as we helped out with our share of chores as we were able.

"What will we do?" Sarah asked me the day after the first group arrived. Billy was sleeping in the room we shared, waking at odd intervals to eat. "The rescuers up there, saving them right now. Did you hear that William Eddy already turned around and headed back up?"

"Yeah, but his wife and daughter died." I winced. "This is his second attempt. I hope he doesn't have to come back down this time, too. That idiot isn't giving himself time to heal before diving back into the mountains."

"Grief is like that," Sarah said. "And don't pretend that you don't want to go."

I froze, my hands plunged into the dough, kneading. I made bread from a stool every single day. It was therapeutic. And I wanted there to be fresh bread at all times, just in case the others made it. "I do want to go back," I said. "Every time I close my eyes, I think about Ma, all by herself, watching all the children."

"I think about little Elizabeth," Sarah said. "I think about Nancy, ordering everyone around, and Jonathan, letting her." She perched on a chair. "Do you think they'll make it here soon?"

The waiting was miserable, especially because it *wasn't* miserable, but we knew what it must be like for them. We'd been there. But then James Reed showed up, gathering his family. We didn't intrude—they'd been separated a long time, and Patty and Thomas were not in great shape. But within a few hours of their arrival, after the small ones were fed and resting, we slowly made our way over.

"You're here to ask about your mother," James Reed said.

I nodded.

He sighed. "I hate this part. We were stuck in a blizzard," he said. "A terrible, awful storm."

It had been bad here, too, but we'd been warm and safe inside. The animals had wailed, scratching at the door. The wind had screamed, but we'd been safe.

It made me think about the blizzard when we lost Pa. "Ma didn't make it."

James Reed shook his head.

It hurt.

Badly.

"The others were alive when I left," he said, "but none of them could walk, and the Breens insisted they had to stay and wait for more rescuers." Mr. Reed winced. "I tried to rouse them, but without luck."

At first, Sarah and I were too upset to do much but cry. But later, hours later, Sarah sat next to me and wrapped an arm around me. "We should tell Billy how Pa died. If Ma had to die too, at least they died in the same way, and they're together now."

Billy had woken up behind us, and he startled me when he said, "Pa thought he was damned. For not rescuing Hardcoop, and for exiling Reed."

"Reed saved you all," I said. "Once we came, he was the one to rally everyone else, including most of the first small rescue attempt."

"Pa's not in hell," Sarah said. "Neither are Jay and Ma."

I knew that was true—we'd already been through hell. There was no way God would punish him after what we'd already endured.

Not long after, Mrs. Breen brought Nancy, Jonathan, and baby Elizabeth. She also brought news that Franklin Junior had died. But holding little Elizabeth in my arms, I was overwhelmed by gratitude. The mountain had claimed too many of us, but thanks to Ma and Pa's love for each other and for us, a lot of us had survived.

We had each other.

The Reed family was about to leave—Mr. Reed had already laid claim on some land or other, and they had a place to go. I had a brief flash of jealousy, but I was happy for Virginia. She had gained quite a bit of weight in just a few weeks, and she had color in her face that brought me joy.

"I'm going to miss you," I said. "A lot. But I wish you and your family well."

"I'm going to miss her too," a man I couldn't quite see said. "But she refuses to marry me, so I'm stuck."

"She's only thirteen," I said.

"I'm not ready to get married," Virginia said. "And I certainly don't want to marry the kind of person who's interested in a skeleton." She flounced her way out, winking at me on the way.

Suddenly, it was just me and the man who wanted to marry Virginia Reed. His face, now that I could see it, was flushed. "I'm embarrassed you saw that," he said. "I feel like an idiot."

"There's a place in this world for idiots," I said. "You could say that all the men who have been aiding the relief effort are idiots. Every one of them has risked his life."

"Not me," the man said. "My pa refused to let me go up into the mountains—I'm all he has. All we've done is run supplies up the hill to the camp they set up just past the base of the mountains."

"That's still important," I said. "And if I was all my pa had, I'd listen to him." A wave of sorrow hit me.

"Edward Pyle Junior." The man held out his hand.

When I shook it, a little thrill ran up my arm. "Nice to meet you."

His eyes darted down, then. "Do you need shoes?" He tilted his head. "My pa makes pretty decent ones. Moccasins, but they're very comfortable. He was taught by this man named—"

I shook my head. "My feet are still healing. I can't handle wearing shoes quite yet."

The man pulled a face. "Of course. I always say the wrong thing, you know."

He really did.

But I'd learned that there were worse things than a little awkward conversation. When the good, kind, only-son-to-his-pa Edward Pyle Junior proposed to me six weeks later, I said yes with a smile and a light heart.

Virginia Reed almost unwittingly stole my fiancé on the first part of our journey, but I was happy to take her cast-off, would-be fiancé here in California and make a life with him.

In fact, I was happy to have a life to live at all.

<h1 style="text-align: center; font-style: italic;">Epilogue</h1>

Dear Mrs. Breen:

I can't believe John struck gold! I'm so pleased he was smart enough to buy that amazing home with his money for all of you. I'm not sure if you heard about poor Mary Ann and her miserable business—I still can't believe that man murdered her sweet husband. Did you hear that she took food to him every single day in jail so he would live long enough to be hanged?

She was devastated after her husband died, and I spent quite a lot of time with her, cheering her up. But she has remarried, and the man she is married to now *adores* her. In fact, he's named the town he founded Marysville for her. How'd you like something like that? She deserves all of it, as I'm sure you agree.

And you already know that I kept my word to both you and God and was baptized a Catholic, but I have even bigger news. While dutifully attending mass, I met a very handsome man.

I waited for Eddie for a while, you know, but clearly he's never going to be ready to have a family, at least, not with me. I do wish him well, and I'll always love him just a little bit. But while I was waiting for your son to wise up, I met a man who does want a family.

And did I already say how handsome he is?

He calls me the Belle of San Jose. Doesn't that just have the nicest ring to it? He's a businessman, and his business is quite a funny one. He takes money from people and in return, if their house burns down, his company pays for it.

It's called 'fire insurance.'

Maybe you'd heard of it before. Papa said it's not a new idea, but it sure sounded new to me. Anyhow, Papa just loved him. He said he was smart and fine and he liked that he was asking me out.

Right up until he found out Mr. John Murphy was a Catholic.

Oh, boy, was he angry after that. He shouted and turned bright red, and he and Mama *forbade* me to marry him. You know me well enough to guess that his anger just made me more determined. Thankfully, with his business and all, Mr. Murphy had options. His pride, though, it almost ruined everything. Right before we were supposed to get married, he bumped into Papa in the street and bragged that he was going to marry me *anyway*.

You'll believe me when I tell you I shouted at John something fierce.

But after I forgave him, we came up with a new plan. I ran across the street, telling my mama I was checking on a sick neighbor. John was supposed to bring a priest, only the dumb old priest was scared of Papa. Can you believe that?

Anyway, we wound up just declaring we were married, and then we got the formal papers and such later. We had to jump onto horses—I have a fine grey that's a lot like Papa's Glaucus—and race away. Papa couldn't find us for three days, and by then, he had to give over. Isn't it all just so terribly romantic and exciting?

I'm going to have nine kids—just wait.

I've been inspired by you, you know. I can't believe that after having seven children and keeping them all safe through that harrowing ordeal. . .you had another one! Eventually, you'll get a letter from me announcing that I've had all *nine* of my children, and then you'll smile. Because if Mrs. Peggy Breen could raise eight of the finest children and be a perfect mother while we were stuck in the mountains in the middle of winter, then I can certainly bring one more into the world in sunny, beautiful California.

My only bad news is that the gorgeous weather here hasn't seemed to help Mama much. Can you believe that she seemed to do better in the middle of that horrible lake camp than she does here, in paradise?

It's true. Her headaches are terrible as ever, and she spends all her time in bed.

Sometimes, when she's asleep and can't hear, Papa will joke that maybe he'll starve Mama, since that's when she seems to feel the best. I know he's kidding, but I do pray a lot for her health. If you have an extra moment, maybe you could too. I think God listens better to you than he does to most people.

And he should.

I do still think back, sometimes, about how many people you saved that horrible winter. Me, for sure. My mother. Patty. Little Thomas, and stubborn James Junior. But not only us. You saved your own children, your cantankerous husband, even when he hardly seemed worth the trouble, Mr. Spitzer (as long as you could), and really anyone who asked for help.

I even heard you helped save Mary Donner and the Graves children after their mother died. I think I maybe said this before, but in case I didn't, *thank you.* For saving us, and also just for being you. Some people have a light or something inside of them, and that's you for sure. Whenever I think about you, it makes me smile.

Keep shining that light, Peggy. Never let it dim.

Yours ever, faithfully and lovingly,

Virginia Blackenstoe Reed Murphy

<h1 style="text-align:center">Donner Party Members</h1>

Names that are underlined perished. Ages at death/escape in parenthesis.

The Breen Family from Ireland by way of Keokuk, Iowa
    Patrick Breen (51)
    Margaret Bulger Breen (40)
    John Breen (14)
    Edward Breen (13)
    Patrick Breen Jr. (9)
    Simon Preston Breen (8)
    James Frederick Breen (5)
    Peter Breen (3)
    Isabella Breen (1)

The Reed Family from Springfield, Illinois
    James Frazier Reed (45)
    Margaret Keyes (Backenstoe) Reed (32)
    Virginia Backenstoe Reed (13)
    Martha Jane "Patty" Reed (8)
    James F. Reed Jr. (6)
    Thomas Keyes Reed (4)
    <u>Sarah (Handley) Keyes (70)</u>, died in Kansas on May 29, 1846.

Reed Family Employees
Milt Elliot (28)
Eliza Williams (31)
Baylis Williams (25)
Walter Herron (27)
James Smith (25), Stayed with Donners at Alder Creek during encampment.

The George Donner Family from Sangamon County, Illinois
George Donner (60-62)
Tamsen (also spelled Tamzene) Donner (44)
Elitha Donner (13)
Leanna Charity Donner (11)
Frances Donner (6)
Georgia Ann Donner (4)
Eliza Poor Donner (3)

The Jacob Donner Family from Sangamon County, Illinois
Jacob Donner (56)
Elizabeth Blue Hook Donner (40)
Solomon Elijah Hook (14)
William Hook (12)
George Donner (9)
Mary Martha Donner (7)
Isaac Donner (5)
Samuel Donner (4)
Lewis Donner (3)

Donner Party Teamsters and Friends
Augustus Spitzer (30) (teamster)
Charles "Dutch Charlie" Burger (30) (teamster)
Jean Baptiste Trudeau (16) (teamster)
Noah James (16) (teamster)
Charles Tyler Stanton (35) (friend)
John Denton (30) (friend)
Hiram Owens Miller (29), Left party at Fort Laramie.
Luke Halloran (25)

Samuel Shoemaker (25)

The Eddy Family from Belleville, Illinois
William Henry Eddy (30)
Eleanor P. Eddy (25)
James Eddy (3)
Margaret Eddy (1)

The Graves Family from Marshall County, Illinois
Franklin Ward Graves (57)
Elizabeth Cooper Graves (45)
Sarah Graves Fosdick (21), wife of Jay Fosdick
Jay Fosdick (23)
Mary Ann Graves (19)
William Cooper Graves (17)
Eleanor Graves (14)
Lovina Graves (12)
Nancy Graves (9)
Jonathan Graves (7)
Franklin W. Graves Jr. (5)
Elizabeth Graves (1)
Graves Teamster
John Snyder (25)

The Murphy Family (Levinah Murphy is Sarah Foster and Harriet Pike's mother)
Levinah Jackson Murphy (36), Widow at start of expedition.
Sarah Ann Murphy (19)
John Landrum Murphy (16)
Lemuel B. Murphy (12)
William Green Murphy (10)
Simon Peter Murphy (8)

The Foster Family
William McFadden Foster (30)
Sarah Ann Foster (19)
Jeremiah Foster (1)

The Pike Family
<u>William M. Pike (32)</u>, Died in a firearms accident in October 1846.
Harriet Frances Murphy (18)
Naomi Levina Pike (2)
<u>Catherine Pike (1)</u>

The McCutchen Family
William "Big Bill" McCutchen (30)
Amanda Henderson McCutchen (23)
<u>Harriet McCutchen (1)</u>

The Wolfinger Family
<u>Jacob Wolfinger</u> (age unknown)
Dorothea Wolfinger (20)

The Keseberg Family
Lewis Keseberg (32)
Philippine Keseberg (23)
<u>Ada (Juliane Karoline) Keseberg (3)</u>
<u>Lewis Keseberg Jr. (1)</u>

Unrelated Individuals:
<u>Antonio (last name unknown) (23)</u>, Joined at Fort Laramie.
<u>Mr. Hardcoop (60)</u>, Possible teamster for Lewis Keseberg.
<u>Joseph Reinhardt (30)</u>
<u>Luis (19) & Salvador (19)</u>, Miwok Indians who came with Charles Stanton under Sutter's direction, along with the supplies and mules. Intended to act as guides and ensure return of Sutter's mules.
<u>Patrick Dolan (35)</u>, Traveled with Patrick Breen and family.

Acknowledgments

I would never have written this book if I hadn't been writing a dragon shifter and needed a prologue... So thanks to romantasy and the good influence it had on me.

Thanks also to my kids, who were great sports when I *obsessed* over the Donner party stories, telling them to new people over and over. I swear, they know them almost as well as I do.

And thanks to my ARC team and readers for being so supportive, even when I write things that are *totally unlike* anything else I've ever written. I love you guys so much for all your support and unwavering excitement.

Thanks to my friend Tamie Dearen for her support and excitement, and to Elana Johnson for cheering me up when I had trouble finding this story a home. Having good friends is so important, and I think this story shows this as well as anything else ever could.

But more than anything else, massive thanks to my husband. He's my strength, my support, my James frigging Reed. I love him forever, and I would *totally* lie and tell him I'd caught a bird if he needed me to do it.

Huge shoutout to the many researchers and champions of history who made so many resources available. I'm especially grateful to Kristen Johnson, who keeps her website updated and live. You can check out a lot of additional information here: https://user.xmission.com/~octa/ DonnerParty/

The letters of Virginia Reed, and the journal of Patrick Breen were also very helpful, as were the accounts of Mr. McGlashan. (Although sometimes a little context and judgement must be applied.)

Bridget's a lawyer, but does as little legal work as possible. She has five kids and soooo many animals that she loses count.

Horses, dogs, cats, rabbits, and so many chickens. Animals are her great love, after the hubby, the kids, and the books.

She makes cookies waaaaay too often and believes they should be their own food group. In a (possibly misguided) attempt at balancing the scales, she kickboxes daily. So if you don't like her books, maybe don't tell her in person.

Bridget is active on social media, and has a facebook group she comments in often. (Her husband even gets on there sometimes.) Please feel free to join her there: https://www.facebook.com/groups/750807222376182

You can also sign up for her newsletter and get a free book at www.Bridgetebakerwrites.com

Also by B. E. Baker

I write women's fiction and clean romance under B. E. Baker (so it's kind of strange that I wrote a Donner Party book, but here we are.)

The Irish Escape (women's fiction with romance):

The Crumbly Old Castle

The Creaky Old Barn

The Scarsdale Fosters Series (romance with women's fiction!):

Seed Money (1)

Nouveau Riche (2)

Minted (3)

Loaded (4)

Filthy Rich (5)

The Finding Home Series (romance with women's fiction):

Finding Grace (1)

Finding Faith (2)

Finding Cupid (3)

Finding Spring (4)

Finding Liberty (5)

Finding Holly (6)

Finding Home (7)

Finding Balance (8)

Finding Peace (9)

The Finding Home Series Boxset Books 1-3

The Finding Home Series Boxset Books 4-6

The Finding Home Series Boxset Books 7-9

The Birch Creek Ranch Series (women's fiction with romance):

The Bequest

The Vow

The Ranch

The Retreat

The Reboot

The Surprise

The Setback

The Lookback

Children's Picture Book

Yuck! What's for Dinner?

I also write romantasy and end of the world fiction under Bridget E. Baker.

The Dragon Captured Series: (dragon shifter romance!)

Ensnared

Entwined

Embroiled

Embattled

The Russian Witch's Curse: (horse shifter romance!)

My Queendom for a Horse

My Dark Horse Prince

My High Horse Czar

My Wild Horse King

My Trojan Horse Majesty

The Magical Misfits Series: (paranormal humor!)

My Pigeon Familiar

My Mongrel Pack

My Itching Scales

The Birthright Series:

Displaced (1)

unForgiven (2)

Disillusioned (3)

misUnderstood (4)

Disavowed (5)

unRepentant (6)

Destroyed (7)

The Birthright Series Collection, Books 1-3

The Anchored Series:

Anchored (1)

Adrift (2)

Awoken (3)

Capsized (4)

The Sins of Our Ancestors Series:

Marked (1)

Suppressed (2)

Redeemed (3)

Renounced (4)

Reclaimed (5) a novella!

A stand alone YA romantic suspense:

Already Gone

9 781949 655865